ROMANCE ISLAND

ZONA GALE

1st WORLD
LIBRARY
Literary Society

Romance Island

Zona Gale

© 1st World Library, 2006
PO Box 2211
Fairfield, IA 52556
www.1stworldlibrary.com
First Edition

LCCN: 2007901848

Softcover ISBN: 978-1-4218-4319-3
Hardcover ISBN: 978-1-4218-4221-9
eBook ISBN: 978-1-4218-4417-6

Purchase *"Romance Island"*
as a traditional bound book at:
www.1stWorldLibrary.com/purchase.asp?ISBN=978-1-4218-4319-3

1st World Library is a literary, educational organization
dedicated to:

- Creating a free internet library of downloadable ebooks

- Hosting writing competitions and offering book
publishing scholarships.

Interested in more 1st World Library books?
contact: literacy@1stworldlibrary.com
Check us out at: www.1stworldlibrary.com

1ˢᵗ World Library Literary Society

Giving Back to the World

"If you want to work on the core problem, it's early school literacy."

- **James Barksdale, former CEO of Netscape**

"No skill is more crucial to the future of a child, or to a democratic and prosperous society, than literacy."

- **Los Angeles Times**

Literacy... means far more than learning how to read and write... The aim is to transmit... knowledge and promote social participation."

- **UNESCO**

"Literacy is not a luxury, it is a right and a responsibility. If our world is to meet the challenges of the twenty-first century we must harness the energy and creativity of all our citizens."

- **President Bill Clinton**

"Parents should be encouraged to read to their children, and teachers should be equipped with all available techniques for teaching literacy, so the varying needs and capacities of individual kids can be taken into account."

- **Hugh Mackay**

"Who that remembers the first kind glance of her whom he loves can fail to believe in magic?"

—NOVALIS

CONTENTS

I. DINNER TIME...... 7

II. A SCRAP OF PAPER 21

III. ST. GEORGE AND THE LADY...... 35

IV. THE PRINCE OF FAR-AWAY 51

V. OLIVIA PROPOSES 65

VI. TWO LITTLE MEN...... 79

VII. DUSK, AND SO ON 95

VIII. THE PORCH OF THE MORNING...... 105

IX. THE LADY OF KINGDOMS 122

X. TYRIAN PURPLE 144

XI. THE END OF THE EVENING...... 159

XII. BETWEEN-WORLDS 178

XIII. THE LINES LEAD UP...... 186

XIV. THE ISLE OF HEARTS...... 197

XV. A VIGIL 215

XVI. GLAMOURIE 226

XVII. BENEATH THE SURFACE...... 236

XVIII. A MORNING VISIT 249

XIX. IN THE HALL OF KINGS 258

XX. OUT OF THE HALL OF KINGS...... 272

XXI. OPEN SECRETS...... 287

CHAPTER I

DINNER TIME

As *The Aloha* rode gently to her buoy among the crafts in the harbour, St. George longed to proclaim in the megaphone's monstrous parody upon capital letters:

"Cat-boats and house-boats and yawls, look here. You're bound to observe that this is my steam yacht. I own her—do you see? She belongs to me, St. George, who never before owned so much as a piece of rope."

Instead—mindful, perhaps, that "a man should not communicate his own glorie"—he stepped sedately down to the trim green skiff and was rowed ashore by a boy who, for aught that either knew, might three months before have jostled him at some ill-favoured lunch counter. For in America, dreams of gold—not, alas, golden dreams—do prevalently come true; and of all the butterfly happenings in this pleasant land of larvae, few are so spectacular as the process by which, without warning, a man is converted from a toiler and bearer of loads to a taker of his *bien*. However, to none, one must believe, is the changeling such gazing-stock as to himself.

Although countless times, waking and sleeping, St. George had humoured himself in the outworn pastime of dreaming what he would do if he were to inherit a million dollars, his imagination had never marveled its way to the situation's less poignant advantages. Chief among his satisfactions had been that with which he had lately seen his mother—an exquisite woman, looking like the old lace and Roman mosaic pins which she had saved from the wreck of her fortune—set off for Europe in the exceptional company of her brother, Bishop Arthur Touchett, gentlest of dignitaries. The bishop, only to look upon whose portrait was a benediction, had at sacrifice of certain of his charities seen St. George through college; and it made the million worth while to his nephew merely to send him to Tuebingen to set his soul at rest concerning the date of one of the canonical gospels. Next to the rich delight of planning that voyage, St. George placed the buying of his yacht.

In the dusty, inky office of the *New York Evening Sentinel* he had been wont three months before to sit at a long green table fitting words about the yachts of others to the dreary music of his typewriter, the while vaguely conscious of a blur of eight telephone bells, and the sound of voices used merely to communicate thought and not to please the ear. In the last three months he had sometimes remembered that black day when from his high window he had looked toward the harbour and glimpsed a trim craft of white and brass slipping to the river's mouth; whereupon he had been seized by such a passion to work hard and earn a white-and-brass craft of his own that the story which he was hurrying for the first edition was quite ruined.

"Good heavens, St. George," Chillingworth, the city editor, had gnarled, "we don't carry wooden type. And nothing else would set up this wooden stuff of yours. Where's some snap? Your first paragraph reads like a recipe. Now put your soul into it, and you've got less than fifteen minutes to do it in."

St. George recalled that his friend Amory, as "one hackneyed in the ways of life," had gravely lifted an eyebrow at him, and the new men had turned different colours at the thought of being addressed like that before the staff; and St. George had recast the story and had received for his diligence a New Jersey assignment which had kept him until midnight. Haunting the homes of the club-women and the common council of that little Jersey town, the trim white-and-brass craft slipping down to the river's mouth had not ceased to lure him. He had found himself estimating the value—in money—of the bric-a-brac of every house, and the self-importance of every alderman, and reflecting that these people, if they liked, might own yachts of white and brass; yet they preferred to crouch among the bric-a-brac and to discourse to him of one another's violations and interferences. By the time that he had reached home that dripping night and had put captions upon the backs of the unexpectant-looking photographs which were his trophies, he was in that state of comparative anarchy to be effected only by imaginative youth and a disagreeable task.

Next day, suddenly as its sun, had come the news which had transformed him from a discontented grappler with social problems to the owner of stocks and bonds and shares in a busy mine and other things soothing to enumerate. The first thing which he had added unto these, after the departure of his mother and the bishop, had been *The Aloha*, which only that day had slipped to the river's mouth in the view from his old window at the *Sentinel* office. St. George had the grace to be ashamed to remember how smoothly the social ills had adjusted themselves.

Now they were past, those days of feverish work and unexpected triumph and unaccountable failure; and in the dreariest of them St. George, dreaming wildly, had not dreamed all the unobvious joys which his fortune had brought to him. For although he had accurately painted, for example, the delight of a cruise in a sea-going yacht of his own, yet to step into his dory in the sunset, to watch *The Aloha's* sides shine in the late light as he was rowed ashore past the lesser crafts in the harbour; to see the man touch his cap and put back to make the yacht trim for the night, and then to turn his own face to his apartment where virtually the entire day-staff of the *Evening Sentinel* was that night to dine—these were among the pastimes of the lesser angels which his fancy had never compassed.

A glow of firelight greeted St. George as he entered his apartment, and the rooms wore a pleasant air of festivity. A table, with covers for twelve, was spread in the living-room, a fire of cones was tossing on the hearth, the curtains were drawn, and the sideboard was a thing of intimation. Rollo, his man—St. George had easily fallen in all the habits which he had longed to assume—was just closing the little ice-box sunk behind a panel of the wall, and he came forward with dignified deference.

"Everything is ready, Rollo?" St. George asked. "No one has telephoned to beg off?"

"Yes, sir," answered Rollo, "and no, sir."

St. George had sometimes told himself that the man looked like an oval grey stone with a face cut upon it.

"Is the claret warmed?" St. George demanded, handing his hat. "Did the big glasses come for the liqueur—and the little ones will set inside without tipping? Then take the cigars to the den—you'll have to get some cigarettes for Mr. Provin. Keep up the fire. Light the candles in ten minutes. I say, how jolly the table looks."

"Yes, sir," returned Rollo, "an' the candles 'll make a great difference, sir. Candles do give out an air, sir."

One month of service had accustomed St. George to his valet's gift of the Articulate Simplicity. Rollo's thoughts were doubtless contrived in the cuticle and knew no deeper operance; but he always uttered his impressions with, under his mask, an air of keen and seasoned personal observation. In his first interview with St. George, Rollo had said: "I always enjoy being kep' busy, sir. *To me*, the busy man is a grand sight," and St. George had at once appreciated his possibilities. Rollo was like the fine print in an almanac.

When the candles were burning and the lights had been turned on in the little ochre den where the billiard-table stood, St. George emerged—a well-made figure, his buoyant, clear-cut face accurately bespeaking both health and cleverness. Of a family represented by the gentle old bishop and his own exquisite mother, himself university-bred and fresh from two years' hard, hand-to-hand fighting to earn an honourable livelihood, St. George, of sound body and fine intelligence, had that temper of stability within vast range which goes pleasantly into the mind that meets it. A symbol of this was his prodigious popularity with those who had been his fellow-workers—a test beside which old-world traditions of the urban touchstones are of secondary advantage. It was deeply significant that in spite of the gulf which Chance had digged the day-staff of the *Sentinel*, all save two or three of which were not of his estate, had with flattering alacrity obeyed his summons to dine. But, as he heard in the hall the voice of Chillingworth, the difficulty of his task for the first time swept over him. It was Chillingworth who had advocated to him the need of wooden type to suit his literary style and who had long ordered and bullied him about; and how was he to play the host to Chillingworth, not to speak of the others, with the news between them of that million?

When the bell rang, St. George somewhat gruffly superseded Rollo.

"I'll go," he said briefly, "and keep out of sight for a few minutes. Get in the bath-room or somewhere, will you?" he added nervously, and opened the door.

At one stroke Chillingworth settled his own position by dominating the situation as he dominated the city room. He chose the best chair and told a good story and found fault with the way the fire burned, all with immediate ease and abandon. Chillingworth's men loved to remember that he had once carried copy. They also understood all the legitimate devices by which he persuaded from them their best effort, yet these devices never failed, and the city room agreed that Chilling-worth's fashion of giving an assignment to a new man would force him to write a readable account of his own entertainment in the dark meadows. Largely by personal magnetism he had fought his way upward, and this quality was not less a social gift.

Mr. Toby Amory, who had been on the Eleven with St. George at Harvard, looked along his pipe at his host and smiled, with flattering content, his slow smile. Amory's father had lately had a conspicuous quarter of an hour in Wall Street, as a result of which Amory, instead of taking St. George to the cemetery at Clusium as he had talked, himself drifted to Park Row; and although he now knew considerably less than he had hoped about certain inscriptions, he was supporting himself and two sisters by really brilliant work, so that the balance of his power was creditably maintained. Surely the inscriptions did not suffer, and what then was Amory that he should object? Presently Holt, the middle-aged marine man, and Harding who, since he had lost a lightweight sparring championship, was sporting editor, solemnly entered together and sat down with the social caution of their class. So did Provin, the "elder giant," who gathered news as he breathed and could not intelligibly put six words together. Horace, who would listen to four lines over the telephone and therefrom make a half-column of American newspaper humour or American newspaper tears, came in roaring pacifically and marshaling little Bud, that day in the seventh heaven of his first "beat." Then followed Crass, the feature man, whose interviews were known to the new men as literature, although he was not above publicly admitting that he was not a reporter, but a special writer. Mr. Crass read nothing in the paper that he had not written, and St. George had once prophesied that in old age he would use his scrap-book for a manual of devotions, as Klopstock used his *Messiah*. With him arrived Carbury, the telegraph editor, and later Benfy, who had a carpet in his office and wrote editorials and who came in evening clothes, thus moving Harding and Holt to instant private conversation. The last to appear was Little Cawthorne who wrote the fiction page and made enchanting limericks about every one on the staff and went about singing one song and behaving, the dramatic man flattered him, like a motif. Little Cawthorne entered backward, wrestling with some wiry matter which, when he had executed a manoeuvre and banged the door, was thrust through the passage in the form of Bennie Todd, the head office boy, affectionately known as Bennietod. Bennietod was in every one's secret, clipped every one's space and knew every one's salary, and he had lately covered a baseball game when the man whose copy he was to carry had, outside the fence, become implicated in allurements. He was greeted with noise, and St. George told him heartily that he was glad he had come.

"He made me," defensively claimed Bennietod; frowning deferentially at Little Cawthorne.

"Hello, St. George," said the latter, "come on back to the office. Crass sits in your place and he wears cravats the colour of goblin's blood. Come back."

"Not he," said Chillingworth, smoking; "the Dead-and-Done-with editor is too keen for that; I won't give him a job. He's ruined. Egg sandwiches will never stimulate him now."

St. George joined in the relieved laugh that followed. They were remembering his young Sing Sing convict who had completed his sentence in time to step in a cab and follow his mother to the grave, where his stepfather refused to have her coffin opened. And St. George, fresh from his Alma Mater, had weighted the winged words of his story with allusions to the tears celestial of Thetis, shed for Achilles, and Creon's grief for Haemon, and the Unnatural Combat of Massinger's father and son; so that Chillingworth had said things in languages that are not dead (albeit a bit Elizabethan) and the composing room had shaken mailed fists.

"Hi, you!" said Little Cawthorne, who was born in the South, "this is a mellow minute. I could wish they came often. This shall be a weekly occurrence—not so, St. George?"

"Cawthorne," Chillingworth warned, "mind your manners, or they'll make you city editor."

A momentary shadow was cast by the appearance of Rollo, who was manifestly a symbol of the world Philistine about which these guests knew more and in which they played a smaller part than any other class of men. But the tray which Rollo bore was his passport. Thereafter, they all trooped to the table, and Chillingworth sat at the head, and from the foot St. George watched the city editor break bread with the familiar nervous gesture with which he was wont to strip off yards of copy-paper and eat it. There was a tacit assumption that he be the conversational sun of the hour, and in fostering this understanding the host took grateful refuge.

"This is shameful," Chillingworth began contentedly. "Every one of you ought to be out on the Boris story."

"What is the Boris story?" asked St. George with interest. But in all talk St. George had a restful, host-like way of playing the role of opposite to every one who preferred being heard.

"I'll wager the boy hasn't been reading the papers these three months," Amory opined in his pleasant drawl.

"No," St. George confessed; "no, I haven't. They make me homesick."

"Don't maunder," said Chillingworth in polite criticism. "This is Amory's story, and only about a quarter of the facts yet," he added in a resentful growl. "It's up at the Boris, in West Fifty-ninth Street—you know the apartment house? A Miss Holland, an heiress, living there with her aunt, was attacked and nearly murdered by a mulatto woman. The woman followed her to the elevator and came uncomfortably near stabbing her from the back. The elevator boy was too quick for her. And at the station they couldn't get the woman to say a word; she pretends not to understand or to speak anything they've tried. She's got Amory hypnotized too—he thinks she can't. And when they searched her," went on Chillingworth with enjoyment, "they found her dressed in silk and cloth of gold, and loaded down with all sorts of barbarous ornaments, with almost priceless jewels. Miss Holland claims that she never saw or heard of the woman before. Now, what do you make of it?" he demanded, unconcernedly draining his glass.

"Splendid," cried St. George in unfeigned interest. "I say, splendid. Did you see the woman?" he asked Amory.

Amory nodded.

"Yes," he said, "Andy fixed that for me. But she never said a word. I *parlez-voused* her, and *verstehen-Sied* her, and she sighed and turned her head."

"Did you see the heiress?" St. George asked.

"Not I," mourned Amory, "not to talk with, that is. I happened to be hanging up in the hall there the afternoon it occurred;" he modestly explained.

"What luck," St. George commented with genuine envy. "It's a stunning story. Who is Miss Holland?"

"She's lived there for a year or more with her aunt," said Chillingworth. "She is a New Yorker and an heiress and a great beauty—oh, all the properties are there, but they're all we've got. What do you make of it?" he repeated.

St. George did not answer, and every one else did.

"Mistaken identity," said Little Cawthorne. "Do you remember Provin's story of the woman whose maid shot a masseuse whom she took to be her mistress; and the woman forgave the shooting and seemed to have her arrested chiefly because she had mistaken her for a masseuse?"

"Too easy, Cawthorne," said Chillingworth.

"The woman is probably an Italian," said the telegraph editor, "doing one of her Mafia stunts. It's time they left the politicians alone and threw bombs at the bonds that back them."

"Hey, Carbury. Stop writing heads," said Chillingworth.

"Has Miss Holland lived abroad?" asked Crass, the feature man. "Maybe this woman was her nurse or ayah or something who got fond of her charge, and when they took it away years ago, she devoted her life to trying to find it in America. And when she got here she wasn't able to make herself known to her, and rather than let any one else—"

"No more space-grabbing, Crass," warned Chillingworth.

"Maybe," ventured Horace, "the young lady did settlement work and read to the woman's kid, and the kid died, and the woman thought she'd said a charm over it."

Chillingworth grinned affectionately.

"Hold up," he commanded, "or you'll recall the very words of the charm."

Bennietod gasped and stared.

"Now, Bennietod?" Amory encouraged him.

"I t'ink," said the lad, "if she's a heiress, dis yere dagger-plunger is her mudder dat's been shut up in a mad-house to a fare-you-well."

Chillingworth nodded approvingly.

"Your imagination is toning down wonderfully," he flattered him. "A month ago you would have guessed that the mulatto lady was an Egyptian princess' messenger sent over here to get the heart from an American heiress as an ingredient for a complexion lotion. You're coming on famously, Todd."

"The German poet Wieland," began Benfy, clearing his throat, "has, in his epic of the *Oberon* made admirable use of much the same idea, Mr. Chillingworth—"

Yells interrupted him. Mr. Benfy was too "well-read" to be wholly popular with the staff.

"Oh, well, the woman was crazy. That's about all," suggested Harding, and blushed to the line of his hair.

"Yes, I guess so," assented Holt, who lifted and lowered one shoulder as he talked, "or doped."

Chillingworth sighed and looked at them both with pursed lips.

"You two," he commented, "would get out a paper that everybody would know to be full of reliable facts, and that nobody would buy. To be born with a riotous imagination and then hardly ever to let it riot is to be a born newspaper man. Provin?"

The elder giant leaned back, his eyes partly closed.

"Is she engaged to be married?" he asked. "Is Miss Holland engaged?"

Chillingworth shook his head.

"No," he said, "not engaged. We knew that by tea-time the same day, Provin. Well, St. George?"

St. George drew a long breath.

"By Jove, I don't know," he said, "it's a stunning story. It's the best story I ever remember, excepting those two or three that have hung fire for so long. Next to knowing just why old

Ennis disinherited his son at his marriage, I would like to ferret out this."

"Now, tut, St. George," Amory put in tolerantly, "next to doing exactly what you will be doing all this week you'd rather ferret out this."

"On my honour, no," St. George protested eagerly, "I mean quite what I say. I might go on fearfully about it. Lord knows I'm going to see the day when I'll do it, too, and cut my troubles for the luck of chasing down a bully thing like this."

If there was anything to forgive, every one forgave him.

"But give up ten minutes on *The Aloha*," Amory skeptically put it, adjusting his pince-nez, "for anything less than ten minutes on *The Aloha*?"

"I'll do it now—now!" cried St. George. "If Mr. Chillingworth will put me on this story in your place and will give you a week off on *The Aloha*, you may have her and welcome."

Little Cawthorne pounded on the table.

"Where do I come in?" he wailed. "But no, all I get is another wad o' woe."

"What do you say, Mr. Chillingworth?" St. George asked eagerly.

"I don't know," said Chillingworth, meditatively turning his glass. "St. George is rested and fresh, and he feels the story. And Amory—here, touch glasses with me."

Amory obeyed. His chief's hand was steady, but the two glasses jingled together until, with a smile, Amory dropped his arm.

"I *am* about all in, I fancy," he admitted apologetically.

"A week's rest on the water," said Chillingworth, "would set you on your feet for the convention. All right, St. George," he nodded.

St. George leaped to his feet.

"Hooray!" he shouted like a boy. "Jove, won't it be good to get back?"

He smiled as he set down his glass, remembering the day at his desk when he had seen the white-and-brass craft slip to the river's mouth.

Rollo, discreet and without wonder, footed softly about the table, keeping the glasses filled and betraying no other sign of life. For more than four hours he was in attendance, until, last of the guests, Little Cawthorne and Bennietod departed together, trying to remember the dates of the English kings. Finally Chillingworth and Amory, having turned outdoors the dramatic critic who had arrived at midnight and was disposed to stay, stood for a moment by the fire and talked it over.

"Remember, St. George," Chillingworth said, "I'll have no monkey-work. You'll report to me at the old hour, you won't be late; and you'll take orders—"

"As usual, sir," St. George rejoined quietly.

"I beg your pardon," Chillingworth said quickly, "but you see this is such a deuced unnatural arrangement."

"I understand," St. George assented, "and I'll do my best not to get thrown down. Amory has told me all he knows about it—by the way, where is the mulatto woman now?"

"Why," said Chillingworth, "some physician got interested in the case, and he's managed to hurry her up to the Bitley Reformatory in Westchester for the present. She's there; and that means, we need not disguise, that nobody can see her.

Those Bitley people are like a rabble of wild eagles."

"Right," said St. George. "I'll report at eight o'clock. Amory can board *The Aloha* when he gets ready and take down whom he likes."

"On my life, old chap, it's a private view of Kedar's tents to me," said Amory, his eyes shining behind his pince-nez. "I'll probably win wide disrespect by my inability to tell a mainsail from a cockpit, but I'm a grateful dog, in spite of that."

When they were gone St. George sat by the fire. He read Amory's story of the Boris affair in the paper, which somewhere in the apartment Rollo had unearthed, and the man took off his master's shoes and brought his slippers and made ready his bath. St. George glanced over his shoulder at the attractively-dismantled table, with its dying candles and slanted shades.

"Gad!" he said in sheer enjoyment as he clipped the story and saw Rollo pass with the towels.

It was so absurdly like a city room's dream of Arcady.

CHAPTER II

A SCRAP OF PAPER

To be awakened by Rollo, to be served in bed with an appetizing breakfast and to catch a hansom to the nearest elevated station were novel preparations for work in the *Sentinel* office. The impossibility of it all delighted St. George rather more than the reality, for there is no pastime, as all the world knows, quite like that of practising the impossible. The days when, "like a man unfree," he had fared forth from his unlovely lodgings clandestinely to partake of an evil omelette, seemed enchantingly far away. It was, St. George reflected, the experience of having been released from prison, minus the disgrace.

Yet when he opened the door of the city room the odour of the printers' ink somehow fused his elation in his liberty with the elation of the return. This was like wearing fetters for bracelets. When he had been obliged to breathe this air he had scoffed at its fascination, but now he understood. "A newspaper office," so a revered American of letters who had begun his life there had once imparted to St. George, "is a place where a man with the temperament of a savant and a recluse may bring his American vice of commercialism and worship of the uncommon, and let them have it out. Newspapers have no other use—except the one I began on." When St. George entered the city room, Crass, of the goblin's blood cravats, had vacated his old place, and Provin was just uncovering his typewriter and banging the tin cover upon everything within reach, and

Bennietod was writhing over a rewrite, and Chillingworth was discharging an office boy in a fashion that warmed St. George's heart.

But Chillingworth, the city editor, was an italicized form of Chillingworth, the guest. He waved both arms at the foreman who ventured to tell him of a head that had one letter too many, and he frowned a greeting at St. George.

"Get right out on the Boris story," he said. "I depend on you. The chief is interested in this too—telephoned to know whom I had on it."

St. George knew perfectly that "the chief" was playing golf at Lenox and no doubt had read no more than the head-lines of the Holland story, for he was a close friend of the bishop's, and St. George knew his ways; but Chillingworth's methods always told, and St. George turned away with all the old glow of his first assignment.

St. George, calling up the Bitley Reformatory, knew that the Chances and the Fates were all allied against his seeing the mulatto woman; but he had learned that it is the one unexpected Fate and the one apostate Chance who open great good luck of any sort. So, though the journey to Westchester County was almost certain to result in refusal, he meant to be confronted by that certainty before he assumed it. To the warden on the wire St. George put his inquiry.

"What are your visitors' days up there, Mr. Jeffrey?"

"Thursdays," came the reply, and the warden's voice suggested handcuffs by way of hospitality.

"This is St. George of the *Sentinel*. I want very much to see one of your people—a mulatto woman. Can you fix it for me?"

"Certainly not," returned the warden promptly. "The *Sentinel* knows perfectly that newspaper men can not be admitted here."

"Ah, well now, of course," St. George conceded, "but if you have a mysterious boarder who talks Patagonian or something, and we think that perhaps we can talk with her, why then—"

"It doesn't matter whether you can talk every language in South America," said the warden bruskly. "I'm very busy now, and—"

"See here, Mr. Jeffrey," said St. George, "is no one allowed there but relatives of the guests?"

"Nobody,"—crisply.

"I beg your pardon, that is literal?"

"Relatives, with a permit," divulged the warden, who, if he had had a sceptre would have used it at table, he was so fond of his little power, "and the Readers' Guild."

"Ah—the Readers' Guild," said St. George. "What days, Mr. Jeffrey?"

"To-day and Saturdays, ten o'clock. I'm sorry, Mr. St. George, but I'm a very busy man and now—"

"Good-by," St. George cried triumphantly.

In half an hour he was at the Grand Central station, boarding a train for the Reformatory town. It was a little after ten o'clock when he rang the bell at the house presided over by Chillingworth's "rabble of wild eagles."

The Reformatory, a boastful, brick building set in grounds that seemed freshly starched and ironed, had a discoloured door that would have frowned and threatened of its own accord, even without the printed warnings pasted to its panels stating that no application for admission, with or without permits, would be honoured upon any day save Thursday. This was Tuesday.

Presently, the chains having fallen within after a feudal rattling, an old man who looked born to the business of snapping up a drawbridge in lieu of a taste for any other exclusiveness peered at St. George through absurd smoked glasses, cracked quite across so that his eyes resembled buckles.

"Good morning," said St. George; "has the Readers' Guild arrived yet?"

The old man grated out an assent and swung open the door, which creaked in the pitch of his voice. The bare hall was cut by a wall of steel bars whose gate was padlocked, and outside this wall the door to the warden's office stood open. St. George saw that a meeting was in progress there, and the sight disturbed him. Then the click of a key caught his attention, and he turned to find the old man quietly and surprisingly swinging open the door of steel bars.

"This way, sir," he said hoarsely, fixing St. George with his buckle eyes, and shambled through the door after him locking it behind them.

If St. George had found awaiting him a gold throne encircled by kneeling elephants he could have been no more amazed. Not a word had been said about the purpose of his visit, and not a word to the warden; there was simply this miraculous opening of the barred door. St. George breathlessly footed across the rotunda and down the dim opposite hall. There was a mistake, that was evident; but for the moment St. George was going to propose no reform. Their steps echoed in the empty corridor that extended the entire length of the great building in an odour of unspeakable soap and superior disinfectants; and it was not until they reached a stair at the far end that the old man halted.

"Top o' the steps," he hoarsely volunteered, blinking his little buckle eyes, "first door to the left. My back's bad. I won't go up."

St. George, inhumanely blessing the circumstance, slipped something in the old man's hand and sprang up the stairs.

The first door at the left stood ajar. St. George looked in and saw a circle of bonnets and white curls clouded around the edge of the room, like witnesses. The Readers' Guild was about leaving; almost in the same instant, with that soft lift and touch which makes a woman's gown seem sewed with vowels and sibilants, they all arose and came tapping across the bare floor. At their head marched a woman with such a bright bonnet, and such a tinkle of ornaments on her gown that at first sight she quite looked like a lamp. It was she whom St. George approached.

"I beg your pardon, madame," he said, "is this the Readers' Guild?"

There was nothing in St. George's grave face and deferential stooping of shoulders to betray how his heart was beating or what a bound it gave at her amazing reply.

"Ah," she said, "how do you do?"—and her manner had that violent absent-mindedness which almost always proves that its possessor has trained a large family of children—"I am so glad that you can be with us to-day. I am Mrs. Manners—forgive me," she besought with perfectly self-possessed distractedness, "I'm afraid that I've forgotten your name."

"My name is St. George," he answered as well as he could for virtual speechlessness.

The other members of the Guild were issuing from the room, and Mrs. Manners turned. She had a fashion of smiling enchantingly, as if to compensate her total lack of attention.

"Ladies," she said, "this is Mr. St. George, at last."

Then she went through their names to him, and St. George bowed and caught at the flying end of the name of the woman nearest him, and muttered to them all. The one nearest was a Miss Bella Bliss Utter, a little brown nut of a woman with bead eyes.

"Ah, Mr. St. George," said Miss Utter rapidly, "it has been a wonderful meeting. I wish you might have been with us. Fortunately for us you are just in time for our third floor council."

It had been said of St. George that when he was writing on space and was in need, buildings fell down before him to give him two columns on the first page; but any architectural manoeuvre could not have amazed him as did this. And too, though there had been occasions when silence or an evasion would have meant bread to him, the temptation to both was never so strong as at that moment. It cost St. George an effort, which he was afterward glad to remember having made, to turn to Mrs. Manners, who had that air of appointing committees and announcing the programme by which we always recognize a leader, and try to explain.

"I am afraid," St. George said as they reached the stairs, "that you have mistaken me, Mrs. Manners. I am not—"

"Pray, pray do not mention it," cried Mrs. Manners, shaking her little lamp-shade of a hat at him, "we make every allowance, and I am sure that none will be necessary."

"But I am with the *Evening Sentinel*," St. George persisted, "I am afraid that—"

"As if one's profession made any difference!" cried Mrs. Manners warmly. "No, indeed, I perfectly understand. We all understand," she assured him, going over some papers in one hand and preparing to mount the stairs. "Indeed, we appreciate it," she murmured, "do we not, Miss Utter?"

The little brown nut seemed to crack in a capacious smile.

"Indeed, indeed!" she said fervently, accenting her emphasis by briefly-closed eyes.

"Hymn books. Now, have we hymn books enough?" plaintively broke in Mrs. Manners. "I declare, those new hymn books don't seem to have the spirit of the old ones, no matter what *any one* says," she informed St. George earnestly as they reached an open door. In the next moment he stood aside and the Readers' Guild filed past him. He followed them. This was pleasantly like magic.

They entered a large chamber carpeted and walled in the garish flowers which many boards of directors suppose will joy the cheerless breast. There were present a dozen women inmates,—sullen, weary-looking beings who seemed to have made abject resignation their latest vice. They turned their lustreless eyes upon the visitors, and a portly woman in a red waist with a little American flag in a buttonhole issued to them a nasal command to rise. They got to their feet with a starched noise, like dead leaves blowing, and St. George eagerly scanned their faces. There were women of several nationalities, though they all looked raceless in the ugly uniforms which those same boards of directors consider *de rigueur* for the soul that is to be won back to the normal. A little negress, with a spirit that soared free of boards of directors, had tried to tie her closely-clipped wool with bits of coloured string; an Italian woman had a geranium over her ear; and at the end of the last row of chairs, towering above the others, was a creature of a kind of challenging, unforgetable beauty whom, with a thrill of certainty, St. George realized to be her whom he had come to see. So strong was his conviction that, as he afterward recalled, he even asked no question concerning her. She looked as manifestly not one of the canaille of incorrigibles as, in her place, Lucrezia Borgia would have looked.

The woman was powerfully built with astonishing breadth of shoulder and length of limb, but perfectly proportioned. She was young, hardly more than twenty, St. George fancied, and of the peculiar litheness which needs no motion to be manifest. Her clear skin was of wonderful brown; and her eyes, large and dark, with something of the oriental watchfulness, were like opaque gems and not more penetrable. Her look was immovably fixed upon St. George as if she divined that in some way his coming affected her.

"We will have our hymn first." Mrs. Manners' words were buzzing and pecking in the air. "What can I have done with that list of numbers? We have to select our pieces most carefully," she confided to St. George, "so to be sure that *Soul's Prison* or *Hands Red as Crimson*, or, *Do You See the Hebrew Captive Kneeling?* or anything personal like that doesn't occur. Now what can I have done with that list?"

Her words reached St. George but vaguely. He was in a fever of anticipation and enthusiasm. He turned quickly to Mrs. Manners.

"During the hymn," he said simply, "I would like to speak with one of the women. Have I your permission?"

Mrs. Manners looked momentarily perplexed; but her eyes at that instant chancing upon her lost list of hymns, she let fall an abstracted assent and hurried to the waiting organist. Immediately St. George stepped quietly down among the women already fluttering the leaves of their hymn books, and sat beside the mulatto woman.

Her eyes met his in eager questioning, but she had that temper of unsurprise of many of the eastern peoples and of some animals. Yet she was under some strong excitement, for her hands, large but faultlessly modeled, were pressed tensely together. And St. George saw that she was by no means a mulatto, or of any race that he was able to name. Her features were classic and of exceeding fineness, and her face was sensitive and highly-bred and filled with repose, like the surprising repose of breathing arrested in marble. There was that about her, however, which would have made one, constituted to perceive only the arbitrary balance of things, feel almost afraid; while one of high organization would inevitably have been smitten by some sense of the incalculably higher organization of her nature, a nature which breathed forth an influence, laid a spell—did something indefinable. Sometimes one stands too closely to a statue and is frightened by the nearness, as by the nearness of one of an alien region. St. George felt this directly he spoke to her. He shook off the impression and set himself practically to the matter in hand. He had never had greater need of his faculty for directness. His low tone was quite matter-of-fact, his manner deferentially reassuring.

"I think," he said softly and without preface, "that I can help you. Will you let me help you? Will you tell me quickly your name?"

The woman's beautiful eyes were filled with distress, but she shook her head.

"Your name—name—name?" St. George repeated earnestly, but she had only the same answer. "Can you not tell me where you live?" St. George persisted, and she made no other sign.

"New York?" went on St. George patiently. "New York? Do you live in New York?"

There was a sudden gleam in the woman's eyes. She extended her hands quickly in unmistakable appeal. Then swiftly she caught up a hymn book, tore at its fly-leaf, and made the movement of writing. In an instant St. George had thrust a pencil in her hand and she was tracing something.

He waited feverishly. The organ had droned through the hymn and the women broke into song, with loose lips and without restraint, as street boys sing. He saw them casting curious,

Romance Island   29

sullen glances, and the Readers' Guild whispering among themselves. Miss Bella Bliss Utter, looking as distressed as a nut can look, nodded, and Mrs. Manners shook her head and they meant the same thing. Then St. George saw the attendant in the red waist descend from the platform and make her way toward him, the little American flag rising and falling on her breast. He unhesitatingly stepped in the aisle to meet her, determined to prevent, if possible, her suspicion of the message. "Is it the barbarism of a gentleman," Amory had once propounded, "or is it the gentleman-like manners of a barbarian which makes both enjoy over-stepping a prohibition?"

"I compliment you," St. George said gravely, with his deferential stooping of the shoulders. "The women are perfectly trained. This, of course, is due to you."

The hard face of the woman softened, but St. George thought that one might call her very facial expression nasal; she smiled with evident pleasure, though her purpose remained unshaken.

"They do pretty good," she admitted, "but visitors ain't best for 'em. I'll have to request you"—St. George vaguely wished that she would say "ask"—"not to talk to any of 'em."

St. George bowed.

"It is a great privilege," he said warmly if a bit incoherently, and held her in talk about an institution of the sort in Canada where the women inmates wore white, the managers claiming that the effect upon their conduct was perceptible, that they were far more self-respecting, and so on in a labyrinth of defensive detail. "What do you think of the idea?" he concluded anxiously, manfully holding his ground in the aisle.

"I think it's mostly nonsense," returned the woman tartly, "a big expense and a sight of work for nothing. And now permit me to say—"

St. George vaguely wished that she would say "let."

"I agree with you," he said earnestly, "nothing could be simpler and neater than these calico gowns."

The attendant looked curiously at him.

"They are gingham," she rejoined, "and you'll excuse me, I hope, but visitors ain't supposed to converse with the inmates."

St. George was vanquished by "converse."

"I beg your pardon," he said, "pray forgive me. I will say good-by to my friend."

He turned swiftly and extended his hand to the strange woman behind him. With the cunning upon which he had counted she gave her own hand, slipping in his the folded paper. Her eyes, with their haunting watchfulness, held his for a moment as she mutely bent forward when he left her.

The hymn was done and the women were seating themselves, as St. George with beating heart took his way up the aisle. What the paper contained he could not even conjecture; but there *was* a paper and it *did* contain something which he had a pleasant premonition would be invaluable to him. Yet he was still utterly at loss to account for his own presence there, and this he coolly meant to do.

He was spared the necessity. On the platform Mrs. Manners had risen to make an announcement; and St. George fancied that she must preside at her tea-urn and try on her bonnets with just that same formal little "announcement" air.

"My friends," she said, "I have now an unexpected pleasure for you and for us all. We have with us to-day Mr. St. George, of New York. Mr. St. George is going to sing for us."

St. George stood still for a moment, looking into the expectant faces of Mrs. Manners and the other women of the Readers'

Guild, a spark of understanding kindling the mirth in his eyes. This then accounted both for his admittance to the home and for his welcome by the women upon their errand of mercy. He had simply been very naturally mistaken for a stranger from New York who had not arrived. But since he had accomplished something, though he did not know what, inasmuch as the slip of paper lay crushed in his hand unread, he must, he decided, pay for it. Without ado he stepped to the platform.

"I have explained to Mrs. Manners and to these ladies," he said gravely, "that I am not the gentleman who was to sing for you. However, since he is detained, I will do what I can."

This, mistaken for a merely perfunctory speech of self-depreciation, was received in polite, contradicting silence by the Guild. St. George, who had a rich, true barytone, quickly ran over his little list of possible songs, none of which he had ever sung to an audience that a canoe would not hold, or to other accompaniment than that of a mandolin. Partly in memory of those old canoe-evenings St. George broke into a low, crooning plantation melody. The song, like much of the Southern music, had in it a semi-barbaric chord that the college men had loved, something—or so one might have said who took the canoe-music seriously—of the wildness and fierceness of old tribal loves and plaints and unremembered wooings with a desert background: a gallop of hoof-beats, a quiver of noon light above saffron sand—these had been, more or less, in the music when St. George had been wont to lie in a boat and pick at the strings while Amory paddled; and these he must have reechoed before the crowd of curious and sullen and commonplace, lighted by that one wild, strange face. When he had finished the dark woman sat with bowed head, and St. George himself was more moved by his own effort than was strictly professional.

"Dear Mr. St. George," said Mrs. Manners, going distractedly through her hand-bag for something unknown, "our secretary will thank you formally. It was she who sent you our request, was it not? She *will* so regret being absent to-day."

"She did not send me a request, Mrs. Manners," persisted St. George pleasantly, "but I've been uncommonly glad to do what I could. I am here simply on a mission for the *Evening Sentinel.*"

Mrs. Manners drew something indefinite from her bag and put it back again, and looked vaguely at St. George.

"Your voice reminds me so much of my brother, younger," she observed, her eyes already straying to the literature for distribution.

With soft exclamatory twitters the Readers' Guild thanked St. George, and Miss Bella Bliss Utter, who was of womankind who clasp their hands when they praise, stood thus beside him until he took his leave. The woman in the red waist summoned an attendant to show him back down the long corridor.

At the grated door within the entrance St. George found the warden in stormy conference with a pale blond youth in spectacles.

"Impossible," the warden was saying bluntly, "I know you. I know your voice. You called me up this morning from the *New York Sentinel* office, and I told you then—"

"But, my dear sir," expostulated the pale blond youth, waving a music roll, "I do assure you—"

"What he says is quite true, Warden," St. George interposed courteously, "I will vouch for him. I have just been singing for the Readers' Guild myself."

The warden dropped back with a grudging apology and brows of tardy suspicion, and the old man blinked his buckle eyes.

"Gentlemen," said St. George, "good morning."

Outside the door, with its panels decorated in positive prohibitions, he eagerly unfolded the precious paper. It bore a single name and address: Tabnit, 19 McDougle Street, New York.

CHAPTER III

ST. GEORGE AND THE LADY

St. George lunched leisurely at his hotel. Upon his return from Westchester he had gone directly to McDougle Street to be assured that there was a house numbered 19. Without difficulty he had found the place; it was in the row of old iron-balconied apartment houses a few blocks south of Washington Square, and No. 19 differed in no way from its neighbours even to the noisy children, without toys, tumbling about the sunken steps and dark basement door. St. George contented himself with walking past the house, for the mere assurance that the place existed dictated his next step.

This was to write a note to Mrs. Medora Hastings, Miss Holland's aunt. The note set forth that for reasons which he would, if he might, explain later, he was interested in the woman who had recently made an attempt upon her niece's life; that he had seen the woman and had obtained an address which he was confident would lead to further information about her. This address, he added, he preferred not to disclose to the police, but to Mrs. Hastings or Miss Holland herself, and he begged leave to call upon them if possible that day. He despatched the note by Rollo, whom he instructed to deliver it, not at the desk, but at the door of Mrs. Hastings' apartment, and to wait for an answer. He watched with pleasure Rollo's soft departure, recalling the days when he had sent a messenger boy to some inaccessible threshold, himself stamping up and down in the cold a block or so away to await the boy's return.

Rollo was back almost immediately. Mrs. Hastings and Miss Holland were not at home. St. George eyed his servant severely.

"Rollo," he said, "did you go to the door of their apartment?"

"No, sir," said Rollo stiffly, "the elevator boy told me they was out, sir."

"Showing," thought St. George, "that a valet and a gentleman is a very poor newspaper man."

"Now go back," he said pleasantly, "go up in the elevator to their door. If they are not in, wait in the lower hallway until they return. Do you get that? Until they return."

"You'll want me back by tea-time, sir?" ventured Rollo.

"Wait," St. George repeated, "until they return. At three. Or six. Or nine o'clock. Or midnight."

"Very good, sir," said Rollo impassively, "it ain't always wise, sir, for a man to trust to his own judgment, sir, asking your pardon. His judgment," he added, "may be a bit of the ape left in him, sir."

St. George smiled at this evolutionary pearl and settled himself comfortably by the open fire to await Rollo's return. It was after three o'clock when he reappeared. He brought a note and St. George feverishly tore it open.

"Whom did you see? Were they civil to you?" he demanded.

"I saw a old lady, sir," said Rollo irreverently. "She didn't say a word to me, sir, but what she didn't say was civiler than many people's language. There's a great deal in manner, sir," declaimed Rollo, brushing his hat with his sleeve, and his sleeve with his handkerchief, and shaking the handkerchief meditatively over the coals.

St. George read the note at a glance and with unspeakable relief. They would see him. A refusal would have delayed and annoyed him just then, in the flood-tide of his hope.

"My Dear Mr. St. George," the note ran. "My niece is not at home, and I can not tell how your suggestion will be received by her, though it is most kind. I may, however, answer for myself that I shall be glad to see you at four o'clock this afternoon.

"Very truly yours,
"MEDORA HASTINGS."

Grateful for her evident intention to waste no time, St. George dressed and drove to the Boris, punctually sending up his card at four o'clock. At once he was ushered to Mrs. Hastings' apartment.

St. George entered her drawing-room incuriously. Three years of entering drawing-rooms which he never thereafter was to see had robbed him of that sensation of indefinable charm which for many a strange room never ceases to yield. He had found far too many tables upholding nothing which one could remember, far too many pictures that returned his look, and rugs that seemed to have been selected arbitrarily and because there was none in stock that the owner really liked. He was therefore pleasantly surprised and puzzled by the room which welcomed him. The floor was tiled in curious blocks, strangely hieroglyphed, as if they had been taken from old tombs. Over the fireplace was set a panel of the same stone, which, by the thickness of the tiles, formed a low shelf. On this shelf and on tables and in a high window was the strangest array of objects that St. George had ever seen. There were small busts of soft rose stone, like blocks of coral. There was a statue or two of some indefinable white material, glistening like marble and yet so soft that it had been indented in several places by accidental pressure. There were fans of strangely-woven silk, with sticks of carven rock-crystal, and hand mirrors of polished copper set in frames of gems that he did not recognize. Upon the wall were mended bits of purple tapestry, embroidered or painted or woven in singular patterns of flora and birds that St. George could not name. There were rolls of parchment, and vases of rock-crystal, and a little apparatus, most delicately poised, for weighing unknown, delicate things; and jars and cups without handles, all baked of a soft pottery having a nap like the down of a peach. Over the windows hung curtains of lace, woven by hands which St. George could not guess, in patterns of such freedom and beauty as western looms never may know. On the floor and on the divans were spread strange skins, some marked like peacocks, some patterned like feathers and like seaweed, all in a soft fur that was like silk.

Mingled with these curios were the ordinary articles of a cultivated household. There were many books, good pictures, furniture with simple lines, a tea-table that almost ministered of itself, a work-basket filled with "violet-weaving" needlework, and a gossipy clock with well-bred chimes. St. George was enormously attracted by the room which could harbour so many pagan delights without itself falling their victim. The air was fresh and cool and smelled of the window primroses.

[Illustration]

In a few moments Mrs. Hastings entered, and if St. George had been bewildered by the room he was still more amazed by the appearance of his hostess. She was utterly unlike the atmosphere of her drawing-room. She was a bustling, commonplace little creature, with an expressionless face, indented rather than molded in features. Her plump hands were covered with jewels, but for all the richness of her gown she gave the impression of being very badly dressed; things of jet and metal bobbed and ticked upon her, and her side-combs were continually falling about. She sat on the sofa and looked at the seat which St. George was to have and began to talk—all without taking the slightest heed of him or permitting him to mention the *Evening Sentinel* or his errand. If St. George had been painted purple he felt sure that she would have acted quite the same. Personality meant nothing to her.

"Now this distressing matter, Mr. St. George," began Mrs. Hastings, "of this frightful mulatto woman. I didn't see her myself—no, I had stopped in on the first floor to visit my lawyer's wife who was ill with neuralgia, and I didn't see the creature. If I had been with my niece I dare say it wouldn't have occurred. That's what I always say to my niece. I always say, 'Olivia, nothing *need* occur to vex one. It always happens because of pure heedlessness.' Not that I accuse my own niece of heedlessness in this particular. It was the elevator boy who was heedless. That is the trouble with life in a great city. Every breath you draw is always dependent on somebody else's doing his duty, and when you consider how many people habitually neglect their duty it is a wonder—I always say that to Olivia— it is a wonder that anybody is alive to *do* a duty when it presents itself. 'Olivia,' I always say, 'nobody needs to die.' And I really believe that they nearly all do die out of pure heedlessness. Well, and so this frightful mulatto creature: you know her, I understand?"

Mrs. Hastings leaned back and consulted St. George through her tortoise-shell glasses, tilting her head high to keep them on her nose and perpetually putting their gold chain over her ear, which perpetually pulled out her side-combs.

"I saw her this morning," St. George said. "I went up to the Reformatory in Westchester, and I spoke with her."

"Mercy!" ejaculated Mrs. Hastings, "I wonder she didn't tear your eyes out. Did they have her in a cage or in a cell? What was the creature about?"

"She was in a missionary meeting at the moment," St. George explained, smiling.

"Mercy!" said Mrs. Hastings in exactly the same tone. "Some trick, I expect. That's what I warn Olivia: 'So few things nowadays are done through necessity or design.' Nearly everything is a trick. Every invention is a trick—a cultured trick, one might say. Murder is a trick, I suppose, to a murderer. That's why civilization is bad for morals, don't you think? Well, and so she talked with you?"

"No, Mrs. Hastings," said St. George, "she did not say one word. But she wrote something, and that is what I have come to bring you."

"What was it—some charm?" cried Mrs. Hastings. "Oh, nobody knows what that kind of people may do. I'll meet any one face to face, but these juggling, incantation individuals appal me. I have a brother who travels in the Orient, and he tells me about hideous things they do—raising wheat and things," she vaguely concluded.

"Ah!" said St. George quickly, "you have a brother—in the Orient?"

"Oh, yes. My brother Otho has traveled abroad I don't know how many years. We have a great many stamps. I can't begin to pronounce all the names," the lady assured him.

"And this brother—is he your niece, Miss Holland's father?" St. George asked eagerly.

"Certainly," said Mrs. Hastings severely; "I have only one brother, and it has been three years since I have seen him."

"Pardon me, Mrs. Hastings," said St. George, "this may be most important. Will you tell me when you last heard from him and where he was?"

"I should have to look up the place," she answered, "I couldn't begin to pronounce the name, I dare say. It was somewhere in the South Atlantic, ten months or more ago."

"Ah," St. George quietly commented.

"Well, and now this frightful creature," resumed Mrs. Hastings, "do, pray, tell me what it was she wrote."

St. George produced the paper.

"That is it," he said. "I fancy you will not know the street. It is 19 McDougle Street, and the name is simply Tabnit."

"Yes. And is it a letter?" his hostess demanded, "and whatever does it say?"

"It is not a letter," St. George explained patiently, "and this is all that it says. The name is, I suppose, the name of a person. I have made sure that there is such a number in the street. I have seen the house. But I have waited to consult you before going there."

"Why, what is it you think?" Mrs. Hastings besought him. "Do you think this person, whoever it is, can do something? And whatever can he do? Oh dear," she ended, "I do want to act the way poor dear Mr. Hastings would have acted. Only I know that he would have gone straight to Bitley, or wherever she is, and held a revolver at that mulatto creature's head, and *commanded* her to talk English. Mr. Hastings was a very determined character. If you could have seen the poor dear man's chin! But of course I can't do that, can I? And that's what I say to Olivia. 'Olivia, one doesn't *need* a man's judgment if one will only use judgment oneself.' What is it you think, Mr. St. George?"

Before St. George could reply there entered the room, behind a low announcement of his name, a man of sixty-odd years, nervous, slightly stooped, his smooth pale face unlighted by little deep-set eyes.

"Ah, Mr. Frothingham!" said Mrs. Hastings in evident relief, "you are just in time. Mr. St. John was just telling me horrible things about this frightful mulatto creature. This is Mr. St. John. Mr. Frothingham is my lawyer and my brother Otho's lawyer. And so I telephoned him to come in and hear all about this. And now do go on, Mr. St. John, about this hideous woman. What is it you think?"

"How do you do, Mr. St. John?" said the lawyer portentously. His greeting was almost a warning, and reminded St. George of the way in which certain brakemen call out stations. St. George responded as blithely to this name as to his own and did not correct it. "And what," went on the lawyer, sitting down with long unclosed hands laid trimly along his knees, "have you to contribute to this most remarkable occurrence, Mr. St. John?"

St. George briefly narrated the events of the morning and placed the slip of paper in the lawyer's hands.

"Ah! We have here a communication in the nature of a confession," the lawyer observed, adjusting his gold pince-nez, head thrown back, eyebrows lifted.

"Only the address, sir," said St. George, "and I was just saying to Mrs. Hastings that some one ought to go to this address at once and find out whatever is to be got there. Whoever goes I will very gladly accompany."

Mr. Frothingham had a fashion of making ready to speak and soliciting attention by the act, and then collapsing suddenly with no explosion, like a bad Roman candle. He did this now, and whatever he meant to say was lost to the race; but he looked very wise the while. It was rather as if he discarded you as a fit listener, than that he discarded his own comment.

"I don't know but I ought to go myself," rambled Mrs. Hastings, "perhaps Mr. Hastings would think I ought. Suppose, Mr. Frothingham, that we both go. Dear, dear! Olivia always sees to my shopping and flowers and everything executive, but I can't let her go into these frightful places, can I?"

There was a rustling at the far end of the room, and some one entered. St. George did not turn, but as her soft skirts touched and lifted along the floor he was tinglingly aware of her presence. Even before Mrs. Hastings heard her light footfall, even before the clear voice spoke, St. George knew that he was at last in the presence of the arbiter of his enterprise, and of how much else he did not know. He was silent, breathlessly waiting for her to speak.

"May I come in, Aunt Dora?" she said. "I want to know to what place it is impossible for me to go?"

She came from the long room's boundary shadow. There was about her a sense of white and gray with a knot of pale colour in her hat and an orchid on her white coat. Mrs. Hastings, taking no more account of her presence than she had of St. George's, tilted back her head and looked at the primroses in the window as closely as at anything, and absently presented him.

"Olivia," she said, "this is Mr. St. John, who knows about that frightful mulatto creature. Mr. St. George," she went on, correcting the name entirely unintentionally, "my niece, Miss Holland. And I'm sure I wish I knew what the necessary thing to be done *is*. That is what I always tell you, you know, Olivia. 'Find out the necessary thing and do it, and let the rest go.'"

"It reminds me very much," said the lawyer, clearing his throat, "of a case that I had on the April calendar—"

Miss Holland had turned swiftly to St. George:

"You know the mulatto woman?" she asked, and the lawyer passed by the April calendar and listened.

"I went to the Bitley Reformatory this morning to see her," St. George replied. "She gave me this name and address. We have been saying that some one ought to go there to learn what is to be learned."

Mr. Frothingham in a silence of pursed lips offered the paper. Miss Holland glanced at it and returned it.

"Will you tell us what your interest is in this woman?" she asked evenly. "Why you went to see her?"

"Yes, Miss Holland," St. George replied, "you know of course that the police have done their best to run this matter down. You know it because you have courteously given them every assistance in your power. But the police have also been very ably assisted by every newspaper in town. I am fortunate to be acting in the interests of one of these—the *Sentinel.* This clue was put in my hands. I came to you confident of your cooeperation."

Mrs. Hastings threw up her hands with a gesture that caught away the chain of her eye-glass and sent it dangling in her lap, and her side-combs tinkling to the tiled floor.

"Mercy!" she said, "a reporter!"

St. George bowed.

"But I never receive reporters!" she cried, "Olivia—don't you know? A newspaper reporter like that fearful man at Palm Beach, who put me in the Courtney's ball list in a blue silk when I never wear colours."

"Now really, really, this intrusion—" began Mr. Frothingham, his long, unclosed hands working forward on his knees in undulations, as a worm travels.

Miss Holland turned to St. George, the colour dyeing her face and throat, her manner a bewildering mingling of graciousness and hauteur.

"My aunt is right," she said tranquilly, "we never have received any newspaper representative. Therefore, we are unfortunate never to have met one. You were saying that we should send some one to McDougle Street?"

St. George was aware of his heart-beats. It was all so

unexpected and so dangerous, and she was so perfectly equal to the circumstance.

"I was asking to be allowed to go myself, Miss Holland," he said simply, "with whoever makes the investigation."

Mrs. Hastings was looking mutely from one to another, her forehead in horizons of wrinkles.

"I'm sure, Olivia, I think you ought to be careful what you say," she plaintively began. "Mr. Hastings never allowed his name to go in any printed lists even, he was so particular. Our telephone had a private number, and all the papers had instructions never to mention him, even if he was murdered, unless he took down the notice himself. Then if anything important did happen, he often did take it down, nicely typewritten, and sometimes even then they didn't use it, because they knew how very particular he was. And of course we don't know how—"

St. George's eyes blazed, but he did not lift them. The affront was unstudied and, indeed, unconscious. But Miss Holland understood how grave it was, for there are women whose intuition would tell them the etiquette due upon meeting the First Syndic of Andorra or a noble from Gambodia.

"We want the truth about this as much as Mr. St. George does," she said quickly, smiling for the first time. St. George liked her smile. It was as if she were amused, not absent-minded nor yet a prey to the feminine immorality of ingra-tiation. "Besides," she continued, "I wish to know a great many things. How did the mulatto woman impress you, Mr. St. George?"

Miss Holland loosened her coat, revealing a little flowery waist, and leaned forward with parted lips. She was very beautiful, with the beauty of perfect, blooming, colourful youth, without line or shadow. She was in the very noon of youth, but her eyes did not wander after the habit of youth; they were direct and steady and a bit critical, and she spoke slowly and with graceful sanity in a voice that was without nationality. She might have been the cultivated English-speaking daughter of almost any land of high civilization, or she might have been its princess. Her face showed her imaginative; her serene manner reassured one that she had not, in consequence, to pay the usury of lack of judgment; she seemed reflective, tender, and of a fine independence, tempered, however, by tradition and unerring taste. Above all, she seemed alive, receptive, like a woman with ten senses. And—above all again—she had charm. Finally, St. George could talk with her; he did not analyze why; he only knew that this woman understood what he said in precisely the way that he said it, which is, perhaps, the fifth essence in nature.

"May I tell you?" asked St. George eagerly. "She seemed to me a very wonderful woman, Miss Holland; almost a woman of another world. She is not mulatto—her features are quite classic; and she is not a fanatic or a mad-woman. She is, of her race, a strangely superior creature, and I fancy, of high cultivation; and I am convinced that at the foundation of her attempt to take your life there is some tremendous secret. I think we must find out what that is, first, for your own sake; next, because this is the sort of thing that is worth while."

"Ah," cried Miss Holland, "delightful. I begin to be glad that it happened. The police said that she was a great brutal negress, and I thought she must be insane. The cloth-of-gold and the jewels did make me wonder, but I hardly believed that."

"The newspapers," Mr. Frothingham said acidly, "became very much involved in their statements concerning this matter."

"This 'Tabnit,'" said Miss Holland, and flashed a smile of pretty deference at the lawyer to console him for her total neglect of his comment, "in McDougle Street. Who can he be?—he *is* a man, I suppose. And where is McDougle Street?"

St. George explained the location, and Mrs. Hastings fretfully commented.

"I'm sure, Olivia," she said, "I think it is frightfully unwomanly in you—"

"To take so much interest in my own murder?" Miss Holland asked in amusement. "Aunt Dora, I'm going to do more: I suggest that you and Mr. Frothingham and I go with Mr. St. George to this address in McDougle Street—"

"My dear Olivia!" shrilled Mrs. Hastings, "it's in the very heart of the Bowery—isn't it, Mr. St. John? And only think—"

It was as if Mrs. Hastings' frustrate words emerged in the fantastic guise of her facial changes.

"No, it isn't quite the Bowery, Mrs. Hastings," St. George explained, "though it won't look unlike."

"I wish I knew what Mr. Hastings would have done," his widow mourned, "he always said to me: 'Medora, do only the necessary thing.' Do you think this *is* the necessary thing— with all the frightful smells?"

"It is perfectly safe," ventured St. George, "is it not, Mr. Frothingham?"

Mr. Frothingham bowed and tried to make non-partisanship seem a tasteful resignation of his own will.

"I am at Mrs. Hastings' command," he said, waving both hands, once, from the wrist.

"You know the place is really only a few blocks from Washington Square," St. George submitted.

Mrs. Hastings brightened.

"Well, I have some friends in Washington Square," she said, "people whom I think a great deal of, and always have. If you really feel, Olivia—"

"I do," said Miss Holland simply, "and let us go now, Aunt Dora. The brougham has been at the door since I came in. We may as well drive there as anywhere, if Mr. St. George is willing."

"I shall be happy," said St. George sedately, longing to cry: "Willing! Willing! Oh, Mrs. Hastings and Miss Holland— *willing!*"

Miss Holland and St. George and the lawyer were alone for a few minutes while Mrs. Hastings rustled away for her bonnet. Miss Holland sat where the afternoon light, falling through the corner window, smote her hair to a glory of pale colour, and St. George's eyes wandered to the glass through which the sun fell. It was a thin pane of irregular pieces set in a design of quaint, meaningless characters, in the centre of which was the figure of a sphinx, crucified upon an upright cross and surrounded by a border of coiled asps with winged heads. The window glittered like a sheet of gems.

"What wonderful glass," involuntarily said St. George.

"Is it not?" Miss Holland said enthusiastically. "My father sent it. He sent nearly all these things from abroad."

"I wonder where such glass is made," observed St. George; "it is like lace and precious stones—hardly more painted than carved."

She bent upon him such a sudden, searching look that St. George felt his eyes held by her own.

"Do you know anything of my father?" she demanded suddenly.

"Only that Mrs. Hastings has just told me that he is abroad—in the South Atlantic," St. George wonderingly replied.

"Why, I am very foolish," said Miss Holland quickly, "we have not heard from him in ten months now, and I am frightfully worried. Ah yes, the glass is beautiful. It was made in one of the South Atlantic islands, I believe—so were all these things," she added; "the same figure of the crucified sphinx is on many of them."

"Do you know what it means?" he asked.

"It is the symbol used by the people in one of the islands, my father said," she answered.

"These symbols usually, I believe," volunteered Mr. Frothingham, frowning at the glass, "have little significance, standing merely for the loose barbaric ideas of a loose barbaric nation."

St. George thought of the ladies of Doctor Johnson's Amicable Society who walked from the town hall to the Cathedral in Lichfield, "in linen gowns, and each has a stick with an acorn; but for the acorn they could give no reason."

He looked long at the glass.

"She," he said finally, "our false mulatto, ought to stand before just such glass."

Miss Holland laughed. She nodded her head a little, once, every time she laughed, and St. George was learning to watch for that.

"The glass would suit any style of beauty better than steel bars," she said lightly as Mrs. Hastings came fluttering back. Mrs. Hastings fluttered ponderously, as humblebees fly. Indeed, when one considered, there was really a "blunt-faced bee" look about the woman.

The brougham had on the box two men in smart livery; the footman, closing the door, received St. George's reply to Mrs. Hastings' appeal to "tell the man the number of this frightful place."

"I dare say I haven't been careful," Mrs. Hastings kept anxiously observing, "I have been heedless, I dare say. And I always think that what one must avoid is heedlessness, don't you think? Didn't Napoleon say that if only Caesar had been first in killing the men who wanted to kill him—something about Pompey's statue being kept clean. What was it—why should they blame Caesar for the condition of the public statues?"

"My dear Mrs. Hastings," Mr. Frothingham reminded her, his long gloved hands laid trimly along his knees as before, "you are in my care."

The statue problem faded from the lady's eyes.

"Poor, dear Mr. Hastings always said you were so admirable at cross-questioning," she recalled, partly reassured.

"Ah," cried Miss Holland protestingly, "Aunt Dora, this is an adventure. We are going to see 'Tabnit.'"

St. George was silent, ecstatically reviewing the events of the last six hours and thinking unenviously of Amory, rocking somewhere with *The Aloha* on a mere stretch of green water:

"If Chillingworth could see me now," he thought victoriously, as the carriage turned smartly into McDougle Street.

CHAPTER IV

THE PRINCE OF FAR-AWAY

No. 19 McDougle Street had been chosen as a likely market by a "hokey-pokey" man, who had wheeled his cart to the curb before the entrance. There, despite Mrs. Hastings' coach-man's peremptory appeal, he continued to dispense stained ice-cream to the little denizens of No. 19 and the other houses in the row. The brougham, however, at once proved a counter-attraction and immediately an opposition group formed about the carriage step and exchanged penetrating comments upon the livery.

"Mrs. Hastings, you and Miss Holland would better sit here, perhaps," suggested St. George, alighting hurriedly, "until I see if this man is to be found."

"Please," said Miss Holland, "I've always been longing to go into one of these houses, and now I'm going. Aren't we, Aunt Dora?"

"If you think—" ventured Mr. Frothingham in perplexity; but Mr. Frothingham's perplexity always impressed one as duty-born rather than judicious, and Miss Holland had already risen.

"Olivia!" protested Mrs. Hastings faintly, accepting St. George's hand, "do look at those children's aprons. I'm afraid we'll all contract fever after fever, just coming this far."

Unkempt women were occupying the doorstep of No. 19. St. George accosted them and asked the way to the rooms of a Mr. Tabnit. They smiled, displaying their wonderful teeth, consulted together, and finally with many labials and uncouth pointings of shapely hands they indicated the door of the "first floor front," whose wooden shutters were closely barred. St. George led the way and entered the bare, unclean passage where discordant voices and the odours of cooking wrought together to poison the air. He tapped smartly at the door.

Immediately it was opened by a graceful boy, dressed in a long, belted coat of dun-colour. He had straight black hair, and eyes which one saw before one saw his face, and he gravely bowed to each of the party in turn before answering St. George's question.

"Assuredly," said the youth in perfect English, "enter."

They found themselves in an ample room extending the full depth of the house; and partly because the light was dim and partly in sheer amazement they involuntarily paused as the door clicked behind them. The room's contrast to the squalid neighbourhood was complete. The apartment was carpeted in soft rugs laid one upon another so that footfalls were silenced. The walls and ceiling were smoothly covered with a neutral-tinted silk, patterned in dim figures; and from a fluted pillar of exceeding lightness an enormous candelabrum shed clear radiance upon the objects in the room. The couches and divans were woven of some light reed, made with high fantastic backs, in perfect purity of line however, and laid with white mattresses. A little reed table showed slender pipes above its surface and these, at a touch from the boy, sent to a great height tiny columns of water that tinkled back to the square of metal upon which the table was set. A huge fan of blanched grasses automatically swayed from above. On a side-table were decanters and cups and platters of a material frail and transparent. Before the shuttered window stood an observable plant with coloured leaves. On a great table in the room's centre were scattered objects which confused the eye. A light curtain stirring in the fan's faint breeze hung at the far end of the room.

In a career which had held many surprises, some of which St. George would never be at liberty to reveal to the paper in whose service he had come upon them, this was one of the most alluring. The mere existence of this strange and luxurious habitation in the heart of such a neighbourhood would, past expression, delight Mr. Crass, the feature man, and no doubt move even Chillingworth to approval. Chillingworth and Crass! Already they seemed strangers. St. George glanced at Miss Holland; she was looking from side to side, like a bird alighted among strange flowers; she met his eyes and dimpled in frank delight. Mrs. Hastings sat erectly beside her, her tortoise-rimmed glasses expressing bland approval. The improbability of her surroundings had quite escaped her in her satisfied discovery that the place was habitable. The lawyer, his thin lips parted, his head thrown back so that his hair rested upon his coat collar, remained standing, one long hand upon a coat lapel.

"Ah," said Miss Holland softly, "it *is* an adventure, Aunt Dora."

St. George liked that. It irritated him, he had once admitted, to see a woman live as if living were a matter of life and death. He wished her to be alive to everything, but without suspiciously scrutinizing details, like a census-taker. To appreciate did not seem to him properly to mean to assess. Miss Holland, he would have said, seemed to live by the beats of her heart and not by the waves of her hair—but another proof, perhaps, of "if thou likest her opinions thou wilt praise her virtues."

It was but a moment before the curtain was lifted, and there approached a youth, apparently in the twenties, slender and delicately formed as a woman, his dark face surmounted by a great deal of snow-white hair. He was wearing garments of grey, cut in unusual and graceful lines, and his throat was closely wound in folds of soft white, fastened by a rectangular green jewel of notable size and brilliance. His eyes, large and of exceeding beauty and gentleness, were fixed upon St. George.

"Sir," said St. George, "we have been given this address as one where we may be assisted in some inquiries of the utmost importance. The name which we have is simply 'Tabnit.' Have I the honour—"

Their host bowed.

"I am Prince Tabnit," he said quietly.

St. George, filled with fresh amazement, gravely named himself and, making presentation of the others, purposely omitted the name of Miss Holland. However, hardly had he finished before their host bowed before Miss Holland herself.

"And you," he said, "you to whom I owe an expiation which I can never make,—do you know it is my servant who would have taken your life?"

In the brief interval following this naive assertion, his guests were not unnaturally speechless. Miss Holland, bending slightly forward, looked at the prince breathlessly.

"I have suffered," he went on, "I have suffered indescribably since that terrible morning when I missed her and understood her mission. I followed quickly—I was without when you entered, but I came too late. Since then I have waited, unwilling to go to you, certain that the gods would permit the possible. And now—what shall I say?"

He hesitated, his eyes meeting Miss Holland's. And in that moment Mrs. Hastings found her voice. She curved the chain of her eye-glasses over her ear, threw back her head until the tortoise-rims included her host, and spoke her mind.

"Well, Prince Tabnit," she said sharply—quite as if, St. George thought, she had been nursery governess to princes all her life—"I must say that I think your regret comes somewhat late in the day. It's all very well to suffer as you say over what your servant has tried to do. But what kind of man must you be to have such a servant, in the first place? Didn't you know that she was dangerous and blood-thirsty, and very likely a maniac-born?"

Her voice, never modulated in her excitements, was so full that no one heard at that instant a quick, indrawn breath from St. George, having something of triumph and something of terror. Even as he listened he had been running swiftly over the objects in the room to fasten every one in his memory, and his eyes had rested upon the table at his side. A disc of bronze, supported upon a carven tripod, caught the light and challenged attention to its delicate traceries; and within its border of asps and goat's horns he saw cut in the dull metal a sphinx crucified upon an upright cross—an exact facsimile of the device upon that strange opalized glass from some far-away island which he had lately noted in the window in Mrs. Hastings' drawing-room. Instantly his mind was besieged by a volley of suppositions and imaginings, but even in his intense excitement as to what this simple discovery might bode, he heard the prince's soft reply to Mrs. Hastings:

"Madame," said the prince, "she is a loyal creature. Whatever she does, she believes herself to be doing in my service. I trusted her. I believed that such error was impossible to her."

"Error!" shrilled Mrs. Hastings, looking about her for support and finding little in the aspect of Mr. Augustus Frothingham, who appeared to be regarding the whole proceeding as one from which he was to extract data to be thought out at some future infinitely removed.

As for St. George, he had never had great traffic with a future infinitely removed; he had a youthful and somewhat imagi-native fashion of striking before the iron was well in the fire.

"Your servant believed, then, your Highness," he said clearly, "that in taking Miss Holland's life she was serving you?"

"I must regretfully conclude so."

St. George rose, holding the little brazen disc which he had taken from the table, and confronted his host, compelling his eyes.

"Perhaps you will tell us, Prince Tabnit," he said coolly, "what it is that the people who use this device find against Miss Holland's father?"

St. George heard Olivia's little broken cry.

"It is the same!" she exclaimed. "Aunt Dora—Mr. Frothingham—it is the crucified sphinx that was on so many of the things that father sent. Oh," she cried to the prince, "can it be possible that you know him—that you know anything of my father?"

To St. George's amazement the face of the prince softened and glowed as if with peculiar delight, and he looked at St. George with admiration.

"Is it possible," he murmured, half to himself, "that your race has already developed intuition? Are you indeed so near to the Unknown?"

He took quick steps away and back, and turned again to St. George, a strange joy dawning in his face.

"If there be some who are ready to know!" he said. "Ah," he recalled himself penitently to Miss Holland, "your father— Otho Holland, I have seen him many times."

"*Seen Otho!*" shrilled Mrs. Hastings, as pink and trembling and expressionless as a disturbed mold of jelly. "Oh, poor, dear Otho! Did he live where there are people like your frightful servant? Olivia, think! Maybe he is lying at the bottom of a gorge, all wounded and bloody, with a dagger in his back! Oh, my poor, dear Otho, who used to wheel me about!"

Mrs. Hastings collapsed softly on the divan, her glasses fallen in her lap, her side-combs slipping silently to the rug. Olivia had risen and was standing before Prince Tabnit.

"Tell me," she said trembling, "when have you seen him? Is he well?"

Prince Tabnit swept the faces of the others and his eyes returned to Miss Holland and dropped to the floor.

"The last time that I saw him, Miss Holland," he answered, "was three months ago. He was then alive and well."

Something in his tone chilled St. George and sent a sudden thrill of fear to his heart.

"He was then alive and well?" St. George repeated slowly. "Will you tell us more, your Highness? Will you tell us why the death of his daughter should be considered a service to the prince of a country which he had visited?"

"You are very wonderful," observed the prince, smiling meditatively at St. George, "and your penetration gives me good news—news that I had not hoped for, yet. I can not tell you all that you ask, but I can tell you much. Will you sit down?"

He turned and glanced at the curtain at the far end of the room. Instantly the boy servant appeared, bearing a tray on which were placed, in dishes of delicate-coloured filigree, strange dainties not to be classified even by a cosmopolitan, with his Flemish and Finnish and all but Icelandic cafes in every block.

"Pray do me the honour," the prince besought, taking the dishes from the hands of the boy. "It gives me pleasure, Miss

Holland, to tell you that your father has no doubt had these very plates set before him."

Upon a little table he deftly arranged the dishes with all the smiling ease of one to whom afternoon tea is the only business toward, and to whom an attempted murder is wholly alien. He impressed St. George vaguely as one who seemed to have risen from the dead of the crudities of mere events and to be living in a rarer atmosphere. The lawyer's face was a study. Mr. Augustus Frothingham never went to the theatre because he did not believe that a man of affairs should unduly stimulate the imagination.

There was set before them honey made by bees fed only upon a tropical flower of rare fragrance; cakes flavoured with wine that had been long buried; a paste of cream, thick with rich nuts and with the preserved buds of certain flowers; and little white berries, such as the Japanese call "pinedews"; there was a tea distilled from the roots of rare exotics, and other things savoury and fantastic. So potent was the spell of the prince's hospitality, and so gracious the insistence with which he set before them the strange and odourous dishes, that even Olivia, eager almost to tears for news of her father, and Mrs. Hastings, as critical and suspicious as some beetle with long antennae, might not refuse them. As for Mr. Augustus Frothingham, although this might be Cagliostro's spagiric food, or "extract of Saturn," for aught that his previous experience equipped him to deny, yet he nibbled, and gazed, and was constrained to nibble again.

When they had been served, Prince Tabnit abruptly began speaking, the while turning the fine stem of his glass in his delicate fingers.

"You do not know," he said simply, "where the island of Yaque lies?"

Mrs. Hastings sat erect.

"Yaque!" she exclaimed. "That was the name of the place where your father was, Olivia. I know I remembered it because it wasn't like the man What's-his-name in *As You Like It*, and because it didn't begin with a J."

"The island is my home," Prince Tabnit continued, "and now, for the first time, I find myself absent from it. I have come a long journey. It is many miles to that little land in the eastern seas, that exquisite bit of the world, as yet unknown to any save the island-men. We have guarded its existence, but I have no fear to tell you, for no mariner, unaided by an islander, could steer a course to its coasts. And I can tell you little about the island for reasons which, if you will forgive me, you would hardly understand. I must tell you something of it, however, that you may know the remarkable conditions which led to the introduction of Mr. Holland to Yaque.

"The island of Yaque," continued the prince, "or Arqua, as the name was written by the ancient Phoenicians, has been ruled by hereditary monarchs since 1050 B.C., when it was settled."

"What date did I understand you to say, sir?" demanded Mr. Augustus Frothingham.

The prince smiled faintly.

"I am well aware," he said, "that to the western mind—indeed, to any modern mind save our own—I shall seem to be speaking in mockery. None the less, what I am saying is exact. It is believed that the enterprises of the Phoenicians in the early ages took them but a short distance, if at all, beyond the confines of the Mediterranean. It is merely known that, in the period of which I speak, a more adventurous spirit began to be manifested, and the Straits of Gibraltar were passed and settlements were made in Iberia. But how far these adventurers actually penetrated has been recorded only in those documents that are in the hands of my people—descendants of the boldest of these mariners who pushed their galleys out into the Atlantic. At this time the king of Tyre was Abibaal, soon to be succeeded by his son Hiram, the friend, you will remember, of King David,—"

Mr. Frothingham, who did not go to the theatre for fear of exciting his imagination, uttered the soft non-explosion which should have been speech.

"King Abibaal," continued the prince, "who maintained his court in great pomp, had a younger and favourite son who bore his own name. He was a wild youth of great daring, and upon the accession of Hiram to the throne he left Tyre and took command of a galley of adventuresome spirits, who were among the first to pass the straits and gain the open sea. The story of their wild voyage I need not detail; it is enough to say that their trireme was wrecked upon the coast of Yaque; and Abibaal and those who joined him—among them many members of the court circle and even of the royal family— settled and developed the island. And there the race has remained without taint of admixture, down to the present day. Of what was wrought on the island I can tell you little, though the time will come when the eyes of the whole world will be turned upon Yaque as the forerunner of mighty things. Ruled over by the descendants of Abibaal, the islanders have dwelt in peace and plenty for nearly three thousand years—until, in fact, less than a year ago. Then the line thus traceable to King Hiram himself abruptly terminated with the death of King Chelbes, without issue."

Again Mr. Frothingham attempted to speak, and again he collapsed softly, without expression, according to his custom. As for St. George, he was remembering how, when he first went to the paper, he had invariably been sent to the anteroom to listen to the daily tales of invention, oppression and projects for which a continual procession of the more or less mentally deficient wished the *Sentinel* to stand sponsor. St. George remembered in particular one young student who soberly claimed to have invented wireless telegraphy and who molested the staff for months. Was this olive prince, he wondered, going to prove himself worth only a half-column on a back page,

Zona Gale

after all?

"I understand you to say," said St. George, with the weary self-restraint of one who deals with lunatics, "that the line of King Hiram, the friend of King David of Israel, became extinct less than a year ago?"

The prince smiled.

"Do not conceal your incredulity," he said liberally, "for I forgive it. You see, then," he went on serenely, "how in Yaque the question of the succession became engrossing. The matter was not merely one of ascendancy, for the Yaquians are singularly free from ambition. But their pride in their island is boundless. They see in her the advance guard of civilization, the peculiar people to whom have come to be intrusted many of the secrets of being. For I should tell you that my people live a life that is utterly beyond the ken of all, save a few rare minds in each generation. My people live what others dream about, what scientists struggle to fathom, what the keenest philosophers and economists among you can not formulate. We are," said Prince Tabnit serenely, "what the world will be a thousand years from now."

"Well, I'm sure," Mrs. Hastings broke in plaintively, "that I hope your servant, for instance, is not a sample of what the world is coming to!"

The prince smiled indulgently, as if a child had laid a little, detaining hand upon his sleeve.

"Be that as it may," he said evenly, "the throne of Yaque was still empty. Many stood near to the crown, but there seemed no reason for choosing one more than another. One party wished to name the head of the House of the Litany, in Med, the King's city, who was the chief administrator of justice. Another, more democratic than these, wished to elevate to the throne a man from whose family we had won knowledge of both perpetual motion and the Fourth Dimension—"

St. George smiled angelically, as one who resignedly sees the last fragments of a shining hope float away. This quite settled it. The olive prince was crazy. Did not St. George remember the old man in the frayed neckerchief and bagging pockets who had brought to the office of the *Sentinel* chart after chart about perpetual motion, until St. George and Amory had one day told him gravely that they had a machine inside the office then that could make more things go for ever than he had ever dreamed of, though they had *not* said that the machine was named Chillingworth.

"You have knowledge of both these things?" asked St. George indulgently.

"Yaque understood both those laws," said the prince quietly, "when William the Conqueror came to England."

He hesitated for a moment and then, regardless of another soft explosion from Mr. Frothingham's lips, he added:

"Do you not see? Will you not understand? It is our knowledge of the Fourth Dimension which has enabled us to keep our island a secret."

St. George suddenly thrilled from head to foot. What if he were speaking the truth? What if this man were speaking the truth?

"Moreover," resumed the prince, "there were those among us who had long believed that new strength would come to my people by the introduction of an inhabitant of one of the continents. His coming would, however, necessitate his sove-reignty among us, in fulfilment of an ancient Phoenician law, providing that the state, and every satrapy therein, shall receive no service, either of blood or of bond, nor enter into the marriage contract with an alien; from which law only the royal house is exempt. Thus were the two needs of our land to be served by the means to which we had recourse. For there being no way to settle the difficulty, we vowed to leave the matter to

Chance, that great patient arbiter of destinies of which your civilization takes no account, save to reduce it to slavery. Accordingly each inhabitant of the island took a solemn oath to await, with an open mind free from choice or prejudice, the settlement of the event, certain that the gods would permit the possible. Five days after this decision our watchers upon the hills sighted a South African transport bound for the Azores to coal. A hundred miles from our coast she was wrecked, and it was thought that all on board had been lost. A submarine was ordered to the spot—"

"Do you mean," interrupted St. George, "that you were able to see the wreck at that distance?"

"Certainly," said the prince. "Pray forgive me," he added winningly, "if I seem to boast. It is difficult for me to believe that your appliances are so immature. We were using steamship navigation and limiting our vision at the time of Pericles, but the futility of these was among our first discoveries."

Involuntarily St. George turned to Miss Holland. What would she think, he found himself wondering. Her eyes were luminous and her breath was coming quickly; he was relieved to find that she had not the infectious vulgarity to doubt the possibility of what seemed impossible. This was one of the qualities of Mr. Augustus Frothingham, who had assumed an air of polite interest and an accurately cynical smile, and the manner of generously lending his professional attention to any of the vagaries of the client. Mrs. Hastings stirred uneasily.

"I'm sure," she said fretfully, "that I must be very stupid, but I simply can *not* follow you. Why, you talk about things that don't exist! My husband, who was a very practical and advanced man, would have shown you at once that what you say is impossible."

Here was the attitude of the Commonplace the world over, thought St. George: to believe in wireless telegraphy simply because it has been found out, and to disbelieve in the Fourth

Dimension because it has not been.

"I can not explain these things," admitted the prince gravely, "and I dare say that you could prove that they do not exist, just as a man from another planet could show us to his own satisfaction that there are no such things as music or colour."

"Go on, please," said Olivia eagerly.

"Olivia, I'm sure," protested Mrs. Hastings, "I think it's very unwomanly of you to show such an interest in these things."

"Will you bear with me for one moment, Mrs. Hastings?" begged the prince, "and perhaps I shall be able to interest you. The submarine returned, bringing the sole survivor of the wreck of the African transport."

"Ah, now," Mrs. Hastings assured him blandly, "you are dealing with things that can happen. My brother Otho, my niece's father, was just this last year the sole survivor of the wreck of a very important vessel."

"I have the honour, Mrs. Hastings, to be narrating to you the circumstances attending the discovery of your brother and Miss Holland's father, after the wreck of that vessel."

"My father?" cried Olivia.

The prince bowed.

"After this manner, Chance had rewarded us. We crowned your father King of Yaque."

CHAPTER V

OLIVIA PROPOSES

Prince Tabnit's announcement was received by his guests in the silence of amazement. If they had been told that Miss Holland's father was secretly acting as King of England they could have been no more profoundly startled than to hear stated soberly that he had been for nearly a year the king of a cannibal island. For the cannibal phase of his experience seemed a foregone conclusion. To St. George, profoundly startled and most incredulous, the possible humour of the situation made first appeal. The picture of an American gentleman seated upon a gold throne in a leopard-skin coat, ordering "oysters and foes" for breakfast, was irresistible.

"But he shaved with a shell when he chose,
'Twas the manner of Primitive Man"

floated through his mind, and he brought himself up sharply. Clearly, somebody was out of his head, but it must not be he.

"What?" cried Mrs. Hastings in two inelegant syllables, on the second of which her uncontrollable voice rose. "My brother Otho, a vestry-man at St. Mark's—"

"Aunt Dora!" pleaded Olivia. "Tell us," she besought the prince.

"King Otho I of Yaque," the prince was begining, but the title was not to be calmly received by Mrs. Hastings.

"*King* Otho!" she articulated. "Then—am I royalty?"

"All who may possibly succeed to the throne Blackstone holds to be royalty," said the lawyer in an edictal voice, and St. George looked away from Olivia.

The Princess Olivia!

"King Otho," continued the prince, "ruled wisely and well for seven months, and it was at the beginning of that time that the imperial submarine was sent to the Azores with letters and a packet to you. The enterprise, however, was attended by so great danger of discovery that it was never repeated. This is why, for so long, you have had no word from the king. And now I come," said the prince with hesitation, "to the difficult part of my narrative."

He paused and Mr. Frothingham rushed to his assistance.

"As the family solicitor," said the lawyer, pursing his lips, and waving his hands, once, from the wrists, "would you not better divulge to my ear alone, the—a—"

"No—no!" flashed Olivia. "No, Mr. Frothingham—please."

The prince inclined his head.

"Will it surprise you, Miss Holland," he said, "to learn that I made my voyage to this country expressly to seek you out?"

"To seek me?" exclaimed Olivia. "But—has anything happened to my father?"

"We hope not," replied the prince, "but what I have to tell will none the less occasion you anxiety. Briefly, Miss Holland, it is more than three months since your father suddenly and mysteriously disappeared from Yaque, leaving absolutely no clue to his whereabouts."

A little cry broke from Olivia's lips that went to St. George's heart. Mrs. Hastings, with a gesture that was quite wild and sent her bonnet hopelessly to one side, burst into a volley of exclamations and demands.

"Who did it?" she wailed. "Who did it? Otho is a gentleman. He would never have the bad taste to disappear, like all those dreadful people's wives, if somebody hadn't—"

"My dear Madame," interposed Mr. Frothingham, "calm—calm yourself. There are families of undisputed position which record disappearances in several generations."

"Please," pleaded Olivia. "Ah, tell us," she begged the prince again.

"There is, unfortunately, but little to tell, Miss Holland," said the prince with sympathetic regret. "I had the honour, three months ago, to entertain the king, your father, at dinner. We parted at midnight. His Majesty seemed—"

"His Majesty!" repeated Mrs. Hastings, smiling up at the opposite wall as if her thought saw glories.

"—in the best of health and spirits," continued the prince. "A meeting of the High Council was to be held at noon on the following day. The king did not appear. From that moment no eye in Yaque has fallen upon him."

"One moment, your Highness," said St. George quickly; "in the absence of the king, who presides over the High Council?"

"As the head of the House of the Litany, the chief administrator of justice, it is I," said the prince with humility.

"Ah, yes," St. George said evenly.

"But what have you done?" cried Olivia. "Have you had search made? Have you—"

"Everything," the prince assured her. "The island is not large. Not a corner of it remains unvisited. The people, who were devoted to the king, your father, have sought night and day. There is, it is hardly right to conceal from you," the prince hesitated, "a circumstance which makes the disappearance the more alarming."

"Tell us. Keep nothing from us, I beg, Prince Tabnit," besought Olivia.

"For centuries," said the prince slowly, "there has been in the keeping of the High Council of the island a casket, containing what is known as the Hereditary Treasure. This casket, with some of the finest of its jewels, was left by King Abibaal himself. Since his time every king of the island has upon his death bequeathed to the casket the finest jewel in his possession; and its contents are now therefore of inestimable value. The circumstance to which I refer is that two days after the disappearance of the king, your father, which spread grief and alarm through all Yaque, it was discovered that the Hereditary Treasure was gone."

"Gone!" burst from the lips of the prince's auditors.

"As utterly as if the Fifth Dimension had received it," the prince gravely assured them. "The loss, as you may imagine, is a grievous one. The High Council immediately issued a proclamation that if the treasure be not restored by a certain date—now barely two weeks away—a heavy tax will be levied upon the people to make good, in the coin of the realm, this incalculable loss. Against this the people, though they are a people of peace, are murmurous."

"Indeed!" cried Mrs. Hastings. "Great loyalty it is that sets up the loss of their trumpery treasure over and above the loss of their king, my brother Otho! If," she shrilled indignantly, "we are not unwise to listen to this at all. What is it you think? What is it your people think?"

She raised her head until she had framed the prince in tortoiseshell. Mrs. Hastings never held her head quite still. It continually waved about a little, so that usually, even in peace, it intimated indignation; and when actual indignation set in, the jet on her bonnet tinkled and ticked like so many angry sparrows.

"Madame," said the prince, "there are those among his Majesty's subjects who would willingly lay down their lives for him. But he is a stranger to us—come of an alien race; and the double disappearance is a most tragic occurrence, which the burden of the tax has emphasized. To be frank, were his Majesty to reappear in Yaque without the treasure having been found—"

"Oh!" breathed Mrs. Hastings, "they would kill him!"

The prince shuddered and set his white teeth in his nether lip.

"The gods forbid," he said. "Such primeval punishment is as unknown among us as is war itself. How little you know my people; how pitifully your instincts have become—forgive me—corrupted by living in this barbarous age of yours, fumbling as you do at civilization. With us death is a sacred rite, the highest tribute and the last sacrifice to the Absolute. Our dying are carried to the Temple of the Worshipers of Distance, and are there consecrated. The limit of our punishment would be aerial exposure—"

"You mean?" cried St. George.

"I mean that in extreme cases we have, with due rite and ceremonial, given a victim to an airship, without ballast or rudder, and abundantly provisioned. Then with solemn ritual we have set him adrift—an offering to the great spirits of space—so that he may come to know. This," the prince paused in emotion, "this is the worst that could befall your father."

"How horrible!" cried Olivia. "Oh, how horrible."

"Oh," Mrs. Hastings moaned, "he was born to it. He was born to it. When he was six he tied kites to his arms and jumped out the window of the cupola and broke his collar bone—oh, Otho,—oh Heaven,—and I made him eat oatmeal gruel three times a day when he was getting well."

"Prince Tabnit," said St. George, "I beg you not to jest with us. Have consideration for the two to whom this man is dear."

"I am speaking truth to you," said the prince earnestly. "I do not wish to alarm these ladies, but I am bound in honour to tell you what I know."

"Ah then," said St. George, his narrowed eyes meeting those of the prince, "since the taking of life is unknown to you in Yaque, will you explain how it was that your servant adopted such unerring means to take the life of Miss Holland? And why?"

"My servant," said the prince readily, "belongs to the lahnas or former serfs of the island. Upon her people, now the owners of rich lands, the tax will fall heavily. Crazed by what she considers her people's wrongs following upon the coming of the stranger sovereign, the poor creature must have developed the primitive instincts of your race. Before coming to this country my servant had never heard of murder save as a superseded custom of antiquity, like the crucifying of lions. Her discovery of your daily practice of murder, and of murder practised as a cure for crime—"

"Sir," began the lawyer imposingly.

"—wakened in her the primitive instincts of humanity, and her instinct took the deplorable and fanatic form of your own courts," finished the prince. "Her bitterness toward his Majesty she sought to visit upon his daughter."

Olivia sprang to her feet.

"I must go to my father. I must go to Yaque," she cried ringingly. "Prince Tabnit, will you take me to him?"

Into the prince's face leaped a fire of admiration for her beauty and her daring. He bowed before her, his lowered lashes making thick shadows on his dark cheeks.

"I insist upon this," cried little Olivia firmly, "and if you do not permit it, Prince Tabnit, we must publish what you have told us from one end of the city to the other."

"Yes, by Jove," thought St. George, "and one's country will have a Yaque exhibit in its own department at the next world's fair."

"Olivia! My child! Miss Holland—," began the lawyer.

The prince spoke tranquilly.

"It is precisely this errand," he said, "that has brought me to America. Do you not see that, in the event of your father's failure to return to his people, you will eventually be Queen of Yaque?"

St. George found himself looking fixedly at Mrs. Hastings' false front as the only reality in the room. If in a minute Rollo was going to waken him by bringing in his coffee, he was going to throttle Rollo—that was all. Olivia Holland, an American heiress, the hereditary princess of a cannibal island! St. George still insisted upon the cannibal; it somehow gave him a foothold among the actualities.

"I!" cried Olivia.

Mrs. Hastings, brows lifted, lips parted, winked with lightning rapidity in an effort to understand.

St. George pulled himself together.

"Your Highness," he said sternly, "there are several things upon which I must ask you to enlighten us. And the first, which I hope you will forgive, is whether you have any direct proof that what you tell us of Miss Holland's father is true."

"That's it! That's it!" Mr. Frothingham joined him with all the importance of having made the suggestion. "We can hardly proceed in due order without proofs, sir."

The prince turned toward the curtain at the room's end and the youth appeared once more, this time bearing a light oval casket of delicate workmanship. It was of a substance resembling both glass and metal of changing, rainbow tints, and it passed through St. George's mind as he observed it that there must be, to give such a dazzling and unreal effect, more than seven colours in the spectrum.

"A spectrum of seven colours," said the prince at the same moment, "could not, of course, produce this surface. I confess that until I came to this country I did not know that you had so few colours. Our spectrum already consists of twelve colours visible to the naked eye, and at least five more are distinguishable through our powerful magnifying glasses."

St. George was silent. It was as if he had suddenly been permitted to look past the door that bars and threatens all knowledge.

The prince unlocked the casket. He drew out first a quantity of paper of extreme thinness and lightness on which, embossed and emblazoned, was the coat of arms of the Hollands—a sheaf of wheat and an unicorn's head—and this was surmounted by a crown.

"This," said the prince, "is now the device upon the signet ring of the King of Yaque, the arms of your own family. And here chances to be a letter from your father containing some instructions to me. It is true that writing has with us been superseded by wireless communication, excepting where there is need of great secrecy. Then we employ the alphabet of any language we choose, these being almost disused, as are the Cuneiform and Coptic to you."

"And how is it," St. George could not resist asking, "that you know and speak the English?"

The prince smiled swiftly.

"To you," he said, "who delve for knowledge and who do not know that it is absolute and to be possessed at will, this can not now be made clear. Perhaps some day..."

Olivia had taken the paper from the prince and pressed it to her lips, her eyes filling with tears. There was no mistaking that evidence, for this was her father's familiar hand.

"Otho always did write a fearful scrawl," Mrs. Hastings commented, "his l's and his t's and his vowels were all the same height. I used to tell him that I didn't know whatever people would think."

"I may, moreover," continued the prince, "call to mind several articles which were included in the packet sent from the Azores by his Majesty. You have, for example, a tapestry representing an ibis hunt; you have an image in pink sutro, or soft marble, of an ancient Phoenician god—Melkarth. And you have a length of stained glass bearing the figure of the Tyrian sphinx, crucified, and surrounded by coiled asps."

"Yes, it is true," said Olivia, "we have all these things."

"Why, the trash must be quite expensive," observed Mrs. Hastings. "I don't care much for so many colours myself, perhaps because I always wear black; though I did wear light colours a good deal when I was a girl."

"What else, Mr. St. George?" inquired the prince pleasantly.

"Nothing else," cried Olivia passionately. "I am satisfied. My father is in danger, and I believe that he is in Yaque, for he would never of his own will desert a place of trust. I must go to him. And, Aunt Dora, you and Mr. Frothingham must go with me."

"Oh, Olivia!" wailed Mrs. Hastings, a different key for every syllable, "think—consider! Is it the necessary thing to do? And what would your poor dear uncle have done? And is there a better way than his way? For I always say that it is not really necessary to do as my poor dear husband would have done, providing only that we can find a better way. Oh," she mourned, lifting her hands, "that this frightful thing should come to me at my age. Otho may be married to a cannibal princess, with his sons catching wild goats by the hair like Tennyson and the whistling parrots—"

"Madame," said the prince coldly, "forgets what I have been saying of my country."

"I do not forget," declared Mrs. Hastings sharply, "but being behind civilization and being ahead of civilization comes to the same thing more than once. In morals it does."

St. George was silent. Olivia's splendid daring in her passionate decision to go to her father stirred him powerfully; moreover, her words outlined a possible course of his own whose magnitude startled him, and at the same time filled him with a sudden, dazzling hope.

"But where is your island, Prince Tabnit?" he asked. "You've naturally no consul there and no cable, since you are not even on the map."

"Yaque," said the prince readily, "lies almost due southwest from the Azores."

Mr. Frothingham stirred skeptically.

"But such an island," he said pompously, "so rich in material for the archaeologist, the anthropologist, the explorer in all fields of antiquity—ah, it is out of the question, out of the question!"

"It is difficult," said the prince patiently, "most difficult for me to make myself intelligible to you—as difficult, if you will forgive me, as if you were to try to explain calculus to one of the street boys outside. But directly your phase of civilization has opened to you the secrets of the Fourth Dimension, much will be discovered to you which you do not now discern or dream, and among these, Yaque. I do not jest," he added wearily, "neither do I expect you to believe me. But I have told you the truth. And it would be impossible for you to reach Yaque save in the company of one of the islanders to whom the secret is known. I can not explain to you, any more than I can explain harmony or colour."

"Well, I'm sure," cried Mrs. Hastings fretfully, "I don't know why you all keep wandering from the subject so. Now, my brother Otho—"

"Prince Tabnit,"—Olivia's voice never seemed to interrupt, but rather to "divide evidence finely" at the proper moment— "how long will it take us to reach Yaque?"

St. George thrilled at that "us."

"My submarine," replied the prince, "is plying about outside the harbour. I arrived in four days."

"By the way," St. George submitted, "since your wireless system is perfected, why can not we have news of your island from here?"

"The curve of the earth," explained the prince readily, "prevents. We have conquered only those problems with which we have had to deal. The curve of the earth has of course never entered our calculation. We have approached the problem from another standpoint."

"We have much to do, Prince Tabnit," said Olivia; "when may we leave?"

"Command me," said Prince Tabnit, bowing.

"To-morrow!" cried Olivia, "to-morrow, at noon."

"Olivia!" Mrs. Hastings' voice broke over the name like ice upon a warm promontory. Mrs. Hastings' voice was suited to say "Keziah" or "Katinka," not Olivia.

"Can you go, Mr. Frothingham?" demanded Olivia.

Mr. Frothingham's long hands hung down and he looked as if she had proposed a jaunt to Mars.

"My physician has ordered a sea-change," he mumbled doubtfully, "my daughter Antoinette—I—really—there is nothing in all my experience—"

"Olivia!" Mrs. Hastings in tears was superintending the search for both side-combs.

"Aunt Dora," said Olivia, "you're not going to fail me now. Prince Tabnit—at noon to-morrow. Where shall we meet?"

St. George listened, glowing.

"May I have the honour," suggested the prince, "of waiting upon you at noon to conduct you? And I need hardly say that we undertake the journey under oath of secrecy?"

"Anything—anything!" cried Olivia.

"Oh, my dear Olivia," breathed Mrs. Hastings weakly, "taking me, at my age, into this awful place of Four Dimentias—or whatever it was you said."

"We will be ready to go with you at noon," said Olivia steadily.

St. George held his peace as they made their adieux. A great many things remained to be thought out, but one was clear enough.

The boy servant ran before them to the door. They made their way to the street in the early dusk. A hurdy-gurdy on the curb was bubbling over with merry discords, and was flanked by garrulous Italians with push-carts, lighted by flaring torches. Men were returning from work, children were quarreling, women were in doorways, and a policeman was gossiping with the footman in a knot of watching idlers. With a sigh that was like a groan, Mrs. Hastings sank back on the cushions of the brougham.

"I feel," she said, eyes closed, "as if I had been in a pagan temple where they worship oracles and what's-his-names. What time is it? I haven't an idea. Dear, dear, I want to get home and feel as if my feet were on land and water again. I want some strong sleep and a good sound cup of coffee, and then I shall know what's actually what."

To St. George the slow drive up town was no less unreal than their visit. His head was whirling, a hundred plans and speculations filled his mind, and through these Mrs Hastings' chatter of forebodings and the lawyer's patterned utterance hardly found their way. At his own street he was set down, with Mrs. Hastings' permission to call next day.

Miss Holland gave him her hand.

"I can not thank you," she said, "I can not thank you. But try to know, won't you, what this has been to me. Until to-morrow."

Until to-morrow. St. George stood in the brightness of the street looking after the vanishing carriage, his hand tingling from her touch. Then he went up to his apartment and met Rollo—sleek, deferential, the acme of the polite barbarism in which the prince had made St. George feel that he and his world were living. Ah, he thought, as Rollo took his hat, this was no way to live, with the whole world singing to be discovered anew.

He sat down before the trim little white table with its pretty china and silver and its one rose-shaded candle, but the doubtful content of comfort was suddenly not enough. The spirit of the road and of the chase was in his veins, and he was aglow with "the taste for pilgriming." He looked about on the simple luxury with which he had surrounded himself, and he welcomed his farewell to it. And when Rollo had gone up stairs to complain in person of the shad-roe, St. George spoke aloud:

"If Miss Holland sails for Yaque to-morrow on the prince's submarine," he said, "*The Aloha* and I will follow her."

CHAPTER VI

TWO LITTLE MEN

Next morning St. George was early astir. He had slept little and his dreams had been grotesques. He threw up his blind and looked across buildings to the grey park. The sky was marked with rose, the still reservoir gave back colour upon its breast, and the tower upon its margin might have been some guttural-christened castle on the Rhine. St. George drew a deep breath of good, new air and smiled for the sake of the things that the day was to bring him. He was in the golden age when the youthful expectation of enjoyment is just beginning to be savoured by the inevitable longing for more light, and he seemed to himself to be alluringly near the verge of both.

His first care the evening before had been to hunt out Chillingworth. He had found him in a theatre and had got him out to the foyer and kept him through the third act, pouring in his ears as much as he felt that it was well for him to know. Chillingworth had drawn his square, brown hands through his hair and, in lieu of copy-paper, had nibbled away his programme and paced the corner by the cloak-room.

"It looks like a great big thing," said the city editor; "don't you think it looks like a great big thing?"

"Extraordinarily so," assented St. George, watching him.

"Can you handle it alone, do you think?" Chillingworth demanded.

"Ah, well now, that depends," replied St. George. "I'll see it through, if it takes me to Yaque. But I'd like you to promise, Mr. Chillingworth, that you won't turn Crass loose at it while I'm gone, with his feverish head-lines. Mrs. Hastings and her niece must be spared that, at all events."

"Don't you be a sentimental idiot," snapped Chillingworth, "and spoil the biggest city story the paper ever had. Why, this may draw the whole United States into a row, and mean war and a new possession and maybe consulates and governorships and one thing or another for the whole staff. St. George, don't spoil the sport. Remember, I'm dropsical and nobody can tell what may happen. By the way, where did you say this prince man is?"

"Ah, I didn't say," St. George had answered quietly. "If you'll forgive me, I don't think I shall say."

"Oh, you don't," ejaculated Chillingworth. "Well, you please be around at eight o'clock in the morning."

St. George watched him walking sidewise down the aisle as he always walked when he was excited. Chillingworth was a good sort at heart, too; but given, as the bishop had once said of some one else, to spending right royally a deal of sagacity under the obvious impression that this is the only wisdom.

At his desk next morning Chillingworth gave to St. George a note from Amory, who had been at Long Branch with *The Aloha* when the letter was posted and was coming up that noon to put ashore Bennietod.

"May Cawthorne have his day off to-morrow and go with me?" the letter ended. "I'll call up at noon to find out."

"Yah!" growled Chillingworth, "it's breaking up the whole

staff, that's what it's doin'. You'll all want cut-glass typewriters next."

"If I should sail to-day," observed St. George, quite as if he were boarding a Sound steamer, "I'd like to take on at least two men. And I'd like Amory and Cawthorne. You could hardly go yourself, could you, Mr. Chillingworth?"

"No, I couldn't," growled Chillingworth, "I've got to keep my tastes down. And I've got to save up to buy kid gloves for the staff. Look here—" he added, and hesitated.

"Yes?" St. George complied in some surprise.

"Bennietod's half sick anyway," said Chillingworth, "he's thin as water, and if you would care—"

"By all means then," St. George assented heartily, "I would care immensely. Bennietod sick is like somebody else healthy. Will you mind getting Amory on the wire when he calls up, and tell him to show up without fail at my place at noon to-day? And to wait there for me."

Little Cawthorne, with a pair of shears quite a yard long, was sitting at his desk clipping jokes for the fiction page. He was humming a weary little tune to the effect that "Billy Enny took a penny but now he hadn't many—Lookie They!" with which he whiled away the hours of his gravest toil, coming out strongly on the "Lookie They!" until Benfy on the floor above pounded for quiet which he never got.

"Cawthorne," said St. George, "it may be that I'm leaving to-night on the yacht for an island out in the southeast. And the chief says that you and Amory are to go along. Can you go?"

Little Cawthorne's blue eyes met St. George's steadily for a moment, and without changing his gaze he reached for his hat.

"I can get the page done in an hour," he promised, "and I can pack my thirty cents in ten minutes. Will that do?"

St. George laughed.

"Ah, well now, this goes," he said. "Ask Chillingworth. Don't tell any one else."

"'Billy Enny took a penny,'" hummed Little Cawthorne in perfect tranquillity.

St. George set off at once for the McDougle Street house. A thousand doubts beset him and he felt that if he could once more be face to face with the amazing prince these might be better cleared away. Moreover, the glimpses which the prince had given him of a world which seemed to lie as definitely outside the bourne of present knowledge as does death itself filled St. George with unrest, spiced his incredulity with wonder, and he found himself longing to talk more of the things at which the strange man had hinted.

The squalor of the street was even less bearable in the early morning. St. George wondered, as he hurried across from the Grand Street station, how the prince had understood that he must not only avoid the great hotels, but that he must actually seek out incredible surroundings like these to be certain of privacy. For only the very poor are sufficiently immersed in their own affairs to be guiltless of curiosity, save indeed a kind of surface morbid wonderment at crepe upon a door or the coming of a well-dressed woman to their neighbourhood. The prince might have lived in McDougle Street for years without exciting more than derisive comment of the denizens, derision being no other than their humour gone astray.

St. George tapped at the door which the night before had admitted him to such revelation. There was no answer, and a repeated summons brought no sound from within. At length he tentatively touched the latch. The door opened. The room was quite empty. No remnant of furniture remained.

Zona Gale

He entered, involuntarily peering about as if he expected to find the prince in a dusty corner. The windows were still shuttered, and he threw open the blinds, admitting rectangles of sunlight. He could have found it in his heart, as he looked blankly at the four walls, to doubt that he had been there at all the night before, so emphatically did the surroundings deny that they had ever harboured a title. But on the floor at his feet lay a scrap of paper, twisted and torn. He picked it up. It was traced in indistinguishable characters, but it bore the Holland coat of arms and crown which the prince had shown them. St. George put the paper in his pocket and questioned a group of boys in the passage.

"Yup," shouted one of the boys with that prodigality of intonation distinguishing the child of the streets, who makes every statement as if his word had just been contradicted out of hand, "he means de bloke wid de black block. Aw, he lef' early dis mornin' wid 's junk follerin'.' Dey's two of 'em. Wot's he t'ink? Dis ain't no Nigger's Rest. Dis yere's all Eyetalian."

St. George hurried to Fifty-ninth Street. It was not yet ten o'clock, but the departure of the prince made him vaguely uneasy and for his life he could not have waited longer. Perhaps it was not true at all; perhaps none of it had happened. The McDougle Street part had vanished; what if the Boris too were a myth? But as he sprang up the steps at the apartment house St. George knew better. The night before her hand had lain in his for an infinitesimal time, and she had said "Until to-morrow."

On sending his name to Mrs. Hastings he was immediately bidden to her apartment. He found the drawing-room in confusion—the furniture covered with linen, the bric-a-brac gone, and three steamer trunks strapped and standing outside the door. All of which mattered to him less than nothing, for Olivia was there alone.

She came down the dismantled room to meet him, smiling a little and very pale but, St. George thought, even more beautiful than she had been the day before. She was dressed for walking and had on a sober little hat, and straightway St. George secretly wondered how he could ever have approved of anything so flagrant as a Gainsborough. She lifted her veil as they sat down, and St. George liked that. To complete his capitulation she turned to a little table set before the bowing flames of juniper branches in the grate.

"This is breakfast," she told him; "won't you have a cup of tea and a muffin? Aunt Medora will be back presently from the chemist's."

For the first time St. George blessed Mrs. Hastings.

"You are really leaving to-day, Miss Holland?" he asked, noting the little ringless hand that gave him two lumps.

"Really leaving," she assented, "at noon to-day. Mr. Frothingham sails with us, and his daughter Antoinette, who will be a great comfort to me. The prince doesn't know about her yet," she added naively, "but he must take her."

St. George nodded approvingly. Unless all signs failed, he reflected, Yaque had some surprises in store at the hands of the daughter of its sovereign.

"Where does the prince appoint?" he asked.

He listened in entire disapproval while she told him of the place below quarantine where they were to board the submarine. The prince, it appeared, had sent his servant early that morning to assure them that all was in readiness, a bit of oriental courtesy which made no impression upon St. George, though it explained the prompt withdrawal from 19 McDougle Street. When she had finished, St. George rose and stood before the fire, looking down at her from a world of uncertainty.

"I don't like it, Miss Holland," he declared, and hesitated, divided between the desire to tell her that he was going too, and the fear lest Mrs. Hastings should arrive from the chemist's.

Olivia made a gesture of throwing it all from her.

"Have a muffin—do," she begged. "This is my last breakfast in America for a time—let me have a pleasant memory of it. Mr. St. George, I want—oh, I want to tell you how greatly I appreciate—"

"Ah, please," urged St. George, and smiled while he protested, "you see, I've been very selfish about the whole matter. I'm selfish now to be here at all when, I dare say, you've no end of things to do."

"No," Olivia disclaimed, "I have not," and thus proved that she was a woman of genius. For a less complex woman always flutters through the hour of her departure. Only Juno can step from the clouds without packing a bag and feeding the peacocks and leaving, pinned to an asphodel, a note for Jupiter.

"Then tell me what you are going to do in Yaque," he besought. "Forgive me—what are you going to do all alone there in that strange land, and such a land?"

He divined that at this she would be very brave and buoyant, and he was lost in anticipative admiration; when she was neither he admired more than ever.

"I don't know," said Olivia gravely, "I only know that I must go. You see that, do you not—that I must go?"

"Ah, yes," St. George assured her, "I do indeed, believe me. Don't you think," he said, "that I might give you a lamp to rub if you need help? And then I'll appear."

"In Yaque?"

He nodded gravely.

"Yes, in Yaque. I shall rise out of a jar like the Evil Genie; and though I shall be quite helpless you will still have the lamp. And I shall be no end glad to have appeared."

"But suppose," said Olivia merrily, "that when I have eaten a pomegranate or a potato or something in Yaque I forget all about America? And when you step out of the jar I say 'Off with his head,' by mistake. How shall I know it is you when the jar is opened?"

"I shall ask you what the population of Yaque is," he assured her, "and how the island compares with Manhattan, and if this is your first visit, and how you are enjoying your stay; and then you will recognize the talk of civilization and spare me."

"No," she protested, "I've longed to say 'Off with his head' to too many people who have said all that to me. And you mustn't say that a holiday always seems like Sunday, either."

Whereat they both laughed, and it seemed an uncommonly pleasant world, and even the sad errand that was taking Olivia to Yaque looked like a hope.

Then the talk ran on pleasantly, and things went very briskly forward, and there was no dearth of fleet little smiles at this and that. What was she to bring him from Yaque—a pet ibis? No, he had no taste for ibises—unless indeed there should be Fourth-Dimension ibises; and even then he begged that she would select instead a magic field-glass, with which one might see what is happening at an infinite distance; although of what use would that be to him, he wanted to know, since it would be his too late to follow her errantry through Yaque? They felt, as they talked, quite like the puppets of the days of Haroun-al-Raschid; only the puppets, poor children of mere magic, had not the traditions of the golden age of science for a setting, and were obliged to content themselves with mere tricks of jars of genii instead of applied electricity and its daring. What an

Zona Gale

Arabian Nights' Entertainment we might have had if only Scheherazade had ever heard of the Present! As for the thousand-and-one-nights, they would not have contained all her invention. No wonder that the time went trippingly for the two who were concerned in such bewildering speculation as the prince had made possible and who were furthering acquaintanceship besides.

"Ah, well now, at all events," begged St. George at length, "will you remember something while you are away?"

"Your kindness, always," she returned.

"But will you remember," said St. George with his boy's eagerness, "that there is some one who hopes no less than you for your success, and who will be infinitely proud of any command at all from you? And will you remember that, though I may not be successful, I shall at least be doing something to try to help you?"

"You are very good," she said gently, "I shall remember. For already you have not only helped me—you have made the whole matter possible."

"And what of that," propounded St. George gloomily, "if I can't help you just when the danger begins? I insist, Miss Holland, that it takes far more good nature to see some one else set off at adventure than it takes to go one's self. Won't you let me come back here at twelve o'clock and go down with you to the boat?"

"By all means," Olivia assented, "my aunt and I shall both be glad, Mr. St. George. Then you can wish us well. What is a submarine like," she wanted to know; "were you ever on one?"

"Never, excepting a number of times," replied St. George, supremely unconscious of any vagueness. He was rapidly losing count of all events up to the present. He was concerned only with these things: that she was here with him, that the time might be measured by minutes until she would be caught away to undergo neither knew what perils, and that at any minute Mrs. Hastings might escape from the chemist's.

Although the commonplace is no respecter of enchantments, it was quite fifteen minutes before the sword fell and Mrs. Hastings did make the moment her prey, as pinkly excited as though her drawing-room had been untenanted. And in the meantime no one knows what pleasantly absurd thing St. George longed to say, it is so perilous when one is sailing away to Yaque and another stands upon the shore for a word of farewell. But, indeed, if it were not for the soberest moments of farewell, journeys and their returns would become very tame affairs. When the first man and maid said even the most formal farewell, providing they were the right man and the right maid, the very stars must have begun their motion. Very likely the fixed stars are nothing but grey-beards with no imagination. Distance lends enchantment, but the frivolous might say that the preliminary farewell is the mint that coins it. And, enchantment being independent of the commonplace, after all, it may have been that certain stars had already begun to sing while St. George sat staring at the little bowing flames of the juniper branches and Olivia was taking her tea. Then in came Mrs. Hastings, a very literal interfering goddess, and her bonnet was frightfully awry so that the parrot upon it looked shockingly coquettish and irreverent and lent to her dignity a flavour of ill-timed waggishness. But it must be admitted that Mrs. Hastings and everything that she wore were "*les antipodes des graces.*" She was followed by a footman, his arms filled with parcels, and she sank among them on the divan and held out her limp, plump hand for a cup of tea. Mrs. Hastings had the hands that are fettered by little creases at the wrists and whose wedding rings always seem to be uncomfortably snug. She sat down, and her former activity dissolved, as it were, into another sort of energy and became fragments of talk. Mrs. Hastings was like the old woman in Ovid who sacrificed to the goddess of silence, but could never keep still; save that Mrs. Hastings did not sacrifice.

"Good morning, Mr. St. George," she said. "I'm sure I've quite forgotten everything. Olivia dear, I've had all the prescriptions made up that I've ever taken to Rutledge's, because no one can tell what the climate will be like, it's so low on the map. I've looked up the Azores—that's where we get some of our choicest cheese. And camphor—I've got a pound of camphor. And I must say positively that I always was against these wars in the far East, because all the camphor comes from Korea or one of those frightful islands and now it has gone up twenty-six cents a pound. And then the flaxseed, Olivia dear. I've got a tin of flaxseed, for no one can tell—"

St. George doubted if she knew when he said good morning, although she named him Mr. St. John, gave him permission to go to the boat, hoped in one breath that he would come again to see them, and in the next that he would send them a copy of whatever the *Sentinel* might publish about them, in serene oblivion of the state of the post-office department in Yaque. Mrs. Hastings, in short, was one of the women who are thrown into violent mental convulsions by the prospect of a journey; this was not at all because she was setting sail specifically for Yaque, for the moment that she saw a porter or a pier, though she was bound only for the Bronx or Staten Island, she was affected in the same way.

As Olivia gave St. George her hand he came perilously near telling her that he would follow her to Yaque; but he reflected that if he were to tell her at all, he would better do so on the way to the submarine. So he went blindly down the hall and rang the elevator bell for so long that the boy deliberately stopped on the floor below and waited, with the diabolical independence of the American lords of the lift, "for to teach 'im a lessing," this one explained to a passing chamber-maid.

St. George hurried to his apartment to leave a note for Amory who was directed upon his arrival to bide there and await his host's return. Then he paced the floor until it was time to go back to the Boris, deaf to Rollo's solemn information that the dust comes up out of the varnish of furniture during the night, like cream out of milk. By the time he had boarded a downtown car, St. George had tortured himself to distraction, and his own responsibility in this submarine voyage loomed large and threatening. Therefore, it suddenly assumed the proportion of mountains yet unseen when, though it wanted ten minutes to twelve when he reached the Boris, his card was returned by a faint polite clerk with the information that Mrs. Hastings and Miss Holland had been gone from the hotel for half an hour. There was a note for him in their box the clerk believed, and presently produced it—a brief, regretful word from Olivia telling him that the prince had found that they must leave fully an hour earlier than he had planned.

Sick with apprehension, cursing himself for the ease and dexterity with which he had permitted himself to be outwitted by Tabnit, St. George turned blindly from the office with some vague idea of chartering all the tugs in the harbour. It came to him that he had bungled the matter from first to last, and that Bud or Bennietod would have used greater shrewdness. And while he was in the midst of anathematizing his characteristic confidence he stepped in the outer hallway and saw that which caused that confidence to balloon smilingly back to support him.

In the vestibule of the Boris, deaf to the hovering attention of a door-boy more curious than dutiful, stood two men of the stature and complexion of Prince Tabnit of Yaque. They were dressed like the youth who had answered the door of the prince's apartment, and they were speaking softly with many gestures and evidently in some perplexity. The drooping spirits of St. George soared to Heaven as he hastened to them.

"You are asking for Miss Holland, the daughter of King Otho of Yaque," he said, with no time to smile at the pranks of the democracy with hereditary titles.

The men stared and spoke almost together.

"We are," they said promptly.

"She is not here," explained St. George, "but I have attended to some affairs for her. Will you come with me to my apartment where we may be alone?"

The men, who somehow made St. George think of tan-coloured greyhounds with very gentle eyes, consulted each other, not with the suspicion of the vulgar but with the caution of the thorough-bred.

"Pardon," said one, "if we may be quite assured that this is Miss Holland's friend to whom we speak—"

St. George hesitated. The hall-boy listened with an air of polite concern, and there were curious over-shoulder glances from the passers-by. Suddenly St. George's face lighted and he went swiftly through his pockets and produced a scrap of paper— the fragment that had lain that morning on the floor of the prince's deserted apartment, and that bore the arms of the King of Yaque. It was the strangers' turn to regard him with amazement. Immediately, to St. George's utmost embarrass-ment, they both bowed very low and pronounced together:

"Pardon, adon!"

"My name is St. George," he assured them, "and let's get into a cab."

They followed him without demur.

St. George leaned back on the cushions and looked at them— lean lithe little men with rapid eyes and supple bodies and great repose. They gave him the same sense of strangeness that he had felt in the presence of the prince and of the woman in the Bitley Reformatory—as if, it whimsically flashed to him, they some way rhymed with a word which he did not know.

"What is it," St. George asked as they rolled away, "what is it that you have come to tell Miss Holland?"

Only one of the men spoke, the other appearing content to show two rows of exceptionally white teeth.

"May we not know, adon," asked the man respectfully, "whether the prince has given her his news? And if the prince is still in your land?"

"The prince's servant, Elissa, has tried to stab Miss Holland and has got herself locked up," St. George imparted without hesitation.

An exclamation of horror broke from both men.

"To stab—to *kill*!" they cried.

"Quite so," said St. George, "and the prince, upon being discovered, disclosed some very important news to Miss Holland, and she and her friends started an hour ago for Yaque."

"That is well, that is well!" cried the little man, nodding, and momentarily hesitated; "but yet his news—what news, adon, has he told her?"

For a moment St. George regarded them both in silence.

"Ah, well now, what news had he?" he asked briefly.

The men answered readily.

"Prince Tabnit was commissioned by the Yaquians to acquaint the princess with the news of the strange disappearance of her father, the king, and to supplicate her in his place to accept the hereditary throne of Yaque."

"Jupiter!" said St. George under breath.

In a flash the whole matter was clear to him. Prince Tabnit had delivered no such message from the people of Yaque, but had contented himself with the mere intimation that in some vanishing future she would be expected to ascend the throne. And he had done this only when Olivia herself had sought him out after an attempt had been made upon her life by his servant. It seemed to St. George far from improbable that the woman had been acting under the prince's instructions and, that failing, he himself had appeared and obligingly placed the daughter of King Otho precisely within the prince's power. Now she was gone with him, in the hope of aiding her father, to meet Heaven knew what peril in this pagan island; and he, St. George, was wholly to blame from first to last.

"Good Heavens," he groaned, "are you sure—but are you sure?"

"It is simple, adon," said the man, "we came with this message from the people of Yaque. A day before we were to land, Akko and I—I am Jarvo—overheard the prince plan with the others to tell her nothing—nothing that the people desire. When they knew that we had heard they locked us up and we have only this morning escaped from the submarine. If the prince has told her this message everything is well. But as for us, I do not know. The prince has gone."

"He told her nothing—nothing," said St. George, "but that her father and the Hereditary Treasure have disappeared. And he has taken her with him. She has gone with him."

Deaf alike to their exclamations and their questions St. George sat staring unseeingly through the window, his mind an abyss of fear. Then the cab drew up at the door of his hotel and he turned upon the two men precipitantly.

"See," he cried, "in a boat on the open sea, would you two be at all able to direct a course to Yaque?"

Both men smiled suddenly and brilliantly.

"But we have stolen a chart," announced Jarvo with great

simplicity, "not knowing what thing might befall."

St. George wrenched at the handle of the cab door. He had a glimpse of Amory within, just ringing the elevator bell, and he bundled the two little men into the lobby and dashed up to him.

"Come on, old Amory," he told him exultingly. "Heaven on earth, put out that pipe and pack. We leave for Yaque tonight!"

CHAPTER VII

DUSK, AND SO ON

Dusk on the tropic seas is a ceremony performed with reverence, as if the rising moon were a priestess come among her silver vessels. Shadows like phantom sails dip through the dark and lie idle where unseen crafts with unexplained cargoes weigh anchor in mid-air. One almost hears the water cunningly lap upon their invisible sides.

To Little Cawthorne, lying luxuriously in a hammock on the deck of *The Aloha*, fancies like these crowded pleasantly, and slipped away or were merged in snatches of remembered songs. His hands were clasped behind his head, one foot was tapping the deck to keep the hammock in motion while strange compounds of tune and time broke aimlessly from his lips.

"Meet me by moonlight alone,
And then I will tell you a tale.
Must be told in the moonlight alone
In the grove at the end of the vale"

he caroled contentedly.

Amory, the light of his pipe cheerfully glowing, lay at full length in a steamer chair. *The Aloha* was bounding briskly forward, a solitary speck on the bosom of darkening purple, and the men sitting in the companionship of silence, which all the world praises and seldom attains, had been engaging in that most entertaining of pastimes, the comparison of present comfort with past toil. Little Cawthorne's satisfaction flowered in speech.

"Two weeks ago to-night," he said, running his hands through his grey curls, "I took the night desk when Ellis was knocked out. And two weeks ago to-morrow morning we were the only paper to be beaten on the Fownes will story. Hi—you."

"Happy, Cawthorne?" Amory removed his pipe to inquire with idle indulgence.

"Am I happy?" affirmed Little Cawthorne ecstatically in four tones, and went on with his song:

"The daylight may do for the gay,
The thoughtless, the heartless, the free,
But there's something about the moon's ray
That is sweeter to you and to me."

"Did you make that up?" inquired Amory with polite interest.

"I did if I want to," responded Little Cawthorne. "Everything's true out here—go on, tell everything you like. I'll believe you."

St. George came out of the dark and leaned on the rail without speaking. Sometimes he wondered if he were he at all, and he liked the doubt. He felt pleasantly as if he had been cut loose from all old conditions and were sailing between skies to some unknown planet. This was not only because of the strange waters rushing underfoot but because of the flowering and singing of something within him that made the world into which he was sailing an alien place, heavenly desirable. A week ago that day *The Aloha* had weighed anchor, and these seven days, in fairly fortunate weather, her white nose had been cleaving seas to traverse which had so long been her owner's dream; and yet her owner, in pleasant apostasy, had turned his back upon the whole matter of what he had been used to dream, and now ungratefully spent his time in trying to count the hours to his journey's end.

Somewhere out yonder, he reflected, as he leaned on the rail, this southern moonlight was flooding whatever scene *she* looked on; the lapping of the same sea was in her ears; and his future and hers might be dependent upon those two perplexed tan-coloured greyhounds below. By which one would have said that matters had been going briskly forward with St. George since the morning that he had breakfasted with Olivia Holland.

Exactly when the end of the journey would be was not evident either to him or to the two strange creatures who proposed to be his guides. Or rather to Jarvo, who was still the spokesman; lean little Akko, although his intelligence was unrivaled, being content with monosyllables for stepping-stones while the stream of Jarvo's soft speech flowed about him. Barnay, the captain, frankly distrusted them both, and confided to St. George that "them two little jool-eyed scuts was limbs av the old gint himself, and they reminded him, Barnay, of a pair of haythen naygurs," than which he could say no more. But then, Barnay's wholesale skepticism was his only recreation, save talking about his pretty daughter "of school age," and he liked to stand tucking his beard inside his collar and indulging in both. In truth, Barnay, who knew the waters of the Atlantic fairly well, was sorely tried to take orders from the two little brown strangers who, he averred, consulted a "haythen apparaytus" which they would cheerfully let him see but of which he could "make no more than av the spach av a fish," and then directed him to take courses which lay far outside the beaten tracks of the high seas.

St. George, who had had several talks with them, was puzzled and doubtful, and more than once confided to himself that the lives of the passenger list of *The Aloha* might be worth no more than coral headstones at the bottom of the South Atlantic. But he always consoled himself with the cheering reflection that he had had to come—there was no other way half so good. So *The Aloha* continued to plow her way as serenely as if she were heading toward the white cliffs of Dover and trim villas and a custom-house. And the sea lay a blue, uninhabited glory save as land that Barnay knew about marked low blades of smoke on the horizon and slipped back into blue sheaths.

This was the evening of the seventh day, and that noon Jarvo had looked despondent, and Barnay had sworn strange oaths, and St. George had been disquieted. He stood up now, going vaguely down into his coat pockets for his pipe, his erect figure thrown in relief against the hurrying purple. St. George was good to look at, and Amory, with the moonlight catching the glass of his pince-nez, smoked and watched him, shrewdly pondering upon exactly how much anxiety for the success of the enterprise was occupying the breast of his friend and how much of an emotion a good bit stronger. Amory himself was not in love, but there existed between him and all who were a special kinship, like that between a lover of music and a musician.

Little Cawthorne rose and shuffled his feet lazily across deck.

"Where is that island, anyway?" he wanted to know, gazing meditatively out to sea.

St. George turned as if the interruption was grateful.

"The island. I don't see any island," complained Little Cawthorne. "I tell you," he confided, "I guess it's just Chillingworth's little way of fixing up a nice long vacation for us."

They smiled at memory of Chillingworth's grudging and snarling assents to even an hour off duty.

From below came Bennietod, walking slowly. The seaman's life was not for Bennietod, and he yearned to reach land as fervently as did St. George, though with other anxiety. He sat down on the moon-lit deck and his face was like that of a little old man with uncanny shrewdness. His week among them had wrought changes in the head office boy. For Bennietod was ambitious to be a gentleman. His covert imitations had always amused St. George and Amory. Now in the comparative freedom of *The Aloha* his fancy had rein and he had adopted all the habits and the phrases which he had long reserved and liked best, mixing them with scraps of allusions to things which Benfy had encouraged him to read, and presenting the whole in his native lower East-side dialect. Bennietod was Bowery-born and office-bred, and this sad metropolitanism almost made of him a good philosopher.

"I'd like immensely to say something," observed St. George abruptly, when his pipe was lighted.

"Oh, yes. All right," shrilled Little Cawthorne with resignation, "I suppose you all feel I'm the Jonah and you thirst to scatter me to the whales."

"I want to know," St. George went on slowly, "what you think. On my life, I doubt if I thought at all when we set out. This all promised good sport, and I took it at that. Lately, I've been wondering, now and then, whether any of you wish yourselves well out of it."

For a moment no one spoke. To shrink from expression is a characteristic in which the extremes of cultivation and mediocrity meet; the reserve of delicacy in St. George and Amory would have been a reserve of false shame in Bennietod, and of an exaggerated sense of humour in Little Cawthorne. It was not remarkable that from the moment the enterprise had been entered upon, its perils and its doubtful outcome had not once been discussed. St. George vaguely reckoned with this as he waited, while Amory smoked on and blew meditative clouds and regarded the bowl of his pipe, and Little Cawthorne ceased the motion of his hammock, and Bennietod hugged his knees and looked shrewdly at the moon, as if he knew more about the moon than he would care to tell. St. George felt his heart sink a little. Then Little Cawthorne rose and squared valiantly up to him.

"What," inquired the little man indignantly, "are you trying to do? Pick a fight?"

St. George looked at him in surprise.

"Because if you are," continued little Cawthorne without preamble, "we're three to one. And three of us are going to Yaque. We'll put you ashore if you say so."

St. George smiled at him gratefully.

"No—Bennietod?" inquired Little Cawthorne.

Bennietod, pale and manifestly weak, grinned cheerfully and fumbled in sudden abashment at an amazing checked Ascot which he had derived from unknown sources.

"Bes' t'ing t'ever I met up wid," he assented, "ef de deck'd lay down levil. I'm de sonny of a sea-horse if it ain't."

"Amory?" demanded the little man.

Amory looked along his pipe and took it briefly from his lips and shook his head.

"Don't say these things," he pleaded in his pleasant drawl, "or I'll swear something horrid."

St. George merely held his pipe by the bowl and nodded a little, but the hearts of all of them glowed.

After dinner they sat long on deck. Rollo, at his master's invitation, joined them with a mandolin, which he had been discovered to play considerably better than any one else on board. Rollo sat bolt upright in a reclining chair to prove that he did not forget his station and strummed softly, and acknowledged approval with:

"Yes, sir. A little music adds an air to any occasion, *I* always think, sir."

The moon was not yet full, but its light in that warm world was brilliant. The air was drowsy and scented with something that might have been its own honey or that might have come from the strange blooms, water-sealed below. Now and then St. George went aside for a space and walked up and down the deck or sent below for Jarvo. Once, as Jarvo left St. George's side, Little Cawthorne awoke and sat upright and inquiring, in his hammock.

"What *is* the matter with his feet?" he inquired peevishly. "I shall certainly ask him directly."

"It's the seventh day out," Amory observed, "and still nobody knows."

For Jarvo and Akko had another distinction besides their diminutive stature and greyhound build. Their feet, clad in soft soleless shoes, made of skins, were long and pointed and of almost uncanny flexibility. It had become impossible for any one to look at either of the little men without letting his eyes wander to their curiously expressive feet, which, like "courtier speech," were expressive without revealing anything.

"I t'ink," Bennietod gave out, "dat dey're lost Eyetalian organ-grinder monkeys, wid huming intelligence, like Bertran's Bimi."

"What a suspicious child it is," yawned Little Cawthorne, and went to sleep again. Toward midnight he awoke, refreshed and happy, and broke into instant song:

"The daylight may do for the gay,
The thoughtless, the heartless, the free,
But there's something about the moon's ray—"

he was chanting in perfect tonelessness, when St. George cried out. The others sprang to their feet.

"Lights!" said St. George, and gave the glass to Amory, his hand trembling, and very nearly snatched it back again.

Far to the southeast, faint as the lost Pleiad, a single golden point pricked the haze, danced, glimmered, was lost, and reappeared to their eager eyes. The impossibility of it all, the impossibility of believing that they could have sighted the lights of an island hanging there in the waste and hitherto known to nobody simply because nobody knew the truth about the Fourth Dimension did not assail them. So absorbed had St. George become in the undertaking, so convincing had been the events that led up to it, and so ready for anything in any dimension were his companions, that their excitement was simply the ancient excitement of lights to the mariner and nothing more; save indeed that to St. George they spoke a certain language sweeter than the language of any island lying in the heart of mere science or mere magic either.

When it became evident that the lights were no will-o'-the-wisps, born of the moon and the void, but the veritable lights that shine upon harbours, Bennietod tumbled below for Jarvo, who came on deck and gazed and doubted and well-nigh wept for joy and poured forth strange words and called aloud for Akko. Akko came and nodded and showed white teeth.

"To-morrow," he said only.

Barnay came.

"Fwhat matther?" He put it cynically, scowling critically at Jarvo and Akko. "All in the way av fair fight, that'll be about Mor-rocco, if I've the full av my wits about me, an' music to my eyes, by the same token."

Jarvo fixed him with his impenetrable look.

"It is the light of the king's palace on the summit of Mount Khalak," he announced simply.

The light of the king's palace. St. George heard and thrilled with thanksgiving. It would be then the light at her very threshold, provided the impossible is possible, as scientists and devotees have every reason to think. But was she there—was she there? If there was an oracle for the answer, it was not St. George. The little white stars danced and signaled faintly on the far horizon. Whatever they had to reveal was for nearer eyes than his.

The glass passed from hand to hand, and in turn they all swept the low sky where the faint points burned; but when some one had cried that the lights were no longer visible, and the others had verified the cry by looking blankly into a sudden waste of milky black—black water, pale light—and turned baffled eyes to Jarvo, the little man spoke smoothly, not even reaching a lean, brown hand for the glass.

"But have no fear, adon," he reassured them, "the chart is not exact—it is that which has delayed us. It will adjust itself. The light may long disappear, but it will come again. The gods will permit the possible."

They looked at one another doubtfully when the two little brown men had gone below, where Barnay had immediately retired, tucking his beard in his collar and muttering sedition. If the two strange creatures were twin Robin Goodfellows perpetrating a monstrous twentieth century prank, if they were gigantic evolutions of Puck whose imagination never went far beyond threshing corn with shadowy flails, at least this very modern caper demanded respect for so perfectly catching the spirit of the times. At all events it was immensely clever of them to have put their finger upon the public pulse and to have realized that the public imagination is ready to believe anything because it has seen so much proved. Still, "science was faith once"; and besides, to St. George, charts and compasses of all known and unknown systems of seamanship were suddenly become but the dead letter of the law. The spirit of the whole matter was that Olivia might be there, under the lights that his own eyes would presently see again. "Who, remembering the first kind glance of her whom he loves, can fail to believe in magic?" It is very likely that having met Olivia at all seemed at that moment so wonderful to St. George that any of the "frolic things" of science were to be accepted with equanimity.

For an hour or more the moon, flooding the edge of the deck of *The Aloha*, cast four shadows sharply upon the smooth boards. Lined up at the rail stood the four adventurers, and the glass passed from one to another like the eye of the three Grey Sisters. The far beacon appeared and disappeared, but its actuality might not be doubted. If Jarvo and Akko were to be trusted, there in the velvet distance lay Yaque, and Med, the King's City, and the light upon the very palace of its American sovereign.

St. George's pulses leaped and trembled. Amory lifted lazy lids and watched him with growing understanding and finally, upon a pretext of sleep, led the others below. And St. George, with a sense of joyful companionship in the little light, paced the deck until dawn.

CHAPTER VIII

THE PORCH OF THE MORNING

By afternoon the island of Yaque was an accomplished fact of distinguishable parts. There it lay, a thing of rock and green, like the islands of its sister latitudes before which the passing ships of all the world are wont to cast anchor. But having once cast anchor before Yaque the ships of all the world would have had great difficulty in landing anybody.

Sheer and almost smoothly hewn from the utmost coast of the island rose to a height of several hundred feet one scarcely deviating wall of rock; and this apparently impregnable wall extended in either direction as far as the sight could reach. Above the natural rampart the land sloped upward still in steep declivities, but cut by tortuous gorges, and afar inland rose the mountain upon whose summit the light had been descried. There the glass revealed white towers and columns rising from a mass of brilliant tropical green, and now smitten by the late sun; but save these towers and columns not a sign of life or habitation was discernible. No smoke arose, no wharf or dock broke the serene outline of the black wall lapped by the warm sea; and there was no sound save that of strong torrents afar off. Lonely, inscrutable, the great mass stood, slightly shelved here and there to harbour rank and blossomy growths of green and presenting a rugged beauty of outline, but apparently as uninhabitable as the land of the North Silences.

Consternation and amazement sat upon the faces of the owner

of *The Aloha* and his guests as they realized the character of the remarkable island. St. George and Amory had counted upon an adventure calling for all diplomacy, but neither had expected the delight of hazard that this strange, fairy-like place seemed about to present. Each felt his blood stirring and singing in his veins at the joy of the possibilities that lay folded before them.

"We shall be obliged to land upon the east coast then, Jarvo?" observed St. George; "but how long will it take us to sail round the island?"

"Very long," Jarvo responded, "but no, adon, we land on this coast."

"How is that possible?" St. George asked.

"Well, hi—you," said Little Cawthorne, "I'm a goat, but I'm no mountain goat. See the little Swiss kid skipping from peak to peak and from crag to crag—"

"Do we scale the wall?" inquired St. George, "or is there a passage in the rock?"

Bennietod hugged himself in uncontrollable ecstasy.

"Hully Gee, a submarine passage, in under de sea, like Jules Werne," he said in a delight that was almost awe.

"There is a way over the rock," said Jarvo, "partly hewn, partly natural, and this is known to the islanders alone. That way we must take. It is marked by a White Blade blazoned on the rock over the entrance of the submarines. The way is cunningly concealed—hardly will the glass reveal it, adon."

Barnay shook his head.

"You've a bad time comin' with the home-sickness," he prophesied, tucking his beard far down in his collar until he looked, for Barnay, smooth-shaven. "I've sailed the sou' Atlantic up an' down fer a matther av four hundhred years, more or less, an' I niver as much as seed hide *nor* hair av the place before this prisint. There ain't map or chart that iver dhrawed breath that shows ut, new or old. Ut's been lifted out o' ground to be afther swallowin' us in—a sweet dose will be the lot av us, mesilf with as foine a gir-rl av school age as iver you'll see in anny counthry."

"Ah yes, Barnay," said St. George soothingly—but he would have tried now to soothe a man in the embrace of a sea-serpent in just the same absent-minded way, Amory thought indulgently.

The sun was lowering and birds of evening were beginning to brood over the painted water when *The Aloha* cast anchor. In the late light the rugged sides of the island had an air of almost sinister expectancy. There was a great silence in their windless shelter broken only by the boom and charge of the breakers and the gulls and choughs circling overhead, winging and dipping along the water and returning with discordant cries to their crannies in the black rock. Before the yacht, blazoned on a dark, water-polished stratum of the volcanic stone, was the White Blade which Jarvo told them marked the subterranean entrance to the mysterious island.

St. George and his companions and Barnay, Jarvo and Akko were on deck. Rollo, whose soul did not disdain to be valet to a steam yacht, was tranquilly mending a canvas cushion.

"The adon will wait until sunrise to go ashore?" asked Jarvo.

"*Sunrise!*" cried St. George. "Heaven on earth, no. We'll go now."

There was no need to ask the others. Whatever might be toward, they were eager to be about, though Rollo ventured to St. George a deprecatory: "You know, sir, one can't be too careful, sir."

"Will you prefer to stay aboard?" St. George put it quietly.

"Oh, no, sir," said Rollo with a grieved face, "one should meet danger with a light heart, sir," and went below to pack the oil-skins.

"Hear me now," said Barnay in extreme disfavour. "It's I that am to lay hereabouts and wait for you, sorr? Lord be good to me, an' fwhat if she lays here tin year', and you somewheres fillin' the eyes av the aygles with your brains blowed out, neat?" he demanded misanthropically. "Fwhat if she lays here on that gin'ral theory till she's rotted up, sorr?"

"Ah well now, Barnay," said St. George grimly, "you couldn't have an easier career."

Little Cawthorne, from leaning on the rail staring out at the island, suddenly pulled himself up and addressed St. George.

"Here we are," he complained, "here has been me coming through the watery deep all the way from Broadway, with an octopus clinging to each arm and a dolphin on my back, and you don't even ask how I stood the trip. And do you realize that it's sheer madness for the five of us to land on that island together?"

"What do you mean?" asked St. George.

The little man shook his grey curls.

"What if it's as Barnay says?" he put it. "What if they should bag us all—who'll take back the glad news to the harbour? Lord, you can't tell what you're about walking into. You don't even know the specific gravity of the island," he suggested earnestly. "How do you know but your own weight will flatten you out the minute you step ashore?"

St. George laughed. "He thinks he is reading the fiction page," he observed indulgently. "Still, I fancy there is good sense on the page, for once. We don't know anything about anything. I suppose we really ought not to put all five eggs in one basket. But, by Jove—"

He looked over at Amory with troubled eyes.

"As host of this picnic," he said, "I dare say I ought to stay aboard and let you fellows—but I'm hanged if I will."

Little Cawthorne reflected, frowning; and you could as well have expected a bird to frown as Little Cawthorne. It was rather the name of his expression than a description of it.

"Suppose," he said, "that Bennietod and I sit rocking here in this bay—if it is a bay—while you two rest your chins on the top of that ledge of rock up there, and look over. And about to-morrow or day after we two will venture up behind you, or you could send one of the men back—"

"My thunder," said Bennietod wistfully, "ain't I goin' to get to climb in de pantry window at de palace—nor fire out of a loophole—"

"Bennietod an' I couldn't talk to a prince anyway," said Little Cawthorne; "we'd get our language twisted something dizzy, and probably tell him 'yes, ma'am.'"

St. George's eyes softened as he looked at the little man. He knew well enough what it cost him to make the suggestion, which the good sense of them all must approve. Not only did Little Cawthorne always sacrifice himself, which is merely good breeding, but he made opportunities to do so, which is both well-bred and virtuous. When Rollo came up with the oil-skins they told him what had been decided, and Rollo, the faithful, the expressionless, dropped his eyelids, but he could not banish from his voice the wistfulness that he might have been one to stay behind.

"Sometimes it *is* best for a person to change his mind, sir," was his sole comment.

Presently the little green dory drew away from *The Aloha*, and they left her lying as much at her ease as if the phantom island before her were in every school-boy's geography, with a scale of miles and a list of the principal exports attached.

"If we had diving dresses, adon," Jarvo suggested, "we might have gone down through the sluice and entered by the lagoon where the submarines pass."

"Jove," said Amory, trying to row and adjust his pince-nez at the same time, "Chillingworth will never forgive us for missing that."

"You couldn't have done it," shouted Little Cawthorne derisively, from the deck of the yacht, "you didn't wear your rubbers. If anybody sticks a knife in you send up a r-r-r-ocket!"

The landing, effected with the utmost caution, was upon a flat stone already a few inches submerged by the rising tide. Looking up at the jagged, beetling world above them their task appeared hopeless enough. But Jarvo found footing in an instant, and St. George and Amory pressed closely behind him, Rollo and little Akko silently bringing up the rear and carrying the oil-skins. Slowly and cautiously as they made their way it was but a few minutes until the three standing on the deck, and Barnay open-mouthed in the dory, saw the sinuous line of the five bodies twist up the tortuous course considerably above the blazoned emblem of the White Blade.

In truth, with Jarvo to set light foot where no foot seemed ever before to have been set, with Jarvo to inspect every twig and pebble and to take sharp turns where no turn seemed possible, the ascent, perilous as it was, proved to be no such super-human feat as from below it had appeared. But it seemed interminable. Even when the sea lay far beneath them and the faces of the watchers on the deck of *The Aloha* were no longer distinguishable, the grim wall continued to stretch upward, melting into the sky's late blue.

The afterglow laid a fair path along the water, and the warm dusk came swiftly out of the east. At snail's pace, now with heads bent to knees, now standing erect to draw themselves up by the arms or to leap a wicked-looking crevice, the four took their way up the black side of the rock. Birds of the cliffs, disturbed from long rest, wheeled and screamed about them, almost brushing their faces with long, fearless wings. There was an occasional shelf where, with backs against the wall spotted with crystals of feldspar, they waited to breathe, hardly looking down from the dizzy ledge. Great slabs of obsidian were piled about them between stretches of calcareous stone, and the soil which was like beds of old lava covered by thin layers of limestone, was everywhere pierced by sharp shoulders of stone lying in savage disarray. Gradually rock-slides and rock-edges yielded a less insecure footing on the upper reaches, but the chasms widened and water dripping from lateral crevasses made the vague trail slippery and the occasional earth sodden and treacherous. For a quarter of a mile their way lay over a kind of porous gravel into which their feet sank, and beyond at the summit of a ridge Jarvo halted and threw back to them a summary warning to prepare for "a long leap." A sharp angle of rock, jutting out, had been split down the middle by some ancient force—very likely a Paleozoic butterfly had brushed it with its wing—and the edges had been worn away in a treacherous slope to the very lip of the crumbling promontory. From this edge to the edge of the opposite abutment there was a gap of wicked width, and between was a sheer drop into space wherefrom rose the sound of tumbling waters. When Jarvo had taken the leap, easily and gracefully, alighting on the other side like the greyhound that he resembled, and the others, following, had cleared the edge by as safe a margin as if the abyss were a minor field-day event, St. George and Amory looked back with sudden wonder over the path by which they had come.

"I feel as if I weighed about ninety pounds," said St. George; "am I fading away or anything?"

Amory stood still.

"I was thinking the same thing," he said. "By Jove—do you suppose—what if Little Cawthorne hit the other end of the nail, as usual? Suppose the specific gravity—suppose there is something—suppose it doesn't hold good in this dimension that a body—by Jove," said Amory, "wouldn't that be the deuce?"

St. George looked at Jarvo, bounding up the stony way as easily as if he were bounding down.

"Ah well now," he said, "you know on the moon an ordinary man would weigh only twenty-six or seven pounds. Why not here? We aren't held down by any map!"

They laughed at the pleasant enormity of the idea and were hurrying on when Akko, behind them, broke his settled silence.

"In America," he said, "a man feels like a mountain. Here he feels like a man."

"What do you mean by that?" demanded St. George uneasily. But Akko said no more, and St. George and Amory, with a disquieting idea that each was laughing at the other, let the matter drop.

From there on the way was easier, leveling occasionally, frequently swelling to gentle ridges, and at last winding up a steep trail that was not difficult to keep in spite of the fast falling night. And at length Jarvo, rounding a huge hummock where converging ridges met, scrambled over the last of these and threw himself on the ground.

"Now," he said simply.

The two men stood beside him and looked down. It seemed to St. George that they looked not at all upon a prospect but upon the sudden memory of a place about which he might have dreamed often and often and, waking, had not been able to remember, though its familiarity had continued insistently to beat at his heart; or that in what was spread before him lay the satisfaction of Burne-Jones' wistful definition of a picture: "... a beautiful, romantic dream of something that never was, never will be, in a light better than any light that ever shone, in a land no one can define or remember, only desire..." yet it was to St. George as if he had reached no strange land, no alien conditions; but rather that he had come home. It was like a home-coming in which nothing is changed, none of the little improvements has been made which we resent because no one has thought to tell us of them; but where everything is even more as one remembers than one knew that one remembered.

At his feet lay a pleasant valley filled with the purple of deep twilight. Far below a lagoon caught the late light and spread it in a pattern among hidden green. In the midst of the valley towered the mountain whose summit, royally crowned by shining towers, had been visible from the open sea. At its feet, glittering in the abundant light shed upon its white wall and dome and pinnacle, stood Med, the King's City—but its light was not the light of the day, for that was gone; nor of the moon, not risen; and no false lights vexed the dark. Yet he was looking into a cup of light, as clear as the light in a gazing-crystal and of a quality as wholly at variance with reality. The rocky coast of Yaque was literally a massive, natural wall; and girt by it lay the heart of the island, fertile and populous and clothed in mystery. This new face which Nature turned to him was a glorified face, and some way *it meant what he meant.*

St. George was off for a few steps, trampling impatiently over the coarse grass of the bank. Somewhere in that dim valley— was she there, was she there? Was she in trouble, did she need him, did she think of him? St. George went through the ancient, delicious list as conscientiously as if he were the first lover, and she were the first princess, and this were the first ascent of Yaque that the world had ever known. For by some way of miracle, the mystery of the island was suddenly to him the very mystery of his love, and the two so filled his heart that he could not have told of which he was thinking. That which had lain, shadowy and delicious, in his soul these many days— not so very many, either, if one counts the suns—was become not only a thing of his soul but a thing of the outside world, almost of the visible world, something that had existed for ever and which he had just found out; and here, wrapped in nameless light, lay its perfect expression. When a shaft of silver smote the long grass at his feet, and the edge of the moon rose above the mountain, St. George turned with a poignant exultation—did a mere victory over half a continent ever make a man feel like that?—and strode back to the others.

"Come on," he called ringingly in a voice that did everything but confess in words that something heavenly sweet was in the man's mind, "let's be off!"

Amory was carefully lighting his pipe.

"I feel sort of tense," he explained, "as if the whole place would explode if I threw down my match. What do you think of it?"

St. George did not answer.

"It's a place where all the lines lead up," he was saying to himself, "as they do in a cathedral."

The four went the fragrant way that led to the heart of the island. First the path followed the high bank the branches of whose tropical undergrowth brushed their faces with brief gift of perfume. On the other side was a wood of slim trunks, all depths of shadow and delicacies of borrowed light in little pools. Everywhere, everywhere was a chorus of slight voices, from bark and air and secret moss, singing no forced notes of monotone, but piping a true song of the gladness of earth, plaintive, sweet, indescribably harmonious. It came to St. George that this was the way the woods at night would always sound if, somehow, one were able to hear the sweetness that poured itself out. Even that familiar sense in the night-woods that something is about to happen was deliciously present with him; and though Amory went on quietly enough, St. George swam down that green way, much as one dreams of floating along a street, above-heads.

The path curved, and went hesitatingly down many terraces. Here, from the dimness of the marge of the island, they gradually emerged into the beginnings of the faint light. It was not like entering upon dawn, or upon the moonlight. It was by no means like going to meet the lights of a city. It was literally "a light better than any light that ever shone," and it wrapped them round first like a veil and then like a mantle. Dimly, as if released from the censer-smoke of a magician's lamp, boughs and glades, lines and curves were set free of the dark; and St. George and Amory could see about them. Yet it did not occur to either to distrust the phenomenon, or to regard it as unnatural or the fruit of any unnatural law. It was somehow quite as convincing to them as is his first sight of electric light to the boy of the countryside, and no more to be regarded as witchcraft.

St. George was silent. It was as if he were on the threshold of Far-Away, within the Porch of the Morning of some day divine. The place was so poignantly like the garden of a picture that one has seen as a child, and remembered as a place past all speech beautiful, and yet failed ever to realize in after years, or to make any one remember, or, save fleetingly in dreams to see once more, since the picture-book is never, never chanced upon again. Sometimes he had dreamed of a great sunny plain, with armies marching; sometimes he had awakened at hearing the chimes, and fancied sleepily that it was infinite music; sometimes, in the country in the early morning, he had had an unreasonable, unaccountable moment of perfect happiness: and now the fugitive element of them all seemed to have been crystallized and made his own in that floating walk down the wooded terraces of this unknown world. And yet he could not have told whether the element was contained in that beauty, or in his thought of Olivia.

At last they emerged upon a narrow, grassy terrace where white steps mounted to a wide parapet. Jarvo ran up the steps and turned:

"Behold Med, adon," he said modestly, as if he had at that moment stirred it up in a sauce-pan and baked it before their astonished eyes.

They were standing at the top of an immense flight of steps extending as far to right and left as they could see, and leading down by easy stages and wide landings to the white-paved city itself. The clear light flooded the scene—lucid, vivid, many-peopled. Far as the eye could see, broad streets extended, lined with structures rivaling in splendour and beauty those unforgotten "topless towers." Temples, palaces, and public buildings rose, storey upon storey, built of hewn stones of great size; and noble arches faced an open square before a temple of colossal masonry crowning an eminence in the centre of the city. Directly in line with this eminence rose the mountain upon whose summit stood the far-seen pillars where burned the solitary light.

If an enchanted city had risen from the waves because some one had chanced to speak the right word, it could have been no more bewildering; and yet the look of this city was so substantial, so adapted to all commonplace needs, so essentially the scene of every-day activity and purpose, that dozens of towns of petty European principalities seem far less actual and practicable homes of men. Busy citizens hurrying, the bark of a dog, the mere tone of a temple bell spoke the ordinary occupations of all the world; and upon the chief street the moon looked down as tranquilly as if the causeway were a continuation of Fifth Avenue.

But it was as if the spirit of adventure in St. George had suddenly turned and questioned him, saying:

"What of Olivia?"

For Olivia gone to a far-away island to find her father was subject of sufficient anxiety; but Olivia in the power of a pretender who might have at command such undreamed resources was more than cool reason could comprehend. That was the principal impression that Med, the King's City, made upon St. George.

"To the right, adon," Jarvo was saying, "where the walls are highest—that is the palace of the prince, the Palace of the Litany."

"And the king's palace?" St. George asked eagerly.

Jarvo lifted his face to the solitary summit light upon the mountain.

"But how does one ascend?" cried St. George.

"By permission of Prince Tabnit," replied Jarvo, "one is borne up by six imperial carriers, trained in the service from birth. One attempting the ascent alone would be dashed in pieces."

"No municipal line of airships?" ventured Amory in slow astonishment.

Jarvo did not quite get this.

"The airships, adon," he said, "belong to the imperial household and are kept at the summit of Mount Khalak."

"A trust," comprehended Amory; "an absolute monarchy is a bit of a trust, anyhow. Of course, it's sometimes an outraged trust..." he murmured on.

"The adon," said Jarvo humbly, "will understand that we, I and Akko, have borne great risk. It is necessary that we make our peace with all speed, if that may be. The very walls are the ears of Prince Tabnit, and it is better to be behind those walls. May the gods permit the possible."

"Do you mean to say," asked St. George, "that we too would better look out the prince at once?"

"The adon is wise," said Jarvo simply, "but nothing is hid from Prince Tabnit."

St. George considered. In this mysterious place, whose ways were as unknown to him and to his companions as was the etiquette of the court of the moon, clearly diplomacy was the better part of valour. It was wiser to seek out Prince Tabnit, if he had really arrived on the island, than to be upon the defensive.

"Ah, very well," he said briefly, "we will visit the prince."

"Farewell, adon," said Jarvo, bowing low, "may the gods permit the possible."

"Of course you will communicate with us to-morrow," suggested St. George, "so that if we wish to send Rollo down to the yacht—"

"The gods will permit the possible, adon," Jarvo repeated gently.

There was a flash of Akko's white teeth and the two little men were gone.

St. George and Amory turned to the descending of the wide white steps. Such immense, impossible white steps and such a curious place for these two to find themselves, alone, with a valet. Struck by the same thought they looked at each other and nodded, laughing a little.

"Alone in the distance," said Amory, emptying his pipe, "and not a cab to be seen."

Rollo thrust forward his lean, shadowed face.

"Shall I look about for a 'ansom, sir?" he inquired with perfect gravity.

St. George hardly heard.

"It's like cutting into a great, smooth sheet of white paper," he said whimsically, "and making any figure you want to make."

Before they reached the bottom of the steps they divined, issuing from an isolated, temple-seeming building below, a train of sober-liveried attendants, all at first glance resembling Jarvo and Akko. These defiled leisurely toward the strangers and lined up irregularly at the foot of the steps.

"Enter Trouble," said Amory happily.

They found themselves confronting, in the midst of the attendants, an olive man with no angles, whose face, in spite of its health and even wealth of contour, was ridiculously grave, as if the *papier-mache* man in the down-town window should have had a sudden serious thought just before his *papier-mache* incarnation.

"Permit me," said the man in perfect English and without bowing, "to bring to you the greeting of his Highness, Prince Tabnit, and his welcome to Yaque. I am Cassyrus, an officer of the government. At the command of his Highness I am come to conduct you to the palace."

"The prince is most kind," said St. George, and added eagerly: "He is returned, then?"

"Assuredly. Three days ago," was the reply.

"And the king—is he returned?" asked St. George.

The man shook his head, and his very anxiety seemed important.

"His Majesty, the King," he affirmed, "is still most lamentably absent from his throne and his people."

"And his daughter?" demanded St. George then, who could not possibly have waited an instant longer to put that question.

"The daughter of his Majesty, the King," said Cassyrus, looking still more as if he were having his portrait painted, "will in three days be recognized publicly as Princess of Yaque."

St. George's heart gave a great bound. Thank Heaven, she was here, and safe. His hope and confidence soared heavenward. And by some miracle she was to take her place as the people of Yaque had petitioned. But what was the meaning of that news of the prince's treachery which Jarvo and Akko had come bearing? The prince had faithfully fulfilled his mission and had conducted the daughter of the King of Yaque safely to her father's country. What did it all mean?

St. George hardly noted the majestic square through which they were passing. Impressions of great buildings, dim white and misty grey and bathed in light, bewilderingly succeeded one another; but, as in the days which followed the news of his inheritance, he found himself now in a temper of unsurprise, in that mental atmosphere—properly the normal—which regards all miracle as natural law. He even omitted to note what was of passing strangeness: that neither the retinue of the minister nor the others upon the streets cast more than casual glances at their unusual visitors. But when the great gates of the palace were readied his attention was challenged and held, for though mere marvels may become the air one breathes, beauty will never cease to amaze, and the vista revealed was of almost disconcerting beauty.

Avenues of brightness, arches of green, glimpses of airy columns, of boundless lawns set with high, pyramidal shrines, great places of quiet and straight line, alleys whose shadow taught the necessity of mystery, the sound of water—the pure, positive element of it all—and everywhere, above, below and far, that delicate, labyrinth light, diffused from no visible source. It was as if some strange compound had changed the character of the dark itself, transmuting it to a subtle essence more exquisite than light, inhabiting it with wonders. And high above their heads where this translucence seemed to mix with the upper air and to fuse with moonbeams, sprang almost joyously the pale domes and cornices of the palace, sending out floating streamers and pennons of colours nameless and unknown.

"Jupiter," said the human Amory in awe, "what a picture for the first page of the supplement."

St. George hardly heard him. The picture held so perfectly the elusive charm of the Question—the Question which profoundly underlies all things. It was like a triumphant burst of music which yet ends on a high note, with imperfect close, hinting passionately at some triumph still loftier.

From either side of the wall of the palace yard came glittering a detachment of the Royal Golden Guard, clad in uniforms of unrelieved cloth-of-gold. These halted, saluted, wheeled, and between their shining ranks St. George and Amory footed quietly on, followed by Rollo carrying the yellow oil-skins. To St. George there was relief in the motion, relief in the vastness, and almost a boy's delight in the pastime of living the hour.

Yet Royal Golden Guard, majestic avenues, and towered palace with its strange banners floating in strange light, held for him but one reality. And when they had mounted the steps of the mighty entrance, and the sound of unrecognized music reached him—a very myth of music, elusive, vagrant, fugued—and the palace doors swung open to receive them, he could have shouted aloud on the brilliant threshold:

"He says she is here in Yaque."

CHAPTER IX

THE LADY OF KINGDOMS

So there were St. George and Amory presently domiciled in a prince's palace such as Asia and Europe have forgotten, as by and by they will forget the Taj Mahal and the Bon Marche. And at nine o'clock the next morning in a certain Tyrian purple room in the west wing of the Palace of the Litany the two sat breakfasting.

"One always breakfasts," observed St. George. "The first day that the first men spend on Mars I wonder whether the first thing they do will be to breakfast."

"Poor old Mars has got to step down now," said Amory. "We are one farther on. I don't know how it will be, but if I felt on Mars the way I do now, I should assent to breakfast. Shouldn't you?"

"On my life, Toby," said St. George, "as an idealist you are disgusting. Yes, I should."

The table had been spread before an open window, and the window looked down upon the palace garden, steeped in the gold of the sunny morning, and formal with aisles of mighty, flowering trees. Within, the apartment was lofty, its walls fashioned to lift the eye to light arches, light capitals, airy traceries, and spaces of the hue of old ivory, held in heavenly quiet. The sense of colour, colour both captive and atmospheric, was a new and persistent delight, for it was colour purified, specialized, and infinitely extended in either direction from the crudity of the seven-winged spectrum. The room was like an alcove of outdoors, not divorced from the open air and set in contra-distinction, but made a continuation of its space and order and ancient repose—a kind of exquisite porch of light.

Across this porch of light Rollo stepped, bearing a covered dish. The little breakfast-table and the laden side-table were set with vessels of rock-crystal and drinking-cups of silver gilt, and breakfast consisted of delicately-prepared sea-food, a pulpy fruit, thin wine and a paste of delicious powdered gums. These things Rollo served quite as if he were managing oatmeal and eggs and china. One would have said that he had been brought up between the covers of an ancient history, nothing in consequence being so old or so new as to amaze him. Upon their late arrival the evening before he had instantly moved about his duties in all the quiet decorum with which he officiated in three rooms and a bath, emptying the oil-skins, disposing of their contents in great cedar chests, and, from certain rich and alien garments laid out for the guests, pretending as unconcernedly to fleck lint as if they had been broadcloth from Fifth Avenue. He stood bending above the breakfast-table, his lean, shadowed hands perfectly at home, his lean, shadowed face all automatic attention.

"Rollo," said St. George, "go and look out the window and see if Sodom is smoking."

"Yes, sir," said Rollo, and moved to the nearest casement and bent his look submissively below.

"Everything quiet, sir," he reported literally; "a very warm day, sir. But it's easy to sleep, sir, no matter how warm the days are if only the nights are cool. Begging your pardon, sir."

St. George nodded.

"You don't see Jezebel down there in the trees," he pressed him, "or Elissa setting off to found Carthage? Chaldea and Egypt all calm?" he anxiously put it.

Rollo stirred uneasily.

"There's a couple o' blue-tailed birds scrappin' in a palm tree, sir," he submitted hopefully.

"Ah," said St. George, "yes. There would be. Now, if you like," he gave his servant permission, "you may go to the festivals or the funeral games or wherever you choose to-day. Or perhaps," he remembered with solicitude, "you would prefer to be present at the wedding-of-the-land-water-with-the-sea-water, providing, as I suspect, Tyre is handy?"

"Thank you, sir," said Rollo doubtfully.

"Mind you put your money on the crack disc-thrower, though," warned St. George, "and you might put up a couple of darics for me."

"No," languidly begged Amory, "pray no. You are getting your periods mixed something horrid."

"A person's recreation is as good for him as his food, sir," proclaimed Rollo, sententious, anxious to agree.

"Food," said Amory languidly, "this isn't food—it's molten history, that's what it is. Think—this is what they had to eat at the cafes boulevardes of Gomorrah. And to think we've been at Tony's, before now. Do you remember," he asked raptly, "those brief and savoury banquets around one o'clock, at Tony's? From where Little Cawthorne once went away wearing two omelettes instead of his overshoes? Don't tell me that Tonycana and all this belong to the same system in space. Don't tell me—"

He stopped abruptly and his eyes sought those of St. George.

It was all so incredible, and yet it was all so real and so essentially, distractingly natural.

"I feel as if we had stepped through something, to somewhere else. And yet, somehow, there is so little difference. Do you suppose when people die *they* don't notice any difference, either?"

"What I want to know," said Amory, filling his pipe, "is how it's going to look in print. Think of Crass—digging for headlines."

St. George rose abruptly. Amory was delicious, especially his drawl; but there were times—

"Print it," he exclaimed, "you might as well try to print the absolute."

Amory nodded.

"Oh, if you're going to be Neoplatonic," he said, "I'm off to hum an Orphic hymn. Isn't it about time for the prince? I want to get out with the camera, while the light is good."

The lateness of the hour of their arrival at the palace the evening before had prevented the prince from receiving them, but he had sent a most courteous message announcing that he himself would wait upon them at a time which he appointed. While they were abiding his coming, Rollo setting aside the dishes, Amory smoking, strolling up and down, and examining the faint symbolic devices upon the walls' tiling, St. George stood before one of the casements, and looked over the aisles of flowering tree-tops to the grim, grey sides of Mount Khalak, inscrutable, inaccessible, now not even hinting at the walls and towers upon its secret summit. He was thinking how heavenly curious it was that the most wonderful thing in his commonplace world of New York—that is, his meeting with Olivia—should, out here in this world of things wonderful beyond all dream, still hold supreme its place as the sovereign wonder, the sovereign delight.

"I dare say that means something," he said vaguely to himself, "and I dare say all the people who are—in love—know what it does mean," and at this his spirit of adventure must have nodded at him, as if it understood, too.

When, in a little time, Prince Tabnit appeared at the open door of the "porch of light," it was as if he had parted from St. George in McDougle Street but the night before. He greeted him with exquisite cordiality and his welcome to Amory was like a welcome unfeigned. He was clad in white of no remembered fashion, with the green gem burning on his breast, but his manner was that of one perfectly tailored and about the most cosmopolitan offices of modernity. One might have told him one's most subtly humourous story and rested certain of his smile.

"I wonder," he asked with engaging hesitation when he was seated, "whether I may have a—cigarette? That is the name? Yes, a cigarette. Tobacco is unknown in Yaque. We have invented no colonies useful for the luxury. How can it be—forgive me—that your people, who seem remote from poetry, should be the devisers and popularizers of this so poetic pastime? To breathe in the green of earth and the light of the dead sun! The poetry of your American smoke delights me."

St. George smiled as he offered the prince his case.

"In America," he said, "we devised it as a vice, your Highness. We are obliged to do the same with poetry, if we popularize it."

And St. George was thinking:

"Miss Holland. He has seen Miss Holland—perhaps yesterday. Perhaps he will see her to-day. And how in this world am I ever to mention her name?"

But the prince was in the idlest and most genial of humours. He spoke at once of the matters uppermost in the minds of his guests, gave them news of the party from New York, told how they were in comfort in the palace on the summit of Mount Khalak, struck a momentary tragic note in mention of the mystery still mantling the absence of the king and repeated the announcement already made by Cassyrus, the premier, that in two days' time, failing the return of the sovereign, the king's daughter would be publicly recognized, with solemn ceremonial, as Princess of Yaque. Then he turned to St. George, his eyes searching him through the haze of smoke.

"Your own coming to Yaque," he said abruptly, "was the result of a sudden decision?"

"Quite so, your Highness," replied St. George. "It was wholly unexpected."

"Then we must try to make it also an unexpected pleasure," suggested the prince lightly. "I am come to ask you to spend the day with me in looking about Med, the King's City."

He dropped the monogrammed stub of his cigarette in a little jar of smaragdos, brought, he mentioned in passing, from a despoiled temple of one of the Chthonian deities of Tyre, and turned toward his guests with a winning smile.

"Come," he said, "I can no longer postpone my own pleasure in showing you that our nation is the Lady of Kingdoms as once were Babylon and Chaldea."

It was as if the strange panorama of the night before had once more opened its frame, and they were to step within. As the prince left them St. George turned to Rollo for the novelty of addressing a reality.

"How do you wish to spend the day, Rollo?" he asked him.

Rollo looked pensive.

"Could I stroll about a bit, sir?" he asked.

"Stroll!" commanded St. George cheerfully.

"Thank you, sir," said Rollo. "I always think a man can best learn by observation, sir."

"Observe!" supplemented his master pleasantly, as a detachment of the guard appeared to conduct Amory and him below.

"Don't black up the sandals," Amory warned Rollo as he left him, "and be back early. We may want you to get us ready for a mastodon hunt."

"Yes, sir," said Rollo with simplicity, "I'll be back quite some time before tea-time, sir."

St. George was smiling as they went down the corridor. He had been vain of his love that, in Yaque as in America, remained the thing it was, supreme and vital. But had not the simplicity of Rollo taken the leap in experience, and likewise without changing? For a moment, as he went down the silent corridors, lofty as the woods, vocal with faint inscriptions on the uncovered stone, the old human doubt assailed him. The very age of the walls was a protest against the assumption that there is a touchstone that is ageless. Even if there is, even if love is unchanging, the very temper of unconcern of his valet might be quite as persistent as love itself. But the gallery emptying itself into a great court open to the blue among graven rafters, St. George promptly threw his doubt to the fresh, heaven-kissing wind that smote their faces, and against mystery and argument and age alike he matched only the happy clamour of his blood. Olivia Holland was on the island, and all the age was gold. In Yaque or on the continents there can be no manner of doubt that this is love, as Love itself loves to be.

They emerged in the appeasing air of that perfect morning, and the sweetness of the flowering trees was everywhere, and wide roads pointed invitingly to undiscovered bournes, and overhead in the curving wind floated the flags and streamers of those joyous, wizard colours.

They went out into the rejoicing world, and it was like penetrating at last into the heart of that "land a great way off" which holds captive the wistful thought of the children of earth, and reveals itself as elusively as ecstasy. If one can remember some journey that he has taken long ago—Long Ago and Far Away are the great touchstones—and can remember the glamourie of the hour and forget the substructure of events, if he can recall the pattern and forget the fabric, then he will understand the spirit that informed that first morning in Yaque. It was a morning all compact of wonder and delight—wonder at that which half-revealed itself, delight in the ever-present possibility that here, there, at any moment, Olivia Holland might be met. As for the wonder, that had taken some three thousand years to accumulate, as nearly as one could compute; and as for the delight, that had taken less than ten days to make possible; and yet there is no manner of doubt which held high place in the mind of St. George as the smooth miles fled away from hurrying wheels.

Such wheels! Motors? St. George asked himself the question as he took his place beside the prince in the exquisitely light vehicle, Amory following with Cassyrus, and the suites coming after, like the path from a lanthorn. For the vehicles were a kind of electric motor, but constructed exquisitely in a fashion which, far from affronting taste, delighted the eye by leading it to lines of unguessed beauty. They were motors as the ancients would have built them if they had understood the trick of science, motors in which the lines of utility were veiled and taught to be subordinate. The speed attained was by no means great, and the motion was gentle and sacrificed to silence. And when St. George ventured to ask how they had imported the first motors, the prince answered that as Columbus was sailing on the waters of the Atlantic at adventure, the people of Yaque were touring the island in electric motors of much the same description, though hardly the clumsiness, of those which he had noticed in New York.

This was the first astonishment, and other astonishments were to follow. For as they went about the island it was revealed that the remainder of the world is asleep with science for a pillow and the night-lamp of philosophy casting shadows. Yet as the prince exhibited wonders, one after another, St. George, dimly conscious that these are the things that men die to discover, would have given them all for one moment's meeting with Olivia on that high-road of Med. If you come to think of it, this may be why science always has moved so slowly, creeping on from point to point.

Thus it came about that when Prince Tabnit indicated a low, pillared, temple-like building as the home of perpetual motion, which gave the power operating the manufactures and water supply of the entire island, St. George looked and understood and resolved to go over the temple before he left Yaque, and then fell a-wondering whether, when he did so, Olivia would be with him. When the prince explained that it is ridiculous to suppose that combustion is the chief means of obtaining light and heat, or that Heaven provided divinely-beautiful forests for the express purpose of their being burned up; and when he told him that artificial light and heat were effected in a certain reservoir (built with a classic regard for the dignity of its use as a link with unspoken forces) St. George listened, and said over with attention the name of the substance acted upon by emanations—and wondered if Olivia were not afraid of it. So it was all through the exhibition of more wonders scientific and economic than any one has dreamed since every one became a victim of the world's habit of being afraid to dream. Although it is true that when St. George chanced to observe that there were about Med few farms of tilled ground, the prince's reply did startle him into absorbed attention:

"You are referring to agriculture?" Prince Tabnit said after a moment's thought. "I know the word from old parchments brought from Phoenicia by our ancestors. But I did not know that the art is in practice anywhere in the world. Do you mean to assure me," cried the prince suddenly, "that the vegetables which I ate in America were raised by what is known as 'tilling the soil'?"

"How else, your Highness?" doubted St. George, wondering if he were responsible for the fading mentality of the prince.

Prince Tabnit looked away toward the splendour of some new thought.

"How beautiful," he said, "to subsist on the sun and the dust. Beautiful and lost, like the dreams of Mitylene. But I feel as if I were reading in Genesis," he declared. "Is it possible that in this 'age of science' of yours it has not occurred to your people that if plants grow by slowly extracting their own elements from the soil, those elements artificially extracted and applied to the seed will render growth and fruitage almost instantaneous?"

"At all events we've speculated about it," St. George hastened to impart with pride, "just as we do about telephones that will let people see one another when they talk. But nearly every one smiles at both."

"Don't smile," the prince warned him. "Yaque has perfected both those inventions only since she ceased to smile at their probability. Nothing can be simpler than instantaneous vegetation. Any Egyptian juggler can produce it by using certain acids. We have improved the process until our fruits and vegetables are produced as they are needed, from hour to hour. This was one of the so-called secrets of the ancient Phoenicians—has it never occurred to you as important that the Phoenician name for Dionysos, the god of wine-growers, was lost?"

Mentally St. George added another barrel to the cargo of *The Aloha*, and wondered if the *Sentinel* would start botanical gardens and a lighting plant and turn them to the account of advertisers.

All the time, mile upon mile, was unrolling before them the unforgetable beauty of the island. So perfectly were its features marshaled and so exact were its proportions that, as in many great experiences and as in all great poems, one might not, without familiarity, recall its detail, but must instead remain wrapped in the glory of the whole. The avenues, wide as a river, swept between white banks of majestic buildings combining with the magic of great mass the pure beauty of virginal line. Line, the joy of line, the glory of line, almost, St. George thought, the divinity of line, was everywhere manifest; and everywhere too the divinity of colour, no longer a quality extraneous, laid on as insecure fancy dictates, but, by some law long unrevealed, now actually identified with the object which it not so much decorated as purified. The most interesting of the thoroughfares led from the Eurychorus, or public square, along the lagoon. This fair water, extending from Med to Melita, was greenly shored and dotted with strange little pleasure crafts with exquisite sweeping prows and silken canopies. Before a white temple, knee-deep in whose flowered ponds the ibises dozed and contemplated, was anchored the imperial trireme, with delicately-embroidered sails and prow and poop of forgotten metals. From within, temple music sounded softly and was never permitted to be silenced, as the flame of the Vestals might never be extinguished. Here on the shores had begun the morning traffic of itinerant merchants of Med and Melita, compelled by law to carry on their exchange in the morning only, when the light is least lovely. Upon canopied wagons drawn by strange animals, with shining horns, were displayed for sale all the pleasantest excuses for commerce—ostrich feathers, gums, gems, quicksilver, papyrus, bales of fair cloth, pottery, wine and oranges. The sellers of salt and fish and wool and skins were forced down under the wharfs of the lagoon, and there endeavoured to attract attention by displaying fanciful and lovely banners and by liberating faint perfumes of the native orris and algum. Street musicians, playing tunefully upon the zither and upon the crowd, wandered, wearing wreaths of fir, and clustered about stalls where were offered tenuous blades, and statues, and temple vessels filled with wine and flowers.

Zona Gale

At the head of the street leading to the temple of Baaltis (My Lady—Aphrodite) the prince's motor was checked while a procession of pilgrims, white-robed and carrying votive offerings, passed before them, the votive tablet to the Lady Tanith and the Face of Baal being borne at the head of the line by a dignitary in a smart electric victoria. This was one of the frequent Festival Embassies to Melita, to combine religious rites with mourning games and the dedication of the tablet, and there was considerable delay incident to the delivery of a wireless message to the dignitary with the tablet of the Semitic inscription. St. George wondered vaguely why, in a world of marvels, progress should not already have outstripped the need of any communication at all. This reminded him of something at which the prince had hinted away off in another aeon, in another world, when St. George had first seen him, and there followed ten minutes of talk not to be forgotten.

"Would it be possible for you to tell me, your Highness," St. George asked,—and thereafter even a lover must have forgiven the brief apostasy of his thought—"how it can be that you know the English? How you are able to speak it here in Yaque?"

The motor moved forward as the procession passed, and struck into a magnificent country avenue bordered by trees, tall as elms and fragrant as acacias.

"I can tell you, yes," said the prince, "but I warn you that you will not in the least understand me. I dare say, however, that I may illustrate by something of which you know. Do there chance to be, for example, any children in America who are regarded as prodigies of certain understanding?"

"You mean," St. George asked, "children who can play on a musical instrument without knowing how they do it, and so on?"

"Quite so," said the prince with interest.

"Many, your Highness," affirmed St. George. "I myself know a child of seven who can play most difficult piano compositions without ever having been taught, or knowing in the least how he does it."

"Do you think of any one else?" asked the prince.

"Yes," said St. George, "I know a little lad of about five, I should say, who can add enormous numbers and instantly give the accurate result. And he has no idea how he does that, and no one has ever taught him to count above twelve. Oh—every one knows those cases, I fancy."

"Has any one ever explained them, Mr. St. George?" asked the prince.

"How should they?" asked St. George simply. "They are prodigies."

"Quite so," said the prince again. "It is almost incredible that these instances seem to suggest to no one that there must be other ways to 'learn' music and mathematics—and, therefore, everything else—than those known to your civilization. Let me assure you that such cases as these, far from being miracles and prodigies, are perfectly normal when once the principle is understood, as we of Yaque understand it. It is the average intelligence among your people which is abnormal, inasmuch as it is unable to perform these functions which it was so clearly intended to exercise."

"Do you mean," asked St. George, "that we need not learn—as we understand 'learn'?"

"Precisely," said the prince simply. "You are accustomed, I was told in New York, to say that there is 'no royal road to learning.' On the contrary, I say to you that the possibilities of these children are in every one. But to my intense surprise I find that we of Yaque are the only ones in the world who understand how to use these possibilities. Our system of education consists simply in mastering this principle. After that, all knowledge—all languages, for instance—everything—belongs to us."

St. George looked away to the rugged sides of Mount Khalak, lying in its clouds of iris morning mist, unreal as a mountain of Ultima Thule. It was all right—what he had just been hearing was a part of this ultimate and fantastic place to which he had come. And yet *he* was real enough, and so, according to certain approved dialectic, perhaps these things were realities, too. He stole a glance at the prince's profile. Here was actually a man who was telling him that he need not have faced Latin and Greek and calculus; that they might have been his of his own accord if only he had understood how to call them in!

"That would make a very jolly thing of college," he pensively conceded. "You could not show me how it is managed, your Highness?" he besought. "That will hardly come in bulk, too—"

The prince shook his head, smiling.

"I could not 'show you,' as you say," he answered, "any more than I could, at present, send a wireless communication without the apparatus—though it will be only a matter of time until that is accomplished, too."

St. George pulled himself up sharply. He glanced over his shoulder and saw Amory polishing his pince-nez and looking quite as if he were leaning over hansom-doors in the park, and he turned quickly to the prince, half convinced that he had been mocked.

"Suppose, your Highness," he said, "that I were to print what you have just told me on the front page of a New York morning paper, for people to glance over with their coffee? Do you think that even the most open-minded among them would believe that there is such a place as Yaque?"

The prince smiled curiously, and his long-fringed lids drooped in momentary contemplation. The auto turned into that majestic avenue which terminates in the Eurychorus before the Palace of the Litany. St. George's eye eagerly swept the long white way. At its far end stood Mount Khalak. *She* must have passed over this very ground.

"There is," the prince's smooth voice broke in upon his dream, "no such place as Yaque—as you understand 'place.'"

"I beg your pardon, your Highness?" St. George doubted blankly. Good Heavens. Maybe there had arrived in Yaque no Olivia, as he understood Olivia.

"You showed some surprise, I remember," continued the prince, "when I told you, in McDougle Street, that we of Yaque understand the Fourth Dimension."

McDougle Street. The sound smote the ear of St. George much as would the clang of the fire patrol in the midst of light opera.

"Yes, yes," he said, his attention now completely chained. Yet even then it was not that he cared so absorbingly about the Fourth Dimension. But what if this were all some trick and if, in this strange land, Olivia had simply been flashed before his eyes by the aid of mirrors?

"I find," said the prince with deliberation, "that in America you are familiar with the argument that, if your people understood only length and breadth and did *not* understand the Third Dimension—thickness—you could not then conceive of lifting, say, a square or a triangle and laying it down upon another square or triangle. In other words, you would not know anything of *up* and *down*."

St. George nodded. This was the familiar talk of college class-rooms.

"As it is," pursued the prince, "your people do perfectly understand lifting a square and placing it upon a square, or a triangle upon a triangle. But you do not know anything about placing a cube upon a cube, or a pyramid upon a pyramid *so that both occupy the same space at the same time.* We of Yaque have mastered that principle also," the prince tranquilly concluded, "and all that of which this is the alphabet. That is why we are able to keep our island unknown to the world— not to say 'invisible.'"

For a moment St. George looked at him speechlessly; then, in spite of himself, a slow smile overspread his face.

"But," he said, "your Highness, there is not a mathematician in the civilized world who has not considered that problem and cast it aside, with the word that if fourth-dimensional space does exist it can not possibly be inhabited."

"Quite so," said the prince, "and yet here we are."

And, if you come to think of it—as St. George did—that is the only answer to a world of impossibilities already proved possible. But the vista which all this opened smote him with irresistible humour.

"Ah well now, I suppose, your Highness," he said, "that our ocean liners sail clean through the island of Yaque, then, and never even have their smoke pushed sidewise?"

The prince laughed pleasantly.

"Have you ever," he asked, "had occasion to explain the principles of hydraulics, or chess, or philosophical idealism to a three-year-old child, or a charwoman? You must forgive me, but really I can think of no better comparison. I am quite as powerless now as you have been if you have ever attempted it. I can only assure you that such things *are.* Without Jarvo or Akko or some one who understood, you might have sailed the high seas all your life and never have come any nearer to Yaque."

St. George reflected.

"Is Yaque the only example of this kind of thing," he asked, "that the Fourth Dimension would reveal?"

"By no means," said the prince in surprise, "the world is literally teeming with like revelations, once the key is in your hands. The Fourth Dimension is only the beginning. We utilize that to isolate our island. But the higher dimensions are gradually being conquered, too. Nearly all of us can pass into the Fifth at will, 'disappearing,' as you have the word, from the lower dimensions. It is well-known to you that in a land whose people knew length and breadth, but no *up* and *down*, an object might be pushed, but never lifted *up* or put *down*. If it were to be lifted, such a people would believe it to have 'disappeared.' So, from you who know only three dimensions, Yaque has 'disappeared,' until one of us guides you here. Also we pass at will into the Fifth Dimension and even higher, and seem to 'disappear'; the only difference is that, there, we should not be able yet to guide one who did not himself understand how to pass there. Just as one who understands how to die and to come to life, as you have the phrase, would not be able to take with him any one who did not understand how to take himself there..."

St. George listened, grasping at straws of comprehension, remembering how he had heard all this theorized about and smiled at; but most of all he was beset by a practical consideration.

"Then," he said suddenly, the question leaping to his lips almost against his will, "if you hold this key to all knowledge, how is it that the king—Mr. Holland—could get away from you, and the Hereditary Treasure be lost?"

The prince sighed profoundly.

"We have by no means," he said, "perfected our knowledge. We are at one with the absolute in knowledge—true. But the affairs of every day most frequently elude us. Not even the most advanced among us are perfect intuitionists. We have by no means reached that desirable and inevitable day when our minds shall flow together, without need of communication, without possibility of secret. We still suffer the disadvantage of a slight barrier of personality."

"And it is into one of these lapses," thought St. George irreverently, "that the king has disappeared." Aloud he asked curiously concerning a matter which was every moment becoming more incomprehensible.

"But how, your Highness," he said simply, "did your people ever consent to have an American for your king?"

Before the prince could reply there occurred a phenomenon that sent all thought of such insubstantialities as the secrets of the Fourth Dimension far in the background.

The prince's motor, closely followed by the others of the train, had reached a little eminence from which the island unrolled in fair patterns. Before them the smooth road unwound in varied light. At their left lay a still grove from whose depths was glimpsed a slim needle of a tower, rising, arrow-like, from the green. In the distance lay Med, with shining domes. The water of the lagoon gave brightness here and there among the hills. And as St. George and the prince looked over the prospect they saw, far down the avenue toward Med, a little, moving speck—a speck moving with a rapidity which neither the prince's motor nor any known motor of Yaque had ever before permitted itself.

In an instant the six members of the Royal Golden Guard, who upon beautiful, spirited horses rode in advance of the train of the prince, wheeled and thundered back, lifting glittering hands of warning. "Aside! Aside!" shrieked the main Golden Guard, "a motor is without control!"

Immediately there was confusion. At a touch the prince's car was drawn to the road's extreme edge, and the Golden Guards rode furiously back along the train, hailing the peaceful, slow-going machines into orderly retreat. They were all sufficiently amenable, for at sight of the alarming and unprecedented onrush of the growing speck that was bearing full down upon them, anxiety sat upon every face.

St. George watched. And as the car drew nearer the thought which, at first sight of its speed, had vaguely flashed into being, took definite shape, and his blood leaped to its music. Whose hand would be upon that lever, whose daring would be directing its flight, whose but one in all Yaque—and that Olivia's?

It was Olivia. That was plain even in the mere instant that it took the great, beautiful motor, at thirty miles an hour, to flash past them. St. George saw her—coat of hunting pink and fluttering veil and shining eyes; he was dimly conscious of another little figure beside her, and of the unmistakable and agonized Mrs. Hastings in the tonneau; but it was only Olivia's glance that he caught as it swept the prince. There was the faintest possible smile, and she was gone; and St. George, his heart pounding, sat staring stupidly after that shining cloud of dust, frantically wondering whether she could just possibly have seen him. For this was no trick of the imagination, his galloping heart told him that. And whether or not Yaque was a place, the world, the world was within his grasp, instinct with possibilities heavenly sweet. His eyes met Amory's in the minute when Cassyrus, prime minister of Yaque, had it borne in upon him this was no runaway machine, but the ordinary and preferred pace of the daughter of their king; and while Cassyrus, at the enormity of the conception, breathed out expostulations in several languages—some of them known to us only by means of inscriptions on tombs—Amory spoke to St. George:

"Who was the other girl?" he asked comprehensively.

"What other girl?" St. George blankly murmured.

And at this, Amory turned away with a look that could be made to mean whatever Amory meant.

On went the imperial train faring back to Med over the road lately stirred to shining dust by the wheels of Olivia's auto. Olivia's auto. St. George was secretly saying over the words with a kind of ecstatic non-comprehension, when the prince spoke:

"That," he said, "may explain why an American has been able to govern us. Chance crowned him, but he made himself king."

Prince Tabnit hesitated and his eyes wandered—and those of St. George followed—to a far winding dot in that opal valley, a mere speck of silver with a prick of pink, fleeing in a cloud of sunny dust.

"I do not know if you will know what I mean," said the prince, "but hers is the spirit, and the spirit of her father, the king, which Yaque had never known. It is the spirit which we of Phoenicia seem to have lost since the wealth of the world accumulated at her ports and she gave her trust to the hands of mariners and mercenaries, and later bowed to the conqueror. It is the spirit that not all the continental races, I fancy, have for endowment, but yours possesses in rich measure. For this we would exchange half that we have achieved."

St. George nodded, glowing.

"It is a great tribute, your Highness," he said simply, and in his heart he laid it at Olivia's feet.

Thereafter, in the long ride to Melita, during luncheon upon a high white terrace overlooking the sailless sea, and in the hours on the unforgetable roads of the islands, St. George, while incommunicable marvels revealed themselves linked with incommunicable beauty, sat in the prince's motor, his eyes searching the horizon for that fleeing speck of silver and pink. It did not appear again. And when the train of the prince rolled into the yard of the Palace of the Litany it trembled upon St. George's lips to ask whether the formalities of the court would permit him that day to scale the skies and call upon the royal household.

"For whatever he says, I've got to do," thought St. George, "but no matter what he says, I shall go. Doesn't Amory realize that we've been more than twelve hours on this island, and that nothing has been done?"

And then as they crossed the grassy court in the delicate hush of the merging light—the nameless radiance already penetrating the dusk—the prince spoke smoothly, as if his words bore no import deeper than his smile:

"You are come," he said courteously, "in time for one of the ceremonies of our regime most important—to me. You will, I hope, do honour to the occasion by your presence. This evening, in the Hall of Kings in the Palace of the Litany, will occur the ceremony of my betrothal."

"Your betrothal, your Highness?" repeated St. George uncertainly.

"You will be attended by an escort," the prince continued, "and Balator, the commander of the guard, will receive you in the hall. May the gods permit the possible."

He swept through the portico before them, and they followed dumbly.

The betrothal of the prince.

St. George heard, and his eager hope went down in foreboding. He turned, hardly daring to read his own dread in the eyes of Amory.

Amory, as St. George had said, was delicious, especially his drawl; but there were times—now, for example, when all that the eyes of Amory expressed was what his lips framed, *sotto-voce*:

"An American heiress, betrothed to the prince of a cannibal island! Wouldn't Chillingworth turn in his grave at his desk?"

CHAPTER X

TYRIAN PURPLE

The "porch of light" proved to be an especially fascinating place at evening. Evening, which makes most places resemble their souls instead of their bodies, had a grateful task in the beautiful room whose spirit was always uppermost, and Evening moved softly in its ivory depths, preluding for Sleep. Here, his lean, shadowed face all anxiety, Rollo stood, holding at arm's length a parti-coloured robe with floating scarfs.

"It seems to me, sir," he said doubtfully, "that this one would 'ave done better. Beggin' your pardon, sir."

St. George shook his head distastefully.

"It doesn't matter," he said, and broke into a slow smile as he looked at Amory. The robes which the prince had provided for the evening were rather harder to become accustomed to than the notion of intuitive knowledge.

"There's an air about this one though, sir," opined Rollo firmly, "there's a cut—a sort of *way* with the seams, so to speak, sir, that the other can't touch. And cut is what counts, sir, cut counts every time."

"Ah, yes, I dare say, Rollo," said St. George, "and as a judge of 'cut' I don't say you can be equaled. But I do say that in the styles of Deuteronomy you aren't necessarily what you might call up."

"Yes, sir," said Rollo, dropping his eyes, "but a well-dressed man was a well-dressed man, sir, then *as* now."

As a matter of fact the well-knit, athletic young figures looked uncommonly well in the garments *a la mode* in Yaque. One would have said that if the garments followed Deuteronomy fashions they had at all events been cut by the scissors of a court tailor to Louis XV. The result was beautiful and bizarre, but it did not suggest stageland because the colours were so good.

"I dare say," said St. George, examining the exquisitely fine cloth whose shades were of curious depth and richness, "that this may be regular Tyrian purple."

Amory waved his long sleeves.

"Stop," he languidly begged, "you make me feel like a golden text."

St. George went back to the row of open casements and resumed his walk up and down before the windows that looked away to the huge threatening bulk of Mount Khalak. Since the prince's announcement that afternoon St. George had done little besides continuing that walk. Now it wanted hardly half an hour to the momentous ceremony of the evening, big with at least one of the dozen portents of which he accused it.

"Amory," he burst out as he walked, "if you didn't know anything about it, would you say that the prince could possibly have made her consent to marry him?"

Amory, left in the middle of the great room, stood polishing his pince-nez exactly as if he had been waiting at the end of Chillingworth's desk of a bright, American morning.

"If I didn't know anything about it," he said cheerfully, "I should say that he had. As it is, having this afternoon watched a certain motor wear its way past me, I should say that nothing in Yaque is more unlikely. And that's about as strong as you could put it."

"We don't know what the man may have threatened," said St. George morosely, "he may have played upon her devotion to her father to some ridiculous extent. He may have refused to land the submarine at Yaque at all otherwise—"

St. George broke off suddenly.

"Toby!" he said.

Amory looked over and nodded. He had seen that look before on St. George's face.

"She's not going to marry the prince," said St. George, "and if her father is alive and in a hole, he's going to be pulled out. And she's *not* going to marry the prince."

"Why, no," assented Amory, "no."

He had guessed a good deal of the truth since he had been watching St. George flee over seas upon a yacht, shod, so to speak, with fire, and he had arrived at the suspicion that *The Aloha* was winged by little Loves and guided under water by plenty of blue and green dragons. But he had not, until now, been thoroughly certain that St. George's spirit of adventure had another name; and though theoretically his sympathies leaped to the look in his friend's eyes, yet he found himself wondering practically what effect romance would be having upon their enterprise. After all, from a newspaper point of view, to relinquish any part of the adventure was a kind of tragedy, and it cost Amory something to emphasize his assent.

"Of course she won't," he said, "and now let's toddle down and see about it."

When the tread of the feet of a detachment of the Royal Golden Guard was heard without, Rollo advanced to the door with a dignity which amounted to melancholy. The setting of a palace and the proximity of a prince had raised his office to the majesty of skilled labour. He always threw open the door now as who should say, "Enter. But mind you have a reason."

At sight of the long liberty of the corridor where the light lay mysteriously touching tiles and tapestries to festal colours, Amory's spirits rose contagiously, and his eyes shone behind his pince-nez.

"Me," he said, looking ahead with enjoyment at the glittering escort, "me—done in a fabric of about the eleventh shade of the Yaque spectrum—made loose and floppy, after a modish Canaanitish model. I'll wager that when the first-born of Canaan was in the flood-tide of glory, this very gown was worn by one of the most beautiful women in the pentapolis of Philistia. I'm going to photograph the model for the Sunday supplement, and name it *The Nebuchadnezzar.*"

Amory murmured on, and St. George hardly heard him. He could almost count by minutes now the time until he should see her. Would she see him, and might he just possibly speak with her, and what would the evening hold for her? As he went forth where she would be, the spell of the place was once more laid upon him, as it had been laid in the hour of his coming. Once more, as in the hour when he had first looked down upon the valley brimming with a light "better than any light that ever shone" he was at one with the imponderable things which, always before, had just eluded him. Now, as then, the thought of Olivia was the symbol for them all. So the two went on through the winding galleries—silent, haunted—to the great staircase, and below into the crowded court. And when they reached the threshold of the audience-chamber they involuntarily stood still.

The hall was like a temple in its sense of space and height and clear air, but its proportions did not impress one, and indeed one could not remember its boundaries as one does not consider the boundaries of a grove. It was amphitheatre-shaped, and about it ran a splendid colonnade, in the niches of whose cornices were beautiful grotesques—but Yaque seemed to be a land whose very grotesques had all the dignity of the ultimate instead of crying for the indulgence due a phase. The roof was inlaid with prisms of clear stone, and on high were pilasters carved with the Tyrian sphinxes crucified upon upright crosses, surmounted by parhelions of burnished metal. All the seats faced a great dais at the chamber's far end where three thrones were set.

But it was the men and women in the great chamber who filled St. George with wonder. The women—they were beautiful women, slow-moving, slow-eyed, of soft laughter and sudden melancholy, and clear, serene profiles and abundant hair. And they were all *alive*, fully and mysteriously alive, alive to their finger-tips. It was as if in comparison all other women acted and moved in a kind of half-consciousness. It was as if, St. George thought vaguely, one were to step through the frame of a pre-Raphaelite tapestry and suddenly find its strange women rejoicing in fulfillment instead of yearning, in noon instead of dusk. As he stood looking down the vast chamber, all springing columns and light lines lifting through the honey-coloured air, it smote St. George that these people, instead of being far away, were all near, surprisingly, unbelievably near to him,—in a way, nearer to his own elusive personality than he was himself. They were all obviously of his own class; he could perfectly imagine his mother, with her old lace and Roman mosaics, moving at home among them, and the bishop, with his wise, kindly smile. Yet he was irresistibly reminded of a certain haunting dream of his childhood in which he had seemed to himself to walk the world alone, with every one else allied against him because they all knew something that he did not know. That was it, he thought suddenly, and felt his pulse quickening at the intimation: *They all knew something that he did not know*, that he could not know. But, as they swept him with their clear-eyed, impersonal look, a look that seemed in some exquisite fashion to take no account of individuality, he was gratefully aware of a curious impression that they would like to have had him know, too.

"They wish I knew—they'd rather I did know," St. George found himself thinking in a strange excitement, "if only I could know—if only I could know."

He looked about him, smiling a little at his folly. He saw the light flash on Amory's glasses as they turned inquisitively on this and that, and somehow the sight steadied him.

"Ah well," he assured himself, "I'll look them up in a thousand years or so, and we'll dine together, and then we'll say: 'Don't you remember how I didn't know?'"

Immediately there presented himself to them a little man who proved to be Balator, lord-chief-commander of the Royal Golden Guard, and now especially directed by the prince, he pleasantly told them, to be responsible for their entertainment and comfort during the ceremony to follow. They were, in fact, his guests for the evening, but St. George and Amory were uncertain whether, considering his office, this was a high honour or a kind of exalted durance. However, as the man was charming the doubt was not important. He had an attenuated face, so conveniently brown by race as to suggest the most soldierly exposure, and he had great, peaceable, slow-lidded eyes. He was, they subsequently learned, an authority upon insect life in Yaque, for he had never had the smallest opportunity to go to war.

As Balator led his guests to their seats near the throne every one looked on them, as they passed, with the serenest fellowship, and no regard persisted longer than a glance, friendly and fugitive. Balator himself not only refrained from stoning the barbarians with commonplaces, but he did not so much as mention America to them or treat them otherwise than as companions, as if his was not only the cosmopolitanism that knows no municipal or continental aliens of its own class, but a kind of inter-dimensional cosmopolitanism as well.

"Which," said Amory afterward, "was enviable. The next man from Trebizond or Saturn or Fez whom I meet I'm going to greet and treat as if he lived the proverbial 'twenty minutes out.'"

A great clock boomed and throbbed through the palace, striking an hour that was no more intelligible than the jargon of a ship's clock to a landsman. Somewhere an orchestra thrilled into haunting sound, poignant with disclosures barely missed. Overhead, through the mighty rafters of the conical roof, the moon looked down.

"That'll be the same old moon," said Amory. "By Jove! Won't it?"

"It will, please Heaven," said St. George restlessly; "I don't know. Will it?"

Near the throne was seated a company of dignitaries who wore upon their breasts great stars and were soberly dressed in a kind of scholar's gown. Some whispered together and nodded and looked as solemn as tithing men; and others were feverishly restless and continually took papers from their graceful sleeves. By developments these were revealed to be the High Council of Yaque, conservative and radical, even in dimensional isolation. Farther back rose tier upon tier of seats sacred to the wives and daughters of the ministry, and St. George even looked hopelessly and mechanically among these for the face that he sought.

To some seats slightly elevated, not far from the dais, his attention was at length challenged by an upheaving and billowing of purple and black. He looked, and in the same instant what seemed to have been a kind of storm centre resolved itself cloudily into Mrs. Medora Hastings, breathlessly resuming her seat, while Mr. Augustus Frothingham, in indescribably gorgeous apparel elaborately bent to receive— and a member of the High Council bent to hand—two glittering articles which St. George was certain were side-combs. There the lady sat, tilting her head to keep her tortoise-shell glasses on her nose, perpetually curving their chain over her ear, a gesture by which the side-combs were perpetually displaced. If the island people had been painted purple, St. George felt sure that she would have acted quite the same. Personality meant nothing to her—not, as with them, because it had been merged in something greater, but because, with her, it was overborne by self. And there sat Mr. Frothingham (who did not attend the play during court because he believed that a man of affairs should not unduly stimulate the imagination), his head thrown back so that his long hair rested on his amazing collar, his hands laid trimly along his knees. In that crystal air, instinct with its delicate, dominant implication of things imponderable, the personality of each persisted undisturbed, in a kind of adamantine unconsciousness. Again, as when he had considered the soul of Rollo, St. George smiled a shade bitterly. Is it then so easy to persist, he wondered? Is love's uttermost gift so little? But as the music swelled with premonitory meaning, he understood something that its very transitoriness disclosed: the persistence of love, love's mere immortality, is the dead letter of the law without that which is elusive, imponderable, even evanescent as the spirit of the land to which he had come, into which he felt himself new-born.

Immediately, bestowing its gift of altered mood, other music, cut by the lift and fall of trumpets, sounded from hidden places all about the walls and from the alcoves of the lofty roof. Then a veil hanging between two pillars was drawn aside, and the prince's train appeared. There were a detachment of the guard, splendid in their unrelieved gold, and the officers of the court, at their head Cassyrus, the premier, who had manifestly been compounded of Heaven to be a drum-major, and had so undeviating a look that he seemed always to have been caught, red-handed, at his post. Last came Prince Tabnit, dressed in pure white save for a collar of precious stones from which hung the strange green gem that St. George remembered. His clear face and the whiteness of his hair lent to him an air of almost unearthly distinction. His delicate hands wearing no jewels were at his sides, and his head was magnificently erect. He mounted the dais as the music sank to silence, and without preface began to speak.

"My people," he said, and St. George felt himself thrilling with the strength and tenderness of that voice, "in the continuance of this our time of trial we come among you that we may win strength and courage from your presence. Since one mind dwells in us all, we have no need of words of cheer. That no message from his Majesty, the King, has come to us is known to you all, with mourning. But the gods—to whom 'here' is the same as 'there'—will permit the possible, and they have permitted to us the presence of the daughter of our sovereign, by the grace of the infinite, heir to the throne of Yaque. In two days, should his Majesty not then have returned to his sorrowing people, she will, in accordance with our custom, be crowned Hereditary Princess of Yaque and, after one year, Queen of Yaque and your rightful sovereign."

As the prince paused, a little breath of assent was in the room, more potent than any crudity of applause.

"Next," pursued the prince, "we would invite your attention to our own affairs, which are of importance solely as they are affected by the immemorial tradition of the House of the Litany. Therefore, in accordance with the custom of our predecessors for two thousand years," lightly pursued the prince, "we have named this day as the day of our betrothal. Moreover, this is determined upon in justice to the daughters of the twenty peers of Yaque, whose marriage the law forbids until the choice of the head of the House of the Litany has been made..."

St. George listened, and his hope soared heavenward as the hope of young love will soar, in spite of itself, at the mere sight of open sky. The daughters of the twenty peers of Yaque! Of course they were to be considered. Why should he fear that, because Olivia was in Yaque, the mere mention of a betrothal referred to Olivia? He was bold enough to smile at his fears, to smile even when, as the prince ceased speaking, the music sounded again, as it were from the air, in a chorus of pure young voices with a ripple of unknown strings in accompaniment.

Suddenly, at the opening of great doors, a flood of saffron light was poured upon a stair, and at the summit appeared the leisurely head of a procession which the two men were destined never to forget. Across the gallery and down the stair—it might have been the Golden Stair linking Near with Far—came a score of exquisite women in all the glory of their youth, of perfect physical beauty and splendid strength and fullness of life; and the wonder was not their beauty more than a kind of dryad delicacy of that beauty, which was yet not frailty but a look of angelic strength. But they were not remote—they were gloriously human, almost, one would say, divinely human, all gentle movement and warmth and tender breath. They were not remote, save as one's own soul would be remote by its very excess of intimacy with life, Little maids, so shy that their actuality was certain, came before them carrying flowers, and these were followed by youths scattering fragrant burning powder whose fallen flames were instantly pounced upon and extinguished by small furry lemurs trained to lay silver discs upon the flames. And as they all ranged themselves about the throne a little figure appeared at the top of the stairway alone, beneath the lifted curtain.

She was veiled; but the elastic step, the girlish grace, the poise and youthful dignity were not to be mistaken. The room whirled round St. George, and then closed in about him and grew dark. For this was the woman advancing to her betrothal; from the manner of her entrance there could be no doubt of that. And it was none of the daughters of the twenty peers. It was Olivia.

She wore a trailing gown of rainbow hues, more like the hues of water than of texture, and the warm light fell upon these as she descended and variously multiplied them to beauty. Her little feet were sandaled and a veil of indescribable thinness was wound about her abundant hair and fell across her face, but the gold of her hair escaped the veil and rippled along her gown. Carven chains and necklaces were upon her throat, and bracelets of beaten gold and jewels upon her arms. About her forehead glittered a jeweled band with pendent gems which, at her moving, were like noon sun upon water.

As he realized that this was indeed she whom he had come to seek, only to find her hedged about with difficulties—and it might be by divinities—which he had not dreamed of coping, a kind of madness seized St. George. The lights danced before his eyes, and his impulse had to do with rushing up to the dais and crying everybody defiance but Olivia. On the moon-lit deck of *The Aloha* he had dreamed out the island and the rescue of the island princess, and a possible home-going on his yacht to a home about which he had even dared to dream, too. But it had not once occurred to him to forecast such a contingency as this, or, later, so to explain to himself Prince Tabnit's change of purpose in permitting her recognition as Princess of Yaque—indeed, if what Jarvo and Akko had told him in New York were accurate, in bringing her to the island at all. And yet what, he thought crazily, if his guess at her part in this betrothal were far wrong? What if her father's safety were not the only consideration? What if, not unnaturally dazzled by the fairy-land which had opened to her ... even while he feared, St. George knew far better. But the number of terrors possible to a man in love is equal to those of battle-fields.

Amory bent toward him, murmuring excitedly.

"Jupiter," he said, "is she the American girl?"

"She's Miss Holland," answered St. George miserably.

"No—no, not the princess," said Amory, "the other."

St. George looked. On the stair was a little figure in rose and silver—very tiny, very fair, and no doubt the lawyer's daughter.

"I dare say it is," he told him, as one would say, "Now what the deuce of it?"

Prince Tabnit had risen to receive Olivia, and St. George had to see him extend his hand and assist her beside him upon the dais. In the absence of her father she was obliged to stand alone. Then the little figure in rose and silver and one of the daughters of the peers advanced and lifted her veil, and St. George wanted to shout with sudden exultation. This then was she—so near, so near. Surely no great harm could come to them so long as the sea and the mystery of the island no longer lay between them. Did she know of his presence? Although he and Amory were seated so near the throne, they were at one side, and her clear, pure profile was turned toward them. And Olivia did not lift her eyes throughout the prime minister's long address, of which St. George and Amory, so lapped were they in wild projects and importunities, heard nothing until, uttered with indescribable pompousness, as if Cassyrus were a dowager and had made the match himself, the concluding words beat upon St. George's heart like stones. They were the formal announcement of the betrothal of Olivia, daughter of his Majesty, Otho I of Yaque, to Tabnit, Prince of Yaque and Head of the House of the Litany.

St. George saw Prince Tabnit kneel before Olivia and place a ring her hand—no doubt the ring which had betrothed the island princesses for three thousand years. He saw the High Council standing with bowed heads, like the necessary archangels in an old painting; he caught the flash of the turquoise-blue ephod of the head of the religious order, as the benediction was pronounced by its wearer. And through it all he said to himself that all would be well if only she understood, if only she had the supreme self-consciousness to play the game. After all he knew her so little. He was certain of her exquisite, playful fancy, but had she imagination? Would she see the value of the moment and watch herself moving through it? Or would she live it with that feminine, unhumourous seriousness which is woman's weakness? She had an exquisite independence, he was certain that she had humour, and he remembered how alive she had seemed to him, receptive, like a woman with ten senses. But after all, would not her graceful sanity of view, that sense of tradition and unerring taste which he so reverenced, yet handicap her now and prevent her from daring whatever she must dare?

Amory was beside himself. It was all very well to feel a great sympathy for St. George, but the sight was more than journalistic flesh and blood could look upon with sympathetic calm.

"An American girl!" he breathed in spite of himself. "Why, St. George, if we can leave this island alive—"

"Well, *you* won't," St. George explained, with brutal directness, "unless you can cut that."

Before silence had again fallen, the prime minister, all his fever of importance still upon him, once more faced the audience. This time his words came to St. George like a thunderbolt:

"In three days' time, at noon, in this the Hall of Kings," he cried, letting each phrase fall as if he were its proud inventor, "immediately following the official recognition of Olivia, daughter of Otho I, as Hereditary Princess of Yaque, there will be solemnized, according to the immemorial tradition of the island last observed six hundred and eighty-four years ago by Queen Pentellaria, the marriage of Olivia of Yaque, to his Highness, Prince Tabnit, head of the House of the Litany, and chief administrator of justice. *For the law prescribes that no unmarried woman shall sit upon the throne of Yaque.* At noon of the third day will be observed the double ceremony of the recognition and the marriage. May the gods permit the possible."

There was a soft insistence of music from above, a stir and breath about the room, the premier backed away to his seat, and St. George, even with the horrified tightening at his heart, was conscious of a vague commotion from the vicinity of Mrs. Medora Hastings. Then he saw the prince rise and turn to

Olivia, and extend his hand to conduct her from the hall. The great banquet room beyond the colonnade was at once thrown open, and there the court circle and the ministry were to gather to do honour to the new princess, whom Prince Tabnit was to lead to the seat at his right hand at the table's head.

To the amazement of his Highness, Olivia made no movement to accept the hand that he offered. Instead, she sat slightly at one side of the great glittering throne, looking up at him with something like the faintest conceivable smile which, while one saw, became once more her exquisite, girlish gravity. When the music sank a little her voice sounded above it with a sweet distinctness:

"One moment, if you please, your Highness," she said clearly.

It was the first time that St. George had heard her voice since its good-by to him in New York. And before her words his vague fears for her were triumphantly driven. The spirit that he had hoped for was in her face, and something else; St. George could have sworn that he saw, but no one else could have seen the look, a glimpse of that delicate roguery that had held him captive when he had breakfasted with her—several hundred years before, was it?—at the Boris. Ah, he need not have feared for her, he told himself exultantly. For this was Olivia—of America—standing in a company of the women who seemed like the women of whom men dream, and whose presence, save in glimpses at first meetings, they perhaps never wholly realize. These were the women of the land which "no one can define or remember." And yet, as he watched her now, St. George was gloriously conscious that Olivia not only held her own among them, but that in some charm of vividness and of *knowledge of laughter*, she transcended them all.

A ripple of surprise had gone round the room. For all the air of the ultimate about the island-women, St. George doubted whether ever in the three thousand years of Yaque's history a woman had raised her voice from that throne upon a like occasion. And such a tender, beguiling, cajoling little voice it was. A voice that held little remarques upon whatever it had just said, and that made one breathless to know what would come next.

"Bully!" breathed Amory, his eyes shining behind his pince-nez.

Prince Tabnit hesitated.

"If the princess wishes to speak with us—" he began, and Olivia made a charming gesture of dissent, and all the jewels in her hair and upon her white throat caught the light and were set glittering.

"No," she said gently, "no, your Highness. I wish to speak in the presence of my people."

She gave the "my" no undue value, yet it fell from her lips with delicious audacity.

"Indeed," she said, "I think, your Highness, that I will speak to my people myself."

CHAPTER XI

THE END OF THE EVENING

The Hall of Kings was very still as Olivia rose. She stood with
one hand touching her veil's hem, the other resting on the low,
carved arm of the throne, and at the coming and going of her
breath her jewels made the light lambent with the indeterminate colours of those strange, joyous banners floating far
above her head.

Her voice was very sweet and a little tremulous—and it is the
very grace of a woman's courage that her voice tremble never
so slightly. It seemed to St. George that he loved her a
thousand times the more for that mere persuasive wavering of
her words. And, while he listened to what he felt to be the
prelude of her message, it seemed to him that he loved her
another thousand times the more—what heavenly ease there is
in this arithmetic of love—for the tender meaning which,
upon her lips, her father's name took on. When, speaking with
simplicity and directness of the subject that lay uppermost in
the minds of them all, she asked their utmost endeavour in
their common grief, it was clear that what she said transcended
whatever phenomena of mere experience lay between her and
those who heard her, and they understood. The *rapport* was
like that among those who hear one music. But St. George
listened, and though his mind applauded, it ran on ahead to
the terrifying future. This was all very well, but how was it to
help her in the face of what was to happen in three days' time?

"Therefore," Olivia's words touched tranquilly among the flying ends of his own thought, "I am come before you to make that sacrifice which my love for my father, and my grief and my anxiety demand. I count upon your support, as he would count upon it for me. I ask that one heart be in us all in this common sorrow. And I am come with the unalterable determination both to renounce my throne there"—never was anything more enchanting than the way those two words fell from her lips—"and to postpone my marriage"—there never was anything more profoundly disquieting than *those* two words in such a connection—"until such time as, by your effort and by my own, we may have news of my father, the king; and until, by your effort or by my own, the Hereditary Treasure shall be restored."

So, serenely and with the most ingenuous confidence, did the daughter of the absent King Otho make disposition of the hour's events. Amory leaned forward and feverishly polished his pince-nez.

"What do you think of that?" he put it, beneath his breath, "what *do* you think of that?"

St. George, watching that little figure—so adorably, almost pathetically little in its corner of the great throne—knew that he had not counted upon her in vain. Over there on the raised seats Mrs. Medora Hastings and Mr. Augustus Frothingham were looking on matters as helplessly as they would look at a thunder-storm or a circus procession, and they were taking things quite as seriously. But Olivia, in spite of the tragedy that the hour held for her, was giving the moment its exact value, guiltless of the feminine immorality of panic. To give a moment its due without that panic, is, St. George knew, a kind of genius, like creating beauty, and divining another's meaning, and redeeming the spirit of a thing from its actuality. But by that time the arithmetic of his love was by way of being in too many figures to talk about. Which is the proper plight of love.

Every one had turned toward Prince Tabnit, and as St. George looked it smote him whimsically that that impassive profile was like the profiles upon the ancient coins which, almost any day, might be cast up by a passing hoof on the island mold. Indeed, St. George thought, one might almost have spent the prince's profile at a fig-stall, and the vender would have jingled it among his silver and never have detected the cheat. But in the next moment the joyous mounting of his blood running riot in audacious whimsies was checked by the even voice of the prince himself.

"The gratitude and love of this people," he said slowly, "are due to the daughter of its sovereign for what she has proposed. It is, however, to be remembered that by our ancient law the State and every satrapy therein shall receive no service, whether of blood or of bond, from an alien. The king himself could serve us only in that he was king. To his daughter as Princess of Yaque and wife of the Head of the House of the Litany, this service in the search for the sovereign and the Hereditary Treasure will be permitted, but she may serve us only from the throne."

"Upon my soul, then that lets *us* out," murmured Amory.

And St. George remembered miserably how, in that dingy house in McDougle Street, he and Olivia had listened once before to the recital of that law from the prince's lips. If they had known how next they would hear it! If they had known then what that law would come to mean to her! What could she do now—what could even Olivia do now but assent?

She could do a great deal, it appeared. She could incline her head, with a bewitching droop of eyelids, and look up to meet the eyes of the prince with a serenity that was like a smile.

"In my country," said Olivia gravely, "when anything special arises they frequently find that there is no law to cover it. It would seem to us"—it was as though the humility of that "us" took from her superb daring—"that this is a matter requiring the advice of the High Council. Therefore," asked little Olivia gently, "will you not appoint, your Highness, a special session of the High Council to convene at noon to-morrow, to consider our proposition?"

There was a scarcely perceptible stir among the members of the High Council, for even the liberals were, it would seem, taken aback by a departure which they themselves had not instituted. Olivia, still in submission to tradition which she could not violate, had gained the time for which she hoped. With a grace that was like the conferring of a royal favour, Prince Tabnit appointed the meeting of the High Council for noon on the following day.

"May the gods permit the possible," he added, and once more extended his hand to Olivia. This time, with lowered eyes, she gave him the tips of her fingers and, as the beckoning music swelled a delicate prelude, she stepped from the dais and suffered the prince to lead her toward the banquet hall.

Amory drew a long breath, and it came to St. George that if he, Amory, said anything about what he would give if he had a leased wire to the *Sentinel* Office, there would no longer be room on the island for them both. But Amory said no such thing. Instead, he looked at St. George in distinct hesitation.

"I say," he brought out finally, "St. George, by Jove, do you know, it seems to me I've seen Miss Frothingham before. And how jolly beautiful she is," he added almost reverently.

"Maybe it was when you were a Phoenician galley slave and she went by in a trireme," offered St. George, trying to keep in sight the bright hair and the floating veil beyond the press of the crowd. Would he see Olivia and would he be able to speak with her, and did she know he was there, and would she be angry? Ah well, she could not possibly be angry, he thought; but with all this in his mind it was hardly reasonable of Amory to expect him to speculate on where Miss Frothingham might have been seen before. If it weren't for this Balator now, St.

George said to himself restlessly, and suddenly observed that Balator was expecting them to follow him. So, in the slow-moving throng, all soft hues and soft laughter, they made their way toward the colonnade that cut off the banquet room. And at every step St. George thought, "she has passed here—and here—and here," and all the while, through the mighty open rafters in the conical roof, were to be seen those strange banners joyously floating in the delicate, alien light. The wine of the moment flowed in his veins, and he moved under strange banners, with a strange ecstasy in his heart.

Therefore, suddenly to hear Rollo's voice at his shoulder came as a distinct shock.

"It's one of them little brown 'uns, sir," Rollo announced in his best tone of mystery. "He's settin' upstairs, sir, an' he's all fer settin' there *till* he sees you. He says it's most important, sir."

Amory heard.

"Shall I go up?" he asked eagerly; "I'd like a whiff of a pipe, anyway. It'll be something to tie to."

"Will you go?" asked St. George in undisguised gratitude. He was prepared to accept most risks rather than to lose sight of the star he was following.

With a word to Balator who explained where, on his return, he could find them, Amory turned with Rollo, and slipped through the crowd. Having reasons of his own for getting back to the hall below, Amory was prepared to speed well the interview with "the little brown 'un" who, he supposed, was Jarvo.

It was Jarvo—Jarvo, in a state of excitement, profound and incredible. The little man, from the annoyingly serene mode of mind in which he had left them, was become, for him, almost agitated. He sprang up from a divan in the great dressing-room of their apartment and approached Amory almost without greeting.

"Adon, adon," he said earnestly, "you must leave the palace at once—at once. But to-night!"

Amory hunted for his pipe, found and lighted it, pressing a cigarette upon Jarvo who accepted, and held it, alight, in the palm of his hand.

"To-night," he repeated, as if it were a game.

"Ah well, now," said Amory reasonably, "why, Jarvo? And we so comfortable."

The little man looked at Amory beseechingly.

"I know what I know," he said earnestly, "many things will happen. There is danger about the palace to-night—danger it may be for you. I do not know all, but I come to warn you, and to warn the adon who has been kind to us. You have brought us here when we were alone in America," said Jarvo simply. "Akko and I will help you now. It was Akko who remembered the tower."

Amory looked down at the bowl of his pipe, and shook his vestas in their box, and turned his eyes to Rollo, listening near by with an air of the most intense abstraction. Yes, all these things were real. They were all real, and here was he, Amory, smoking. And yet what was all this amazing talk about danger in the palace, and being warned, and remembering the tower?

"Anybody would think I was Crass, writing head-lines," he told himself, and blew a cloud of smoke through which to look at Jarvo.

"What are you talking about?" he demanded sternly.

Jarvo had a little key in his hand, which he shook. The key was on a slender, carved ring, and it jingled. And when he offered it to him Amory abstractedly took it.

"See, adon," said Jarvo, "see! In the ilex grove on the road that we took last night there is a white tower—it may be that you have noticed it to-day. That tower is empty, and this is the key. There may be guards, but I shall know how to pass among them. You must come with me there to-night, the three. Even then it may be too late, I do not know. The gods will permit the possible. But this I know: the Royal Guard are of the lahnas, on whom the tax to make good the Hereditary Treasure will fall most heavily. They are filled with rage against your people—you and the king who is of your people. I do not know what they will do, but you are not safe for one moment in the palace. I come to warn you."

Amory's pipe went out. He sat pulling at it abstractedly, trying to fit together what St. George had told him of the Hereditary Treasure situation. And more than at any other time since his arrival on the island his heart leaped up at the prospect of promised adventure. What if St. George's romantic apostasy were not, after all, to spoil the flavour of the kind of adventure for which he, Amory, had been hoping? He leaned eagerly forward.

"What would you suggest?" he said.

Jarvo's eyes brightened. At once he sprang to his feet and stood before Amory, taking soft steps here and there as he talked, in movement graceful and tenuous as the greyhound of which he had reminded St. George.

"In the palace yard," explained the little man rapidly, "is a motor which came from Melita, bringing guests for the ceremony of to-night. They will remain in the palace until after the marriage of the prince, two days hence. But the motor—that must go back to-night to Melita, adon. I have made for myself permission to take it there. But you—the three—must go with me. At the tower in the ilex grove I shall leave you, and I shall return. Is this good?"

"Excellent. But what afterward?" demanded Amory. "Are we all to keep house in the tower?"

Jarvo shook his head, like a man who has thought of everything.

"Through to-morrow, yes," he said, "but to-morrow night, when the dark falls—"

He bent forward and spoke softly.

"Did not the adon wish to ascend the mountain?" he asked.

"Rather," said Amory, "but how, good heavens?"

"I and Akko wish to ascend also; the prince has sent us no message, and we fear him," said Jarvo simply. "There are on the island, adon, six carriers, trained from birth to make the ascent. They are the sons of those whose duty it was to ascend, and they the sons for many generations. The trail is very steep, very perilous. Six were taught to go up with messages long before the knowledge of the wireless way, long before the flight of the airships. They are become a tradition of the island. It is with them that you must ascend—if you have no fear."

"Fear!" cried Amory. "But these men, what of them? They are in the employ of the State. How do you know they will take us?"

Jarvo dropped his eyes.

"I and Akko," he said quietly, "we are two of these six carriers, adon."

Then Amory leaped up, scattering the ashes of his pipe over the tiles. This, then, was what was the matter with the feet of the two men, about which they had all speculated on the deck of *The Aloha*, the feet trained from birth to make the ascent of the steep trail, feet become long, tenuous, almost prehensile—

"It's miracles, that's what it is," declared Amory solemnly. "How on earth did they come to take you to New York?" he could not forbear asking.

"The prince knew nothing of your country, adon," answered Jarvo simply. "He might have needed us to enter it."

"To climb the custom-house," said Amory abstractedly, and laughed out suddenly in sheer light-heartedness. Here was come to them an undertaking to which St. George himself must warm as he had warmed at the prospect of the voyage. To go up the mountain to the threshold of the king's palace, where lived the daughter of the king.

Amory bent himself with a will to mastering each detail of the little man's proposals. Rollo, they decided, was at once to make ready a few belongings in the oil-skins. Immediately after the banquet St. George and Amory were to mingle with the throng and leave the palace—no difficult matter in the press of the departures—and, on the side of the courtyard beneath the windows of the banquet room, Jarvo, already joined by Rollo, would be awaiting them in the motor bound for Melita.

"It sounds as if it couldn't be done," said Amory in intense enjoyment. "It's bully."

He paced up and down the room, talking it over. He folded his arms, and looked at the matter from all sides and wondered, as touching a story being "covered" for Chillingworth, whether he were leaving anything unthought.

"Chillingworth!" he said to himself in ecstasy. "Wouldn't Chillingworth dote to idolatry upon this sight?"

Then Amory stood still, facing something that he had not seen before. He had come, in his walk, upon a little table set near the room's entrance, and bearing a decanter and some cups.

"Hello," he said, "Rollo, where did this come from?"

Rollo came forward, velvet steps, velvet pressing together of his hands, face expressionless as velvet too.

"A servant of 'is 'ighness, sir," he said—Rollo did that now and then to let you know that his was the blood of valets—"left it some time ago, with the compliments of the prince. It looks like a good, nitzy Burgundy, sir," added Rollo tolerantly, "though the man did say it was bottled in something B.C., sir, and if it was it's most likely flat. You can't trust them vintages much farther back than the French Revolootion, beggin' your pardon, sir."

Amory absently lifted the decanter, and then looked at it with some curiosity. The decanter was like a vase, ornamented with gold medallions covered with exquisite and precise engraving of great beauty and variety of design. Serpents, men contending with lions, sacred trees and apes were chased in the gold, and the little cups of sard were engraved in pomegranates and segments of fruit and pendent acorns, and were set with cones of cornelian. The cups were joined by a long cord of thick gold.

Amory set his hand to the little golden stopper, perhaps hermetically sealed, he thought idly, at about the time of the accidental discovery of glass itself by the Phoenicians. Amory was not imaginative, but as he thought of the possible age of the wine, there lay upon him that fascination communicable from any link between the present and the living past.

"Solomon and Sargon," he said to himself, "the geese in the capitol, Marathon, Alexander, Carthage, the Norman conquest, Shakespeare and Miss Frothingham!"

He smiled and twisted the carven stopper.

"And the girl is alive," he said almost wonderingly. "There has been so much Time in the world, and yet she is alive now. Down there in the banquet room."

The odour of the contents of the vase, spicy, penetrating, delicious, crept out, and he breathed it gratefully. It was like no odour that he remembered. This was nothing like Rollo's "good, nitzy Burgundy"—this was something infinitely more wonderful. And the odour—the odour was like a draught. And wasn't this the wine of wines, he asked himself, to give them courage, exultation, the most superb daring when they started up that delectable mountain? St. George must know; he would think so too.

"Oh, I say," said Amory to himself, "we must put some strength in Jarvo's bones too—poor little brick!"

With that Amory drew the carven stopper, fitted in the little funnel that hung about the neck of the vase, poured a half-finger of the wine in each cup, and lifted one in his hand. But the mere odour was enough to make a man live ten lives, he thought, smiling at his own strange exultation. He must no more than touch it to his lips, for he wanted a clear head for what was coming.

"Come, Jarvo," he cried gaily—was he shouting, he wondered, and wasn't that what he was trying to do—to shout to make some far-away voice answer him? "Come and drink to the health of the prince. Long may he live, long may he live—without us!"

Amory had stood with his back to the little brown man while he poured the wine. As he turned, he lifted one cup to his lips and Rollo gravely presented the other to Jarvo. But with a bound that all but upset the velvet valet, the little man cleared the space between him and Amory and struck the cup from Amory's hand.

"Adon!" he cried terribly, "adon! Do not drink—do

not drink!"

The precious liquid splashed to the floor with the falling cup and ran red about the tiles. Instantly a powerful and delightful fragrance rose, and the thick fumes possessed the air. Amory threw out his hands blindly, caught dizzily at Rollo, and was half dragged by Jarvo to the open window.

"Oh, I say, sir—" burst out Rollo, more upset over the loss of the wine than he was alarmed at the occurrence. If it came to losing a good, nitzy Burgundy, Rollo knew what that meant.

"Adon," cried Jarvo, shaking Amory's shoulders, "did you taste the liquor—tell me—the liquor—did you taste?"

Amory shook his head. Jarvo's face and the hovering Rollo and the whole room were enveloped in mist, and the wine was hot on his lips where the cup had touched them. Yet while he stood there, with that permeating fragrance in the air, it came to him vaguely that he had never in his life known a more perfectly delightful moment. If this, he said to himself vaguely, was what they meant by wine in the old days, then so far as his own experience went, the best "nitzy" Burgundy was no more than a flabby, *vin ordinaire* beside it. Not that "flabby" was what he meant to call it, but that was the word that came. For he felt as if no less than six men were flowing in his veins, he summed it up to himself triumphantly.

But after all, the effect was only momentary. Almost as quickly as those strange fumes had arisen they were dissipated. And when presently Amory stood up unsteadily from the seat of the window, he could see clearly enough that Jarvo, with terrified eyes, was turning the vase in his hands.

"It is the same," he was saying, "it must be the same. The gods have permitted the possible. I was here to tell you."

"Tell me what?" demanded Amory with ungrateful irritation. "Is the stuff poison?" he asked, tottering in spite of himself as he crossed the floor toward him. But Jarvo turned his face, and upon it was such an incongruous terror that Amory involuntarily stood still.

"There are known to be two," said Jarvo, holding the vase at arm's length, "and the one is abundant life, if the draught is not over-measured. But the other is ten thousand times worse than death."

"What do you mean?" cried Amory roughly. "What are you talking about? If the stuff is poison can't you say so?"

Jarvo looked at him swiftly.

"These things are not spoken aloud in Yaque," he said simply, and after that he held his peace. Amory threatened him and laughed at him, but Jarvo shook his head. At last Amory scoffed at the whole matter and stretched out his hand for the vase.

"Come," he said, "at all events I'll take it with me. It can't be very much worse than the American liqueurs."

"My word for it, sir, beggin' your pardon," said Rollo earnestly, "it's a kind of what you might call med-i-eval Burgundy, sir."

"It is not well," said Jarvo, handing the vase with reluctance, "yet take it—but see that it touches no lips. I charge you that, adon."

Amory smiled and slipped the little vase in his coat pocket.

"It's all right," he said, "I won't let it get away from me. I can find my legs now; I'll go back down. Look sharp, Rollo. Be down there with the oil-skins. We put on this Tyrian purple stuff over the whole outfit," he explained to Jarvo, "and I suppose, you know, that you can get both robes back here for us, if we escape in them?"

"Assuredly, adon," said Jarvo, "and you must escape without delay. This wine must mean that the prince, too, wishes you harm. Now let me be before you for a little, so that no one may see us together. I shall go now, immediately, to the motor—it is waiting already by the wall on the side of the courtyard opposite the windows of the banquet hall. I shall not fail you."

"On the side of the courtyard opposite the windows of the banquet room," repeated Amory. "Thanks, Jarvo. You're all kinds of a good fellow."

"Yes, adon," gravely assented the little man from the threshold.

Ten minutes later Amory followed. Already Rollo had packed the oil-skins, and Amory, his nerves steadied and the excitement of all that the night promised come upon him, hurried before him down the corridor, his thoughts divided in their allegiance between the delight of telling St. George what was toward, and the new and alluring delight of seeing Antoinette Frothingham near at hand in the banquet room. After all, he had had only the vaguest glimpse of a little figure in rose and silver, and he doubted if he could tell her from the princess, but for the interpreting gown.

Amory looked up with an irrepressible thrill of delight. He was just at that moment crossing the high white audience-hall, the anteroom to the Hall of Kings—he, Amory, in Tyrian purple garments. If anything were needed to complete the picture it would be to meet face to face, there in that big, lonely room, a little figure in rose and silver. It made his heart beat even to think of the possibilities of that situation. He skirted the Hall of Kings, and stood in one of the archways of the colonnade, facing the banquet room.

The banquet-table extended about three sides of the room, whose centre the guests faced. The middle space was left pure, unvexed by columns or furnishing. At the room's far end Amory glimpsed the prince, at his side Olivia's white veil, and her women about her; and, nearer, St. George and Balator in the place appointed. A guard came to conduct him, and he crossed to his seat and sank down with the look that could be made to mean whatever Amory meant.

"I expect to be served," murmured the journalist in him, "by beautiful tame megatheriums, in sashes. And is that glyptodon salad?"

St. George's eyes were upon the guests, so tranquilly seated, aware of the hour.

"I fancy," he said in half-voice, "that presently we shall see little flames issuing from their hair, as there used from the hair of the ladies in Werner's ballets."

Then as Balator leaned toward him in his splendid leisure, fostering his charm, there came an amazing interruption.

The low key of the room was electrically raised by a cry, loosed from some other plight of being, like an odour of burning encroaching upon a garden.

"Why have you not waited?" some one called, and the voice—clear, equal, imperious—evened its way upon the air and reduced to itself the soft speech of the others. Silence fell upon them all, and their eyes were toward a figure standing in the open interval of the room—a figure whose aspect thrilled St. George with sudden, inexplicable emotion.

It was an old man, incredibly old, so that one thought first of his age. His beard and hair were not all grey, but he had grotesquely brown and wrinkled flesh. His stuff robe hung in straight folds about his singularly erect figure, and there was in his bearing the dignity of one who has understood all fine and gentle things, all things of quietude. But his look was vacant, as if the mind were asleep.

"Why have you not waited?" he repeated almost wonderingly.

"Why have you not sent for me?" and his eyes questioned one and another, and rested on the face of the prince upon the dais, with Olivia by his side. The guard, whom in some fashion the strange old man had eluded, hurried from the borders of the room. But he broke from them and was off up half the length of the hall toward the prince's seat.

"Do you not know?" he cried as he went, "I am Malakh. Read one another's eyes and you will know. I am Malakh."

As the guards closed about him he tottered and would have fallen save that they caught him roughly and pressed to a door, half carrying him, and he did not resist. But as speech was renewed another voice broke the murmur, and with great amazement St. George knew that this was Olivia's voice.

"No," she cried—but half as if she distrusted her own strange impulse, "let him stay—let him stay."

St. George saw the prince's look question her. He himself was unable to account for her unexpected intercession, and so, one would have said, was Olivia. She looked up at the prince almost fearfully, and down the length of the listening table, and back to the old man whose eyes were upon her face.

"He is an old man, your Highness," St. George heard her saying, "let him stay."

Prince Tabnit, who gave a curious impression of doing everything that he did in obedience to inertia rather than in its defiance, indicated some command to the puzzled guards, and they led old Malakh to a stone bench not far from the dais, and there he sank down, looking about him without surprise.

"It is well," he said simply, "Malakh has come."

While St. George was marveling—but not that the old man spoke the English, for in Yaque it was not surprising to find the very madmen speaking one's own tongue—Balator explained the man.

"He is a poor mad creature," Balator said. "He walks the streets of Med saying 'Melek, Melek,' which is to say, 'king,' and so he is seeking the king. But he is mad, and they say that he always weeps, and therefore they pretend to believe that he says 'Malakh,' which is to say 'salt.' And they call him that for his tears. Doubtless the princess does not understand. Her Highness has a tender heart."

St. George was silent. The incident was trivial, but Olivia had never seemed so near.

Sometimes in the world of commonplace there comes an extreme hour which one afterward remembers with "Could that have been I? But could it have been I who did that?" And one finds it in one's heart to be certain that it was not one's self, but some one else—some one very near, some one who is always sharing one's own consciousness and inexplicably mixing with one's moments. "Perhaps," St. George would have said, "there is some such person who is nearly, but not quite, I myself. And if there is, it was he and not I who was at that banquet!" It was one of the hours which seem to have been made with no echo. It was; and then passed into other ways, and one remembered only a brightness. For example, St. George listened to what Balator said, and he heard with utmost understanding, and with the frequent pleasure of wonder, and was now and then exquisitely amused as one is amused in dreams. But even as he listened, if he tried to remember the last thing that was said, and the next to the last thing, he found that these had escaped him; and as he rose from the table he could not recall ten words that had been spoken. It was as if the some one very near, who is always sharing one's consciousness and inexplicably mixing with one's moments, had taken St. George's part at the banquet while he, himself, sat there in the role of his own outer consciousness. But neither he nor that hypothetical "some one else," who was also he, lost for one instant the heavenly knowledge that Olivia was up there at the head of the table.

Amory, in spite of diplomatic effort, had not succeeded in imparting to St. George anything of his talk with Jarvo. Balator was too near, and the place was somehow too generally attentive to permit a secret word. So, as they rose from the table, St. George was still in ignorance of what was toward and knew nothing of either the Ilex Tower or the possibilities of the morrow. He had only one thought, and that was to speak with Olivia, to let her know that he was there on the island, near her, ready to serve her—ah well, chiefly, he did not disguise from himself, what he wanted was to look at her and to hear her speak to him. But Amory had depended on the confusion of the rising to communicate the great news, and to tell about Jarvo, waiting in a motor out there in the palace courtyard, by the wall on the side opposite the windows of the banquet room. In an auspicious moment Amory looked warily about, thrilling with premonition of his friend's enthusiasm.

Before he could speak, St. George uttered a startled exclamation, caught at Amory's arm, sprang forward, and was off up the long room, dragging Amory with him.

About the dais there was suddenly an appalling confusion. Push of feet, murmurs, a cry and, visible over the heads between, a glistening of gold uniforms closing about the throne seats, flashing back to the long, open windows, disappearing against the night...

"What is it?" cried Amory as he ran. "What is it?"

"Quick," said St. George only, "I don't know. They've gone with her."

Amory did not understand, but he saw that Olivia's seat was empty; and when he swept the heads for her white veil, it was not there.

"Who has?" he said.

St. George swerved to the side of the room toward the

windows, and old Malakh stood there, crying out and pointing.

"The guard, I think," St. George answered, and was over the low sill of a window, running headlong across the courtyard, Amory behind him. "There they go," St. George cried. "Good God, what are we to do? There they go."

Amory looked. Down a side avenue—one of those tunnels of shadow that taught the necessity of mystery—a great motor car was speeding, and in the dimness the two men could see the white of Olivia's floating veil.

At this, Amory wheeled and searched the length of wall across the yard. If only—if only—

There on the side of the courtyard opposite the windows of the banquet room stood the motor that was that night to go back to Melita. Bolt upright on the seat was Jarvo, and climbing in the tonneau, with his neck stretched toward the confusion of the palace, was Rollo. Jarvo saw Amory, who beckoned; and in an instant the car was beside them and the two men were over the back of the tonneau in a flash.

"That way," cried St. George, with no time to waste on the miracle of Jarvo's appearance, "that way—there. Where you see the white."

At a touch the motor plunged away into the fragrant darkness. Amory looked back. Figures crowded the windows of the palace, and streamed from the banquet hall into the courtyard. Men hurried through the hall, and there was clamour of voices, and in the honey-coloured air the great bulk of the palace towered like a faithless sentinel, the alien banners in nameless colours sending streamers into the moon-lit upper spaces.

On before, down nebulous ways, went the whiteness of the floating veil.

CHAPTER XII

BETWEEN-WORLDS

Down nebulous ways they went, the thin darkness flowing past them. The sloping avenue ran all the width of the palace grounds, and here among slim-trunked trees faint fringes of the light touched away the dimness in the open spaces and expressed the borders of the dusk. Always the way led down, dipping deeper in the conjecture of shadow, and always before them glimmered the mist of Olivia's veil, an eidolon of love, of love's eternal Vanishing Goal.

And St. George was in pursuit. So were Amory and Jarvo, and Rollo of the oil-skins, but these mattered very little, for it was St. George whose eyes burned in his pale face and were striving to catch the faintest motion in that fleeing car ahead.

"Faster, Jarvo," he said, "we're not gaining on them. I think they're gaining on us. Put ahead, can't you?"

Amory vexed the air with frantic questionings. "How did it happen?" he said. "Who did it? Was it the guard? What did they do it for?"

"It looks to me," said St. George only, peering distractedly into the gloom, "as if all those fellows had on uniforms. Can you see?"

Jarvo spoke softly.

"It is true, adon," he said, "they are of the guard. This is what they had planned," he added to Amory. "I feared the harm would be to you. It is the same. Your turn would be the next."

"What do you mean?" St. George demanded.

Amory, with some incoherence, told him what Jarvo had come to them to propose, and heightened his own excitement by plunging into the business of that night and the next, as he had had it from the little brown man's lips.

"Up the mountain to-morrow night," he concluded fervently, "what do you think of that? Do you see us?"

"Maniac, no," said St. George shortly, "what do we want to go up the mountain for if Miss Holland is somewhere else? Faster, Jarvo, can't you?" he urged. "Why, this thing is built to go sixty miles an hour. We're creeping."

"Perhaps it's better to start in gentle and work up a pace, sir," observed Rollo inspirationally, "like a man's legs, sir, beggin' your pardon."

St. George looked at him as if he had first seen him, so that Amory once more explained his presence and pointed to the oil-skins. And St. George said only:

"Now we're coming up a little—don't you think we're coming up a little? Throw it wide open, Jarvo—now, go!"

"What are you going to do when you catch them?" demanded Amory. "We can't lunge into them, for fear of hurting Miss Holland. And who knows what devilish contrivance they've got—dum-dum bullets with a poison seal attachment," prophesied Amory darkly. "What are you going to do?"

"I don't know what we're going to do," said St. George doggedly, "but if we can overtake them it won't take us long to find out."

Never so slightly the pursuers were gaining. It was impossible to tell whether those in the flying car knew that they were followed, and if they did know, and if Olivia knew, St. George wondered whether the pursuit were to her a new alarm, or whether she were looking to them for deliverance. If she knew! His heart stood still at the thought—oh, and if they had both known, that morning at breakfast at the Boris, that *this* was the way the genie would come out of the jar. But how, if he were unable to help her? And how could he help her when these others might have Heaven knew what resources of black art, art of all the colours of the Yaque spectrum, if it came to that? The slim-trunked trees flew past them, and the tender branches brushed their shoulders and hung out their flowers like lamps. Warm wind was in their faces, sweet, reverberant voices of the wood-things came chorusing, and ahead there in the dimness, that misty will-o'-the-wisp was her veil, Olivia's veil. St. George would have followed if it had led him between-worlds.

In a manner it did lead him between-worlds. Emerging suddenly upon a broader avenue their car followed the other aside and shot through a great gateway of the palace wall—a wall built of such massive blocks that the gateway formed a covered passageway. From there, delicately lighted, greenly arched, and on this festal night, quite deserted, went the road by which, the night before, they had entered Med.

"Now," said St. George between set teeth, "now see what you can do, Jarvo. Everything depends on you."

Evidently Jarvo had been waiting for this stretch of open road and expecting the other car to take it. He bent forward, his wiry little frame like a quivering spring controlling the motion. The motor leaped at his touch. Away down the road they tore with the wind singing its challenge. Second by second they saw their gain increase. The uniforms of the guards in the car became distinguishable. The white of Olivia's veil merged in the brightness of her gown—was it only the shining of the gold of the uniforms or could St. George see the floating gold of her hair? Ah, wonderful, past all speech it was wonderful to be fleeing toward her through this pale light that was like a purer element than light itself. With the phantom moving of the boughs in the wood on either side light seemed to dance and drip from leaf to leaf—the visible spirit of the haunted green. The unreality of it all swept over him almost stiflingly. Olivia—was it indeed Olivia whom he was following down lustrous ways of a land vague as a star; or was his pursuit not for her, but for the exquisite, incommunicable Idea, and was he following it through a world forth-fashioned from his own desire?

Suddenly indistinguishable sounds were in his ears, words from Amory, from Jarvo certain exultant gutturals. He felt the car slacken speed, he looked ahead for the swift beckoning of the veil, and then he saw that where, in the delicate distance, the other motor had sped its way, it now stood inactive in the road before them, and they were actually upon it. The four guards in the motor were standing erect with uplifted faces, their gold uniforms shining like armour. But this was not all. There, in the highway beside the car, the mist of her veil like a halo about her, Olivia stood alone.

St. George did not reckon what they meant to do. He dropped over the side of the tonneau and ran to her. He stood before her, and all the joy that he had ever known was transcended as she turned toward him. She threw out her hands with a little cry—was it gladness, or relief, or beseeching? He could not be certain that there was even recognition in her eyes before she tottered and swayed, and he caught her unconscious form in his arms. As he lifted her he looked with apprehension toward the car that held the guards. To his bewilderment there was no car there. The pursued motor, like a winged thing of the most innocent vagaries, had taken itself off utterly. And on before, the causeway was utterly empty, dipping idly between murmurous green. But at the moment St. George had no time to spend on that wonder.

He carried Olivia to the tonneau of Jarvo's car, jealous when

Rollo lifted her gown's hem from the dust of the road and when Amory threw open the door. He held her in his arms, half kneeling beside her, profoundly regardless where it should please the others to dispose themselves. He had no recollection of hearing Jarvo point the way through the trees to a path that led away, as far from them as a voice would carry, to the Ilex Tower whose key burned in Amory's pocket, promising radiant, intangible things to his imagination. St. George understood with magnificent unconcern that Amory and Rollo were gone off there to wait for the return of him and Jarvo; he took it for granted that Jarvo had grasped that Olivia must be taken back to her aunt and her friends at the palace; and afterward he knew only, for an indeterminate space, that the car was moving across some dim, heavenly foreground to some dim, ultimate destination in which he found himself believing with infinite faith.

For this was Olivia, in his arms. St. George looked down at her, at the white, exquisite face with its shadow of lashes, and it seemed to him that he must not breathe, or remember, or hope, lest the gods should be jealous and claim the moment, and leave him once more forlorn. That was the secret, he thought, not to touch away the elusive moment by hope or memory, but just to live it, filled with its ecstasies, borne on the crest of its consciousness. It seemed to him in some intimately communicated fashion, that the moment, the very world of the island, was become to him a more intense object of consciousness than himself. And somehow Olivia was its expression—Olivia, here in his arms, with the stir of her breath and the light, light pressure of her body and the fall of her hair, not only symbols of the sovereign hour, but the hour's realities.

On either side the phantom wood pressed close about them, and its light seemed coined by goblin fingers. Dissolving wind, persuading little voices musical beyond the domain of music that he knew, quick, poignant vistas of glades where the light spent itself in its longed-for liberty of colour, labyrinthine ways of shadow that taught the necessity of mystery. There was something lyric about it all. Here Nature moved on no formal lines, understood no frugality of beauty, but was lavish with a divine and special errantry to a divine and special understanding. And it had been given St. George to move with her merely by living this hour, with Olivia in his arms.

The sweet of life—the sweet of life and the world his own. The words had never meant so much. He had often said them in exultation, but he had never known their truth: the world was literally his own, under the law. Nothing seemed impossible. His mind went back to the unexplained disappearing of that other motor and, however it had been, that did not seem impossible either. It seemed natural, and only a new doorway to new points of contact. In this amazing land no speculation was too far afield to be the food of every day. Here men understood miracle as the rest of the world understands invention. Already the mere existence of Yaque proved that the space of experience is transcended—and with the thought a fancy, elusive and profound, seized him and gripped at his heart with an emotion wider than fear. What had become of the other car? Had it gone down some road of the wood which the guards knew, or ... The words of Prince Tabnit came back to him as they had been spoken in that wonderful tour of the island. "The higher dimensions are being conquered. Nearly all of us can pass into the fifth at will, 'disappearing,' as you have the word." Was it possible that in the vanishing of the pursued car this had been demonstrated before him? Into this space, inclusive of the visible world and of Yaque as well, had the car passed *without the pursuers being able to point* to the direction which it had taken? St. George smiled in derision as this flashed upon him, and it hardly held his thought for a moment, for his eyes were upon Olivia's face, so near, so near his own ... Undoubtedly, he thought vaguely, that other motor had simply swerved aside to some private opening of the grove and, from being hard-pressed and almost overtaken, was now well away in safety. Yet if this were so, would they not have taken Olivia with them? But to that strange and unapparent hyperspace they could not have taken her, because she did not understand. "...just as one," Prince Tabnit had said, "who understands how to die and come to life again would not be able to take with him any one who himself did not understand how to accompany him..."

Some terrifying and exalting sense swept him into a new intimacy of understanding as he realized glimmeringly what heights and depths lay about his ceasing to see that car of the guard. Yet, with Olivia's head upon his arm, all that he theorized in that flash of time hung hardly beyond the border of his understanding. Indeed, it seemed to St. George as if almost—almost he could understand, as if he could pierce the veil and know utterly all the secrets of spirit and sense that confound. "We shall all know *when we are able to bear it*," he had once heard another say, and it seemed to him now that at last he was able to bear it, as if the sense of the uninterrupted connection between the two worlds was almost a part of his own consciousness. A moment's deeper thought, a quicker flowing of the imagination, a little more poignant projecting of himself above the abyss and he, too, would understand. It came to him that he had almost understood every time that he had looked at Olivia. Ah, he thought, and how exquisite, how matchless she was, and what Heaven beyond Heaven the world would hold for him if only she were to love him. St. George lifted the little hand that hung at her side, and stooped momentarily to touch his cheek to the soft hair that swept her shoulder. Here for him lay the sweet of life—the sweet of the world, ay, and the sweet of all the world's mysteries. This alien land was no nearer the truth than he. His love was the expression of its mystery. They went back through the great archway, and entered the palace park. Once more the slim-trunked trees flew past them with the fringes of light expressing the borders of the dusk. St. George crouched, half-kneeling, on the floor of the tonneau, his free hand protecting Olivia's face from the leaning branches of heavy-headed flowers. He had been so passionately anxious that she should know that he was on the island, near her, ready to serve her; but now, save for his alarm and anxiety about her, he felt a shy, profound gratitude that the hour had fallen as it had fallen. Whatever was to come, this nearness to her would be his to remember and possess. It had been his supreme hour. Whether she had recognized him in that moment on the road, whether she ever knew what had happened made, he thought, no difference. But if she was to open her eyes as they reached the border of the park, and if she was to know that it was like this that the genie had come out of the jar—the mere notion made him giddy, and he saw that Heaven may have little inner Heaven-courts which one is never too happy to penetrate.

But Olivia did not stir or unclose her eyes. The great strain of the evening, the terror and shock of its ending, the very relief with which she had, at all events, realized herself in the hands of friends were more than even an island princess could pass through in serenity. And when at last from the demesne of enchantment the car emerged in the court of the palace, Olivia knew nothing of it and, as nearly as he could recall afterward, neither did St. George. He understood that the courtyard was filled with murmurs, and that as Olivia was lifted from the car the voice of Mrs. Medora Hastings, in all its excesses of tone and pitch, was tilted in a kind of universal reproving. Then he was aware that Jarvo, beseeching him not to leave the motor, had somehow got him away from all the tumult and the questioning and the crush of the other motors setting tardily off down the avenue in a kind cf majestic pursuit of the princess. After that he remembered nothing but the grateful gloom of the wood and the swift flight of the car down that nebulous way, thin darkness flowing about him.

He was to go back to join Amory in some kind of tower, he knew; and he was infinitely resigned, for he remembered that this was in some way essential to his safety, and that it had to do with the ascent of Mount Khalak to-morrow night. For the rest St. George was certain of nothing save that he was floating once more in a sea of light, with the sweet of the world flowing in his veins; and upon his arm and against his shoulder he could still feel the thrill of the pressure of Olivia's head.

The genie had come out of the jar—and never, never would he go back.

CHAPTER XIII

THE LINES LEAD UP

In the late hours of the next afternoon Rollo, with a sigh, uncoiled himself from the shadow of the altar to the god Melkarth, in the Ilex Temple, and stiffly rose. Vicissitudes were not for Rollo, who had not fathomed the joys of adaptability; and the savour of the sweet herbs which, from Jarvo's wallet, he had that day served, was forgotten in his longing for a drop of tarragan vinegar and a bulb of garlic with which to dress the herbs. His lean and shadowed face wore an expression of settled melancholy.

"Sorrow's nothing," he sententiously observed. "It's trouble that does for a man, sir."

St. George, who lay at full length on a mossy sill of the king's chapel counting the hours of his inaction, continued to look out over the glistening tops of the ilex trees.

"Speaking of trouble," he said, "what would you say, Rollo, to getting back to the yacht to-night, instead of going up the mountain with us?"

Rollo dropped his eyes, but his face brightened under, as it were, his never-lifted mask.

"Oh, sir," he said humbly, "a person is always willing to do whatever makes him the most useful."

"Little Cawthorne and Bennietod," went on St. George, "ten to one will take to the trail to-night, if they haven't already. They'll be coming to Med and reorganizing the police force, or raising a standing army or starting a subway. You'd do well to drop down and give them some idea of what's happened, and I fancy you'd better all be somewhere about on the day after to-morrow, at noon. Not that there will be any wedding at that time," explained St. George carefully, "although there may be something to see, all the same. But you might tell them, you know, that Miss Holland is due to marry the prince then. Can you get back to the yacht alone?"

Rollo hadn't thought of that, and his mask fell once more into its lines of misery.

"I don't know, sir," he said doubtfully, "most men can go up a steep place all right. It's comin' down that's hard on the knees. And if I was to try it alone, sir—"

Jarvo made a sign of reassurance.

"That is not well," he said, "you would be dashed to pieces. Ulfin, one of the six, will wait for us to-night on the edge of the grove. He can conduct the way to the vessel."

"Ah, sir," said Rollo, not without a certain self-satisfaction, "something is always sure to turn up, sir."

From a tour of the temple Amory came listlessly back to the king's chapel. There, where the descendants of Abibaal had worshiped until their idols had been refined by Time to a kind of decoration, the Americans and Jarvo had spent the night. They had slept stretched on benches of beveled stone. They had waked to trace the figures in a length of tapestry representing the capture of Io on the coast of Argolis, doubtless woven by an eye-witness. They had bathed in a brook near the entrance where stood the altar for the sacrifice round which the priests and *hierodouloi* had been wont to dance, and where huge architraves, metopes and tryglyphs, massive as those at

Gebeil and Tortosa and hewn from living rock, rose from the fragile green of the wood like a huge arm signaling its eternal "Alas!" They had partaken of Jarvo's fruit and sweet herbs, and Rollo had served them, standing with his back to the niche where once had looked augustly down the image of the god. And now Amory, with a smile, leaned against a wall where old vines, grown miraculously in crannies, spread their tendrils upon the friendly hieroglyphic scoring of the crenelated stone, and summed up his reflections of the night.

"I've got it," he announced, "I think it was up in the Adirondacks, summer before last. I think I was in a canoe when she went by in a launch, with the Chiswicks. Why, do you know, I think I dreamed about Miss Frothingham for weeks."

St. George smiled suddenly and radiantly, and his smile was for the sake of both Rollo and Amory—Rollo whose sense of the commonplace nothing could overpower, Amory who talked about the Chiswicks in the Adirondacks. Why not? St. George thought happily. Here in the temple certain precious and delicate idols were believed to be hidden in alcoves walled up by mighty stone; and here, Jarvo was telling them, were secret exits to the road contrived by the priests of the temple at the time of their oppression by the worshipers of another god; but yet what special interest could he and Amory have in brooding upon these, or the ancient Phoenicians having "invited to traffic by a signal fire," when they could sit still and remember?

"To-night," he said aloud, feeling a sudden fellowship for both Amory and Rollo, "to-night, when the moon rises, we shall watch it from the top of the mountain."

Then he wondered, many hundred times, whether Olivia could possibly have recognized him.

When the dark had fallen they set out. The ilex grove was very still save for a fugitive wind that carried faint spices, and they took a winding way among trunks and reached the edge of the wood without adventure. There Ulfin and another of the six carriers were waiting, as Jarvo had expected, and it was decided that they should both accompany Rollo down to the yacht.

Rollo handed the oil-skins to St. George and Amory, and then stood crushing his hat in his hands, doing his best to speak.

"Look sharp, Rollo," St. George advised him, "don't step one foot off a precipice. And tell the people on the yacht not to worry. We shall expect to see them day after to-morrow, somewhere about. Take care of yourself."

"Oh, sir," said Rollo with difficulty, "good-by, sir. I 'ope you'll be successful, sir. A person likes to succeed in what they undertake."

Then the three went on down the glimmering way where, last night, they had pursued the floating pennon of the veil. There were few upon the highway, and these hardly regarded them. It occurred to St. George that they passed as figures in a dream will pass, in the casual fashion of all unreality, taking all things for granted. Yet, of course, to the passers-by upon the road to Med, there was nothing remarkable in the aspect of the three companions. All that was remarkable was the adventure upon which they were bound, and nobody could possibly have guessed that.

Almost a mile lay between them and the point where the ascent of the mountain was to be begun. The road which they were taking followed at the foot of the embankment which girt the island, and it led them at last to a stretch of arbourescent heath, piled with black basaltic rocks. Here, where the light was dim like the glow from light reflected upon low clouds, they took their way among great branching cacti and nameless plants that caught at their ankles. A strange odour rose from the earth, mineral, metallic, and the air was thick with particles stirred by their feet and more resembling ashes than dust. This was a waste place of the island, and if one were to lift a handful of the soil, St. George thought, it was very likely that one might detect its elements; as, here the dust of a temple, here of a book, here a tomb and here a sacrifice. He felt himself near the earth, in its making. He looked away to the sugar-loaf cone of the mountain risen against the star-lit sky. Above its fortress-like bulk with circular ramparts burned the clear beacon of the light on the king's palace. As he saw the light, St. George knew himself not only near the earth but at one with the very currents of the air, partaker of now a hope, now a task, now a spell, and now a memory. It was as if love had made him one with the dust of dead cities and with their eternal spiritual effluence.

At length they crossed the broad avenue that led from the Eurychorus to Melita, and struck into the road that skirted the mountain; and where a thicket of trees flung bold branches across the way, three figures rose from the ground before them, and Akko stepped forward and saluted, his white teeth gleaming. Immediately Jarvo led the way through a strip of underbrush at the base of the mountain, and they emerged in a glade where the light hardly penetrated.

Here were distinguishable the palanquins in which the ascent was to be made. These were like long baskets, upborne by a pole of great flexibility broadening to a wider support beneath the body of the basket and provided with rubber straps through which the arms were passed. When St. George and Amory were seated, Jarvo spoke hesitatingly:

"We must bandage your eyes, adon," he said.

"Oh really, really," protested St. George, "we don't understand half we do see. Do let us see what we can."

"You must be blindfolded, adon," repeated Jarvo firmly.

Amory, passing his arms reflectively through the rubber straps which Akko held for him, spoke cheerfully:

Zona Gale

"I'll go up blindfold," he submitted, "if I can smoke."

"Neither of us will," said St. George with determination. "See here, Jarvo, we are both level-headed. We pledge you our word of honour, in addition, not to dive overboard. Now—lead on."

"It has never been done," said the little brown man with obstinacy, "you will lose your reason, adon."

"Ah well now, if we do," said St. George, "pitch us over and leave us. Besides, I think we have. Lead on, please."

Against the will of the others, he prevailed. The light oil-skins were placed in the baskets, each of which was shouldered by two men, Jarvo bearing the foremost pole of St. George's palanquin. All the carriers had drawn on long, soft shoes which, perhaps from some preparation in which they had been dipped, glowed with light, illuminating the ground for a little distance at every step.

"Are you ready, adon?" asked Jarvo and Akko at the same moment.

"Ready!" cried St. George impatiently.

"Ready," said Amory languidly, and added one thought more: "I hope for Chillingworth's sake," he said, "that Frothingham is a notary public. We'll have to have somebody's seal at the bottom of all this copy."

The baskets were lightly lifted. Jarvo gave a sharp command, and all four of the men broke into a rhythmic chant. Jarvo, leading the way, sprang immediately upon the first foothold, where none seemed to be, and without pause to the next. So perfectly were the men trained that it was as if but one set of muscles were inspiring the movements made to the beat of that monotonous measure. In their strong hands the flexible pole seemed to give as their bodies gave, and so lightly did they leap upward that the jar of their alighting was hardly perceptible, as if, as had occurred to St. George as they ascended the lip of the island, gravity were here another matter. So, without pause, save in the rhythm of that strange march music, the remarkable progress was begun.

St. George threw one swift glance upward and looked down, shudderingly. Beetling above them in the great starlight hung the gigantic pile, wall upon wall of rock hewn with such secret foothold that it was a miracle how any living thing could catch and cling to its forbidding surface. Only lifelong practice of the men, who from childhood had been required to make the ascent and whose fathers and fathers' fathers before them had done the same, could have accounted for that catlike ability to cling to the trail where was no trail. The sensation of the long swinging upward movement was unutterably alien to anything in life or in dreams, and the sheer height above and the momently-deepening chasm below were presences contending for possession.

Strange fragrance stole from gum and bark of the decreasing vegetation. Dislodged stones rolled bounding from rock to rock into the abyss. To right and left the way went. There was not even the friendly beacon of the summit to beckon them. It seemed to St. George that their whole safety lay in motion, that a moment's cessation from the advance would hurl them all down the sides of the declivity. Since the ascent began he had not ceased to look down; and now as they rose free of the tree-tops that clothed the base of the mountain he could see across the plain, and beyond the bounding embankment of the island to the dark waste of the sea. Somewhere out there *The Aloha* was rocking. Somewhere, away to the northwest, the lights of New York harbour shone. *Did* they, St. George wondered vaguely; and, when he went back, how would they look to him? It seemed to him in some indeterminate fashion that when he saw them again there would be new lines and sides of beauty which he had never suspected, and as if all the world would be changed, included in this new world that he had found.

Half-way up the ascent a resting-place was contrived for the carriers. The projection upon which the baskets were lowered was hardly three feet in width. Its edge dropped into darkness. Within reach, leaves rustled from the summit of a tree rooted somewhere in the chasm. The blackness below was vast and to be measured only by the memory of that upward course. Gemmed by its lighted hamlets the fair plain of the island lay, with Med and Melita glowing like lamps to the huge dusk.

"St. George," said Amory soberly, "if it's all true—if these people do understand what the world doesn't know anything about—"

"Yes," said St. George.

"It makes a man feel—"

"Yes," said St. George, "it does."

This, they afterward remembered, was all that they said on the ascent. One wonders if two, being met among the "strengthless tribes of the dead," would find much more to say.

Then they went on, scaling that invisible way, with the twinkling feet of the carriers drawing upward like a thread of thin gold which they were to climb. What, St. George thought as the way seemed to lengthen before them, what if there were no end? What if this were some gigantic trick of Destiny to keep him for the rest of his life in mid-air, ceaselessly toiling up, a latter-day Sisyphus, in a palanquin? He had dreamed of stairs in the darkness which men mounted and found to have no summits, and suppose this were such a stair? Suppose, among these marvels that were related to his dreams, he had, as it were, tossed a ball of twine in the air and, like the Indian jugglers, climbed it? Suppose he had built a castle in the clouds and tenanted it with Olivia, and were now foolhardily attempting to scale the air? Ah well, he settled it contentedly, better so. For this divine jugglery comes once into every life, and one must climb to the castle with madness and singing if he would attain to the temples that lie on the castle-plain.

Gradually, as they approached the summit, the ascent became less precipitous. As they neared the cone their way lay over a kind of natural fosse at the cone's base; and, although the mountain did not reach the level of perpetual snow, yet an occasional cool breath from the dark told where in some natural cavern snow had lain undisturbed since the unremembered eruption of the sullen, volcanic peak. Then came a breath of over-powering sweetness from some secret thicket, and something was struck from the feet of the bearers that was like white pumice gravel. St. George no longer looked downward; the plain and the waste of the sea were in a forgotten limbo, and he searched eagerly on high for the first rays of the light that marked the goal of his longing.

Yet he was unprepared when, swerving sharply and skirting an immense shoulder of rock, Jarvo suddenly emerged upon a broad retaining wall of stone bordering a smooth, moon-lit terrace extending by shallow flights of steps to the white doors of the king's palace itself.

As St. George and Amory freed themselves and sprang to their feet their eyes were drawn to a glory of light shining over the low parapet which surrounded the terrace.

"Look," cried St. George victoriously, "the moon!"

From the sea the moon was momently growing, like a giant bubble, and a bright path had issued to the mountain's foot. "See," she would doubtless have said if she could, "I would have shown you the way here all your life if only you had looked properly." But at all events St. George's prophecy was fulfilled: From the top of Mount Khalak they were watching the moon rise. St. George, however, was not yet in the company whose image had pleasantly besieged him when he had prophesied. He turned impatiently to the palace. Jarvo, resting on the stones where he had sunk down, signaled them to go on, and the two needed no second bidding. They set off briskly across the plateau, Amory looking about him with eager curiosity, St. George on the crest of his divine expectancy.

The palace was set on the west of the gentle slope to which the mountain-top had been artificially leveled. The terrace led up on three sides from the marge of the height to the great portals. Over everything hung that imponderable essence that was clearer and purer than any light—"better than any light that ever shone." In its glamourie, with that far ocean background, the palace of pale stone looked unearthly, a sky thing, with ramparts of air. The principle of the builders seemed not to have been the ancient dictum that "mass alone is admirable," for the great pile was shaped, with beauty of unknown line, in three enormous cylinders, one rising from another, the last magnificently curved to a huge dome on whose summit burned with inconceivable brilliance the light which had been a beacon to the longing eyes turned toward it from the deck of *The Aloha*. In the shadow of the palace rose two high towers, obelisk-shaped from the pure white stone. Scattered about the slope were detached buildings, consisting of marble monoliths resting upon double bases and crowned with carved cornices, or of truncated pyramids and pyramidions. These had plinths of delicately-coloured stone over which the light diffused so that they looked luminous, and the small blocks used to fill the apertures of the courses shone like precious things. Adjacent to one of the porches were two conical shrines, for images and little lamps; and, near-by, a fallen pillar of immense proportions lay undisturbed upon the court of sward across which it had some time shivered down.

But if the palace had been discovered to be the preserved and transported Temple of Solomon it could not have stayed St. George for one moment of admiration. He was off up the slope, seeing only the great closed portals, and with Amory beside him he ran boldly up the long steps. It was a part of the unreality of the place that there seemed absolutely no sign of life about the King's palace. The windows glowed with the soft light within, but there were no guards, no servants, no sign of any presence. For the first time, when they reached the top of the steps, the two men hesitated.

"Personally," said Amory doubtfully, "I have never yet tapped at a king's front door. What does one do?"

St. George looked at the long stone porches, uncovered and girt by a parapet following the curve of the facade.

"Would you mind waiting a minute?" he said.

With that he was off along the balcony to the south—and afterward he wondered why, and if it is true that Fate tempts us in the way that she would have us walk by luring us with unseen roses budding from the air.

Where the porch abruptly widened to a kind of upper terrace, like a hanging garden set with flowering trees, three high archways opened to an apartment whose bright lights streamed across the grass-plots. St. George felt something tug at his heart, something that urged him forward and caught him up in an ecstasy of triumph and hope fulfilled. He looked back at Amory, and Amory was leaning on the parapet, apparently sunk in reflections which concerned nobody. So St. George stepped softly on until he reached the first archway, and there he stopped, and the moment was to him almost past belief. Within the open doorway, so near that if she had lifted her eyes they must have met his own, was the woman whom he had come across the sea to seek.

St. George hardly knew that he spoke, for it was as if all the world were singing her name.

"Olivia!" he said.

Zona Gale

CHAPTER XIV

THE ISLE OF HEARTS

The room in which St. George was looking was long and lofty and hung with pale tapestries. White pillars supporting the domed white ceiling were wound with garlands. The smoke from a little brazen tripod ascended pleasantly, and about the windows stirred in the faint wind draperies of exceeding thinness, woven in looms stilled centuries ago.

Olivia was crossing before the windows. She wore a white gown strewn with roses, and she seemed as much at home on this alien mountain-top as she had been in her aunt's drawing-room at the Boris. But her face was sad, and there was not a touch of the piquancy which it had worn the night before in the throne-room, nor of its delicious daring as she had sped past him in the big Yaque touring car. Save for her, the room was deserted; it was as if the prince had come to the castle and found the Sleeping Princess the only one awake.

If in that supreme moment St. George had leaped forward and taken her in his arms no one—no one, that is, in the fairy-tale of what was happening—would greatly have censured him. But he stood without for a moment, hardly daring to believe his happiness, hardly knowing that her name was on his lips.

He had spoken, however, and she turned quickly, her look uncertainly seeking the doorway, and she saw him. For a moment she stood still, her eyes upon his face; then with a little incredulous cry that thrilled him with a sudden joyous hope that was like belief, she came swiftly toward him.

St. George loved to remember that she did that. There was no waiting for assurance and no fear; only the impulse, gloriously obeyed, to go toward him.

He stepped in the room, and took her hands in his and looked into her eyes as if he would never turn away his own. In her face was a dawning of glad certainty and welcome which he could not doubt.

"You," she cried softly, "you. How is it possible? But how is it possible?"

Her voice trembled a little with something so sweet that it raced through his veins with magic.

"Did you rub the lamp?" he said. "Because I couldn't help coming."

She looked at him breathlessly.

"Have you," he asked her gravely, "eaten of the potatoes of Yaque? And are you going to say, 'Off with his head'? And can you tell me what is the population of the island?"

At that they both laughed—the merry, irrepressible laugh of youth which explains that the world is a very good place indeed and that one is glad that one belongs there. And the memory of that breakfast on the other side of the world, of their happy talk about what would happen if they two were impossibly to meet in Yaque came back to them both, and set his heart beating and flooded her face with delicate colour. In her laugh was a little catching of the breath that was enchanting.

"Not yet," she said, "your head is safe till you tell me how you got here, at all events. Now tell me—oh, tell me. I can't believe it until you tell me."

She moved a little away from the door.

"Come in," she said shyly, "if you've come all the way from America you must be very tired."

St. George shook his head.

"Come out," he pleaded, "I want to stand on top of a high mountain and show you the whole world."

She went quite simply and without hesitation—because, in Yaque, the maddest things would be the truest—and when she had stepped from the low doorway she looked up at him in the tender light of the garden terrace.

"If you are quite sure," she said, "that you will not disappear in the dark?"

St. George laughed happily.

"I shall not disappear," he promised, "though the world were to turn round the other way."

They crossed the still terrace to the parapet and stood looking out to sea with the risen moon shining across the waters. The light wind stirred in the cedrine junipers, shaking out perfume; the great fairy pile of the palace rose behind them; and before them lay the monstrous moon-lit abyss than whose depths the very stars, warm and friendly, seemed nearer to them. To the big young American in blue serge beside the little new princess who had drawn him over seas the dream that one is always having and never quite remembering was suddenly come true. No wonder that at that moment the patient Amory was far enough from his mind. To St. George, looking down upon Olivia, there was only one truth and one joy in the universe, and she was that truth and that joy.

"I can't believe it," he said boyishly.

"Believe—what?" she asked, for the delight of hearing him say so.

"This—me—most of all, you!" he answered.

"But you must believe it," she cried anxiously, "or maybe it will stop being."

"I will, I will, I am now!" promised St. George in alarm.

Whereat they both laughed again in sheer light-heartedness. Then, resting his broad shoulders against a prism of the parapet, St. George looked down at her in infinite content.

"You found the island," she said; "what is still more wonderful you have come here—but *here*—to the top of the mountain. Oh, did you bring news of my father?"

St. George would have given everything save the sweet of the moment to tell her that he did.

"But now," he added cheerfully, and his smile disarmed this of its over-confidence, "I've only been here two days or so. And, though it may look easy, I've had my hands full climbing up this. I ought to be allowed another day or two to locate your father."

"Please tell me how you got here," Olivia demanded then.

St. George told her briefly, omitting the yacht's ownership, explaining merely that the paper had sent him and that Jarvo and Akko had pointed the way and, save for that journey down nebulous ways in the wake of her veil the night before, sketching the incidents which had followed his arrival upon the island.

"And one of the most agreeable hours I've had in Yaque," he

finished, "was last night, when you were chairman of the meeting. That was magnificent."

"You *were* there!" cried Olivia, "I thought—"

"That you saw me?" St. George pressed eagerly.

"I think that I thought so," she admitted.

"But you never looked at me," said St. George dolefully, "and I had on a forty-two gored dress, or something."

"Ah," Olivia confessed, "but I had thought so before when I knew it couldn't be you."

St. George's heart gave a great bound.

"When before?" he wanted to know ecstatically.

"Ah, before," she explained, "and then afterward, too."

"When afterward?" he urged.

(Smile if you like, but this is the way the happy talk goes in Yaque as you remember very well, if you are honest.)

"Yesterday, when I was motoring, I thought—"

"I was. You did," St. George assured her. "I was in the prince's motor. The procession was temporarily tied up, you remember. Did you really think it was I?"

But this the lady passed serenely over.

"Last night," she said, "when that terrible thing happened, who was it in the other motor? Who was it, there in the road when I—was it you? Was it?" she demanded.

"Did you think it was I?" asked St. George simply.

"Afterward—when I was back in the palace—I thought I must have dreamed it," she answered, "and no one seemed to know, and *I* didn't know. But I did fancy—you see, they think father has taken the treasure," she said, "and they thought if they could hide me somewhere and let it be known, that he would make some sign."

"It was monstrous," said St. George; "you are really not safe here for one moment. Tell me," he asked eagerly, "the car you were in—what became of that?"

"I meant to ask you that," she said quickly. "I couldn't tell, I didn't know whether it turned aside from the road, or whether they dropped me out and went on. Really, it was all so quick that it was almost as if the motor had stopped being, and left me there."

"Perhaps it did stop being—in this dimension," St. George could not help saying.

At this she laughed in assent.

"Who knows," she said, "what may be true of us—*nous autres* in the Fourth Dimension? In Yaque queer things are true. And of course you never can tell—"

At this St. George turned toward her, and his eyes compelled hers.

"Ah, yes, you can," he told her, "yes, you can."

Then he folded his arms and leaned against the stone prisms again, looking down at her. Evidently the magician, whoever he was, did not mind his saying that, for the palace did not crumble or the moon cease from shining on the white walls.

"Still," she answered, looking toward the sea, "queer things *are* true in Yaque. It is queer that you are here. Say that it is."

"Heaven knows that it is," assented St. George obediently.

Presently, realizing that the terrace did not intend to turn into a cloud out-of-hand, they set themselves to talk seriously, and St. George had not known her so adorable, he was once more certain, as when she tried to thank him for his pursuit the night before. He had omitted to mention that he had brought her back alone to the Palace of the Litany, for that was too exquisite a thing, he decided, to be spoiled by leaving out the most exquisite part. Besides, there was enough that was serious to be discussed, in all conscience, in spite of the moon.

"Tell me," said St. George instead, "what has happened to you since that breakfast at the Boris. Remember, I have come all the way from New York to interview you, Mademoiselle the Princess."

So Olivia told him the story of the passage in the submarine which had arrived in Yaque two days earlier than *The Aloha*; of the first trip up Mount Khalak in the imperial airship; of Mrs. Hastings' frantic fear and her utter refusal ever to descend; and of what she herself had done since her arrival. This included a most practical account of effort that delighted and amazed St. George. No wonder Mrs. Hastings had said that she always left everything "executive" to Olivia. For Olivia had sent wireless messages all over the island offering an immense reward for information about the king, her father; she had assigned forty servants of the royal household to engage in a personal search for such information and to report to her each night; she had ordered every house in Yaque, not excepting the House of the Litany and the king's palace itself, to be searched from dungeon to tower; and, as St. George already knew, she had brought about a special meeting of the High Council at noon that day.

"It was very little," said the American princess apologetically, "but I did what I could."

"What about the meeting of the High Council?" asked St.

George eagerly; "didn't anything come of that?"

"Nothing," she answered, "they were like adamant. I thought of offering to raise the Hereditary Treasure by incorporating the island and selling the shares in America. Nobody could ever have found what the shares stood for, but that happens every day. Half the corporations must be capitalized chiefly in the Fourth Dimension. That is all," she added wearily, "save that day after to-morrow I am to be married."

"That," St. George explained, "is as you like. For if your father is on the island we shall have found him by day after to-morrow, at noon, if we have to shake all Yaque inside out, like a paper sack. And if he isn't here, we simply needn't stop."

Olivia shook her head.

"You don't know the prince," she said. "I have heard enough to convince me that it is quite as he says. He holds events in the hollow of his hand."

"Amory proposed," said St. George, "that we sit up here and throw pebbles at him for a time. And Amory is very practical."

Olivia laughed—her laugh was delicious and alluring, and St. George came dangerously near losing his head every time that he heard it.

"Ah," she cried, "if only it weren't for the prince and if we had news of father, what a heavenly, heavenly place this would be, would it not?"

"It would, it would indeed," assented St. George, and in his heart he said, "and so it is."

"It's like being somewhere else," she said, looking into the abyss of far waters, "and when you look down there—and when you look up, you nearly *know*. I don't know what, but you nearly know. Perhaps you know that 'here' is the same as 'there,' as all these people say. But whatever it is, I think we might have come almost as near knowing it in New York, if we had only known how to try."

"Perhaps it isn't so much knowing," he said, "as it is being where you can't help facing mystery and taking the time to be amazed. Although," added St. George to himself, "there are things that one finds out in New York. In a drawing-room, at the Boris, for instance, over muffins and tea."

"It will be delightful to take all this back to New York," Olivia vaguely added, as if she meant the fairy palace and the fairy sea.

"It will," agreed St. George fervently, and he couldn't possibly have told whether he meant the mystery of the island or the mystery of that hour there with her. There was so little difference.

"Suppose," said Olivia whimsically, "that we open our eyes in a minute, and find that we are in the prince's room in McDougle Street, and that he has passed his hand before our faces and made us dream all this. And father is safe after all."

"But it isn't all a dream," St. George said softly, "it can't possibly all be a dream, you know."

She met his eyes for a moment.

"Not your coming away here," she said, "if the rest is true I wouldn't want that to be a dream. You don't know what courage this will give us all."

She said "us all," but that had to mean merely "us," as well. St. George turned and looked over the terrace. What an Arabian night it was, he was saying to himself, and then stood in a sudden amazement, with the uncertain idea that one of the Schererazade magicians had answered that fancy of his by appearing.

A little shrine hung thick with vines, its ancient stone chipped and defaced, stood on the terrace with its empty, sightless niche turned toward the sea. Leaning upon its base was an old man watching them. His eyes under their lowered brows were peculiarly intent, but his look was perfectly serene and friendly. His stuff robe hung in straight folds about his singularly erect figure, and his beard and hair were not all grey. But he was very old, with incredibly brown and wrinkled flesh, and his face was vacant, as if the mind were asleep.

As he looked, St. George knew him. Here on the top of this mountain was that amazing old man whom he had last seen in the banquet hall at the Palace of the Litany—that old Malakh for whom Olivia had so unexplainably interceded.

"What is that man doing here?" St. George asked in surprise.

"He is a mad old man, they said," Olivia told him, "down there they call him Malakh—that means 'salt'—because they said he always weeps. We had stopped to look at a metallurgist yesterday—he had some zinc and some metals cut out like flowers, and he was making them show phosphorescent colours in his little dark alcove. The old man was watching him and trying to tell him something, but the metallurgist was rude to him and some boys came by and jostled him and pushed him about and taunted him—and the metallurgist actually explained to us that every one did that way to old Malakh. So I thought he was better off up here," concluded Olivia tranquilly.

St. George was silent. He knew that Olivia was like this, but everything that proved anew her loveliness of soul caught at his heart.

"Tell me," he said impulsively, "what made you let him stay last night, there in the banquet hall?"

She flushed, and shook her head with a deprecatory gesture.

"I haven't an idea," she said gravely, "I think I must have done it so the fairies wouldn't prick their feet on any new sorrow. One has to be careful of the fairies' feet."

St. George nodded. It was a charming reason for the left hand to give the right, and he was not deceived.

"Look at him," said St. George, almost reverently, "he looks like a shade of a god that has come back from the other world and found his shrine dishonoured."

Some echo of St. George's words reached the old man and he caught at it, smiling. It was as if he had just been thinking what he spoke.

"There are not enough shrines," he said gently, "but there are far too many gods. You will find it so."

Something in his words stirred St. George strangely. There was about the old creature an air of such gentleness, such supreme repose and detachment that, even in that place of quiet, his presence made a kind of hush. He was old and pallid and fragile, but there lingered within him, while his spirit lingered, the perfume of all fine and gentle things, all things of quietude. When he had spoken the old man turned and moved slowly down the ways of strange light, between the fallen temples builded to forgotten gods, and he seemed like the very spirit of the ancient mountain, ignorant of itself and knowing all truth.

"How strange," said St. George, looking after him, "how unutterably strange and sad."

"That is good of you," said Olivia. "Aunt Dora and Antoinette thought I'd gone quite off my head, and Mr. Frothingham wanted to know why I didn't bring back some one who could have been called as a witness."

"Witness," St. George echoed; "but the whole place is made of witnesses. Which reminds me: what is the sentence?"

"The sentence?" she wondered.

"The potatoes of Yaque," he reminded her, "and my head?"

"Ah well," said Olivia gravely, "inasmuch as the moon came up in the east to-night instead of the west, I shall be generous and give you one day's reprieve."

"Do you know, I *thought* the moon came up in the east to-night," cried St. George joyfully.

* * * * *

It was half an hour afterward that Amory's languid voice from somewhere in the sky broke in upon their talk. As he came toward them across the terrace St. George saw that he was miraculously not alone.

Afterward Amory told him what had happened and what had made him abide in patience and such wondrous self-effacement.

When St. George had left him contemplating the far beauties of the little blur of light that was Med, Mr. Toby Amory set a match to one of his jealously expended store of Habanas and added one more aroma to the spiced air. To be standing on the doorstep of a king's palace, confidently expecting within the next few hours to assist in locating the king himself was a situation warranting, Amory thought, such fragrant celebration, and he waited in comparative content.

The moon had climbed high enough to cast a great octagonal shadow on the smooth court, and the Habana was two-thirds memory when, immediately back of Amory, a long window opened outward, releasing an apparition which converted the remainder of the Habana into a fiery trail ending out on the terrace. It was a girl of rather more than twenty, exquisitely petite and pretty, and wearing a ruffley blue evening gown whose skirt was caught over her arm. She stopped short when she saw Amory, but without a trace of fear. To tell the truth, Antoinette Frothingham had got so desperately bored within-doors that if Amory had worn a black mask or a cloak of flame she would have welcomed either.

For the last two hours Mrs. Medora Hastings and Mr. Augustus Frothingham had sat in a white marble room of the king's palace, playing chess on Mr. Frothingham's pocket chess-board. Mr. Frothingham, who loathed chess, played it when he was tired so that he might rest and when he was rested he played it so that he might exercise his mind—on the principle of a cool drink on a hot day and a hot drink on a cool day. Mrs. Hastings, who knew nothing at all about the game, had entered upon the hour with all the suave complacency with which she would have attacked the making of a pie. Mrs. Hastings had a secret belief that she possessed great aptitude.

Antoinette Frothingham, the lawyer's daughter, had leaned on the high casement and looked over the sea. The window was narrow, and deep in an embrasure of stone. To be twenty and to be leaning in this palace window wearing a pale blue dinner-gown manifestly suggested a completion of the picture; and all that evening it had been impressing her as inappropriate that the maiden and the castle tower and the very sea itself should all be present, with no possibility of any knight within an altitude of many hundred feet.

"The dear little ponies' heads!" Mrs. Hastings had kept saying. "What a poetic game chess is, Mr. Frothingham, don't you think? That's what I always said to poor dear Mr. Hastings—at least, that's what he always said to me: 'Most games are so *needless*, but chess is really up and down poetic'"

Mr. Frothingham made all ready to speak and then gave it up in silence.

"Um," he had responded liberally.

"I'm sure," Mrs. Hastings had continued plaintively, "neither he nor I ever thought that I would be playing chess up on top of a volcano in the middle of the ocean. It's this awful feeling," Mrs. Hastings had cried querulously, "of being neither on earth nor under the water nor in Heaven that I object to. And nobody can get to us."

"That's just it, Mrs. Hastings," Antoinette had observed earnestly at this juncture.

"Um," said Mr. Frothingham, then, "not at all, not at all. We have all the advantages of the grave and none of its discomforts."

Whereupon Antoinette, rising suddenly, had slipped out of the white marble room altogether and had found the knight smoking in loneliness on the very veranda.

Amory put his cap under his arm and bowed.

"I hope," he said, "that I haven't frightened you."

He was an American! Antoinette's little heart leaped.

"I am having to wait here for a bit," explained Amory, not without vagueness.

Miss Frothingham advanced to the veranda rail and contrived a shy scrutiny of the intruder.

"No," she said, "you didn't frighten me in the least, of course. But—do you usually do your waiting at this altitude?"

"Ah, no," answered Amory with engaging candour, "I don't. But I—happened up this way." Amory paused a little desperately. In that soft light he could not tell positively whether this was Miss Holland or that other figure of silver and rose which he had seen in the throne room. The blue gown was not interpretative. If she was Miss Holland it would be very shabby of him to herald the surprise. Naturally, St. George would appreciate doing that himself. "I'm looking about a bit," he neatly temporized.

Antoinette suddenly looked away over the terrace as her eyes met his, smiling behind their pince-nez. Amory was good to look at, and he had never been more so than as he towered above her on the steps of the king's palace. Who was he—but who was he? Antoinette wondered rapidly. Had a warship arrived? Was Yaque taken? Or had—she turned eyes, round with sudden fear, upon Amory.

"Did Prince Tabnit send you?" she demanded.

Amory laughed.

"No, indeed," he said. Amory had once lived in the South, and he accented the "no" very takingly. "I came myself," he volunteered.

"I thought," explained Antoinette, "that maybe he opened a door in the dark, and you walked out. It *is* rather funny that you should be here."

"You are here, you know," suggested Amory doubtfully.

"But I may be a cannibal princess," Antoinette demurely pointed out. It was not that her astonishment was decreasing; but why—modernity and the democracy spoke within her— waste the possibilities of a situation merely because it chances to be astonishing? Moments of mystery are rare enough, in all conscience; and when they do arrive all the world misses them by trying to understand them. Which is manifestly ungrateful and stupid. They do these things better in Yaque.

"You maybe," agreed Amory evenly, "though I don't know that I ever met a desert island princess in a dinner frock. But then, I am a beginner in desert islands."

"Are you an American?" inquired Antoinette earnestly.

Amory looked up at the frowning facade of the king's palace, and he could have found it in his heart to believe his own answer.

"I'm the ghost," he confessed, "of a poor beggar of a Phoenician who used to make water-jars in Sidon. I have been condemned to plow the high seas and explore the tall mountains until I find the Pitiful Princess. She must be up at the very peak, in distress, and I—"

Amory stopped and looked desperately about him. Would St. George never come? How was he, Amory, to be accountable for what he told if he were left here alone in these extraordinary circumstances?

Then Antoinette lightly clapped her hands.

"A ghost!" she exclaimed with pleasure. "Miss Holland hoped the place was haunted. A Phoenician ghost with an Alabama accent."

She had said "Miss Holland hoped."

"Aren't you—aren't you Miss Holland?" demanded Amory promptly, a joyful note of uncertainty in his voice.

Antoinette shook her head.

"No," she said, "though I don't know why I should tell you that."

From Amory's soul rolled a burden that left him treading air on Mount Khalak. She was not Miss Holland. What did he care how long St. George stayed away?

"I am Tobias Amory," he said, "of New York. Most people don't know about the Sidonian ghost part. But I've told you because I thought, perhaps, you might be the Pitiful Princess."

Antoinette's heart was beating pleasantly. Of New York! How—oh, how did he get here? Was there, then, a wishing-stone in that window embrasure where she had been sitting, and had the knight come because she had willed it? How much did he know? How much ought she to tell? Nothing whatever, prudently decided the lawyer's daughter.

"I've had, I'm almost certain, the pleasure of seeing you before," imparted Amory pleasantly, adjusting his pince-nez and looking down at her. She was so enchantingly tiny and he was such a giant.

"In New York?" demanded Antoinette.

"No," said Amory, "no. Do desert island princesses get to New York occasionally, then? No, I think I saw you in Yaque. Yesterday. In a silver automobile. Did I?"

Antoinette dimpled.

"We frightened them all to death," she recalled. "Did we frighten you?"

"So much," admitted Amory, "that I took refuge up here."

"Where were you?" Antoinette asked curiously. Really, he was very amusing—this big courtly creature. How agreeable of Olivia to stay away.

"Ah, tell me how you got here," she impetuously begged. "Desert island people don't see people from New York every day."

"Well then, O Pitiful Princess," said the Shade from Sidon, "it was like this—"

It was easy enough to fleet the time carelessly, and assuredly that high moon-lit world was meant to be no less merry than the golden. Whoever has chanced to meet a delightful companion on some silver veranda up in the welkin knows this perfectly well; and whoever has not is a dull creature. But there are delightful folk who are wont to suspect the dullest of harbouring some sweet secret, some sense of "those sights which alone (says the nameless Greek) make life worth enduring," and this was akin to such a sight.

After a time, at Antoinette's conscientious suggestion, they strolled the way that St. George had taken. And to Olivia and the missing adventurer over by the parapet came Amory's soft query:

"St George, may I express a friendly concern?"

"Ah, come here, Toby," commanded St. George happily, "her Highness and I have been discussing matters of state."

"Antoinette!" cried Olivia in amazement. From time immemorial royalty has perpetually been surprised by the behaviour of its ladies-in-waiting.

"I've been remembering a verse," said Amory when he had been presented to Olivia, "may I say it? It goes:

"'I'll speak a story to you,
Now listen while I try:
I met a Queen, and she kept house
A-sitting in the sky.'"

"Come in and say it to my aunt," Olivia applauded. "Aunt Dora is dying of ennui up here."

They crossed the terrace in the hush of the tropic night. Through the fairy black and silver the four figures moved, and it was as if the king's palace—that sky thing, with ramparts of air—had at length found expression and knew a way to answer the ancient glamourie of the moon.

CHAPTER XV

A VIGIL

Upon Mrs. Hastings and Mr. Augustus Frothingham, drowsing over the pocket chess-board, the sound of footsteps and men's voices in the corridor acted with electrical effect. Then the door was opened and behind Olivia and Antoinette appeared the two visitors who seemed to have fallen from the neighbouring heavens. The two chess-pretenders looked up aghast. If there were a place in the world where chaperonage might be relaxed the uninformed observer would say that it would be the top of Mount Khalak.

"Mercy around us!" cried Mrs. Medora Hastings, "if it isn't that newspaper man! He's probably come over here to cable it all over the front page of every paper in New York. Well," she added complacently, as if she had brought it all about, "it seems good to see some of your own race. How *did* you get here? Some trick, I suppose?"

"My dear fellows," burst out Mr. Augustus Frothingham fervently, "thank God! I'm not, ordinarily, unequal to my situations, but I confess to you, as I would not to a client, that I don't object to sharing this one. How did you come?"

"It's a house-party!" said Antoinette ecstatically.

Amory looked at her in her blue gown in the light of the white room, and his spirits soared heavenward. Why should St.

George have an idea that he controlled the hour?

From a tumult of questioning, none of which was fully answered before Mrs. Hastings put another query, the lawyer at length elicited the substance of what had occurred.

"You came up the side of the mountain, carried by four of those frightful natives?" shrilled Mrs. Hastings. "Olivia, think. It's a wonder they didn't murder you first and throw you over afterward, isn't it, Olivia? Oh, and my poor dear brother. To think of his lying somewhere all mangled and bl—"

Emotion overcame Mrs. Hastings. Her tortoise-shell glasses fell to her lap and both her side-combs tinkled melodiously to the tiled floor.

"This reminds me," said Mr. Frothingham, settling back and finding a pencil with which to emphasize his story, "this reminds me very much of a case that I had on the June calendar—"

In half an hour St. George and Amory saw that all serious consideration of their situation must be accomplished alone with Olivia; for in that time Mr. Frothingham had been reminded of two more cases and Mrs. Hastings had twice been reduced to tears by the picture of the possible fate of her brother. Moreover, there presently appeared supper—a tray of the most savoury delicacies, to produce which Olivia had slipped away and, St. George had no doubt, said over some spell in the kitchens. Supper in the white marble room of the king's palace was almost as wonderful as muffins and tea at the Boris.

There were Olivia in her gown of roses on one side of the table and Antoinette on the other and between them the hungry and happy adventurers. Across the room under a tall silver vase that might have been the one proposed by Achilles at the funeral games for Patroclus ("that was the work of the 'skilful Sidonians'" St. George recalled with a thrill), Mrs. Hastings and Mr. Frothingham were conscientiously finishing their chess, since the lawyer believed in completing whatever he undertook, if for nothing more than a warning never to undertake it again. Manifestly the little ivory kings and queens and castles were in league with all the other magic of the night, for the game prolonged itself unconscionably, and the supper party found it far from difficult to do the same. St. George looked at Olivia in her gown of roses, and his eyes swept the high white walls of the room with its frescoes and inscriptions, its broken statues and defaced chests of stone and ancient armour, and so back to Olivia in her gown of roses, with her little ringless hands touching and lifting among the alien dishes as she ministered to him. What a dear little gown of roses and what beautiful hands, St. George thought; and as for the broken statues and the inscriptions and the contents of the stone chests, nobody had paid any attention to them for so long that they could hardly have missed his regard. Nor Amory's. For Amory was in the midst of a reminiscent reference to the Chiswicks, in the Adirondacks, and to Antionette Frothingham in a launch.

At last they all were aware that the chess-board was being closed and Mrs. Hastings had risen.

"I suppose," she was saying, "that they have an idea here, the poor deluded creatures, that it is very late. But I tell Olivia that we are so much farther east it *can't* be very late in New York at this minute, and I intend to go to bed by my watch as I always do, and that is New York time. If I were in New York I wouldn't be sleepy now, and I'm no different here, am I? I don't think people are half independent enough."

Mrs. Hastings stepped round a stone god, almost faceless, that stood in a little circular depression in the floor.

"Olivia, where," she inquired, patting the bobbing, ticking jet on her gown, "where do you think that frightful, mad, old man is?"

"I heard him cross the corridor a little while ago," Olivia answered. "I think he went to his room."

"I must say, Olivia," said Mrs. Hastings with a damp sigh, "that you are very selfish where I am concerned—in *this* matter."

"Ah," said Olivia, "please, Aunt Dora. He is far too feeble to harm any one. And he's away there on the second floor."

"I'm sure he's a murderer," protested Mrs. Hastings. "He has the murderer's eye. Mr. Hastings would have said he has. We all sleep on the ground floor here," she continued plaintively, "because we are so high up anyway that I think the air must be just as pure as it would be up stairs. I always leave my window up the width of my handkerchief-box."

As they went out to the great corridor Olivia spoke softly to St. George.

"Look up," she said.

He looked, and saw that the vast circular chamber was of incalculable height, extending up to the very dome of the palace, and shaping itself to the lines of the topmost of the three huge cones. It was a great well of light, playing over strange frescoes of gods and daemons, of constellations and of beasts, and exquisite with all the secret colours of some other way of vision. As high as the eye could see, the precious metals upon the skeleton of the open roof shone in the bright light that was set there—the light on the summit of the king's palace.

St. George turned from the glory of it and looked into her eyes.

"'A new Heaven and a new earth,'" he said; but he did not mean the dome of light nor yet the splendour of the palace.

*　*　*　*　*

Manifestly, there is no use in being asleep when one can dream rather better awake. St. George wandered aimlessly between his room and Amory's and took the time to reflect that when a man looks the way Amory did he might as well have Cupids painted on his coat.

"St. George," Amory said soberly, "is this the way you've been feeling all the way here? Is this what you came for? Then, on my soul, I forgive you everything. I would have climbed ten mountains to meet Antoinette Frothingham."

"I've been watching you, you son of Dixie," said St. George darkly; "don't you lose your head just when you need it most."

"I have a notion yours is gone," defended Amory critically, "and mine is only going."

"That's twice as dangerous," St. George wisely opined; "besides—mine is different."

"So is mine," said Amory, "so is everybody's."

St. George stepped through the long window to the terrace. Amory didn't care whether anybody listened; he simply longed to talk, and St. George had things to think about. He crossed the terrace to the south, and went back to the very spot where he and Olivia had stood; and there, because the night would have it no other way, he stretched along the broad wall among the vines, and lit his pipe, and lay looking out at sea. Here he was, liberated from the business of "buzzing in a corner, trifling with monosyllables," set upon a field pleasant with hazard and without paths, to move in the primal experiences where words themselves are born. Better and more intimate names for everything seemed now almost within his ken.

He had longed unspeakably to go pilgriming, and he had forthwith been permitted to leave the world behind with its thickets and thresholds, its hesitations and confusions, its marching armies, breakfasts, friendships and the like, and to live on the edge of what will be. He thought of his mother, in her black gowns and Roman mosaic pins with a touch of yellow lace at her throat, listening to the bishop as he examined the dicta of still cloisters, and he told himself that he knew a heresy or two that were like belief. His mother and the bishop at Tuebingen and on the Baltic! Curiously enough, they did not seem very remote. He adored his mother and the bishop, and so the thought of them was a part of this fairy tale. All pleasant thoughts whether of adventure or impression boast kinship, perhaps have identity. And the name of that identity was Olivia. So he "drove the night along" on the leafy parapet.

He was not far from asleep, nor perhaps from the dream of the Roman emperor who believed the sea to have come to his bedside and spoken with him, when something—he was not sure whether it was a voice or a touch—startled him awake. He rose on his elbow and looked drowsily out at the glorified blackness—as if black were no longer absence cf colour but, the veil of negative definitions having been pierced, were found to be a mystic union of colour and more inclusive than white. The very dark seemed delicately vocal and to "fill the waste with sound" no less than the wash of the waves. St. George awoke deliciously confused by a returning sense of the sweet and the joy of the night.

"'This was the loneliest beach between two seas,'" there flitted through his mind, "'and strange things had been done there in the ancient ages.'" He turned among the vines, half listening. "And in there is the king's daughter," he told himself, "and this is certainly 'the strangest thing that ever befell between two seas.' And I have a great mind to look up the old woman of that tale who must certainly be hereabout, dancing 'widdershins.'"

Then, like a bright blade unsheathed in a quiet chamber, a cry of great and unmistakable fear rang out from the palace—a woman's cry, uttered but once, and giving place to a silence that was even more terrifying. In an instant St. George was on his feet, running with all his might.

"Coming!" he called, "where are you—where are you?" And his heart pounded against his side with the certainty that the voice had been Olivia's.

It was unmistakably Olivia's voice that replied to him.

"Here!" she cried clearly, and St. George followed the sound and dashed through the long open window of the room next that in which he had first seen her that night.

"Here," she repeated, "but be careful. Some one is in this room."

"Don't be afraid," he cried cheerily into the dark. "It's all right," which is exactly what he would have said if there had been about dragons and real shades from Sidon.

The room was now in darkness, and in the dim light cast by the high moon he could at first discern nothing. He heard a silken rustling and the tap of slippered feet. The next instant the apartment was quick with light, and in the curtained entrance to an inner room, Olivia, in a brown dressing-gown, her hair vaguely bright about her flushed face, stood confronting him.

Between them, his thin hand thrown up, palm outward, to protect his eyes from the sudden light, was the old man whom St. George had last seen by the shrine on the terrace.

St. George was prepared for a mere procession of palace ghosts, but at this strange visitor he stared for an uncomprehending moment.

"What are you doing here?" he said wonderingly to him; "what in the world are you doing here?"

The old man looked uncertainly about him, one hand spread against the pillar behind him, the other fumbling at his throat.

"I think," he answered almost indistinguishably, "I think that I meant to sit here—to sit in the room beyond, where the mock stars shine."

Olivia uttered an exclamation.

"How could he possibly know that?" she said.

"But what does he mean?" asked St. George.

She crossed swiftly to a portiere hanging by slender rings from the full height of the lofty room, and at her bidding St. George followed her. She pushed aside the curtain, revealing a huge cave of the dark, a room whose walls were sunk in shadow. But overhead the ceiling was constellated in stars, so that it seemed to St. George as if he were looking into a nearer heaven, homing the far lights that he knew. The Pleiades, Orion, and the Southern Cross, blazing down with inconceivable brilliance, were caught and held captive in the cup of this nearer sky.

"It is like this at night," Olivia said, "but we see nothing in the daytime, save the vague outlines of here and there a star. But how could he have known? There is no other door save this."

The old man had followed them and stood, his eyes fixed on the shining points.

"It is done well," he said softly, "it makes one feel the firmament."

St. George, thrilling with the strangeness of what he saw, and the strangeness of being there with Olivia and this weird old man of the mountain, turned toward him almost fearfully.

How did he know, indeed?

"Ah well," he said, striving to reassure her, "I've no doubt he has wandered in here some evening, while you were at dinner. No doubt—"

He stopped abruptly, his eyes fixed on the old man's hand. For as he lifted it St. George had thought that something glittered. Without hesitation he caught the old man's arm about the wrist, and turned his hand in his own palm. In the thin fingers he found a small sealed tube, filled with something that looked like particles of nickel.

"Do you mind telling me what that is?" asked St. George.

Old Malakh's eyes, liquid and brown and very peaceful, met his own without rebuke.

"Do you mean the gem?" he asked gently. "It is a very beautiful ruby."

Then St. George saw upon the hand that held the sealed tube a ring of matchless workmanship, set with a great ruby that smouldered in the shadow where they stood. Olivia looked at St. George with startled eyes.

"He was not wearing this when we first saw him," she said. "I haven't seen him wearing it at all."

St. George confronted the old man then and spoke with some determination.

"Will you please tell us," he said, "what there is in this tube, and how you came by this ring?"

Old Malakh looked down reflectively at his hand, and back to St. George's face. It was wonderful, the air of courtliness and urbanity and delicate breeding which persisted through age and infirmity and the fallow mind.

"I wish that I might tell you," he said humbly, "but I have only little lights in my head, instead of words. And when I say them, they do not mean—what they *shine*. Do you not see? That is why every one laughs. But I know what the lights say."

St. George looked at Olivia helplessly.

"Will you tell me where his room is?" he said, "and I'll go back with him. I don't know what to make of this, quite, but don't be frightened. It's all right. Didn't you say he is on the second floor?"

"Yes, but don't go alone with him," begged Olivia suddenly, "let me call some of the servants. We don't know what he may do."

St. George shook his head, smiling a little in sheer boyish delight at that "we." "We" is a very wonderful word, when it is not put to unimportant uses by kings, editors and the like.

"I'd rather not, thank you," he said. "I'll have a talk with him, I think."

"His room is at the top of the stair, on the left," said Olivia reluctantly, "but I wish—"

"We shall get on all right," St. George assured her, "and don't let this worry you, will you? I was smoking on the terrace. I'll be there for a while yet. Good night," he said from the doorway.

"Good night," said Olivia. "Good night—and, oh, I thank you."

St. George's expectation of having a talk with the old man was, however, unfounded. Old Malakh led the way to his room—a great place of carven seats and a frowning bed-canopy and high windows, and doors set deep in stone; and he begged St. George to sit down and permitted him to examine the sealed tube filled with little particles that looked like nickel, and spoke with gentle irrelevance the while. At the last St. George left him, feeling as if he were committing not so much an indignity as a social solecism when he locked the door upon the lonely creature, using for the purpose a key-like implement chained to the lock without and having a ring about the size of the iron crown of the Lombards.

"Good night," old Malakh told him courteously, "good night. But yet all nights are good—save the night of the heart."

St. George went back to the terrace. For hours he paced the paths of that little upper garden or lay upon the wall among the pungent vines. But now he forgot the iridescent dark and the companion-sea and the high moon and the king's palace, for it was not these that made the necromancy of the night. It was permitted him to watch before the threshold while Olivia slept, as lovers had watched in the youth of the world. Whatever the morrow held, to-night had been added to yesternight. Not until the dawn of that morrow whitened the sky and drew from the vapourous plain the first far towers of Med, the King's City, did St. George say good night to her glimmering windows.

CHAPTER XVI

GLAMOURIE

There is a certain poster, all stars and poppies and deep grass; and over these hangs a new moon which must surely have been cut by fairy scissors, for it looks as much like a cake or a cowslip as it looks like a moon. But withal it sheds a light so eery and strangely silver that the poster seems, in spite of the poppies, to have been painted in Spring-wind.

"Never," said some chance visitors vehemently, "have I seen such a moon as that!"

"But ah, sir, and ah, madame," was the answer—it is not recorded whether the poster spoke or whether some one spoke for it—"wouldn't you like to?"

Now, therefore, concerning the sweet of those hours in the king's palace the Vehement may be tempted to exclaim that in life things never happen like that. Ah—do they not so? You have only to go back to the days when young love and young life were yours to recall distinctly that the most impossible things were every-day occurrences. What about the time that you went down one street instead of up another and *that* changed the entire course of your days and brought you two together? What about the song, the June, the letter that touched the world to gold before your eyes and caught you up in a place of clouds? Remembering that magic, it is quite impossible to assert that any charming thing whatever would not have happened. Is there not some wonderland in every life? And is not the ancient citadel of Love-upon-the-Heights that common wonderland? One must believe in all the happiness that one can.

But if the Most Vehement—who are as thick as butterflies— still remain unconvinced and persist that they never heard of things fallen out thus, there is left this triumph:

"Ah, sir, or ah, madame, wouldn't you like to?"

* * * * *

A fugitive wind rollicking in from sea next morning swept through the palace and went on around the world; and thereafter it had an hundred odourous ways of attracting attention, which were merely its own tale of what pleasant things it had seen and heard on high.

For example, that breakfast. A cloth had been laid at one end of the long stone table whereat, since the days of Abibaal, brother to Hiram, friend to David, kings had breakfasted and banqueted, and this cloth had now been set with the ancient plate of the palace—dishes that looked like helmets and urns and discs. Here Olivia and Antoinette, in charming print frocks, made a kind of tea in a kind of biblical samovar and served it in vessels that resembled individual trophies of the course. And here St. George and Amory praised the admirable English muffins which some one had taught the dubious cook to make; and Mr. Augustus Frothingham tip-fingered his way about his plate among alien fruits and queer-shaped cakes. "Are they cookies or are they manna?" Amory wondered, "for they remind me of coriander seeds." And here Mrs. Hastings, who always awoke a thought impatient and became ultra-complacent with no interval of real sanity, wistfully asked for a soft-boiled egg and added plaintively:

"Though I dare say the very hens in Yaque lay something besides eggs—pineapples, very likely."

"I suppose," speculated Amory, "that when we get perfectly intuitionized we won't have to eat either one because we'll know beforehand exactly how they both taste."

"A *reductio ad absurdum*, my young friend," said the lawyer sternly; "the real purpose of eating will remain for ever unchanged."

Later, while Mrs. Hastings and Mr. Frothingham went out on the terrace in the sun and wished for a morning paper ("I miss the weather report so," complained Mrs. Hastings) the four young people with Jarvo and Akko for guides set out to explore the palace. For St. George had risen from his two hours' sleep with some clearly-defined projects, and he meant first to go over every niche and corner of the great pile where one—say a king—might be hidden with twenty other kings, and no one be at all the wiser.

What a morning it was! When the rollicking wind got to that part of the story it must have told about it in such intimating perfumes that even the unimaginative were constrained to sit idle, "thinking delicate thoughts." There never was a fairer temple of romance, a very temple of Young Love's Plaisaunce; and since the coming of St. George and Amory all the cavernous chambers and galleries were become homes of hope that the king would be found and all would yet be well.

To the main part of the palace there were storey after storey, all octagons and pentagons and labyrinths, so that incredulity and amazement might increase with every step. How they had ever raised those massive blocks of stone to that great height no one can guess unless, indeed, Amory's theory were correct and the palace had originally been built upon level ground and had had its surroundings blasted neatly away to make a mountain. At all events there were the walls of the great airy rooms made of the naked stone, exquisitely beveled and chiseled, and frescoed with the planetary deities—Eloti, the Moon with her chariot drawn by white bulls, the Sun and his four horses, with his emblem of a column in the form of a rising flame—types

　　　　　Zona Gale

taken from the heavens and from the abyss. There were roofs of sound fir and sweet cedar, carven cornices, cave-like window embrasures with no glass, and little circular rooms built about shrines in which sat broken images of Baal the sun god, of a sandaled Astarte, and a ravening Melkarth, with the lion's skin.

From a great upper corridor there went a stairway, each deep step of which was placed on the back of a stone lion of increasing size, until the tallest lion's head extended close to the painted ceiling, and there were comfortable benches cut in his gigantic paws. Many of the rooms were without furnishing, some were filled with vague, splendid stuff mouldering away, and others with most luxuriously-devised ministries to beauty and comfort. The palace was curiously and wonderfully an habitation of more than two thousand years ago, furnished with a taste and luxury in advance of this moment's civilization of the world. The heart of that elder world beat strangely in one of the upper chambers where they came upon a little work-shop, strewn with unknown metals and tools and empty crucibles, and in their midst a rectangular metallic plate partly traced with a device of boughs, appearing, in one light, slightly fluorescent.

"It is the work of the Princess Simyra, adon," said Jarvo. "She was the daughter of King Thabion, and when she died what she had touched in this room was left unmoved. But it was very many years ago—I have forgotten. Every one has forgotten."

They went down among the very roots of the palace, three full storeys below the surface of the summit. Jarvo went before, lighting the way, and they threaded vaulted corridors and winding passages, and emerged at last in a silent, haunted chamber whose stones had been hewn and sunken there, before Issus. This was the chamber of the tombs of the kings, and its floor echoed to their footsteps, now hollowly, now with ringing clearness. Three sides of the mighty hall were lined with *loculi* or niches, each as deep as the length of a man. About the floor stood stone sarcophagi and beneath the long flags kings were sleeping, each with his abandoned name graven on the stones, washed year-long by the dark. In the room's centre was a lofty cylindrical tomb, mounted by four steps, and this was the resting-place of King Abibaal, the younger son of King Abibaal of Tyre, and the brother to King Hiram, who ruled in Tyre when the Phoenicians who settled Yaque, or Arqua, first passed the Straits of Gibraltar and gained the open sea. ("Dear me," said Mrs. Hastings when they told her, "I was at Mount Vernon once, and the Washingtons' tombs there impressed me very deeply, but they were nothing to these in point of age, were they?") Sunken in the wall was a tomb of white marble hewn in a five-faced pyramidion, where slept Queen Mitygen, who ruled in Yaque while Alexander was king of Persia. There was said to have been buried with her a casket of love-letters from Alexander, who may have known Yaque and probably at one time visited it and, in that case, was entertained in the very palace. And if this is true the story of his omission to conquer the island may one day divert the world.

Jarvo bent before a low tomb whose stone was delicately scored with winged circles.

"Perhaps," he said, "you will recall the accounts of the kidnapped Egyptian priestesses sold to the Theoprotions by Phoenician merchants in the heroic age of Greece? They were not all sold. Here lie the bones of four, given royal burial because of their holy office."

Nothing was unbelievable—nothing had been unbelievable for so long that these four had almost learned that everything is possible. Which, if you come to think of it, and no matter how absurdly you learn it, is a thing immeasurably worth realizing in this world of possibilities. It is one of our two magics.

"And this," Jarvo said softly, pausing before a vacant niche opposite the tomb of King Abibaal, "this will be the receptacle for the present king of Yaque, his Majesty, King Otho, by the grace of God."

Olivia suddenly looked up at St. George, her face pale in the ghostly light. There it had been, waiting for them all the while, the sense of the vivid personal against the vague eternal. But her involuntary appeal to him, slight as it was, thrilled St. George with tenderness as vivid as this tragic element itself.

They went back to the sun and the sweet messengering air above, and crossed a little vacant grassy court on the north side of the mountain. Here they saw that the palace climbed down the northern slope from the summit, and literally overhung the precipice where the supports were made fast by gigantic girders run in the living rock. A little observatory was built below the edge of the mountain, and this box of a place had a glass floor, and one felt like a fly on the sky as one stood there. It was said that a certain king of Yaque, sometime in the course of the Punic Wars, had thrown himself from this observatory in a rage because his court electrician had died, but how true this may be it is impossible to say because so little is known about electricity. Below the building lay quite the most wonderful part of the king's palace.

Here in the long north rooms, hermetically quiet, was the heart of the treasure of the ancient island. Here, saved inexplicably from the wreck of the past, were a thousand testimonies to that lost and but half-guessed art of the elder world. Beautiful things, made in the days when King Solomon built the Temple at Jerusalem, lined the walls, and filled the stone shelves, together with curios of that later day when Phoenicia stood first in knowledge of the plastic and glyptic arts. Workers in gold and ivory, in gems and talismans, in brass and fine linen and purple had done the marvels which those courtier adventurers brought with them over the sea, and to these, from year to year, had been added the treasure of private chests—necklaces and coronals and hair-loops, bottles and vases of glass coloured with metallic oxides, and patterned aggry-beads, now sometimes found in ancient tombs on the Ashantee coasts. Beneath an altar set with censers and basins of gold was a chest brought from Amathus, its ogive lid carved with *bigae* or two-horsed chariots, and it was in this chest,

Jarvo told them, that the Hereditary Treasure had been kept. The chamber walls were covered with bas-reliefs in the ill-proportioned and careful carving of the Phoenician artists not yet under Greek influence, and all about were set the wonderful bronzes, such as Tyrian artificers made for the Temple. The other chambers gave still deeper utterance to days remote, for it was there that the king's library had been collected in case after case, filled with parchment rolls preserved and copied from age to age. What might not be there, they wondered—annals, State documents, the Phoenician originals of histories preserved elsewhere only in fragments of translation or utterly lost, the secrets of science and magic known to men the very forms of whose names have perished; and not only the longed-for poems of Sido and Jopas, but of who could tell how many singing hearts, lyric with joy and love and still voiceful here in these strange halls? These were chambers such as no one has ever entered, for this was the vexing of no unviolated tomb and no buried city, but the actual return to the Past, watching lonely on the mountain.

"Clusium," said Amory softly. "I had actually wanted to go to the cemetery at Clusium, to see some inscriptions!"

"No, you didn't, Toby," said St. George pleasantly, "you wanted to go somewhere and you called it Clusium. You wanted an adventure and you thought Clusium was the name of it."

"I know," said Amory shamelessly, "and there are no end of names for it. But it's always the same thing. *Excepting this.*"

"Excepting this," St. George repeated fervently as they turned to go; and if, in singing of that morning, the rollicking wind sang that, it must have breathed and trembled with a chorus of faint voices from every shelf in the room,—voices that of old had thrilled with the same meaning and woke now to the eternal echo.

Woke now to the eternal echo—an echo that touched

delicately through the events of that afternoon and laid strange values on all that happened. Otherwise, if they four were not all a little echo-mad, how was it that in the shadow of doubt, in the face of danger, and near the inextinguishable mystery they yet found time for the little, wing-like moments that never hold history, because they hold revelation. There were, too, some events; but an event is a clumsy thing at best, unless it has something intangible about it. The delicious moments are when the intangibilities prevail and pervade and possess. In the king's palace there must have been shrines to intangibilities—as there should be everywhere—for they seemed to come there, and belong.

The mere happenings included, for example, a talk that St. George had with Mr. Augustus Frothingham on the terrace after luncheon, in which St. George laid before the lawyer a plan which he had virtually matured and of which he himself thought very well. Thought so well, because of its possibilities, that his face was betrayingly eager as he told about it. It was, briefly, that inasmuch as four of the six men who could scale the mountain were now on its summit, and inasmuch as all the airships were there also, now, therefore, they, the guests on the island of Yaque, were in a perfectly impregnable position— counting out Fifth Dimension contingencies, which of course might include appearings as well as disappearings—and why shouldn't they stay there, and let the ominous noon of the following day slip by unmarked? And when the lawyer said, "But, my dear fellow," as he was bound to say, St. George answered that down there in Med there would be, by noon of the following day, two determined persons who, if Jarvo would get word to them, would with perfect certainty find Mr. Otho Holland, the king, if he were on the island. And when "Well, but my dear fellow" occurred again, St. George replied with deference that he knew it, but although he never had managed an airship he fancied that perhaps he might help with one; and down there in the harbour was a yacht waiting to sail for New York, and therefore no one need even set foot on the island who didn't wish. And Mr. Frothingham laid one long hand on each coat-lapel and threw back his head until his hair rested on his collar, and he looked at the palace—that Titan thing of the sky with ramparts of air—and said, "Nothing in all my experience—" and St. George left him, deep in thought.

On the way back he chanced upon Mrs. Hastings, seated on a bench of lapidescent wood in the portico—and a Titanic portico it looked by day—and, having sent for the palace chef, she was attempting to write down the recipe for the salad of that day's luncheon, although it was composed chiefly of fowls now extinct everywhere excepting in Yaque.

"But my poultry man will get them for me," she urged with determination; "I have only to tell him the name of what I want, and he can always produce it in tins, nicely labeled."

Later, St. George came upon old Malakh, leaning on the terrace wall, looking out to sea, and stood close beside him, marveling at the pallor and the thousand wrinkles of the man's strange face. The face was stranger by day than it had been by night—this St. George had felt when he went that morning to release him, and the old man leaned from the frowning bed-hangings to bid him a gentle good morning. Could he be, St. George now wondered vaguely, a citizen of the fifteenth or twentieth dimension, and, there, did they live to his incredible age? Then he noticed that the old man was not wearing the ruby ring.

"I wear it only when I wish to see it shine, sir," old Malakh answered, and St. George marveled at that courteous "sir," and at other things.

To everything that he asked him the old man returned only his urbane, unmeaning replies, touched with their melancholy symbolism. When St. George left him it was in the hope that Olivia would consent to have him sent down the mountain, although St. George himself was half inclined to agree with Amory's "But, really, I would far rather talk with one madman with this madman's manners than to sup with uncouth sanity" and "After all, if he should murder us, probably no one could do it with greater delicacy." And Olivia had no intention of sending old Malakh back to Med. "How could one possibly do that?" she wanted to know, and there was no oracle.

All the while the world of intangibilities was growing, growing as only that world can grow from the abysmal silence of life that went before. St. George was saying to himself that at last the *Here* and the *Now* were infinitely desirable; and as for the fear for the morrow, what was that beside the promise of the days beyond? At noon they all climbed the Obelisk Tower with its ceiling of carved leaves above carved leaves, and the real heavens a little farther up. They leaned on the broad wall, cut by mock bastions and faced the glory of the sunny, trembling sea, starred with the dipping wings of gulls. Blue sky, blue sea, eyes that saw looks that eyes did not know they gave—ah, what a day it was! When the rollicking wind told about that, down on the dun earth, surely it echoed their young courage, their young belief in the future, the incorruptibility of their understanding that the future was theirs, under the law. For the wind always teaches that. The wind is the supreme believer, and one has only to take a walk in it at this moment to know the truth. Yet in spite of the wind, in spite of their high security, in spite of the little wing-like moments that hold not history but revelation, they were all going down the hours beneath the pendent sword of "To-morrow, at noon."

CHAPTER XVII

BENEATH THE SURFACE

Up came the dusk to the doors of the king's palace—a hurry of grey banners flowing into the empty ways where the sun had been. Upon this high dominion Night could not advance unheralded, and here the Twilight messengered her coming long after the dark lay thick on the lowland and on the toiling water.

St. George, leaning from Amory's window, looked down on the shadows rising in exquisite hesitation, as if they came curling from the lighted censer of Med. There is no doubt at all, Olivia had said gravely, that the dusk is patterned, if only one could see it—figured in unearthly flowers, in wandering stars, in upper-air sprites, grey-winged, grey-bodied, so that sometimes glimpsing them one fancies them to be little living goblins. He smiled, remembering her words, and glanced over his shoulder down the long room where the other light was now beginning to creep about, first expressing, then embracing the chamber dusk. It seemed precisely the moment when something delicate should be caught passing from gloom to radiance, to be thankfully remembered. But only many-winged colours were visible, though he could hear a sound like little murmurous speech in the dusky roof where the air had a recurrent fashion of whispering knowingly.

Indeed, the air everywhere in the palace had a fashion of whispering knowingly, for it was a place of ghostly draughts and blasts creeping through chambers cleft by yawning courts and open corridors and topped by that skeleton dome. And as St. George turned from the window he saw that the door leading into the hall, urged by some nimble gust, imaginative or prying, had swung ajar.

St. George mechanically crossed the room to close the door, noting how the pale light warmed the stones of that cave-like corridor. With his hand upon the latch his eyes fell on something crossing the corridor, like a shadow dissolving from gloom to gloom. Well beyond the open door, stealing from pillar to pillar in the dimness and moving with that swiftness and slyness which proclaim a covert purpose as effectually as would a bell, he saw old Malakh.

Now St. George was in felt-soled slippers and he was coatless, because in the adjoining room Jarvo, with a heated, helmet-like apparatus, was attempting to press his blue serge coat. In that room too was Amory, catching glimpses of himself in a mirror of polished steel, but within reach, on the divan where Jarvo had just laid it, was Amory's coat; and St. George caught that up, slipped it on, and was off down the corridor after the old man, moving as swiftly and slyly as he. St. George had no great faith in him or in what he might know, but the old man puzzled him, and mystification is the smell of a pleasant powder.

The palace was very still. Presumably, Mrs. Hastings and Mr. Frothingham were already at chess in the drawing-room awaiting dinner. St. George heard a snatch of distant laughter, in quick little lilts like a song, and it occurred to him that its echo there was as if one were to pin a ruffle of lace to the grim stones. Some one answered the laugh, and he heard the murmurous touching of soft skirts entering the corridor as he dived down the ancient dark of one of the musty passages. There the silence was resumed. In the palace it was as though the stillness were some living sleeper, waking with protests, thankful for the death of any echo.

No one was in the gallery. St. George, stepping softly, followed as near as he dared to that hurrying figure, flitting down the dark. A still narrower hallway connected the main portion of the palace with a shoulder of the south wing, and into this the old man turned and skirted familiarly the narrow sunken pool that ran the length of the floor, drawing the light to its glassy surface and revealing the shadows sent clustering to the indistinguishable roof.

Midway the gallery sprang a narrow stairway, let in the wall and once leading to the ancient armoury, but now disused and piled with rubbish. Old Malakh went up two steps of this old stairway, turned aside, and slipped away so swiftly that his amazed pursuer caught no more than an after-flutter of his dun-coloured garments. St. George, his softly-clad feet making no noise upon the stones, bounded forward and saw, through a triangular aperture in the stones, and set so low that a man must crouch upon the step to enter, a yawning place of darkness.

He might very well have been taking his life in his hands, for he could have no idea whether the aperture led to the imperial dungeons or to the imperial rain-water cistern; but St. George instantly bent and slipped down into that darkness, thick with the dust of the flight of the old man. With the distinctly pleasurable sensation of being still alive he found himself standing upright upon an uneven floor of masonry. He thrust out his arms and touched sides of mossy rock. Then just before him a pale flame flickered. The old man had kindled a little taper that hardly did more than make shallow hollows in the darkness through which he moved.

It was easy to follow now, and St. George went breathlessly on past the rudely-hewn walls and giant pillars of that hidden way. He might have been lost with ease in any of the lower processes of the palace which they had that morning visited; but he could not be deceived about the chambers which he had once seen, and this subterranean course was new to him. Was it, he wondered, new to Olivia, and to Jarvo? Else why had it

Zona Gale

been omitted in that morning's search? And was this strange guide going on at random, or did he know—something? A suspicion leaped to St. George's mind that made his heart beat. The king—might he be down here after all, and might this weird old man know where? His own consciousness became chiefly conjecture, and every nerve was alert in the pursuit; not the less because he realized that if he were to lose this strange conductor who went on before, either in secure knowledge or in utter madness, he himself might wander for the rest of his life in that nether world.

Past grim latchless doors sealing, with appropriate gestures, their forgotten secrets, past outlying passages winding into the heart of the mountain, past niches filled with shapeless crumbling rubbish they hurried—the mad old man and his bewildered pursuer. Twice the way turned, gradually narro-wing until two could hardly have passed there, and at last apparently terminated in a short flight of steps. Old Malakh mounted with difficulty and St. George, waiting, saw him standing before a blank stone wall. Immediately and without effort the old man's scanty strength served to displace one of the wall's huge stones which hung upon a secret pivot and rolled noiselessly within. He stepped through the aperture, and St. George sprang behind him, watched his moment to cross the threshold, crouched in the leaping shadow of the displaced stone and looked—looked with the undistinguishing amaze-ment that a man feels in the panorama of his dreams.

The room was small and low and set with a circular bench, running about a central pillar. On the table was a confusion of things brilliantly phosphorescent, emitting soft light, and mingled with bulbs, coils and crucibles lying in a litter of egg-shells, feathers, ivory and paper. But it was not these that held St. George incredulous; it was the fire that glowed in their midst—a fire that leaped and trembled and blazed inextin-guishable colour, smouldering, sparkling, tossing up a spray of strange light, lambent with those wizard hues of the pennons and streamers floating joyously from the dome of the Palace of the Litany—the fire from the subject hearts of a thousand jewels. There could be no doubting what he saw. There, flung on the table from the mouth of a carven casket and harbouring the captive light of ages gone, glittered what St. George knew would be the gems of the Hereditary Treasure of the kings of Yaque.

But for old Malakh to know where the jewels were—that was as amazing as was their discovery. St. George, breathing hard in his corner, watched the long, fine hands of the old man trembling among the delicate tubes and spindles, lingering lovingly among the stones, touching among the necklaces and coronals of the dead queens whose dust lay not far away. It was as if he were summoning and discarding something shining and imponderable, like words. The contents of the casket which all Yaque had mourned lay scattered in this secret place of which only this strange, mad creature, a chance pensioner at the palace, had knowledge.

Suddenly the memory of Balator's words smote St. George with new perception. "He walks the streets of Med," Balator had told him at the banquet, "saying 'Melek, Melek,' which is to say 'king,' and so he is seeking the king. But he is mad, and he weeps; and therefore they pretend to believe that he says, 'Malakh,' which is to say 'salt,' and they call him that, for his tears."

Could old Malakh possibly know something of the king? The hope returned to St. George insistently, and he watched, spending his thought in new and extravagant conjecture, his mental vision blurring the details of that heaped-up, glistening confusion; and on the opposite side of the table the old man lifted and laid down that rainbow stuff of dreams, delighting in it, speaking softly above it. Had he been the king's friend, St. George was asking—but why did no one know anything of him? Or had he been an enemy who had done the king violence—but how was that possible, in his age and feebleness? Mystifying as the matter was, St. George exulted as much as he marveled; for it would be his, at all events, to place the jewels in Olivia's hands and clear her father's name; he longed to step out of the dark and confront the old man and seize the casket out of hand, and he would probably have done so and taken his chances at getting back to the upper world, had he not been chained to his corner by the irresistible hope that the old man knew something more—something about the king. And while he wondered, reflecting that at any cost he must prevent the replacing of the pivotal stone, he saw old Malakh take up his taper, turn away from the table, and open a door which the room's central pillar had cut from his view.

He was around the table in an instant. The open door revealed three stone steps which the old man was ascending, one at a time. Following him cautiously St. George heard a door grate outward at the head of the stair, saw the taper move forward in darkness, and the next moment found himself standing in the room of the tombs of the kings of Yaque. And he saw that the panel which had swung inward to admit them was set low in the monolithic tomb of King Abibaal himself.

Old Malakh had crossed swiftly to the wall opposite the tomb, and stood before the vacant niche which was to be occupied, as Jarvo had announced, by "His Majesty, King Otho, by the grace of God." There, setting aside his taper, the old man stretched his arms upward to the empty shelf and with a gesture of inconceivable weariness bowed his head upon them and stood silent, the leaping candle-light silvering his hair.

"Upon my soul," thought St George with finality, "he's murdered him. Old Malakh has murdered the king, and it's driven him crazy."

With that he did step out of the dark, and he laid his hand suddenly upon the old man's shoulder.

"Malakh," he said, "what have you done with the king?"

The old man lifted his head and turned toward St. George a face of singular calm. It was as if so many phantoms vexed his brain that a strange reality was of little consequence. But as his eyes met those of St. George a sudden dimness came over them, the lids fluttered and dropped, and his lips barely formed his words:

"The king," he said. "I did not leave the king. It was the king who somehow went away and left me here—"

He threw out his hands blindly, tottered and swayed from the wall; and St. George received him as he fell, measuring his length upon the stones before King Otho's future tomb.

St. George caught down the light and knelt beside him. Death seemed to have come "pressing within his face," and breathing hardly disquieted his breast. St. George fumbled at the old man's robe, and beneath his fingers the heart fluttered never so faintly. He loosened the cloth at the withered throat, passed his hand over the still forehead, and looked desperately about him.

The other inmates of the palace were, he reflected, about two good city blocks from him; and he doubted if he could ever find his unaided way back to them. Mechanically, though he knew that he carried no flask, he felt conscientiously through his pockets—a habit of the boy in perplexity which never deserts the man in crises. In the inside pocket of the coat that he was wearing—Amory's coat—his fingers suddenly closed about something made of glass. He seized it and drew it forth.

It was a little vase of rock-crystal, ornamented with gold medallions, covered with exquisite and precise engraving of great beauty and variety of design—gryphons, serpents, winged discs, men contending with lions. St. George stared at it uncomprehendingly. In the press of events of the last eight-and-forty hours Amory had quite forgotten to mention to him the prince's intended gift of wine, almost three thousand years old, sealed in Phoenicia.

St. George drew the stopper. In an instant an odour, spicy, penetrating, delicious, saluted him and gave life to the dead air of the room. For a moment he hesitated. He knew that the flask had not been among Amory's belongings and that he himself had never seen it before. But the odour was, he thought, unmistakable, and so powerful that already he felt as if the liquor were racing through his own veins. He touched it to his lips; it was like a full draught of some marvelous elixir. Sudden confidence sat upon St. George, and thanking his guiding stars for the fortunate chance, he unhesitatingly set the flask to the old man's lips.

There was a long-drawn, shuddering breath, a fluttering of the eyelids, a movement of the limbs, and after that old Malakh lay quite still upon the stones. Once more St. George thrust his hand within the bosom of the loose robe, and the heart was beating rapidly and regularly and with amazing force. In a moment deep breaths succeeded one another, filling the breast of the unconscious man; but the eyelids did not unclose, and St. George took up the taper and bent to scan the quiet face.

St. George looked, and sank to his knees and looked again, holding the light now here, now there, and peering in growing bewilderment. What he saw he was wholly unable to define. It was as if a mask were slowly to dissolve and yet to lie upon the features which it had covered, revealing while it still made mock of concealing. Colour was in the lips, colour was stealing into the changed face. The *changed* face—changed, St. George could not tell how; and the longer he looked, and though he rubbed his eyes and turned them toward the dark and then looked again, moving the taper, he could neither explain nor define what had happened.

He set the candle on the floor and sprang away from the quiet figure, searching the dark. The great silent place, with its shoulders of sarcophagi jutting from the gloom was black save for the little ring of pallid light about that prostrate form. St. George sent his hand to his forehead, and shook himself a bit, and straightened his shoulders with a smile.

"It must be the stuff you've tasted," he addressed himself

solemnly. "Heaven knows what it was. It's the stuff you've tasted."

Though he had barely touched his lips to the rock-crystal vase St. George's blood was pounding through his veins, and a curious exhilaration filled him. He looked about at the rims and corners of the tombs caught by the light, and he laughed a little—though this was not in the least what he intended—because it passed through his mind that if King Abibaal and Queen Mitygen, for example, might be treated with the contents of the mysterious vase they would no doubt come forth, Abibaal with memories of the Queen of Sheba in his eyes, and Queen Mitygen with her casket of Alexander's letters. Then St. George went down on his knees again, and raised the old man's head until it rested upon his own breast, and he passed the candle before his face, his hand trembling so that the light flickered and leaped up.

This time there was no mistaking. The tissues of old Malakh's ashen face and throat and pallid hands were undergoing some subtle transfiguration. It was as if new blood had come encroaching in their veins. It was as if the muscles were become firm and full, as if the wrinkled skin had been made smooth, the lips grown fresh, as if—the word came to St. George as he stared, spell-stricken—as if *youth* had returned.

St. George slipped down upon the stones and sat motionless. There was a little blue, forked vein on the man's forehead, and upon this he fastened his eyes, mechanically following it downward and back. Lines had crossed it, and there had been a deep cleft between the eyes, but these had disappeared, leaving the brow almost smooth. The cheeks were now tinged with colour, and the throat, where he had pulled aside the robe, showed firm and white. Mechanically St. George passed his hand along the inert arm, and it was no more withered than his own—the arm of no greybeard, but of a man in the prime of life. What did it mean—what did it mean? St. George waited, the blood throbbing in his temples, a mist before his eyes. What did it mean?

The minutes dragged by and still the unconscious man did not stir or unclose his eyes. From time to time St. George pressed his hand to the heart, and found it beating on rhythmically, powerfully. When he found himself sitting with averted head, as if he were afraid to look back at that changing face, a fear seized him that he had lost his reason and that what he imagined himself to see was a phase of madness. So he left the old man's side and sturdily tramped away into the huge dark of the room, resolutely explaining to himself that this was all very natural; the old man had been ill, improperly nourished, and the powerful stimulant of the wine had partly restored him. But even while he went over it St. George knew in his heart that what had happened was nothing that could be so explained, nothing that could be explained at all by anything within his ken.

His footsteps echoed startlingly on the stones, and the chill breath of the place smote his face as he moved. He stumbled on a displaced tile and pitched forward upon a jagged corner of sarcophagus, and reeled as if at a blow from some arm of the darkness. The taper rays struck a length of wall before him, minting from the gloom a sheet of pale orchids clinging to the unclean rock. St. George remembered a green slope, spangled with crocuses and wild strawberries, coloured like the orchids but lying under free sky, in free air. It seemed only a trick of Chance that he was not now lying on that far slope, wherever it was, instead of facing these ghost blooms in this ghost place. Back there, where the light glimmered beside the tomb of King Abibaal, nobody could tell what awaited him. If the man could change like this, might he not take on some shape too hideous to bear in the silence? St. George stood still, suddenly clenching his hands, trying to reach out through the dark and to grasp—himself, the self that seemed slipping away from him. But was he mad already, he wondered angrily, and hurried back to the far flickering light, stumbling, panting, not daring to look at the figure on the floor, not daring not to look.

He resolutely caught up the candle and peered once more at

the face. As steadily and swiftly as change in the aspect of the sky the face had gone on changing. St. George had followed to the chamber an old tottering man; the figure before him was a man of not more than fifty years.

St. George let fall the candle, which flickered down, upright in its socket; and he turned away, his hand across his eyes. Since this was manifestly impossible he must be mad, something in the stuff that he had tasted had driven him mad. He felt strong as a lion, strong enough to lift that prostrate figure and to carry it through the winding passages into the midst of those above stairs, and to beg them in mercy to tell him how the man looked. What would *she* say? He wondered what Olivia would say. Dinner would be over and they would be in the drawing-room—Olivia and Amory and Antoinette Frothingham; already the white room and the lights and Antoinette's laughter seemed to him of another world, a world from which he had irrevocably passed. Yet there they were above, the same roof covering them, and they did not know that down here in this place of the dead he, St. George, was beyond all question going mad.

With a cry he pulled off Amory's coat, flung it over the unconscious man, and rushed out into the blackness of the corridor. He would not take the light—the man must not die alone there in the dark—and besides he had heard that the mad could see as well in the dark as in the light. Or was it the blind who could see in the dark? No doubt it was the blind. However, he could find his way, he thought triumphantly, and ran on, dragging his hand along the slippery stones of the wall—he could find his way. Only he must call out, to tell them who it was that was lost. So he called himself by name, aloud and sternly, and after that he kept on quietly enough, serene in the conviction that he had regained his self-control, fighting to keep his mind from returning to the face that changed before his eyes, like the appearances in the puppet shows. But suddenly he became conscious that it was his own name that he went shouting through the passages; and that was openly absurd, he reasoned, since if he wanted to be found he must call some one else's name. But he must hurry—hurry—hurry; no one could tell what might be happening back there to that face that changed.

"Olivia!" he shouted, "Amory! Jarvo—oh, Jarvo! Rollo, you scoundrel—"

Whereat the memory that Rollo was somewhere on a yacht assailed him, and he pressed on, blindly and in silence, until glimmering before him he saw a light shining from an open door. Then he rushed forward and with a groan of relief threw himself into the room. Opposite the door loomed the grim sarcophagus of King Abibaal, and beside it on the floor lay the figure with the face that changed. He had gone a circle in those tortuous passages, and this was the room of the tombs of the kings.

He dragged himself across the chamber toward the still form. He must look again; no one could tell what might have happened. He pulled down the coat and looked. And there was surely nothing in the delicate, handsome, English-looking face upturned to his to give him new horror. It was only that he had come down here in the wake of a tottering old creature, and that here in his place lay a man who was not he. Which was manifestly impossible.

Mechanically St. George's hand went to the man's heart. It was beating regularly and powerfully, and deep breaths were coming from the full, healthily-coloured lips. For a moment St. George knelt there, his blood tingling and pricking in his veins and pulsing in his temples. Then he swayed and fell upon the stones.

*   *   *   *   *

When St. George opened his eyes it was ten o'clock of the following morning, though he felt no interest in that. There was before him a great rectangle of light. He lifted his head and saw that the light appeared to flow from the interior of the tomb of King Abibaal. The next moment Amory's cheery voice, pitched high in consternation and relief, made havoc among the echoes with a background of Jarvo's smooth thanksgiving for the return of adon.

St. George, coatless, stiff from the hours on the mouldy stones, dragged himself up and turned his eyes in fear upon the figure beside him. It flashed hopefully through his mind that perhaps it had not changed, that perhaps he had dreamed it all, that perhaps ...

By his first glance that hope was dispelled. From beneath Amory's coat on the floor an arm came forth, pushing the coat aside, and a man slenderly built, with a youthful, sensitive face and somewhat critically-drooping lids, sat up leisurely and looked about him in slow surprise, kindling to distinct amusement.

"Upon my soul," he said softly, "what an admission—what an admission! I can not have made such a night of it in years."

Upon which Jarvo dropped unhesitatingly to his knees.

"Melek! Melek!" he cried, prostrating himself again and again. "The King! The King! The gods have permitted the possible."

CHAPTER XVIII

A MORNING VISIT

In an upper room in the Palace of the Litany, fair with all the burnished devices of the early light, Prince Tabnit paced on that morning of mornings of his marriage day. Because of his great happiness the whole world seemed to him like some exquisite intaglio of which this day was the design.

The room, "walled with soft splendours of Damascus tiles," was laid with skins of forgotten animals and was hung with historic tapestries dyed by ancient fingers in the spiral veins of the Murex. There were frescoes uniting the dream with its actuality, columns carved with both lines and names of beauty, pilasters decorated with chain and checker-work and golden nets. A stairway led to a high shrine where hung the crucified Tyrian sphinx. The room was like a singing voice summoning one to delights which it described. But whatever way one looked all the lines neither pointed nor seemed to have had beginning, but being divorced from source and direction expressed merely beauty, like an altar "where none cometh to pray."

Prince Tabnit, in his trailing robe of white embroidered by a thousand needles, looked so akin to the room that one suspected it of having produced him, Athena-wise, from, say, the great black shrine. When he paused before the shrine he seemed like a child come to beseech some last word concerning the Riddle, rather than a man who believed himself to have mastered all wisdom and to have nailed the world-sphinx to her cross.

"Surely there is a vein for the silver
And a place for the gold where they fine it.
Iron is taken out of the earth
And brass is moulton out of the stone.
Man setteth an end to darkness
And searcheth out all perfection:
The stones of darkness and of the shadow of death,"

he was repeating softly. "So it is," he added, "'and searcheth to the farthest bound.' Have I not done so? And do I not triumph?"

Then the youth who had once admitted St. George and his friends to that far-away house in McDougle Street—with the hokey-pokey man outside the door—entered with the poetry of deference; and if, as he bent low, there was a lift and droop of his eyelids which tokened utter bewilderment, not to say agitation, he was careful that the prince should not see that.

"Her Highness, the Princess of Yaque, Mrs. Hastings, Mr. Augustus Frothingham and Miss Frothingham ask audience, your Highness," he announced clearly.

Prince Tabnit turned swiftly.

"Whom do you say, Matten?" he questioned and when the boy had repeated the names, meditated briefly. He was at a loss to fathom what this strange visit might portend; beyond doubt, he reflected (in a world which was an intaglio of his own designing) it portended nothing at all. He hastened forward to wait upon them and paused midway the room, for the highest tribute that a Prince of the Litany could pay to another was to receive him in this chamber of the Crucified Sphinx.

"Conduct them here, Matten," he commanded, and took up his station beside an hundred-branched candlestick made in

Curium. There he stood when, having been led down corridors of ivory and through shining anterooms, Mrs. Hastings and Olivia and Antoinette appeared on the threshold of the chamber, followed by Mr. Frothingham. As the prince hastened forward to meet them with sweepings of his gown embroidered by a thousand needles and bent above their hands uttering gracious words, assuredly in all the history of Med and of the Litany the room of the Crucified Sphinx had never presented a more peculiar picture.

Into that tranquil atmosphere, dream-pervaded, Mrs. Medora Hastings swept with all the certainty of an opinion bludgeoning the frail security of a fact. She had refused to have her belongings sent to the apartments in the House of the Litany placed that day at her disposal, preferring to dress for the coronation before she descended from Mount Khalak. She was therefore in a robe of black samite, trimmed with the fur of a whole chapter of extinct animals, and bangles and pendants of jewels bobbed and ticked all about her. But on her head she wore the bonnet trimmed with a parrot, set, as usual, frightfully awry. Beside her, with all the timidity of charming reality in the presence of fantasy, came Olivia and Antoinette—Olivia in a walking frock of white broadcloth, with an auto coat of hunting pink, and a cap held down by yards of cloudy veiling; Antoinette in a blue cloth gown, and about them both—stout little boots and suede gloves and smart shirtwaists—such an air of actuality as this chamber, prince and Sphinx and tradition and all, could not approach. Mr. Augustus Frothingham had struck his usual incontestable middle-ground by appearing in the blue velvet of a robe of State, over which he had slipped his light covert top-coat, and he carried his immaculate top-hat and a silver-headed stick.

"Prince Tabnit," said Mrs. Medora Hastings without ceremony, "what have they done with that poor young man? Ask him, Olivia," she besought, sinking down upon a chair of verd antique and extending a limp, plump hand to the niece who always did everything executive.

Olivia was very pale. She had hardly slept, night-long. Alarm at the inexplicable disappearance of St. George at dinner-time the day before and at the discovery that old Malakh was nowhere about had, by morning, deepened to unreasoning fear among them all. And then Olivia, knowing nothing of what had taken place in the room of the tombs, had resolved upon a desperate expedient, had bundled into an airship her almost prostrate aunt, Mr. Frothingham and his excited little daughter, and had borne down upon the Palace of the Litany two hours before noon. Amory, frantic with apprehension, had stayed behind with Jarvo, certain that St. George could not have left the mountain. But now that Olivia stood before the prince it required but a moment to convince her that Prince Tabnit really knew nothing of St. George's whereabouts. Indeed, since his gift of Phoenician wine, sealed three thousand years ago, and the immediate evanishment of the two Americans, his Highness had no longer vexed his thought with them, and he was genuinely amazed to know that (in a world which was an intaglio of his own designing) these two had actually spent yesterday at the king's palace on Mount Khalak. He perceived that he must give them more definite attention than his half-idle device of the wine—intended as that had been as a mere hyperspatial practical joke, not in the least irreconcilable with his office of host.

"Mr. St. George came to Yaque to help me find my father," Olivia was concluding earnestly, "and if anything has happened to him, Prince Tabnit, I alone am responsible."

The prince reflected for a moment, his eyes fixed upon the hundred-branched candlestick. Then:

"Mr. St. George's disappearance," he said, "has prevented a still more unpleasant catastrophe."

"Catastrophe!" repeated Mrs. Hastings, quite without tucking in her voice at the corners, "I have thought of no other word since I got to be royalty."

"A world experience, a world experience, dear Madame," contributed Mr. Frothingham, his hands laid trimly along his blue velvet lap.

"But that doesn't make it any easier to bear, no matter what anybody says," retorted the lady.

"Inasmuch," pursued Prince Tabnit with infinite regret, "as these Americans have, as you say, assisted in the search for your father, the king, they have most unfortunately violated that ancient law which provides that no State or satrapy shall receive aid, whether of blood or of bond, from an alien. The Royal House alone is exempt."

"And the penalty," demanded Olivia fearfully. "Is there a penalty? What is that, Prince Tabnit?"

The voice of the prince was never more mellow.

"Do not be alarmed, I beg," he hastened his reassurance. "Upon the return of Mr. St. George, he and his friend will simply be set adrift in a rudderless airship, an offering to the great idea of space."

Mrs. Hastings swayed toward the prince in her chair of verd antique, and her voice seemed to become brittle in the air.

"Oh, is that what you call being ahead of the time," she demanded shrilly, "getting behind science to behave like Nero? And for my part I don't see anything whatever about the island that is ahead of the times. You haven't even got silk shoe-laces. I actually had to use a cloth-of-gold sandal strap to lace my oxfords, and when I lost a cuff-link I was obliged to make shift with two sides of one of Queen Agothonike's ear-rings that I found in the museum at the palace. And that isn't all," went on the lady, wrong kindling wrong, "what do you do for paper and envelopes? There is not a quire to be found in Med. They offered me *wireless blanks*—an ultra form that Mr. Hastings would never have considered in good taste. And how about visiting cards? I tried to have a plate made, and they showed me a wireless apparatus for flashing from the doorstep the name of the visitor—an electrical entrance which Mr. Hastings would have considered most inelegant. Ahead of the times, with your rudderless airships! I have always said that the electric chair is a way to be barbarous and good form at the same time, and that is what I think about Yaque!"

Mr. Frothingham's hands worked forward convulsively on his blue velvet knees.

"My dear Madame," he interposed earnestly, "the history of criminal jurisprudence, not to mention the remarkable essay of the Marquis Beccaria—proves beyond doubt that the extirpation of the offender is the only possible safety for the State—"

Olivia rose and stood before the prince, her eyes meeting his.

"You will permit this sentence?" she asked steadily. "As head of the House of the Litany, you will execute it, Prince Tabnit?"

"Alas!" said the prince humbly, "it is customary on the day of the coronation to set adrift all offenders. I am the servant of the State."

"Then, Prince Tabnit, I can not marry you."

At this Mrs. Hastings looked blindly about for support, and Mr. Frothingham and Antoinette flew to her side. In that moment the lady had seen herself, prophetically, in black samite and her parrot bonnet, set adrift in the penitential airship with her rebellious niece.

For a moment Prince Tabnit hesitated: he looked at Olivia, who was never more beautiful than as she defied him; then he walked slowly toward her, with sweep and fall of his garments embroidered by a thousand needles. Antoinette and her father, ministering to Mrs. Hastings, heard only the new note that had crept into his voice, a thrill, a tremour—

"Olivia!" he said.

Her eyes met his in amazement but no fear.

"In a land more alien to me than the sun," said the prince, "I saw you, and in that moment I loved you. I love you more than the life beyond life upon which I have laid hold. I brought you to this island to make you my wife. Do you understand what it is that I offer you?"

Olivia was silent. She was trembling a little at the sheer enormity of the moment. Suddenly, Prince Tabnit seemed to her like a name that she did not know.

"Will you not understand what I mean?" he besought with passionate earnestness. "Can I make my words mean nothing to you? Do you not see that it is indeed as I say—that I have grasped the secret of life within life, beyond life, transcending life, as his understanding transcends the man? The wonder of the island is but the alphabet of wisdom. The secrets of life and death and being itself are in my grasp. The hidden things that come near to you in beauty, in dream, in inspiration are mine and my people's. All these I can make yours—I offer you life of a fullness such as the people of the world do not dream. I will love you as the gods love, and as the gods we will live and love—it may be for ever. Nothing of high wisdom shall be unrevealed to us. We shall be what the world will be when it nears the close of time. Come to me—trust me—be beside me in all the wonder that I know. But above all, love me, for I love you more than life, and wisdom, and mystery!"

Olivia understood, and she believed. The mystery of life had always been more real to her than its commonplaces, and all her years she had gone half-expecting to meet some one, unheralded, to whom all things would be clear, and who should make her know by some secret sign that this was so, and should share with her. She had no doubt whatever that

Prince Tabnit spoke the truth—just as the daughter of the river-god Inachus knew perfectly that she was being wooed by a voice from the air. Indeed, the world over, lovers promise each other infinite things, and are infinitely believed.

"I do understand you, Prince Tabnit," Olivia said simply, "I do understand something of what you offer me. I think that these things were not meant to be hidden from men always, so I can even believe that you have all that you say. But—there is something more."

Olivia paused—and swiftly, as if some little listening spirit had released the picture from the air, came the memory of that night when she had stood with St. George on that airy rampart beside the wall of blossoming vines.

"There is something more," she repeated, "when two love each other very much I think that they have everything that you have said, and more."

He looked at her in silence. The stained light from some high window caught her veil in meshes of rose and violet—fairy colours, witnessing the elusive, fairy, invincible truth of what she said.

"You mean that you do not love me?" said the prince gently.

"I do not love you, your Highness," said Olivia, "and as for the wisdom of which you speak, that is worse than useless to you if you can do as you say with two quite innocent men." She hesitated, searching his face. "Is there no way," she said, "that I, the daughter of your king, can save them? I will appeal to the people!"

The prince met her eyes steadily, adoringly.

"It would avail nothing," he said, "they are at one with the law. Yet there is a way that I can help you. If Mr. St. George returns, as he must, he and his friends shall be set adrift with due ceremony—but in an imperial airship, with a man secretly in control. By night they can escape to their yacht. This I will do—upon one condition."

"Oh—what is that?" she asked, and for all the reticence of her eagerness, her voice was a betrayal.

Prince Tabnit turned to the window. Below, in the palace grounds, and without, in the Eurychorus, a thousand people awaited the opening of the palace doors. They filled the majestic avenue, poured up the shadowed alleys that taught the necessity of mystery, were grouped beneath the honey-sweet trees; and above their heads, from every dome and column in the fair city, flowed and streamed the joyous, wizard, nameless colours of the pennons blown heavenward against the blue. They were come, this strange, wise, elusive people, to her marriage.

The prince was smiling as he met her eyes; for the world was always the exquisite intaglio, and to-day was its design.

"They know," he said simply, "what was to have been at noon to-day. Do you not understand my condition?"

CHAPTER XIX

IN THE HALL OF KINGS

Somewhat before noon the great doors of the Palace of the Litany and of the Hall of Kings were thrown open, and the people streamed in from the palace grounds and the Eury-chorus. Abroad among them—elusive as that by which we know that a given moment belongs to dawn, not dusk—was the sense of questioning, of unrest, of expectancy that belongs to the dawn itself. Especially the youths and maidens—who, besides wisdom, knew something of spells—waited with a certain wistfulness for what might be, for Change is a kind of god even to the immortals. But there were also those who weighed the departures incident to the coming of the strange people from over-seas; and there were not lacking conservatives of the old regime to shake wise heads and declare that a barbarian is a barbarian, the world over.

All that rainbow multitude, clad for festival, rose with the first light music that stole, winged and silken, from hidden cedar alcoves, and some minutes past the sounding of the hour of noon the chamfered doors set high in the south wall of the Hall of Kings were swung open, and at the head of the stair appeared Olivia.

She was alone, for the custom of Yaque required that the island princesses should on the day of their recognition first appear alone before their people in token of their mutual faith. From the wardrobes at the castle Olivia had chosen the coronation gown of Queen Mitygen herself. It was of fine lace woven in a single piece, and it lay in a foam of shining threads traced with pure lines of shadow. On her head were a jeweled coronal and jeweled hair-loops in the Phoenician fashion, once taken from a king's casket and sent secretly, upon the decline of Assyrian ascendancy, to be bartered in the marts of Coele-Syria. Chains of jewels, in a noon of colour, lay about her throat, as once they lay upon the shoulders of the dead queens of Yaque and, before them, of the women of the elder dynasties long since recorded in indifferent dust. Girdling her waist was a zone of rubies that burned positive in the tempered light. With all her delicacy, Olivia was like her rubies—vivid, graphic, delineated not by light but by line.

The members of the High Council rustled in their colour and white, and flashed their golden stars; the Golden Guards (save the apostate few who were that day sentenced to be set adrift) were filling the stairway like a bank of buttercups; and Olivia's women, led by Antoinette in a gown of colours not to be lightly denominated, were entering by an opposite door. In the raised seats near the High Council, Mrs. Hastings and Mr. Frothingham leaned to wave a sustaining greeting. Until that high moment Mrs. Medora Hastings had been by no means certain that Olivia would appear at all, though she openly nourished the hope that "everything would go off smoothly." ("I don't care much for foreigners and never have," she confided to Mr. Frothingham, "still, I was thinking while I was at breakfast, after all, to the prince *we are* the foreigners. There is something in that, don't you think? And then the dear prince—he is so very metaphysical!")

Upon the beetling throne Olivia took her place, and her women sank about her like tiers of sunset clouds. She was so little and so beautiful and so unconsciously appealing that when Prince Tabnit and Cassyrus and the rest of the court entered, it is doubtful if an eye left Olivia, to homage them. But Prince Tabnit was the last to note that, for he saw only Olivia; and the world—the world was an intaglio of his own designing.

With due magnificence the preliminary ceremonies of the coronation proceeded—musty necessities, like oaths and historical truths, being mingled with the most delicate observances, such as the naming of the former princesses of the island, from Adija, daughter of King Abibaal, to Olivia, daughter of King Otho; and such as counting the clouds for the misfortunes of the regime. This last duty fell to the office of the lord chiefchancellor, and from an upper porch he returned quickening with the intelligence that there was not a cloud in the sky, a state of the heavens known to no coronation since Babylon was ruled by Assyrian viceroys. The lord chief-chancellor and Cassyrus themselves brought forth the crown—a beautiful crown, shining like dust-in-the-sun—and Cassyrus, in a voice that trumpeted, rehearsed its history: how it had been made of jewels brought from the coffers of Amasis and Apries, when King Nebuchadnezzar wrested Phoenicia from Egypt, and, too, of all manner of precious stones sent by Queen Atossa, wife of Darius, when the Crotoniat Democedes, with two triremes and a trading vessel, visited Yaque before they went to survey Hellenic shores, with what disastrous result. And Olivia, standing in the queen's gown, listened without hearing one word, and turned to have her veil lifted by Antoinette and the daughter of a peer of Yaque; and she knelt before the people while the lord chief-chancellor set the crown on her bright hair. It was a picture that thrilled the lord chief-chancellor himself—who was a worshiper of beauty, and a man given to angling in the lagoon and making metric translations of the inscriptions.

Then it was in the room as if a faint flame had been breathed upon and had upleaped in a thousand ways of expectancy, and as if a secret sign had been set in the lift and dip of the music—the music that was so like the great chamber with its lift and dip of carven line. The thrill with which one knows the glad news of an unopened letter was upon them all, and they heard that swift breath of an event that stirs before its coming. When Olivia's women fell back from the dais with wonder and murmur, the murmur was caught up in the great hall, and ran from tier to tier as amazement, as incredulity, and as thanksgiving.

For there, beside the beetling throne, was standing a man, slenderly built, with a youthful, sensitive face and critically-drooping lids, and upon them all his eyes were turned in faint amusement warmed by an idle approbation.

"Perfect—perfect. Quite perfect," he was saying below his breath.

Olivia turned. The next moment she stood with outstretched arms before her father; and King Otho, in his long, straight robe, encrusted with purple amethysts, bent with exquisite courtesy above his daughter's hands.

"My dear child," he murmured, "the picture that you make entirely justifies my existence, but hardly my absence. Shall we ask his Highness to do that?"

It mattered little who was to do that so long as it was done. For to that people, steeped in dream, risen from the crudity of mere events to breathe in the rarer atmosphere of their significance, here was a happening worthy their attention, for it had the dignity of mystery. Even Mrs. Medora Hastings, billowing toward the throne with cries, was less poignantly a challenge to be heard. Upon her the king laid a tranquillizing hand and, with a droop of eyelids in recognition of Mr. Frothingham, he murmured: "Ah, Medora—Medora! Delight in the moment—but do not embrace it," while beside him, star-eyed, Olivia stood waiting for Prince Tabnit to speak.

To Olivia, trembling a little as she leaned upon his arm, King Otho bent with some word, at which she raised to his her startled face, and turned from him uncertainly, and burned a heavenly colour from brow to chin. Then, her father's words being insistent in her ear, and her own heart being tumultuous with what he had told her, she turned as he bade her, and, following his glance, slipped beneath a shining curtain that cut from the audience chamber the still seclusion of the King's

Alcove, a chamber long sacred to the sovereigns of Yaque.

Confused with her wonder and questioning, hardly daring to understand the import of her father's words, Olivia went down a passage set between two high white walls of the palace, open to-day to the upper blue and to the floating pennons of the dome. Here, prickly-leaved plants had shot to the cornices with uncouth contorting of angled boughs, and in their inner green ruffle-feathered birds looked down on her with the uncanny interest of myriapods. She caught about her the lace of her skirts and of her floating veil, and the way echoed musically to the touch of her little sandals and was bright with the shining of her diadem. And at the end of the passage she lifted a swaying curtain of soft dyes and entered the King's Alcove.

The King's Alcove laid upon one the delicate demands of calm open water—for its floor of white transparent tiles was cunningly traced with the reflected course of the carven roof, and one seemed to look into mirrored depths of disappearing line between spaces shaped like petals and like chevrons. In the King's Alcove one stood in a world of white and one's sight was exquisitely won, now by a niche open to a blue well of sea and space, now by silver plants lucent in high casements. And there one was spellbound with this mirroring of the Near which thus became the Remote, until one questioned gravely which was "there" and which was "here," for the real was extended into vision, and vision was quickened to the real, and nothing lay between. But to Olivia, entering, none of these things was clearly evident, for as the curtain of many dyes fell behind her she was aware of two figures—but the one, with a murmured word which she managed somehow to answer without an idea what she said or what it had said either, vanished down the way that she had come. And she stood there face to face with St. George.

He had risen from a low divan before a small table set with figs and bread and a decanter of what would have been bordeaux if it had not been distilled from the vineyards of Yaque. He was very pale and haggard, and his eyes were darkly circled and still fever-bright. But he came toward her as if he had quite forgotten that this is a world of danger and that she was a princess and that, little more than a week ago, her name was to him the unknown music. He came toward her with a face of unutterable gladness, and he caught and crushed her hands in his and looked into her eyes as if he could look to the distant soul of her. He led her to a great chair hewn from quarries of things silver and unremembered, and he sat at her feet upon a bench that might have been a stone of the altar of some forgotten deity of dreams, at last worshiped as it should long have been worshiped by all the host that had passed it by. He looked up in her face, and the room was like a place of open water where heaven is mirrored in earth, and earth reflects and answers heaven.

St. George laughed a little for sheer, inextinguishable happiness.

"Once," he said, "once I breakfasted with you, on tea and—if I remember correctly—gold and silver muffins. Won't you breakfast with me now?"

Olivia looked down at him, her heart still clamourous with its anxiety of the night and of the morning.

"Tell me where you can have been," she said only; "didn't you know how distressed we would be? We imagined everything—in this dreadful place. And we feared everything, and we—" but yet the "we" did not deceive St. George; how could it with her eyes, for all their avoidings, so divinely upon him?

"Did you," he said, "ah—did you wonder? I wish I knew!"

"And my father—where did you find him?" she besought. "It was you? You found him, did you not?"

St. George looked down at a fold of her gown that was fallen across his knee. How on earth was he ever to move, he wondered vaguely, if the slightest motion meant the withdrawing of that fold. He looked at her hand, resting so near, so near, upon the arm of the chair; and last he looked again into her face; and it seemed wonderful and before all things wonderful, not that she should be here, jeweled and crowned, but that he should so unbelievably be here with her. And yet it might be but a moment, as time is measured, until this moment would be swept away. His eyes met hers and held them.

"Would you mind," he said, "now—just for a little, while we wait here—not asking me that? Not asking me anything? There will be time enough in there—when *they* ask me. Just for now I only want to think how wonderful this is."

She said: "Yes, it is wonderful—unbelievable," but he thought that she might have meant the white room or her queen's robe or any one of all the things which he did not mean.

"*Is* it wonderful to you?" he asked, and he said again: "I wish—I wish I knew!"

He looked at her, sitting in the moon of her laces and the stars of her gems, and the sense of the immeasurableness of the hour came upon him as it comes to few; the knowledge that the evanescent moment is very potent, the world where the siren light of the Remote may at any moment lie quenched in some ashen present. To him, held momentarily in this place that was like shoreless, open water, the present was inestimably precious and it lay upon St. George like the delicate claim of his love itself. What the next hour held for them neither could know, and this universal uncertainty was for him crystallized in an instant of high wisdom; over the little hand lying so perilously near, his own closed suddenly and he crushed her fingers to his lips.

"Olivia—dear heart," he said, "we don't know what they may do—what will happen—oh, may I tell you *now*?"

There was no one to say that he might not, for the hand was not withdrawn from his. And so he did tell her, told her all his heart as he had known his heart to be that last night on *The Aloha*, and in that divine twilight of his arriving on the island, and in those hours beside the airy ramparts of the king's palace, and in the vigil that followed, and always—always, ever since he could remember, only that he hadn't known that he was waiting for her, and now he knew—now he knew.

"Must you not have known, up there in the palace," he besought her, "the night that I got there? And yesterday, all day yesterday, you must have known—didn't you know? I love you, Olivia. I couldn't have told you, I couldn't have let you know, only now, when we can't know what may come or what they may do—oh, say you forgive me. Because I love you—I love you."

She rose swiftly, her veil floating about her, silver over the gold of her hair; and the light caught the enchantment of the gems of the strange crown they had set upon her head, and she looked down at him in almost unearthly beauty. He stood before her, waiting for the moment when she should lift her eyes. And the eyes were lifted, and he held out his arms, and straight to them, regardless of the coronation laces of Queen Mitygen, went Olivia, Princess of Yaque. He put aside her shining hair, as he had put it aside in that divine moment in the motor in the palace wood; and their lips met, in that world that was like the shoreless open sea where earth reflects heaven, and heaven comes down.

They sat upon the white-cushioned divan, and St. George half knelt beside her as he had knelt that night in the fleeing motor, and there were an hundred things to say and an hundred things to hear. And because this fragment of the past since they had met was incontestably theirs, and because the future hung trembling before them in a mist of doubt, they turned happy, hopeful eyes to that future, clinging to each other's hands. The little chamber of translucent white, where one looked down to a mirrored dome and up to a kind of sky, became to them a place bounded by the touch and the look and the voice of each other, as every place in the world is bounded for every heart that beats.

"Sweetheart," said St. George presently, "do you remember that you are a princess, and I'm merely a kind of man?"

Was it not curious, he thought, that his lips did not speak a new language of their own accord?

"I know," corrected Olivia adorably, "that I'm a kind of princess. But what use is that when it only makes trouble for us?"

"Us"—"makes trouble for us." St. George wondered how he could ever have thought that he even guessed what happiness might be when "trouble for us" was like this. He tried to say so, and then:

"But do you know what you are doing?" he persisted. "Don't you see—dear, don't you see that by loving me you are giving up a world that you can never, never get back?"

Olivia looked down at the fair disordered hair on his temples. It seemed incredible that she had the right to push it from his forehead. But it was not incredible. To prove it Olivia touched it back. To prove that *that* was not incredible, St. George turned until his lips brushed her wrist.

"Don't you know, don't you, dear," he pressed the matter, "that very possibly these people here have really got the secret that all the rest of the world is talking about and hoping about and dreaming they will sometime know?"

Olivia heard of this likelihood with delicious imperturbability.

"I know a secret," she said, just above her breath, "worth two of that."

"You'll never be sorry—never?" he urged wistfully, resolutely denying himself the entire bliss of that answer.

"Never," said Olivia, "never. Shall you?"

That was exceptionally easy to make clear, and thereafter he whimsically remembered something else:

"You live in the king's palace now," he reminded her, "and this is another palace where you might live if you chose. And you might be a queen, with drawing-rooms and a poet laureate and all the rest. And in New York—in New York, perhaps we shall live in a flat."

"No," she cried, "no, indeed! Not 'perhaps,' I *insist* upon a flat." She looked about the room with its bench brought from the altar of a forgotten deity of dreams, with its line and colour dissolving to mirrored point and light—the mystic union of sight with dream—and she smiled at the divine incongruity and the divine resemblance. "It wouldn't be so very different— a flat," she said shyly.

Wouldn't it—wouldn't it, after all, be so very different?

"Ah, if you only think so, really," cried St. George.

"But it will be different, just different enough to like better," she admitted then. "You know that I think so," she said.

"If only you knew how much I think so," he told her, "how I have thought so, day and night, since that first minute at the Boris. Olivia, dear heart—when did you think so first—"

She shook her head and laid her hands upon his and drew them to her face.

"Now, now—now!" she cried, "and there never was any time but now."

"But there will be—there will be," he said, his lips upon her hair.

After a time—for Time, that seems to have no boundaries in the abstract, is a very fiend for bounding the divine concrete—after a time Amory spoke hesitatingly on the other side of the curtain of many dyes.

"St. George," he said, "I'm afraid they want you. Mr. Holland—the king, he's got through playing them. He wants you to get up and give 'em the truth, I think."

"Come in—come in, Amory," St. George said and lifted the curtain, and "I beg your pardon," he added, as his eyes fell upon Antoinette in a gown of colours not to be lightly denominated. She had followed Olivia from the hall, and had met Amory midway the avenue of prickly trees, and they had helpfully been keeping guard. Now they went on before to the Hall of Kings, and St. George, remembering what must happen there, turned to Olivia for one crowning moment.

"You know," she said fearfully, "before father came the prince intended the most terrible things—to set you and Mr. Amory adrift in a rudderless airship—"

St. George laughed in amusement. The poor prince with his impossible devices, thinking to harm him, St. George—*now.*

"He meant to marry you, he thought," he said, "but, thank Heaven, he has your father to answer to—and me!" he ended jubilantly.

And yet, after all, Heaven knew what possibilities hemmed them round. And Heaven knew what she was going to think of him when she heard his story. He turned and caught her to him, for the crowning moment.

"You love me—you love me," he said, "no matter what happens or what they say—no matter what?"

She met his eyes and, of her own will, she drew his face down to hers.

"No matter what," she answered. So they went together toward the chamber which they had both forgotten.

When they reached the Hall of Kings they heard King Otho's voice—suave, mellow, of perfect enunciation:

"—some one," the king was concluding, "who can tell this considerably better than I. And it seems to me singularly fitting that the recognition of the part eternally played by the 'possible' be temporarily deferred while we listen to—I dislike to use the word, but shall I say—the facts."

It seemed to St. George when he stood beside the dais, facing that strange, eager multitude with his strange unbelievable story upon his lips—the story of the finding of the king—as if his own voice were suddenly a part of all the gigantic incredibility. Yet the divinely real and the fantastic had been of late so fused in his consciousness that he had come to look upon both as the normal—which is perhaps the only sane view. But how could he tell to others the monstrous story of last night, and hope to be believed?

None the less, as simply as if he had been narrating to Chillingworth the high moment of a political convention, St. George told the people of Yaque what had happened in that night in the room of the tombs with that mad old Malakh whom they all remembered. It came to him as he spoke that it was quite like telling to a field of flowers the real truth about the wind of which they might be supposed to know far more than he; and yet, if any one were to tell the truth about the wind who would know how to listen? He was not amazed that, when he had done, the people of Yaque sat in a profound silence which might have been the silence of innocent amazement or of utter incredulity.

But there was no mistaking the face of Prince Tabnit. Its cool tolerant amusement suddenly sent the blood pricking to St. George's heart and filled him with a kind of madness. What he did was the last thing that he had intended. He turned upon the prince, and his voice went cutting to the farthest corner of the hall:

"Men and women of Yaque," he cried, "I accuse your prince of the knowledge that can take from and add to the years of man at will. I accuse him of the deliberate and criminal use of that knowledge to take King Otho from his throne!"

St. George hardly knew what effect his words had. He saw only Olivia, her hands locked, her lips parted, looking in his face in anguish; and he saw Prince Tabnit smile. Prince Tabnit sat upon the king's left hand, and he leaned and whispered a smiling word in the ear of his sovereign and turned a smiling face to Olivia upon her father's right.

"I know something of your American newspapers, your Majesty," the prince said aloud, "and these men are doing their part excellently, excellently."

"What do you mean, your Highness?" demanded St. George curtly.

"But is it not simple?" asked the prince, still smiling. "You have contrived a sensation for the great American newspaper. No one can doubt."

King Otho leaned back in the beetling throne.

"Ah, yes," he said, "it is true. Something has been contrived. But—is the sensation of *his* contriving, Prince?"

Olivia stood silent. It was not possible, it was not possible, she said over mechanically. For St. George to have come with this story of a potion—a drug that had restored youth to her father, had transformed him from that mad old Malakh—

"Father!" she cried appealingly, "don't you remember—don't you know?"

King Otho, watching the prince, shook his head, smiling.

"At dawn," he said, "there are few of us to be found remaining still at table with Socrates. I seem not to have been of that number."

"Olivia!" cried St. George suddenly.

She met his eyes for a moment, the eyes that had read her own, that had given message for message, that had seen with her the glory of a mystic morning willingly relinquished for a diviner dawn. Was she not princess here in Yaque? She laid her hand upon her father's hand; the crown that they had given her glittered as she turned toward the multitude.

"My people," she said ringingly, "I believe that that man speaks the truth. Shall the prince not answer to this charge before the High Council now—here—before you all?"

At this King Otho did something nearly perceptible with his eyebrows. "Perfect. Perfect. Quite perfect," he said below his breath. The next instant the eyelids of the sovereign drooped considerably less than one would have supposed possible. For from every part of the great chamber, as if a storm long-pent had forced the walls of the wind, there came in a thousand murmurs—soft, tremulous, definitive—the answering voice to Olivia's question:

"Yes. Yes. Yes..."

CHAPTER XX

OUT OF THE HALL OF KINGS

In Prince Tabnit's face there was a curious change, as if one were suddenly to see hieroglyphics upon a star where before there had been only shining. But his calm and his magnificent way of authority did not desert him, as so grotesque a star would still stand lonely and high in the heavens. He spoke, and upon the multitude fell instant silence, not the less absolute that it harboured foreboding.

"Whatever the people would say to me," said the prince simply, "I will hear. My right hand rests in the hand of the people. In return I decree allegiance to the law. Your princess stands before you, crowned. This most fortunate return of his Majesty, the King, can not set at naught the sacred oath which has just left her lips. Henceforth, in council and in audience, her place shall be at his Majesty's right hand, as was the place of that Princess Athalme, daughter of King Kab, in the dynasty of the fall of Rome. Is it not, therefore, but the more incumbent upon your princess to own her allegiance to the law of the island by keeping her troth with me—that troth witnessed and sanctioned by you yourselves? This ceremony concluded I will answer the demands of the loyal subjects whose interests alone I serve. For we obey that which is higher than authority—the law, born in the Beginning—"

Prince Tabnit's voice might almost have taken his place in his absence, it was so soft, so fine of texture, no more consciously

Zona Gale

modulated than is the going of water or the way of a wing. It was difficult to say whether his words or, so to say, their fine fabric of voice, begot the silence that followed. But all eyes were turned upon Olivia. And, Prince Tabnit noting this, before she might speak he suddenly swept his flowing robes embroidered by a thousand needles to a posture of humility before his sovereign.

"Your Majesty," he besought, "I pray your consent to the bestowal upon my most unworthy self of the hand of your daughter, the Princess Olivia."

King Otho leaned upon the arm of his carven throne. Against its strange metal his hand was cameo-clear.

"For the king," he was remembering softly, "'the Pyrenees, or so he fancied, ceased to exist.' For another 'the mountains of Daphne are everywhere.' Each of us has his impossible dream to prove that he is an impossible creature. Why not I? To be normal is the cry of all the hobgoblins ... And what does the princess say?" he asked aloud.

"Her Highness has already given me the great happiness to plight me her troth," said Prince Tabnit.

King Otho's eyebrows flickered from their parallel of repose.

"In Yaque or in America," he murmured, "the Americans do as the Americans do. None of us is mentioned in Deuteronomy, but what is the will of the princess?" the American Sovereign asked.

Mrs. Hastings, seated near the dais, heard; and as she turned, a rhinestone side-comb slipped from her hair, tinkled over the jewels of her corsage and shot into the lap of a member of the High Council. He, never having seen a side-comb, fancied that it might be an infernal machine which he had never seen either, and, palpitating, flashed it to the guardian hand of Mr. Frothingham. At the same moment:

"Ah, why, Otho," said Mrs. Hastings audibly, "we had two ancestors at Bannockburn!"

"Bannockburn!" argued Mr. Augustus Frothingham, below the voice, "Bannockburn. But what, my dear Mrs. Hastings, is Bannockburn beside the Midianites and the Moabites and the Hittites and the Ammonites and the Levites?"

In this genealogical moment the prince leaned toward Olivia.

"Choose," he said significantly, but so softly that none might hear, "oh, my beloved, choose!"

The faces of the great assembly blurred and wavered before Olivia, and the low hum of the talk in the room was relative, like the voices of passers-by. She looked up at the prince and away from him in mute appeal to something that ought to help her and would not. For Olivia was of those who, never having seen the face of Destiny very near, are accustomed to look upon nothing as wholly irrevocable; and—for one of her graces—she had the feminine expectation that, if only events can be sufficiently postponed, something will intervene; which is perhaps a heritage of the gentlest women descended from Homeric days. If the island was so historic, little Olivia may have said, where was the interfering goddess? She looked unseeingly toward St. George and toward her father, and the sense of the bitter actuality of the choice suddenly wounded her, as the Actual for ever wounds the woman and the dream.

Then suddenly, above the stir of expectation of the people, and the associate bustling of the High Council there came a vague confusion and trampling from outside, and the far outer doors of the hall were thrown open with a jar and a breath, vibrant as a murmur. There was a cry, the determined resistance of some of the Golden Guard, and shouts of expostulation and warning as they were flung aside by a powerful arm. In the disorder that followed, a miraculously-familiar figure—that familiarity and strangeness are both miracles ought to explain certain mysteries—was beside St. George and a thankful voice said in his ear:

"Mr. St. George, sir, for the mercy of Heaven, sir—come back to the yacht. No person can tell what may happen ten minutes ahead, sir!"

The oracle of this universal truth was Rollo, palpitating, his immaculate coat stained with earth, earth-stains on his cheeks, and his breast labouring in an excitement which only anxiety for his master could effect. But St. George hardly saw him. His eyes were fixed on some one who stood towering before the dais, like the old prints of the avenging goddesses. Clad in the hideous stripes which boards of directors consider *de rigueur* for the soul that is to be won back to the normal, stood the woman Elissa, who, by all counts of Prince Tabnit, should have been singing a hymn with Mrs. Manners and Miss Bella Bliss Utter in the Bitley Reformatory, in Westchester County, New York.

"Stop!" she cried in that perfect English which is not only a rare experience but a pleasant adventure, "what new horror is this?"

To Prince Tabnit's face, as he looked at her, came once more that indefinable change—only this time nearer and more intimately explainable, as if something ethereal, trained to delicate lines, like smoke, should suddenly shape itself to a menace. St. George saw the woman step close to the dais, he saw Olivia's eyes questioning him, and in the hurried rising of the peers and of the High Council he heard Rollo's voice in his ear:

"It's a gr'it go, sir," observed Rollo respectfully, "the woman has things to tell, sir, as people generally don't know. She's flew the coop at the place she was in—it seems she's been shut up some'eres in America, sir; an' she got 'old of the capting of a tramp boat o' some kind—one o' them boats as smells intoxicating round the 'atches—an' she give 'im an' the mate a 'andful o' jewelry that she'd on 'er when she was took in an' 'ad someways contrived to 'ang on to, an' I'm blessed hif she wasn't able fer to steer fer the island, sir—we took 'er aboard the yacht only this mornin' with 'er 'air down her back, an' we've brought 'er on here. An' she says—men can be gr'it beasts, sir, an' no manner o' mistake," concluded Rollo fervently.

And a little hoarse voice said in St. George's ear:

"Mr. St. George, sir—we ain't late, are we? We been flirtin' de ger-avel up dat ka-liff since de car-rack o' day."

And there was Bennietod, with an edge of an old horse pistol showing beneath his cuff; and, round-eyed and alert as a bird newly alighted on a stranger sill, Little Cawthorne stood; and the sight put strength into St. George, and so did Little Cawthorne's words:

"I didn't know whether they'd let us in or not," he said, "unless we had on a plaited decollette, with biases down the back."

Clearly and confidently in the silent room rang the voice of the woman confronting Prince Tabnit, and her eyes did not leave his face. St. George was struck with the change in her since that day in the Reformatory chapel. Then she had been like a wild, alien thing in dumb distress; now she was unchained and native. Her first words explained why, in the extreme dilemma in which St. George had last seen her, she had yet remained mute.

"I release myself," she cried, "from my oath of silence, though until to-day I have spoken only to those who helped me to come back to you—my master. Have you nothing to say to me? Has the time seemed long? Is it a weary while since I left you to do your will and murder the woman whom you were now about to make your wife?"

A cry of horror rose from the people, and then stillness

came again.

"Take the woman away," said Prince Tabnit only, "she is speaking madness."

"I am speaking the truth," said the woman clearly. "I was of Melita—there are those here who will know my face. And it is not I alone who have served the State. I challenge you, Tabnit—here, before them all! Where are Gerya and Ibera, Cabulla and Taura? Have not their people, weeping, besought news of them in vain? And what answer have you given them?"

Murmurs and sobs rose from the assembly, stilled by the tranquil voice of the prince.

"Where are they?" he repeated gently, his voice vibrant in its rise and fall, its giving of delicate values. "But the people know where they are. They have attained to the perfect life and died the perfect death. For I have raised them to the supreme estate."

Prince Tabnit, with uplifted face, sat motionless, looking out over the throng from beneath lowered lids; then his eyes, confident and a little mocking, returned to the woman. But they had for her no terror. She turned from him, confronting the pale, eager faces of the people; and in her beauty and distinction she was like Olivia's women, crowded beside the dais.

"Men and women of Yaque," cried Elissa, "I will tell you to what 'supreme estate' these friends whom you seek have long been raised. For here in Med and in Melita you will find many of those whom you have mourned as dead—you will find them as you yourselves have met and passed them, it may have been countless times, on your streets of Yaque—not young and beautiful as when they left you, but men and women of incredible age. Withered, shaken by palsy, infirm, they creep upon their lonely ways or go at will to drag themselves unrecognized along your highways, as helpless as the dead themselves. They number scores, and they are those who have displeased your prince by some little word, some little wrong, or, more than these, by some thwarting of the way of his ambition: Oblo, who disappeared from his place as keeper at the door; Ithobal, satrap of Melita; young Prince Kaal—ay, and how many more? You do not understand my words? I say that your prince has knowledge of some secret, accursed drug that can call back youth or make actual age—*age*, do you understand—just as we of Yaque bring both flowers and fruit to swift maturity!"

Olivia uttered a little cry, not at the grotesque horror of what the woman had said but at the miracle of its unconscious support of the story and theory of St. George. And St. George heard; and suddenly, because another had voiced his own fantastic message, its incredibility and unreality became appalling, and yet he felt infinitely reconciled to both because he interpreted aright that little muffled exclamation from Olivia. What did it matter—oh, what did it matter whether or not the reality were grotesque? What seems to be happening is always the reality, if only one understands it sufficiently. And at all events there had been that hour in the King's Alcove. At last, as he weighed that hour against the fantasy of all the rest, St. George understood and lived the divine madness of all great moments, the madness that realizes one star and is content that all the heavens shall march unintelligibly past so long as that single shining is not dimmed.

But King Otho was riding no such griffin with sun-gold wings. King Otho was genuinely and personally interested in the woman's words. He turned to Prince Tabnit with animation.

"Really, Prince," he said, "is it so? Pray do not deny it unless there is no other way, for I am before all things interested. It is far more important to me that you tell me as much as you can tell, than that you deny or even disprove it."

Prince Tabnit smiled in the eagerly interested face of his sovereign, and rose and came to the edge of the dais, his garments embroidered by a thousand needles touching and floating about him; and it was as if he reached those before him by a kind of spiritual magnetism, not without sublimity.

"My people," he said—and his voice had all the tenderness that they knew so well—"this is some conspiracy of those to whom we have shown the utmost hospitality. I would have shielded your king, for he was also my sovereign and I owed him allegiance. But now that is no longer possible, and the time is come. Know then, oh my people of Yaque, that which my loyalty has led me wrongfully to conceal: that in the strange disappearance and return of your sovereign, King Otho, he who will may trace the loss of that which the island has mourned without ceasing. I accuse your king—he is no longer mine—of being now in possession of the Hereditary Treasure of Yaque."

Then St. George came back with a thrill to actuality. In the press of the events of this morning, after his awakening in the room of the tombs, he had completely forgotten the soft fire of gems that had burned beneath the hands of old Malakh in that dark chamber under King Abibaal's tomb. He and Amory and Jarvo had, with the king, left the chamber by the upper passages, and Amory and Jarvo knew nothing of the jewels. Yet St. George was certain that he could not have been mistaken, and he listened breathlessly for what the king would say.

King Otho, with a smile, nodded in perfect imperturbability.

"That is true," he said, "I had forgotten all about it."

They waited for him to speak, the people in amazed silence, Mrs. Medora Hastings saying unintelligible things in whispers, for which she had a genius.

"It is true," said King Otho, "that I am responsible for the disappearance of the Hereditary Treasure. You will find it at this moment in a basement dungeon of the palace on Mount Khalak. On the very day, three months ago, that I dined with your prince I had made a discovery of considerable importance to me, namely, that the little island of Yaque is richer in most of the radio-active substances than all the rest of the world. The discovery gave me keener pleasure than I had known in years—I had suspected it for some time after I found the noctilucous stars on the ceiling of my sitting-room at the palace. And in the work-shop of the Princess Simyra I came upon a quantity of metallic uranium, and a great many other things which I question the taste of taking the time to describe. But my experiments there with the very perfect gems of your admirable collection had evidently been antedated by some of your own people, for the apparatus was intact. I shall be glad to show some charming effects to any one who cares to see them. I have succeeded in causing the diamonds of Darius to phosphoresce most wonderfully."

The phosphorescence of the diamonds of Darius was to the people far less important than the joyous fact which they were not slow to grasp, that the Hereditary Treasure was, if they might believe the king's words, restored to them, and the burden of the tax averted. They did not understand, nor did they seek to understand; because they knew the inefficiency of details and they also knew the value of mere import.

But the king, child of a social order that wreaks itself on particularizations, returned to his quest for a certain recounting.

"Prince Tabnit," he said, "the High Council and the people of Yaque are impatient for your answer to this woman's words."

"I rejoice with them and with your Majesty," replied Prince Tabnit softly, "that the treasure is safe. My own explanation is far less simple. If what this woman says is true, yet it is true in such wise as, strive as I may, I can not speak; nor, strive as you may, can you fathom. Therefore I say that the claim which she has made is idle, and not within my power to answer."

At this St. George bounded to his feet. Amory looked up at

him in terror, and Little Cawthorne and Bennietod went a step or two after him as he sprang forward, and Rollo's lean shadowed face, obvious as his way of speech, was wrinkled in terrified appeal.

"An idle claim!" St. George thundered as he strode before the dais. "Is this woman's story and mine an idle claim, and one not within your power to answer? Then I will tell you how to answer, Prince Tabnit. I challenge you now, in the presence of your people—taste this!"

Upon the carven arm of Prince Tabnit's throne St. George set something that he had taken from his pocket. It was the vase of rock-crystal from which, the night before in the room of the tombs, the king had drunk.

What followed was the last thing that St. George had expected. It was as if his defiance had unlocked flood-gates. In an instant the vast assembly was in motion. With a sound of garments that was like far wind they were upon their feet and pressing toward the throne. With all the passion of their "Yes! Yes! Yes!" in response to Olivia's appeal they came, resistlessly demanding the answer to some dreadful question long shrouded in their hearts. Their armour was their silence; they made no sound save that ominous sweep of their robes and the conspiracy of their sandaled feet upon the tiles.

St. George did not turn. Indeed, it did not once cross his mind that their hostility could possibly be toward him. Besides, his look was fixed upon the prince's face, and what he read there was enough. The peers, the High Council and those nearest the throne wavered and swerved from the man, leaving him to face what was to come.

Whatever was to come he would have met nobly. He was of those infrequent folk of some upper air who exhibit a certain purity even in error, or in worse. He stood with his exquisite pale face uplifted, his white hair in a glory about it, his white gown embroidered by a thousand needles falling in virginal lines against the warm, pure colour of that room with its wraiths of hue and light. And he opened the heart of the green jewel that burned upon his breast.

"Not for me the wine of youth," he said slowly, "but the poison of age. The poison which, without me to unlock the secret, all mankind must drink alone. May you drink it late, my friends!" he cried. "I, who hold in my soul the secret of the passing of time and youth, drink now to those among you and among all men who have won and kept the one thing dearer than these."

He touched the green gem to his lips, and let it fall upon the embroidered laces on his breast. Then quietly and in another voice he began to speak.

With the first words there came to St. George the thrill of something that had possessed him—when? In that ecstatic moment on *The Aloha* when he had seen the light in the king's palace; in the instant when the Isle of Yaque had first lain subject before him, "a land which no one can define or remember—only desire;" in the divine time of his triumph in having scaled the heights to the palace, that sky-thing, with ramparts of air; above all, in the hour of his joy in the King's Alcove, when Olivia had looked in his eyes and touched his lips. Inexplicably as the way that eternity lies barely unrevealed in some kin-thing of its own—a shell, a duty, a vista—he suddenly felt it now in what the prince was saying. He listened, and for one poignant stab of time he knew that he touched hands with the elemental and saw the ancient kindliness of all those people naked in their faces and knew himself for what he was.

He listened, and yet there was no making captive the words of the prince in understanding. Prince Tabnit was speaking the English, and every word was clearly audible and, moreover, was probably daily upon St. George's lips. But if it had been to ransom the rest of the world from its night he could not have understood what the prince was saying. Every word was a word that belonged as much to St. George as to the prince; but in some unfathomable fashion the inner sense of what he said for ever eluded, dissolving in the air of which it was a part. And yet, past all doubting, St. George knew that he was hearing the essence of that strange knowledge which the Isle of Yaque had won while all the rest of mankind struggled for it—he knew with the certainty with which we recognize strange forces in a dozen of the every-day things of life, in electricity, in telepathy, in dreams. With the same certainty he realized that what the prince was saying would, if he could understand, lift a certain veil. Here, put in words at last, was manifestly the secret, that catch of understanding without which men are groping in the dark, perhaps that mere pointing of relations which would make clear, without blasphemy, time and the future, rebirth and old existence, it might be; and certainly the accident of personality. Here, crystallized, were the things that men almost know, the dream that has just escaped every one, the whisper in sleep that would have explained if one could remember when one woke, the word that has been thrillingly flashed to one in moments of absorption and has fled before one might catch the sound, the far hope of science, the glimpse that comes to dying eyes and is voiced in fragments by dying lips. Here without penetrating the great reserve or tracing any principle to its beginning, was the truth about both. And St. George was powerless to receive it.

He turned fearfully to Olivia. Ah—what if she did not guess anything of the meaning of what she was hearing? For one instant he knew all the misery of one whose friend stands on another star. But when he saw her uplifted face, her eager eyes and quick breath and her look divinely questioning his, he was certain that though she might not read the figures of the veil, yet she too knew how near, how near they Stood; and to be with her on this side was dearer—nay, was nearer the Secret— than without her to pass the veil that they touched. Then he looked at Amory; wouldn't old Amory know, he wondered. Wouldn't his mere understanding of news teach him what was happening? But old Amory, the light flashing on his pince-nez, was keeping one eye on the prince and wondering if the chair that he had just placed for Antoinette was not in the draught of the dome; and little Antoinette was looking about her like a rosebud, new to the butterflies of June; and King Otho was listening, languid, heavy-lidded, sensitive to little values, sophisticating the moment; and Little Cawthorne stood with eyes raised in simple, tolerant wonder; and the others, Bennietod, Mrs. Hastings and Mr. Augustus Frothingham, showed faces like the pools in which pebbles might be dropped, making no ripples—one must suppose that there are such pools, since there are certainly such faces. St. George saw how it was. Here, spoken casually by the prince, just as the Banal would speak of the visible and invisible worlds, here was the Sesame of understanding toward which the centuries had striven, the secret of the link between two worlds; and here, of all mankind, were only they two to hear—they two and that motionless company who knew what the prince knew and who kept it sealed within their eyes.

St. George looked at the multitude in swift understanding. They were like a Greek chorus, signifying what is. They knew what the prince was saying, they had the secret and yet—they were *no nearer, no nearer* than he. With their ancient kindliness naked in their faces, St. George knew that through his love he was as near to the Source as were they. And it was suddenly as it had been that first night when he had stridden buoyantly through the island; for he could not tell which was the secret of the prince and of these people and which was the blessedness of his love.

None the less he clung desperately to the last words of Prince Tabnit in a vain effort to hold, to make clear, to sophisticate one single phrase, as one waking in the night says over, in a vain effort to fix it, some phantom sentence cried to him in dreams by a shadowy band destined to be dissolved when, in bright day, he would reclaim it. He even managed frantically to write down a jumble of words of which he could make nothing, save here and there a phrase like a touch of hands from the silence: "...the infinite moment that is pending" ... "all is become a window where had been a wall" ... "the wintry vision" ... they were all words that beckon without replying. And all the time it was curiously as if the Something Silent within St. George himself, that so long had striven to speak, were crying out at last in the prince's words—and he could not understand. Yet in spite of it all, in spite of this imminent satisfying of the strange, dreadful curiosity which possesses all mankind, St. George, even now, was far less keen to comprehend than he was to burst through the throng with Olivia in his arms, gain the waiting *Aloha* and sail into the New York harbour with the prize that he had won. "I drink now to those among you and among all men who have won and kept that which is greater than these," the prince had said, and St. George perfectly understood. He had but to look at Olivia to be triumphantly willing that the gods should keep their secrets about time and the link between the two worlds so long as they had given him love. What should he care about time? He had this hour.

When the prince ceased speaking the hall was hushed; but because of the tempest in the hearts of them all the silence was as if a strong wind, sweeping powerfully through a forest, were to sway no boughs and lift no leaves, only to strive noiselessly round one who walked there.

Prince Tabnit wrapped his white mantle about him and sat upon his throne. Spell-stricken, they watched him, that great multitude, and might not turn away their eyes. Slowly, imperceptibly, as Time touches the familiar, the face of the prince took on its change—and one could not have told wherein the change lay, but subtly as the encroachment of the dark, or the alchemy of the leaves, or the betrayal of certain modes of death, the finger was upon him. While they watched he became an effigy, the hideous face of a fantasy of smoke against the night sky, with a formless hand lifted from among the delicate laces in farewell. There was no death—the horror was that there was no death. Only this curse of age drying and withering at the bones.

A long, whining cry came from Cassyrus, who covered his face with his mantle and fled. The spell being broken, by common consent the great hall was once more in motion—St. George would never forget that tide toward all the great portals and the shuddering backward glances at the white heap upon the beetling throne. They fled away into the reassuring sunlight, leaving the echoless hall deserted, save for that breathing one upon the throne.

There was one other. From somewhere beside the dais the woman Elissa crept and knelt, clasping the knees of the man.

CHAPTER XXI

OPEN SECRETS

"Will you have tea?" asked Olivia.

St. George brought a deck cushion and tucked it in the willow steamer chair and said adoringly that he would have tea. Tea. In a world where the essentials and the inessentials are so deliciously confused, to think that tea, with some one else, can be a kind of Heaven.

"Two lumps?" pursued Olivia.

"Three, please," St. George directed, for the pure joy of watching her hands. There were no tongs.

"Aren't the rest going to have some?" Olivia absently shared her attention, tinkling delicately about among the tea things. "Doesn't every one want a cup of tea?" she inquired loud enough for nobody to hear. St. George, shifting his shoulder from the rail, looked vaguely over the deck of *The Aloha*, sighed contentedly, and smiled back at her. No one else, it appeared, would have tea; and there was none to regret it.

St. George's cursory inspection had revealed the others variously absorbed, though they were now all agreed in breathing easily since Barnay, interlarding rational speech with Irishisms of thanksgiving, had announced five minutes before that the fires were up and that in half an hour *The Aloha* might weigh anchor. The only thing now left to desire was to slip clear of the shadow of the black reaches of Yaque, shouldering the blue.

Meanwhile, Antoinette and Amory sat in the comparative seclusion of the bow with their backs to the forward deck, and it was definitely manifest to every one how it would be with them, but every one was simply glad and dismissed the matter with that. Mr. Frothingham, in his steamer chair, looked like a soft collapsible tube of something; Bennietod, at ease upon the uncovered boards of the deck, was circumspectly having cheese sandwiches and wastefully shooting the ship's rockets into the red sunset, in general celebration; and Rollo, having taken occasion respectfully to submit to whomsoever it concerned that fact is ever stranger than fiction, had gone below. Mr. Otho Holland and Little Cawthorne—but their smiles were like different names for the same thing—were toasting each other in something light and dry and having a bouquet which Mr. Holland, who ought to know, compared favourably with certain vintages of 1000 B.C. In a hammock near them reclined Mrs. Medora Hastings, holding two kinds of smelling salts which invariably revived her simply by inducing the mental effort of deciding which was the better. Her hair, which was exceedingly pretty, now rippled becomingly about her flushed face and was guiltless of side-combs—she had lost them both down a chasm in that headlong flight from the cliff's summit, and they irrecoverably reposed in the bed of some brook of the Miocene period. And Mrs. Hastings, her hand in that of her brother, lay in utter silence, smiling up at him in serene content.

For King Otho of Yaque was turning his back upon his island domain for ever. In that hurried flight across the Eurychorus among his distracted subjects, his resolution had been taken. Jarvo and Akko, the adieu to whom had been every one's sole regret in leaving the island, had miraculously found their way to the king and his party in their flight, and were despatched to Mount Khalak for such of their belongings as they could collect, and the island sovereign was well content.

"Ah well now," he had just observed, languidly surveying the tropical horizon through a cool glass of winking amber bubbles, "one must learn that to touch is far more delicate than to lift. It is more wonderful to have been the king of one moment than the ruler of many. It is better to have stood for an instant upon a rainbow than to have taken a morning walk through a field of clouds. The principle has long been understood, but few have had—shall I say the courage?—to practise it. Yet 'courage' is a term from-the-shoulder, and what I require is a word of finger-tips, over-tones, ultra-rays—a word for the few who understand that to leave a thing is more exquisite than to outwear it. It is by its very fineness circum-scribed—a feminine virtue. Women understand it and keep it secret. I flatter myself that I have possessed the high moment, vanished against the noon. Ah, my dear fellow—" he added, lifting his glass to St. George's smile.

But little Cawthorne—all reality in his heliotrope outing and duck and grey curls—raised a characteristic plaint.

"Oh, but I've done it," he mournfully reviewed. "When'll I ever be in another island, in front of another vacated throne? Why didn't I move into the palace, and set up a natty, up-to-date little republic? I could have worn a crown as a matter of taste—what's the use of a democracy if you aren't free to wear a crown? And what kind of American am I, anyway, with this undeveloped taste for acquiring islands? If they ever find this out at the polls my vote'll be challenged. What?"

"Aw whee!" said Bennietod, intent upon a Roman candle, "wha' do you care, Mr. Cawt'orne? You don't hev to go back fer to be a child-slave to Chillingwort'. Me, I've gotta good call to jump overboard now an' be de sonny of a sea-horse, dead to rights!"

St. George looked at them all affectionately, unconscious that already the experience of the last three days was slipping back into the sheathing past, like a blade used. But he was dawningly aware, as he sat there at Olivia's feet in glorious content, that he was looking at them all with new eyes. It was as if he had found new names for them all; and until long afterward one does not know that these moments of bestowing new names mark the near breathing of the god.

The silence of Mrs. Hastings and her quiet devotion to her brother somehow gave St. George a new respect for her. Over by the wheel-house something made a strange noise of crying, and St. George saw that Mr. Frothingham sat holding a weird little animal, like a squirrel but for its stumpy tail and great human eyes, which he had unwittingly stepped on among the rocks. The little thing was licking his hand, and the old lawyer's face was softened and glowing as he nursed it and coaxed it with crumbs. As he looked, St. George warmed to them all in new fellowship and, too, in swift self-reproach; for in what had seemed to him but "broad lines and comic masks" he suddenly saw the authority and reality of homely hearts. The better and more intimate names for everything which seemed now within his grasp were more important than Yaque itself. He remembered, with a thrill, how his mother had been wont to tell him that a man must walk through some sort of fairy-land, whether of imagination or of the heart, before he can put much in or take much from the market-place. And lo! this fairy-land of his finding had proved—must it not always prove?—the essence of all Reality.

His eyes went to Olivia's face in a flash of understanding and belief.

"Don't you see?" he said, quite as if they two had been talking what he had thought.

She waited, smiling a little, thrilled by his certainty of her sympathy.

"None of this happened really," triumphantly explained St. George, "I met you at the Boris, did I not? Therefore, I think that since then you have graciously let me see you for the proper length of time, and at last we've fallen in love just as every one else does. And true lovers always do have trouble, do they not? So then, Yaque has been the usual trouble and happiness, and here we are—engaged."

"I'm not engaged," Olivia protested serenely, "but I see what you mean. No, none of it happened," she gravely agreed. "It couldn't, you know. Anybody will tell you that."

In her eyes was the sparkle of understanding which made St. George love her more every time that it appeared. He noted, the white cloth frock, and the coat of hunting pink thrown across her chair, and he remembered that in the infinitesimal time that he had waited for her outside the Palace of the Litany, she must have exchanged for these the coronation robe and jewels of Queen Mitygen. St. George liked that swift practicality in the race of faery, though he was completely indifferent to Mrs. Hastings' and Antoinette's claims to it; and he wondered if he were to love Olivia more for everything that she did, how he could possibly live long enough to tell her. When one has been to Yaque the simplest gifts and graces resolve themselves into this question.

The Aloha gently freed herself from the shallow green pocket where she had lain through three eventful days, and slipped out toward the waste of water bound by the flaunting autumn of the west. An island wind, fragrant of bark and secret berries, blew in puffs from the steep. A gull swooped to her nest in a cranny of the basalt. From below a servant came on deck, his broad American face smiling over a tray of glasses and decanters and tinkling ice. It was all very tranquil and public and almost commonplace—just the high tropic seas at the moment of their unrestrained sundown, and the odour of tea-cakes about the pleasantly-littered deck. And for the moment, held by a common thought, every one kept silent. Now that *The Aloha* was really moving toward home, the affair seemed suddenly such a gigantic impossibility that every one resented every one else's knowing what a trick had been played. It was as if the curtain had just fallen and the lights of the auditorium had flashed up after the third act, and they had all caught one another breathless or in tears, pretending that the tragedy had really happened.

"Promise me something," begged St. George softly, in sudden alarm, born of this inevitable aspect; "promise me that when we get to New York you are not going to forget all about Yaque—and me—and believe that none of us ever happened."

Olivia looked toward the serene mystery of the distance.

"New York," she said only, "think of seeing you in New York—now."

"Was I of more account in Yaque?" demanded St. George anxiously.

"Sometimes," said Olivia adorably, "I shall tell you that you were. But that will be only because I shall have an idea that in Yaque you loved me more."

"Ah, very well then. And sometimes," said St. George contentedly, "when we are at dinner I shall look down the table at you sitting beside some one who is expounding some baneful literary theory, and I shall think: What do I care? He doesn't know that she is really the Princess of Far-Away. But I do."

"And he won't know anything about our motor ride, alone, the night that I was kidnapped, either—the literary-theory person," Olivia tranquilly took away his breath by observing.

St. George looked up at her quickly and, secretly, Olivia thought that if he had been attractive when he was courageous he was doubly so with the present adorably abashed look in his eyes.

"When—alone?" St. George asked unconvincingly.

She laughed a little, looking down at him in a reproof that was all approbation, and to be reproved like that is the divinest praise.

"How did you know?" protested St. George in fine indignation. "Besides," he explained, "I haven't an idea what you mean."

"I guessed about that ride," she went on, "the night before last, when you were walking up and down outside my window. I don't know what made me—and I think it was very forward of me. Do you want to know something?" she demanded, looking away.

"More than anything," declared St. George. "What?"

"I think—" Olivia said slowly, "that it began—then—just when I first thought how wonderful that ride would have been. Except—that it had begun a great while before," she ended suddenly.

And at these enigmatic words St. George sent a quick look over the forward deck. It was of no use. Mr. Frothingham was well within range.

"Heavens, good heavens, how happy I am," said St. George instead.

"And then," Olivia went on presently, "sometimes when there are a lot of people about—literary-theory persons and all—I shall look across at you, differently, and that will mean that you are to remember the exact minute when you looked in the window up at the palace, on the mountain, and I saw you. Won't it?"

"It will," said St. George fervently. "Don't try to persuade me that there wasn't any such mountain," he challenged her. "I suppose," he added in wonder, "that lovers have been having these secret signs time out of mind—and we never knew."

Olivia drew a little breath of content.

"Bless everybody," she said.

So they made invasion of that pure, dim world before them; and the serene mystery of the distance came like a thought, drawn from a state remote and immortal, to clasp the hand of There in the hand of Here.

"And then sometimes," St. George went on, his exultation proving greater than his discretion, "we'll take the yacht and pretend we're going back—"

He stopped abruptly with a quick indrawn breath and the hope that she had not noticed. He was, by several seconds, too late.

"Whose yacht is it?" Olivia asked promptly. "I wondered."

St. George had dreaded the question. Someway, now that it was all over and the prize was his, he was ashamed that he had not won it more fairly and humiliated that he was not what she believed him, a pillar of the *Evening Sentinel*. But Amory had miraculously heard and turned himself about.

"It's his," he said briefly, "I may as well confess to you, Miss Holland," he enlarged somewhat, "he's a great cheat. *The Aloha* is his, and so am I, busy body and idle soul, for using up his yacht and his time on a newspaper story. You were the 'story,' you know."

"But," said Olivia in bewilderment, "I don't understand. Surely—"

"Nothing whatever is sure, Miss Holland," Amory sadly assured her, but his eyes were smiling behind his pince-nez. "You would think one might be sure of him. But it isn't so. Me, you may depend upon me," he impressed it lightly. "I'm what I say I am—a poor beggar of a newspaper man, about to be held to account by one Chillingworth for this whole millenial occurrence, and sent off to a political convention to steady me, unless I'm fired. But St. George, he's a gay dilettante."

Then Amory resumed a better topic of his own; and Olivia, when she understood, looked down at her lover as miserably as one is able when one is perfectly happy.

"Oh," she said, "and up there—in the palace to-day—I did think for a minute that perhaps you wanted me to marry the prince so that—they could—."

One could smile now at the enormity of that.

"So that I could put it in the paper?" he said. "But, you see, I never could put it in any paper, even if I didn't love you. Who would believe me? A thousand years from now—maybe less— the *Evening Sentinel*, if it is still in existence, can publish the story, perhaps. Until then I'm afraid they'll have to confine themselves to the doings of the precincts."

Olivia waived the whole matter for one of vaster importance.

"Then why did you come to Yaque?" she demanded.

Mr. Frothingham had left his place by the wheel-house and wandered forward. The steamer chair had a back that was both broad and high, and one sitting in its shadow was hermetically veiled from the rest of the deck. So St. George bent forward, and told her.

After that they sat in silence, and together they looked back toward the island with its black rocks smitten to momentary gold by a last javelin of light. There it lay—the land locking away as realities all the fairy-land of speculation, the land of the miracles of natural law. They had walked there, and had glimpsed the shadowy threshold of the Morning. Suppose, St. George thought, that instead of King Otho, with his delicate sense of the merely visible, a great man had chanced to be made sovereign of Yaque? And instead of Mr. Frothingham, slave to the contestable, and Little Cawthorne in bondage to humour, and Amory and himself swept off their feet by a heavenly romance, suppose a party of savants and economists had arrived in Yaque, with a poet or two to bring away the fire—what then? St. George lost the doubt in the noon of his own certainty. There could be no greater good, he chanted to the god who had breathed upon him, than this that he and Amory shared now with the wise and simple world, the world of the resonant new names. He even doubted that, save in degree, there could be a purer talisman than the spirit that inextinguishably shone in the face of the childlike old lawyer as the strange little animal nestled in his coat and licked his hand. And these were open secrets. Open secrets of the ultimate attainment.

They watched the land dissolving in the darkness like a pearl in wine of night. But at last, when momentarily they had turned happy eyes to each other's faces, they looked again and found that the dusk, taking ancient citadels with soundless tread, had received the island. And where on the brow of the mountain had sprung the white pillars of the king's palace glittered only the early stars.

"Crown jewels," said Olivia softly, "for everybody's head."

Choose from Thousands of 1stWorldLibrary Classics By

A. M. Barnard
Ada Leverson
Adolphus William Ward
Aesop
Agatha Christie
Alexander Aaronsohn
Alexander Kielland
Alexandre Dumas
Alfred Gatty
Alfred Ollivant
Alice Duer Miller
Alice Turner Curtis
Alice Dunbar
Allen Chapman
Alleyne Ireland
Ambrose Bierce
Amelia E. Barr
Amory H. Bradford
Andrew Lang
Andrew McFarland Davis
Andy Adams
Angela Brazil
Anna Alice Chapin
Anna Sewell
Annie Besant
Annie Hamilton Donnell
Annie Payson Call
Annie Roe Carr
Annonaymous
Anton Chekhov
Archibald Lee Fletcher
Arnold Bennett
Arthur C. Benson
Arthur Conan Doyle
Arthur M. Winfield
Arthur Ransome
Arthur Schnitzler
Arthur Train
Atticus
B.H. Baden-Powell
B. M. Bower
B. C. Chatterjee
Baroness Emmuska Orczy
Baroness Orczy
Basil King
Bayard Taylor
Ben Macomber
Bertha Muzzy Bower
Bjornstjerne Bjornson

Booth Tarkington
Boyd Cable
Bram Stoker
C. Collodi
C. E. Orr
C. M. Ingleby
Carolyn Wells
Catherine Parr Traill
Charles A. Eastman
Charles Amory Beach
Charles Dickens
Charles Dudley Warner
Charles Farrar Browne
Charles Ives
Charles Kingsley
Charles Klein
Charles Hanson Towne
Charles Lathrop Pack
Charles Romyn Dake
Charles Whibley
Charles Willing Beale
Charlotte M. Braeme
Charlotte M. Yonge
Charlotte Perkins Stetson
Clair W. Hayes
Clarence Day Jr.
Clarence E. Mulford
Clemence Housman
Confucius
Coningsby Dawson
Cornelis DeWitt Wilcox
Cyril Burleigh
D. H. Lawrence
Daniel Defoe
David Garnett
Dinah Craik
Don Carlos Janes
Donald Keyhoe
Dorothy Kilner
Dougan Clark
Douglas Fairbanks
E. Nesbit
E. P. Roe
E. Phillips Oppenheim
E. S. Brooks
Earl Barnes
Edgar Rice Burroughs
Edith Van Dyne
Edith Wharton

Edward Everett Hale
Edward J. O'Biren
Edward S. Ellis
Edwin L. Arnold
Eleanor Atkins
Eleanor Hallowell Abbott
Eliot Gregory
Elizabeth Gaskell
Elizabeth McCracken
Elizabeth Von Arnim
Ellem Key
Emerson Hough
Emilie F. Carlen
Emily Bronte
Emily Dickinson
Enid Bagnold
Enilor Macartney Lane
Erasmus W. Jones
Ernie Howard Pie
Ethel May Dell
Ethel Turner
Ethel Watts Mumford
Eugene Sue
Eugenie Foa
Eugene Wood
Eustace Hale Ball
Evelyn Everett-green
Everard Cotes
F. H. Cheley
F. J. Cross
F. Marion Crawford
Fannie E. Newberry
Federick Austin Ogg
Ferdinand Ossendowski
Fergus Hume
Florence A. Kilpatrick
Fremont B. Deering
Francis Bacon
Francis Darwin
Frances Hodgson Burnett
Frances Parkinson Keyes
Frank Gee Patchin
Frank Harris
Frank Jewett Mather
Frank L. Packard
Frank V. Webster
Frederic Stewart Isham
Frederick Trevor Hill
Frederick Winslow Taylor

Friedrich Kerst
Friedrich Nietzsche
Fyodor Dostoyevsky
G.A. Henty
G.K. Chesterton
Gabrielle E. Jackson
Garrett P. Serviss
Gaston Leroux
George A. Warren
George Ade
Geroge Bernard Shaw
George Cary Eggleston
George Durston
George Ebers
George Eliot
George Gissing
George MacDonald
George Meredith
George Orwell
George Sylvester Viereck
George Tucker
George W. Cable
George Wharton James
Gertrude Atherton
Gordon Casserly
Grace E. King
Grace Gallatin
Grace Greenwood
Grant Allen
Guillermo A. Sherwell
Gulielma Zollinger
Gustav Flaubert
H. A. Cody
H. B. Irving
H.C. Bailey
H. G. Wells
H. H. Munro
H. Irving Hancock
H. R. Naylor
H. Rider Haggard
H. W. C. Davis
Haldeman Julius
Hall Caine
Hamilton Wright Mabie
Hans Christian Andersen
Harold Avery
Harold McGrath
Harriet Beecher Stowe
Harry Castlemon
Harry Coghill
Harry Houidini

Hayden Carruth
Helent Hunt Jackson
Helen Nicolay
Hendrik Conscience
Hendy David Thoreau
Henri Barbusse
Henrik Ibsen
Henry Adams
Henry Ford
Henry Frost
Henry James
Henry Jones Ford
Henry Seton Merriman
Henry W Longfellow
Herbert A. Giles
Herbert Carter
Herbert N. Casson
Herman Hesse
Hildegard G. Frey
Homer
Honore De Balzac
Horace B. Day
Horace Walpole
Horatio Alger Jr.
Howard Pyle
Howard R. Garis
Hugh Lofting
Hugh Walpole
Humphry Ward
Ian Maclaren
Inez Haynes Gillmore
Irving Bacheller
Isabel Cecilia Williams
Isabel Hornibrook
Israel Abrahams
Ivan Turgenev
J.G.Austin
J. Henri Fabre
J. M. Barrie
J. M. Walsh
J. Macdonald Oxley
J. R. Miller
J. S. Fletcher
J. S. Knowles
J. Storer Clouston
J. W. Duffield
Jack London
Jacob Abbott
James Allen
James Andrews
James Baldwin

James Branch Cabell
James DeMille
James Joyce
James Lane Allen
James Lane Allen
James Oliver Curwood
James Oppenheim
James Otis
James R. Driscoll
Jane Abbott
Jane Austen
Jane L. Stewart
Janet Aldridge
Jens Peter Jacobsen
Jerome K. Jerome
Jessie Graham Flower
John Buchan
John Burroughs
John Cournos
John F. Kennedy
John Gay
John Glasworthy
John Habberton
John Joy Bell
John Kendrick Bangs
John Milton
John Philip Sousa
John Taintor Foote
Jonas Lauritz Idemil Lie
Jonathan Swift
Joseph A. Altsheler
Joseph Carey
Joseph Conrad
Joseph E. Badger Jr
Joseph Hergesheimer
Joseph Jacobs
Jules Vernes
Julian Hawthrone
Julie A Lippmann
Justin Huntly McCarthy
Kakuzo Okakura
Karle Wilson Baker
Kate Chopin
Kenneth Grahame
Kenneth McGaffey
Kate Langley Bosher
Kate Langley Bosher
Katherine Cecil Thurston
Katherine Stokes
L. A. Abbot
L. T. Meade

L. Frank Baum
Latta Griswold
Laura Dent Crane
Laura Lee Hope
Laurence Housman
Lawrence Beasley
Leo Tolstoy
Leonid Andreyev
Lewis Carroll
Lewis Sperry Chafer
Lilian Bell
Lloyd Osbourne
Louis Hughes
Louis Joseph Vance
Louis Tracy
Louisa May Alcott
Lucy Fitch Perkins
Lucy Maud Montgomery
Luther Benson
Lydia Miller Middleton
Lyndon Orr
M. Corvus
M. H. Adams
Margaret E. Sangster
Margret Howth
Margaret Vandercook
Margaret W. Hungerford
Margret Penrose
Maria Edgeworth
Maria Thompson Daviess
Mariano Azuela
Marion Polk Angellotti
Mark Overton
Mark Twain
Mary Austin
Mary Catherine Crowley
Mary Cole
Mary Hastings Bradley
Mary Roberts Rinehart
Mary Rowlandson
M. Wollstonecraft Shelley
Maud Lindsay
Max Beerbohm
Myra Kelly
Nathaniel Hawthrone
Nicolo Machiavelli
O. F. Walton
Oscar Wilde

Owen Johnson
P.G. Wodehouse
Paul and Mabel Thorne
Paul G. Tomlinson
Paul Severing
Percy Brebner
Percy Keese Fitzhugh
Peter B. Kyne
Plato
Quincy Allen
R. Derby Holmes
R. L. Stevenson
R. S. Ball
Rabindranath Tagore
Rahul Alvares
Ralph Bonehill
Ralph Henry Barbour
Ralph Victor
Ralph Waldo Emmerson
Rene Descartes
Ray Cummings
Rex Beach
Rex E. Beach
Richard Harding Davis
Richard Jefferies
Richard Le Gallienne
Robert Barr
Robert Frost
Robert Gordon Anderson
Robert L. Drake
Robert Lansing
Robert Lynd
Robert Michael Ballantyne
Robert W. Chambers
Rosa Nouchette Carey
Rudyard Kipling
Saint Augustine
Samuel B. Allison
Samuel Hopkins Adams
Sarah Bernhardt
Sarah C. Hallowell
Selma Lagerlof
Sherwood Anderson
Sigmund Freud
Standish O'Grady
Stanley Weyman
Stella Benson
Stella M. Francis

Stephen Crane
Stewart Edward White
Stijn Streuvels
Swami Abhedananda
Swami Parmananda
T. S. Ackland
T. S. Arthur
The Princess Der Ling
Thomas A. Janvier
Thomas A Kempis
Thomas Anderton
Thomas Bailey Aldrich
Thomas Bulfinch
Thomas De Quincey
Thomas Dixon
Thomas H. Huxley
Thomas Hardy
Thomas More
Thornton W. Burgess
U. S. Grant
Upton Sinclair
Valentine Williams
Various Authors
Vaughan Kester
Victor Appleton
Victor G. Durham
Victoria Cross
Virginia Woolf
Wadsworth Camp
Walter Camp
Walter Scott
Washington Irving
Wilbur Lawton
Wilkie Collins
Willa Cather
Willard F. Baker
William Dean Howells
William le Queux
W. Makepeace Thackeray
William W. Walter
William Shakespeare
Winston Churchill
Yei Theodora Ozaki
Yogi Ramacharaka
Young E. Allison
Zane Grey